16⁹⁹

AG13

*

BEST NEW
ZΘMBIE
TALES

Volume One

*

*

- BOOKS of the DEAD -

BEST NEW ZOMBIE TALES Volume One

Cover art by Tom Melnick

FIRST EDITION

BOOKS of the DEAD

10 9 8 7 6 5 4 3 2 1

For more information subscribe to:
booksofthedead.blogspot.com

Become part of the message board community:
booksofthedeadforum.yuku.com

For direct sales and inquiries contact:
besthorror@gmail.com

This book is dedicated to zombie author Z. A. Recht.
Feb 4th 1983 ~ Dec 10th 2009

This series was inspired by Stephen Jones and Ramsey Campbell for their work in *Best New Horror*, and by Richard Davis, Gerald W. Page, and Karl Edward Wagner for their work in *The Year's Best Horror Stories*.

IV

COPYRIGHT ACKNOWLEDGEMENTS

'Working Stiff' by Robert Elrod, © 2003. * First appeared in All Dressed Up and Nowhere to Go.

'Introduction' by James Roy Daley, © 2010. ** Original for this anthology.

'Zombie Love' by Ray Garton, © 2003. * First appeared as a limited edition by Subterranean Press.

'Feeding Frenzy' by Matt Hults, © 2007. * First appeared in Fried! Fast Food, Slow Death by Graveside Tales.

'Wings' by Jessica Brown, © 2009. * First appeared in the Nocturnal Lyric #39.

'The Man Who Breaks the Bad News' by Kealan Patrick Burke, © 2003. * First appeared in author's collection: Ravenous Ghosts by 3F Publications.

'Immunity' by Jeff Strand, © 2008. * First appeared in Bits of the Dead by Coscom Entertainment.

'In the Land of the Blind' by Robert Swartwood, © 2004. * First appeared in ChiZine #22.

'Nowhere People' by Gary McMahon, © 2004. * First appeared in Supernatural Tales #10.

'Muddy Waters' by Brian Knight, © 2003. * First appeared in author's collection: Dragonfly by Dominion.

'Darkness Comprehended' Harry Shannon and Gord Rollo, © 2005. * First appeared in City Slab magazine #2.

'Connections' by Simon McCaffery, © 2006. * First appeared Mondo Zombie by Cemetery Dance.

'Sign of the Times' by John Grover, © 2002. * First published in The Eternal Night – E-zine.

'After, Life' by Jeff Parish, © 2008. * First published in Every Day Fiction.

'Paradise Denied' by John L French, © 2004. * First appeared Futures Mystery Anthology Magazine, Spring Edition.

'On the Usefulness of Old Books' by Kim Paffenroth, © 2010. ** Original for this anthology.

"The Revelations of Dr. Maitland' by Charles Black, © 2007. * First appeared in Fiction – E-zine.

'Pegleg and Paddy Save the World' by Jonathan Maberry, © 2007. * First appeared in History is Dead by Permuted Press.

'SKN-3' by Steven E Wedel, © 1997. * First appeared in Mausoleum magazine.

'Fishing' by Jason Brannon, © 2008. * First appeared in Alien Skin Magazine.

'Groundwood' by Bev Vincent, © 2008. * First appeared in Inflation, Wrong World.

* Reprinted by permission of author.
** Used by permission of author.

*

EDITED BY
JAMES ROY
DALEY

*

*

- BOOKS of the DEAD -

Sleepwalk
"Working Stiff"

by Robert Elrod

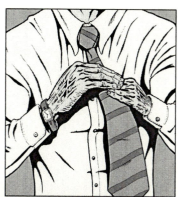

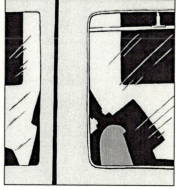

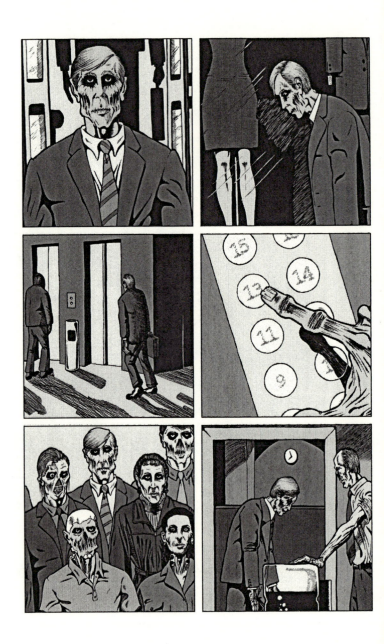

VIII

- BOOKS OF THE DEAD -

ZOMBIE #1

½ OZ OVER-PROOF RUM

1 OZ PINEAPPLE JUICE

1 OZ ORANGE JUICE

½ OZ APRICOT BRANDY

½ TABLESPOON CRUSHED BONE MARROW

½ TABLESPOON SUGAR

1 OZ DARK RUM

2 OZ LIGHT RUM

~

1. SHAKE LIGHT RUM, DARK RUM, APRICOT BRANDY, PINEAPPLE JUICE, ORANGE JUICE, LIMEJUICE, AND POWDERED SUGAR WITH ICE.

2. STRAIN INTO A COLLINS GLASS.

3. SPRINKLE BONE MARROW INTO OVER-PROOF RUM AND FLOAT ON TOP

4. GARNISH WITH A FRUIT SLICE, SPRING OF MINT AND A CHERRY.

5. SERVE.

Also By
James Roy Daley

~

NOVELS

The Dead Parade

UPCOMING ANTHOLOGIES

Best New Zombie Tales #2
Best New Zombie Tales #3
Best New Vampire Tales #1

Best New Zombie Tales
CONTENTS

VII
Sleepwalk: Working Stiff ~ **ROBERT ELROD**

17
Introduction ~ **JAMES ROY DALEY**

23
Zombie Love ~ **RAY GARTON**

118
Feeding Frenzy ~ **MATT HULTS**

146
Wings ~ **JESSICA BROWN**

151
The Man Who Breaks The Bad News ~
KEALAN PATRICK BURKE

166
Immunity ~ **JEFF STRAND**

169
In The Land Of The Blind ~ **ROBERT SWARTWOOD**

180
Nowhere People ~ **GARY McMAHON**

197
Muddy Waters ~ **BRIAN KNIGHT**

211
Darkness Comprehended ~
HARRY SHANNON & GORD ROLLO

223
Connections ~ **SIMON McCAFFERY**

238
Sign of the Times ~ **JOHN GROVER**

247
After, Life ~ **JEFF PARISH**

249
Paradise Denied ~ **JOHN L. FRENCH**

273
On The Usefulness Of Old Books ~ **KIM PAFFENROTH**

288
The Revelations of Dr. Maitland ~ **CHARLES BLACK**

298
Pegleg And Paddy Save The World ~
JONATHAN MABERRY

319
SKN-3 ~ **STEVEN E. WEDEL**

328
Fishing ~ **JASON BRANNON**

335
Groundwood ~ **BEV VINCENT**

- BOOKS OF THE DEAD -

Introduction
JAMES ROY DALEY

SLEEP DISSIPATES and there he is: H. P. fucking Lovecraft.
The old boy is looking down at me with anger and shame
stamped across his weird little face in equal portions. I drag my
knuckles across my eyes, snug in my bed, hoping to wipe some
of the gorp from my lashes, wondering if it's really him. Before
I've drawn a conclusion he grabs me by the wrist and hauls me
from my sheets. A pillow falls to the floor as I stumble across
the bedroom and into the shadows of the hallway. My feet slap
against the hardwood, creating sharp echoes that forge through
the night as I head towards my kitchen.

Staggering and sleepy, I say, "Hey, man. What's going on?"

H. P. flicks on a light and says, "Don't give me any lip, you
obtuse, half-wit, twerp."

In a world that seems far too bright and dynamic, I say,
"Twerp?" I don't care much for *that*. Honestly, I don't care for
the 'half-wit' remark either, but what can I say? On the 'obtuse'
slur he might be accurate. I don't know. What the hell does
obtuse mean...rounded at the free end?

I say, "Why am I a twerp?"

"You know why."

"No, really, I don't."

Now we're in the kitchen. He drags me towards a blender,
which is sitting on the counter between the sink and the stove.
It's plugged into to an outlet and ready for use. I wonder if he
planning on making a fruit smoothie but I don't have a chance

to ask because H. P. wastes no time saying, "Zombies? Are you kidding me? Is that the best you can do?"

For a moment I'm confused, but then a light bulb inside my head comes to life. I know what this is about: the book. He wants to talk to me about my anthology, Best New Zombie Tales. Sure he does. And I'm willing to talk to *him* about my little project, too. But I've got a few questions of my own, fusing together the way questions do. The most obvious inquiry, it seems, would revolve around the fact that Mr. Lovecraft has been dead for decades. What is he, back from the grave? That's ridiculous. The walking departed don't exist... right? *Right?*

I say, "Listen H. P., zombies are big right now. Real big. Do you know—"

He gives my arm a quick yank, cuffing my train of thought. He's livid now; I can see it in his face.

"I gave the world *Cthulhu* and you're serving up *zombies*? I created *Yog-Sothoth*, and all you've got is *the living-dead*? Is that the best you can do?"

For a moment I just stare, as if I'm waiting for someone else to answer the question for me. When nobody does, I reluctantly say, "You don't understand. It's not like I don't know how to be creative...I do. But the horror industry is a funny place right now, you know? The truth of the matter—"

H.P. growls like an animal from the jungle. Then he says, "SHUT UP, idiot! On an off day I could shit out *Shub-Niggurath*, *Y'golonac*, and *Azathoth*, and the most preeminent idea rattling around your infinitesimal, diminutive, nano-scholastic, brain-nugget is *zombies*? Are you on crack? What the hell is wrong with you? Don't you think this planet has suffered through a sufficient quantity of zombies?"

He lifts the lid from the blender, switches the dial from 'off' to 'mulch' and rams my hand inside before I realize what's happening.

I scream, while trying to pull away. Doesn't work. H. P. is stronger than he looks and my hand is getting mulched.

Let me repeat—

My *HAND*…is getting: **M-U-L-C-H-E-D**.

This means that my fingers—all four, plus the tip of my thumb—are getting…*MULCHED*…off.

Connected to the colossal ambush of pain are my eyes, which mature to enormity. I can't help but watch. Now my knuckles are getting chewed. Now the middle of my hand is taking a beating. Oops…there goes the rest of my thumb. There's blood. Not just inside the blender, but everywhere: splashing the walls, the ceiling, the floor, my chest, my face…

Inside the blender I can see bone fragments spinning around in a circle. A moment ago those fragments were inside my hand, not orbiting it.

It may come as no surprise that I want to tell him to stop, to let me go, to turn off that goddamn machine, which, by the way, is very powerful and apparently worth every penny I paid––thank you very much 'Home Shopping Channel.' But I don't tell him to stop. Oh no, I can't. All I can do is cry, and scream, and try to pull away.

And fail miserably, I should add. H. P.'s grip is absolute.

A little FYI here: my screaming doesn't bother Mr. Love-craft—who was kind enough to give us *Shub-Niggurath*, *Y'golonac*, and *Yog-Sothoth*, as he didn't hesitate to point out. No, no. He seems adequately happy with my pain and terror. And oddly enough, he decides to do some screaming of his own.

He unloads: "TELL ME YOU WON'T PUBLISH ANOTHER STUPID *ZOMBIE* BOOK! *TELL ME!*"

I should be saying: *No problem, Mr. Lovecraft. You want me to scrap the book idea? Consider it done. Anything else you need? A backrub? The keys to my car? A thousand dollars? A night with my girl-friend…no questions asked—? Whatever you need, H. P., just name it and it's yours! Oh boy!*

19

Instead, what comes out of my mouth is, "Ahhhhh…I have to release the zombie book!"

Lovecraft is pissed. He changes the dial from 'mulch' to 'mince.' Then from 'mince' to 'liquefy.'

I didn't even know my blender *had* 'liquefy.'

I scream more.

But he screams louder: "NO MORE ZOMBIES! DON'T YOU *HEAR* WHAT I'M TELLING YOU! ZOMBIES ARE PLAYED OUT! TEDIOUS! OVERDONE! **ZOMBIES ARE BORING!!!**"

I'm crying now. *Crying.* Full on. Tears streaming. My hand is gone. My wrist is gone. In another fifteen seconds my elbow will be turned into bone stew. Liquefied. My eyes are burning as snot runs from my nose. Panicking. Terrified. I'm not sure where I find the strength to argue, but I do. "Everybody *loves* zombies!"

He kicks me in the shin.

It's almost funny, really. The kick. It doesn't do much. I don't even feel it, truth be told. Not while my arm is getting shredded. But I see him do it and I understand—he wants to hurt me *more*, somehow. But he's grasping at straws now. Obviously. It's hard to elevate a situation when you've started negotiations by destroying a hand. He's left himself no room to maneuver, so he says, "*Nobody* loves zombies."

Oh, but he's *wrong*. And I *know* he's wrong.

I say, "Yes they do!"

"The market is *saturated!* Do something good…something *original!*"

"My book will be good!"

'DO. SOMETHING. ORIGINAL!"

An unexpected change of heart comes like an adjustment in the wind. He turns the blender off and releases me. Thank heaven. It's quiet now. The silence is a gift but my ears are ringing and my stump is throbbing. I pull my arm out to appraise the damage.

Wait. Let me try that again: I pull *what's left of my arm* out to appraise the damage. What I see looks like a cross between Cthulhu's tentacle-beard and a ketchup sundae.

Lovecraft leans in. In a gentle voice, he asks, "Are you going to publish zombies?"

I'm not sure why, but I stick to my guns. With a tremble in my voice, I say, "Yeah. I guess so."

"You sure?"

Nodding my head now. "Yes. It's the right thing to do."

"Then make sure your zombie book is amazing...you get me?"

"Yeah."

"Say it."

"Yes, yes. I get you. My zombie book will be amazing."

Lovecraft spits on the floor. "I played gentle this time, fucker," he says with a smirk. "If I have to come back here, don't count on getting off so easy. Next time I won't have a blender. I'll have a chainsaw. I'll saw your empty head off."

∞∞∞☉∞∞∞

A*hem.*

Let me clear my throat.

Dear literate zombie fans; my name is James Roy Daley. What you're looking at is a little idea of mine, brought to life by the power of hard work. If you're a zombie purist this compilation will probably piss you off a bunch 'cause I've put together stories that are not afraid to break traditional rules. Question: if you chop a zombie in half and both sections attack, are you fighting two zombies now? What if you chop the sucker into a hundred pieces? What if you're attacked by hair and skin? Are zombies allowed to run? Do they think? Can they talk? Can they use tools? Do they experience emotions? Can they team up? Drive a car? Have sex?

Ah, the questions are endless. And with each comes a plethora of unverified answers. The debate never ends.

Like I said, some of these stories will piss off the traditionalists, no doubt. But if you're a collector of zombie goodness this book will add some brilliant tales to your collection, tales you do *not* have.

I went *digging*.

And found stories inside anthologies you can't buy, and compilations you've never heard of. I've got stories from websites that no longer exist and magazines that haven't put out an issue in ages. I went *digging*, brothers and sisters. *Digging*. And yeah, some of the tales are easy to get. *Some*. Not many.

This book contains funny tales and nightmares, artsy pieces and screamers, big stories and small. I tried to hit different emotions. Straight up, I pulled together the best work I could get my hands on—*I don't want the horror gods to kick my ass, don't you know*. My goal, a simple one: to put together the best zombie tales ever written. Don't care what year the story was written. Don't care who wrote it. Don't care if the story follows Romero's un-written rules of what a zombie is supposed to do. Don't care if it's offensive, or filled with naughty language. All I care about is *High Quality Fiction*. Simple.

And with that, my rant has ended. I did my part. Now it's your turn.

Get comfy.

Get ready.

Get reading.

First up, a Ray Garton masterpiece…

Zombie Love
RAY GARTON

- ONE -

1.

A COLD, GUSTY DECEMBER wind blew the falling rain through the night. Just outside the small northern California town of Anderson, atop what the local children called Witch's Hill, and near the dead-end of narrow seldom-used Hilltop Road, Mrs. Kobylka's little house stood blanketed with ivy. The house was so covered by the white-speckled green leaves it seemed to have grown up out of the earth with the vines. Wisps of smoke were swept away by the wind as they rose out of the small chimney on the right side of the house. Four cracked concrete steps led up through an ivy-coated arch onto a small enclosed porch. The porch was flanked by windows— the one on the left was dark, while a soft glow shone through the drapes on the other. An enormous weeping willow, its branches swaying in the wind, stood in the small yard, which was overrun by weeds. The pickets of a once-white fence surrounding the yard were dark and broken, like old neglected teeth. An old blue pickup truck that had seen better days a long time ago was parked in front of the house.

Three young people sat in a silver Ford Focus Sedan SE parked across the pot-holed road from the house. The rain was loud inside the car as they stared silently at the house—Randy Satifoy at the wheel, his girlfriend Liz Poole in the passenger seat, and Kirk Mundy behind her. Kirk was stretched over the backseat, his nose to the glass on the other side. They were each 17 years old. They had grown up there in Anderson, and since they were small children, they had heard stories about creepy old Mrs. Kobylka, that she was a witch who had lived in that run-down house for over a hundred years.

When they were kids, it had been customary to see who was brave enough to egg Mrs. Kobylka's house each Halloween and risk falling under her evil spell. The old woman had been there when Kirk's dad was a boy, and kids had told the same stories about her back then. One story in particular had stood out, a story about a dead dog. It was passed down from generation to generation of children who rode their bikes up the hill to see the run-down old house, who dared each other to go up and knock on the door. Sometimes they spotted her coming out to get her mail from the rusted old box on the crooked post in front of her house. They watched from hidden vantage points as she shuffled through the weeds that grew up between the cracks in the concrete walk that led to the gate—a plump, slightly hunched old woman with a wild tangle of white hair, always in a simple housedress with a shawl across her shoulders. Sometimes she drove into town in her old pickup truck and was seen at the post office or drugstore, and the whispering children kept a healthy distance from her as she went about her business.

Kirk's dad had told him more than once to stay away from Mrs. Kobylka's place. He'd said she was a crazy old woman and she shouldn't be bothered. It had done no good, of course.

In the Focus, Randy spoke just loud enough to be heard above the sound of the rain: "Are you sure you want to do this, Kirk?"

"Yes." There was no hesitation in his response.

Liz said, "You guys do what you want, but I'm staying here." She ran a brush through her short strawberry-blonde hair. She was a pretty girl with a small round face, tense now as she looked at Randy. She'd been crying earlier, after the news about Natalie, and her blue eyes were puffy. "There's no fuckin' way I'm going in there."

"I'll go alone, I don't care," Kirk said. He sat up in the backseat and opened the door.

"Wait," Randy said, "don't you want me to go with you?"

"If you want. You don't have to. But I've got to do it now, before I lose my nerve." He got out of the car and closed the door.

"All right, I'm coming, I'm coming," Randy said as he got out.

"Leave the keys," Liz said. "If you don't come out in ten or fifteen minutes, I'm getting the hell out of here."

"They're in the ignition," Randy said as turned up the collar of his denim jacket. "But don't leave, we'll be right back."

"I'm glad *you're* so sure," she said.

Randy closed the door as Kirk came around the rear of the car and started across the road, hands in the pockets of his down jacket, head down and shoulders hunched against the rain. Randy hurried to catch up.

Kirk was handsome in a sad way—everything about him was sad lately—tall and slender and subtly muscled, an avid swimmer, with short dark brown hair. But he seemed to have shrunk somehow since the accident. He was pale and drawn from lack of sleep. He limped slightly—his only injury from the accident had been a badly bruised knee. Randy was a little shorter, stockier, with a mop of blond hair, a round face, and wire-framed glasses. They were quickly soaked by the rain as they crossed the road.

"Do you know what you're gonna say to her?" Randy asked as they hurried through the gate, which stood open crookedly, one hinge broken.

"Not really," Kirk said. "I guess I'll just tell her what I want.

She'll either help me or she won't."

They went up the walk and paused at the bottom of the porch steps.

"It's about ten-thirty," Randy said. "What if she's asleep?"

"We'll wake her," Kirk said.

"What if everything we've heard about her is bullshit?"

"Then I'll apologize and we'll go."

"What do you want me to say?"

"Nothing, unless you want to."

Kirk went up the steps and into the small cave formed by the ivy-covered arch, out of the rain, and Randy followed. On the other side of a rickety old screen door, the front door had a square window in the top with white curtains, the glass smudged. He knocked on the frame of the screen and it rattled noisily. A dog barked loudly inside, and Kirk could hear a television playing. The dog sounded big and vicious. The television's volume was high and sounded like the news. There was movement, then footsteps came toward the door.

"She's coming," Randy whispered. "Our last chance to haul ass outta here."

One of the white curtains in the window was tugged aside and a wide, rheumy, deep-set eye peered out at them.

"Who are you?" she asked in a dry, cracked voice. "What you want?" Even though she'd lived there for what seemed like forever, she still spoke with a heavy eastern-European accent: *Vot you vant?*

"My name is Kirk Mundy, Mrs. Kobylka. This is my friend Randy. Can I talk to you, please?"

"Mundy, eh? What you want to talk about?"

"I want to ask you something."

She dropped the curtain and fumbled with locks, muttering to herself. The door opened and she stood before them, a squat, backlit silhouette. She flipped a switch on the wall and the naked yellow bulb in a socket above the door blinked on.

"You come to egg my house?" she said. "Halloween's over. It's *Christmas* time." A couple of her upper front teeth were the only teeth remaining in her head and her wrinkled cheeks and lower lip sunk loosely into her mouth. Her face resembled a decaying old Jack-o-lantern.

Kirk said, "I've come to ask for your help."

"My *help*? What is this, some kinda charity drive?" *Vot ith dith, thome kynt uff choddity drife?*

"No, ma'am," Kirk said. "It's a...a personal favor."

Her eyes darted back and forth between them several times, then she stared at Kirk for a long moment. She wore a pale green housedress, slippers, and a dark shawl on her shoulders. Somewhere behind her the dog continued to bark. "Mundy. You come for Mrs. Kobylka's help, eh?" she said, looking Kirk up and down. "What you want that I should help you with?"

"Would it be all right if we came in?" Kirk said.

"Why should I let you in?"

"So I can tell you what I want."

Kirk watched her as she thought it over. She was stout, short, and hunched, and her face was impossibly lined and creased. Her bleary right eye was wide, her left a narrow slit. Her white hair was long and tangled and went in every direction, like Medusa's snakes. Standing before him in the yellow glow of the porch light, she looked more pathetic than frightening, and it seemed impossible that she was the woman feared by children all over town.

She shrugged one of her round shoulders and said, "Okay. But when I say you go, you go."

"Sure," Kirk said.

They stepped back as she pushed the screen door open, then went inside.

The house was dark and smelled of cooked cabbage. On the left, a small, messy kitchen was lit only by a fluorescent light over a counter, beneath a bank of cupboards. Straight ahead

27

was a dark hallway. On the right was a cluttered living room with a wood stove. At the couch's end nearest them, a lamp with a red shade glowed on an endtable. In the shadowy corner at the other end of the couch stood a large round cage, tall and fat, and inside on a perch was an enormous dark bird. The bird barked in throaty bursts, like a large dog. A small black-and-white TV with rabbit-ears stood on a TV tray in front of the couch playing the news with the volume high. The heat in the house was smothering.

Mrs. Kobylka led them into the living room, where she clapped her hands and shouted, "Baltazar! Stop!"

The bird stopped barking, meowed like a cat once, then fell silent.

"What you want with Mrs. Kobylka?" she said, turning to them.

"Um, it's my girlfriend," Kirk said. "Her name is…was …Natalie Gilbert."

Mrs. Kobylka went to the end of the sagging old couch by the lamp and grunted as she lowered herself onto the flattened cushion. She leaned forward and turned down the television's volume. She had been crocheting when they knocked—the skein of yarn, the crocheting hook, and what looked like the beginning of an afghan lay beside her. She did not invite them to sit.

"What she got to do with me?" she said.

Kirk said, "She…died tonight."

Mrs. Kobylka's thick white eyebrow rose high above her wide eye.

"We were on our way to a Christmas party last night," Kirk said, "and we had a car accident." He thought he'd cried all the tears he had to shed, but more burned his throat. He swallowed a couple times before continuing. "I…I was driving. We were hit by a drunk driver. He ran a stop sign. I was wearing a seatbelt, but…she wasn't."

Baltazar the dark, hulking bird in the cage shouted, "Stumbling bumblefucks!" in what sounded like the voice of an old man.

Kirk's eyes had adjusted to the dull red-tinted light in the room and could see the bird in more detail. He had thought, at first, that it was a parrot of some kind, but it looked like no parrot he had ever seen. It was black, all the way down to its legs and wicked talons, except for red crescents beneath its black eyes, a curved, blood-red blade of a beak, and a patch of crimson feathers on its back and tail. But those seemed to be the only feathers on the bird. It didn't even have feathers on its wings. Instead, its wings seemed to be folds of leathery black flesh. Almost like a bat's wings. But that couldn't be—what kind of bird had wings like a bat?

"Stumbling bumblefucks!" the bird shouted again.

"Hush, Balty," Mrs. Kobylka said. She looked up at Kirk. "You hurt?"

"I got a bump on the knee," Kirk said. "Natalie was…she went into a coma. She had internal injuries. And tonight, she…" He clenched his teeth and took a deep breath. "She died. Just a little while ago. In the hospital."

"Too bad. Mrs. Kobylka feel sad for you. But what this got to do with me?"

"We've…heard things about you," Kirk said, glancing at Randy.

Randy's eyes widened and he spread his arms slightly, as if to say, *What're you looking at* me *for?*

Mrs. Kobylka's frown deepened. "Heard things? We? You two?"

Eye's still wide, Randy looked down at her and nodded.

"Yes," Kirk said. "Since we were kids. We've heard stories about you."

The black-and-red bird giggled in a child's voice, and the sound gave Kirk a chill.

Smirking, Mrs. Kobylka ignored the bird and said, "Stories? What kind of stories?"

Kirk cleared his throat, shifted his weight from foot to foot. "Um, well, since we were kids, people have said that you're… that you can do things."

Mrs. Kobylka sat as far forward as she could and rolls of fat pressed against her housedress. "Spit it out, boy, it's late."

"There's a story about a dog," Kirk said. "According to the, um, the story, years ago a boy's dog got sick and died, and he brought it to you, and you, uh…well, according to the story, you…brought it back." Kirk heard his own words and was suddenly embarrassed. He bowed his head a moment, then looked at her again. "Is that true, Mrs. Kobylka?"

"True?" Her laugh sounded like dry leaves being crushed. "What you saying?"

"Is it true that…" He took another deep breath, then let the words tumble out of him. "Is it true that you're a witch and you can bring back dead things?"

She laughed again as she stood. She stepped in front of Kirk and cocked her head to the left, looked up at him with her round, watery eye. "You come here for my magic?" she whispered, smiling.

"It's…it's true, then?" Kirk said.

"Why you want I should help you bring this girl back?"

"Because…I love her. And I feel responsible for what happened. I should've told her to put her seatbelt on, I should have…I…" His voice dropped to a whisper. "We've known each other since we were in first grade. I can't…live…without her. I love her." He pressed his lips together hard and blinked back tears.

"Love," she said as she turned away and left the living room. She waved a gnarled, liver-spotted hand in the air and said, "Love messes up your head. Scrambles the brains like eggs." She flipped a switch on the wall and turned on the overhead fluorescent in the kitchen, then turned to Kirk and Randy again. "You want I should do my magic for you. Can you pay the price?"

Kirk said, "I don't have much money, but—"

"I'm not talking about *money*. What about you two?" She pointed at them with the first two fingers of her right hand. "What you gonna do for *me*, I do this for you? Kids in this town—they egg my house, call me names, leave dog shit on my porch. And I should do this for you?"

Kirk went to her and said, "We'll try to get the kids to leave you alone."

"You can do that?"

"We can do that. I've got a little brother, and Randy, here, has a younger brother and sister. They have lots of friends. We can tell them to leave you alone. We'll get the word out."

"You tell them stay away from Mrs. Kobylka or I cut them up and feed them to Baltazar," she said with a mischievous smile. Her laugh became a phlegmy cough.

The bird wailed like a baby crying at the top of its lungs.

"Baltazar, stop showing off!" Mrs. Kobylka crossed her small kitchen. "You know what you getting into, boy?" She opened a cupboard and removed a couple jars, put them on the counter.

"What do you mean?" Kirk said.

She closed the cupboard and came to him, stood close. He smelled her sour breath as she said, "This girl, she will be your responsibility, not mine. No one else's. Just yours. And once it is done...there is no undoing it. You understand? She comes back, she is *yours*."

"She was mine when she died," he said.

"Not like this. That story you hear, what happen to that dog?"

"I...I don't know."

"Your girlfriend...she's no dog. I do this for you, boy, it is

31

on your head. Whatever happens, you must live with it the rest of your life."

Kirk suddenly felt impatient. He hadn't slept the night before and his nerves felt raw. "Are you going to help me or not?"

"I do this for you, but I don't know if it is *helping* or not." She went back to the kitchen counter and unscrewed the lid off one of the jars. "I come here when I was just a girl, younger than you, I think. I live here ever since. My husband die. My baby die. I been alone since then." She took the lid off the other jar. Leaning an arm on the edge of the counter, she bent down and opened a cupboard, and used both hands to lift out a stone mortar and pestle, which she put on the counter. "All this town ever give me was shit." She looked at Kirk again. "I do this for you, but you remember—you *ask* for it." Her thin, frayed lips peeled back over her few yellow teeth, and she laughed.

The bird shouted, "Stumbling bumblefucks!"

2.

Their first time together was on a hot summer afternoon under a small bridge near their homes. They lived only four houses apart on River Valley Drive, a rural area just outside Anderson's city limits. The bridge was only three yards long and so low they had to duck when they walked under it. It passed over a small creek that ran all year long and sometimes flooded during the rainier winters.

It had been Natalie's idea to come, and she had brought lunch in a brown grocery bag with the top rolled up. They found a sandy patch among all the rocks and she took a rolled-up towel from the bag and spread it out. They sat cross-legged facing each other with the bag between them.

Looking at her there in the shade of the bridge, it was hard for Kirk to believe she was the same girl who had climbed on the monkeybars with him when they were children. In second grade, he had dropped a live frog down the back of her dress and laughed hysterically as she danced around to get rid of it. In fourth grade, he'd put earthworms in her Power Rangers lunchbox and laughed at her shrieks.

But now they were both 15—his birthday had been the day before, hers a few months ago—and nothing about Natalie made him laugh. Smile, yes, but not laugh the way he used to. They'd been 13 when, as if overnight, Natalie had changed, and as a result, it seemed, so had Kirk. One day, he'd looked at her and had been unable to take his eyes off her ever since. Her smiles made his stomach flutter, and when she held his hand, he was unable to feel the ground beneath his feet. The two had been inseparable since then, and after two years, she could still make him clumsy and weak-kneed and stuttery.

Just an inch shorter than Kirk, she had long, thick hair so black it sometimes looked purple in the sun. It was early August and she had a golden tan. Her round breasts pushed gently against the tanktop she wore, her narrow midriff bare above a pair of white shorts, legs long and silky. When he looked at her now, he saw a young woman, not a girl—and yet, when he was around her, he still felt like a boy. They had been together for two years, and yet everything they did together felt new. And they did almost everything together. Except for one thing—until that summer afternoon.

"What'd you bring?" Kirk asked, nodding toward the bag.

"Chicken salad sandwiches, Dorritos, a couple Cokes, and a little surprise."

"A surprise?"

She smiled. "You'll see," she said.

Natalie moved the bag aside and crawled to him on hands and knees, grinning. She kissed him and their tongues played tag for a moment.

"Happy birthday, Frog Boy," she said with a giggle.

He laughed. "You've never forgiven me for that, have you?"

"Nope. Ever had a slimy frog slide down your spine? It's gross."

"My birthday was yesterday."

"Yeah, but I didn't get a chance to give you a present, did I? So I'm giving it to you now." As she kissed him again, she reached down and unbuttoned his denim cut-offs, slid her hand beneath his boxers and gently squeezed him.

Kirk's lungs seemed to deflate and he hardened instantly as she tugged on his cut-offs.

"Take them off," she said.

As he got up and fumbled his clothes off, Natalie reached into the bag and removed a condom in a bright blue wrapper.

"We're always gonna use one of these, 'kay?" she said. "We are so *not* ready to be a mommy and daddy."

Kirk nodded. He would have agreed to almost anything at that moment. His mouth hung open as he watched her stand and undress. Her breasts bobbed as she slipped the tanktop up over them and took it off.

They made love for the first time there beside the gently burbling creek, in the cool shade of the bridge.

3.

"She just got here a few minutes ago," Luanne Richmond whispered as she let Kirk in through the back door of the Richmond Funeral Home. She closed the door, then led him down a short hall and through a doorway to the left. As they went downstairs to the basement, she whispered, "You can't stay long. My dad could come down here anytime. You can have a couple minutes alone with her but no more."

Luanne was a short, chubby girl with round eyeglasses, her brown hair cut in a pageboy. Natalie and Luanne had been good friends, and Natalie's death had hit her hard. Even now, her eyes were red and swollen from crying. She had been at the hospital earlier when Natalie died, along with a number of other kids from school, and Kirk had taken her aside and asked her for this favor—a few minutes alone with Natalie before she was embalmed and prepared for viewing.

"They wouldn't let me see her here," he'd told her at the hospital. "Only her family. I just want a chance to say goodbye. Alone. Do you understand?" Luanne probably would have thought he was crazy if he'd told her the truth. Luanne had promised to do what she could. She told him to park down the street from the funeral home, where she and her family lived on the second floor. He was to come to the back door and wait in an hour, and be very quiet.

He had left Randy and Liz in the Focus parked at the curb around the corner from the funeral home. All the way from Mrs. Kobylka's, Randy had said, over and over, "Did you see that fuckin' bird? It was like Rodan's short, ugly cousin." Randy had wanted to come into the funeral home with him, but Kirk decided to do it alone.

Luanne led him through a door at the bottom of the stairs and into the cold, white, clinical-looking basement. The air was sour with the smell of formaldehyde and something else, something Kirk did not want to think about.

Natalie lay beneath a white sheet on a shiny stainless-steel table with a gutter around the edges to catch draining fluids. Kirk froze ten feet away and stared open-mouthed at the still, covered form.

"C'mon," Luanne whispered as she grabbed his hand and tugged, "let's go, we have to hurry."

Kirk walked on numb legs to Natalie's side. Luanne pulled the sheet down just below Natalie's shoulders.

Luanne squeezed his upper arm and whispered, "Two minutes, no more. I'm going back upstairs to make sure Dad doesn't come down here, but I can't make any promises. If he catches you, remember what we agreed—you tell him you found the back door unlocked and you came in on your own, and I didn't have anything to do with it. When you're done, just go out the way we came in."

Kirk nodded and tried to say "Thank you," but his voice failed him and he only mouthed the words. Luanne's footsteps faded as she went back up the stairs.

He pulled the sheet back and left it in a heap at her feet, then stared down at her for a long moment. She did not look real.

Last summer, Kirk's family had gone to San Francisco for a weekend, and Natalie had come along. They'd gone to the wax museum at Fisherman's Wharf and had *ooohed* and *aaahed* at the lifelike figures that stood behind glass in the museum. Natalie looked like one of them now—a meticulously crafted wax figure with a grayish-yellow hue. It did not look like the body Kirk had held so many times, the face and neck and breasts he'd kissed, the silky skin he'd stroked.

Her full lips had become thin and gray, with a hint of purple. Her breasts looked deflated and lay flat on her chest, like nippled pancakes of empty flesh. There was an ugly gash on her forehead above her right brow, and another on her right shoulder. A dark maroon bruise had blossomed on her right side, just below her breast. She looked surprisingly good considering the drunk had slammed into her door—the injuries that had killed her were internal.

Heart pounding, breath short, Kirk wasted no time. He reached into the pocket of his jacket and removed a small baby-food jar half-filled with a gray paste Mrs. Kobylka had made.

"Dip your finger in," she had told him. In the fluorescent

light of her kitchen, she'd been a color quite similar to Natalie's. "Make an X over her heart. Then say these words three times." *Den thay dethe verdth tree times.* She had written out the words phonetically on a Post-It note, then spoke them once, slowly, folded the square of yellow paper over and handed it to him.

Kirk removed the lid from the baby-food jar and got a whiff of the paste inside—a mixture of a licorice-like odor and a foul cheesy smell, as well as others he couldn't identify. He wrinkled his nose as he dipped his right index finger into the paste. His hand, finger extended, hovered over Natalie's chest for a moment, then he drew an X slightly left of her sternum. Her flesh was cold and no longer felt like flesh. Instead of the soft, supple skin he was accustomed to, it felt papery and ungiving. He thought again of the wax figures in the museum.

He quickly rubbed the excess paste off his finger onto the edge of the jar's mouth, then replaced the lid and stuffed it back into his pocket. At the same time, he reached into the other pocket for the Post-It. He looked at the eight nonsense syllables on the paper: Zin-bra show-tik mah-fu low-rem. They meant nothing to him, but he did not care. He said them just above a whisper, three times.

4.

Natalie's black hair made her large, pale-turquoise eyes stand out above her high cheekbones. Kirk often stared into them for long minutes, unable to look away.

"You're staring again," she said once as they lay on their sides facing each other. They were on a towel on the shore of Whiskeytown Lake.

"Sorry. But…do you have any idea how beautiful your eyes are?"

"Do you have any idea how unnerving that is?" she said with a laugh. "Besides, my parents could come over here anytime. They'll see you undressing me with your eyes and you'll embarrass me."

But the truth was, Natalie did not embarrass easily. She had a laugh that was pleasant but loud and could be heard throughout the school's cafeteria at lunchtime. It was a laugh that turned heads, but she didn't care, not a bit. And when it came to sex she had no shame; she wanted it when she wanted it, and as a result, they'd had sex in some risky places. The riskier the better, as far as Natalie was concerned. They'd done it a few times in Natalie's bedroom while her parents were downstairs in the living room watching television, and Kirk wasn't sure if the door had been locked. Once on her living room floor in front of the television while her parents were in bed. Several times in the navy-blue Volkswagen Jetta her parents had given her for her sixteenth birthday, while it was parked in some public places—a couple times in the school parking lot, once in the parking lot of the Mt. Shasta Mall, once in the parking lot of the Cinemark Movies 10, all in broad daylight. Twice, she had come to his bedroom window in the middle of the night—he'd always left it open and she'd climbed in and they'd made love in his bed while his parents slept two doors down. She'd wanted him to come to her room at night, but it was on the second floor of her house, unreachable without a ladder, and Kirk wasn't *that* daring. Their closest call had been in one of the janitor's utility closets at school. The janitor, Mr. Edgerly, had been approaching the closet when they came out, and he'd given them his most threatening glare, but had said nothing. Kirk was always against it at first, always worried about getting caught. But Natalie always said, "C'mon, let's do it here, it'll be exciting." He couldn't say no to her when she looked into his eyes and smiled. He couldn't say no to her, period.

But he should have said *something* when she didn't put on her seatbelt last night. He should have noticed and told her to fasten it, should have refused to put the car in gear until she'd done it.

Should-haves ate at his guts like acid.

5.

Natalie opened her eyes.

Kirk stepped back and sucked in a loud gasp. He dropped the Post-It note and it fluttered to the floor. His heart pounded in his ears and he breathed loudly through his mouth.

He had not expected it to work, not really. Although he'd grown up believing Mrs. Kobylka to be a witch, a voice in the back of his mind—the same voice that had told him there was no Santa Claus or Easter Bunny when he was a kid—had told him she was just a weird old woman who'd decided to have a little fun with him. As much as he wanted it, that voice had not allowed him to truly believe Mrs. Kobylka's spell would work.

Natalie slowly, clumsily rolled onto her side, swung her legs over the edge of the table, and sat up. Her back, buttocks, and the backs of her legs were a dark purple where blood had settled in her body. Her eyes moved from side to side, up and down, as she looked around the room. They did not look the same—the sparkle was gone from them, they looked dulled, their bright turquoise paled, diluted. And they did not blink. Her movements were stiff and awkward and she did not turn her head. There was a stiffness to her face and the corners of her mouth were pulled back slightly in a frozen grimace. She did not make a sound, did not even breathe.

"Nat?" Kirk whispered.

She made a small clicking sound in her throat as she tried unsuccessfully to speak.

Kirk took the sheet from the table and draped it over her shoulders, then helped her to her feet. He wrapped her in the sheet and put an arm around her. She felt cold through the cotton. "Come on, let's get out of here," he whispered. Before leaving the basement, he bent down and grabbed the yellow Post-It note off the floor.

- TWO -

1.

It had stopped raining shortly before Kirk entered the funeral home. Natalie's bare feet slapped the wet sidewalk as she walked stiffly beside him, wrapped in the sheet, stumbling now and then. Her arms did not move at her sides and she did not bend her knees as she walked, and the only sound she made was a small gurgle in her throat. She appeared to be unable to move her mouth and her neck remained stiff. Kirk was still reeling from the fact that she'd sat up on the bed, that she had walked out of the funeral home with him, but he was starting to become concerned about her condition.

Kirk could hear Randy and Liz inside the Focus well before he got there. Liz screamed when she saw Natalie, then babbled loudly, while Randy sat behind the wheel with bulging eyes repeating something over and over.

Kirk opened the back door on the passenger side and said to Natalie, "Get in, honey, get in."

"Holy shit!" Randy said.

Natalie had difficulty bending, but finally fell into the car and bent her knees with effort.

Liz was crying as she babbled. "—my God, I can't believe this, I can't fucking believe it, oh my God, this isn't real, this isn't happening!"

"Holy shit!" Randy said.

Kirk persuaded Natalie to scoot over. He got into the car beside her and pulled the door shut. "Let's get out of here," he said.

"Holy shit! Holy shit!"

"Oh, Jesus," Liz said, turned around in her seat so she could gape at Natalie, "this can't be real, this is so fucked up, oh God, I can't believe—"

Kirk said, "Randy, get us out of here before someone sees us. And let's roll down all the windows."

Randy continued to mutter, "Holy shit," to himself as he started the car and put it in gear. The radio came on loudly, startling all of them, and he turned it off.

Liz knelt in her seat, clutching the back of it as she gawked at Natalie. "Jesus, is that really her? Nat? Is it you, Nat?"

"Just *go*, dammit," Kirk said. "And sit down and put on your seatbelt, Liz." He bent over Natalie and pulled the belt across her, buckled her in, then fastened his own.

Liz reluctantly turned around in her seat and put on her belt.

Randy pulled away from the curb, made a U-turn, and drove away from the funeral home. His wide eyes flashed in the rearview mirror as he glanced repeatedly at Natalie's reflection.

"Holy shit," Randy said again, his voice a dry rasp. "She's not bleeding, is she? My mom'll kill me if I get blood in her car."

"Just drive, Randy," Kirk said. "Everything's fine."

With her head craned around, Liz stared at Natalie. "Nobody's gonna believe this. *I* can't believe it, and I'm *seeing* it."

"Well, we're not going to *tell* anyone, are we, Liz?" Kirk said.

Randy said, "Don't you think Luanne's dad is gonna wonder what happened to her? Even Luanne will wonder. She'll think you *took* her. I mean, they're not gonna think Natalie just got up and walked out. Even though…she did."

"What time is it?" Kirk said.

"She doesn't blink," Liz said.

"What time is it," Kirk asked again.

"She doesn't fucking *blink*, that's so *creepy*." She glanced at her watch. "It's about ten minutes after eleven."

"Okay," Kirk said, "my parents are in bed by now."

"Are you sure they aren't up wondering where you are?" Randy asked.

"I told them I'd be out late, and they were cool about it." Kirk turned to Natalie. She sat rigidly and stared at the back of Randy's head. He put a hand on her shoulder and said, "Nat? Natalie?"

Her mouth was still drawn back in a grimace. She made another gurgling sound in her throat, but did not move.

"She's not gonna be sick, is she?" Randy said. "My mom'll kill me—"

"Stop worrying about your mom," Kirk said. "Everything's going to be fine. She's just…well, maybe she's confused." He turned to her again. "Natalie? Look at me."

Still no movement. She stopped making the sound.

Kirk touched her chin to turn her head, but jerked his hand away. She felt so cold, so…*wrong*. There was tension in her facial muscles that he could feel when he touched her. He tried again and did not pull away the second time. But he could not turn her head. He closed his hand gently on her right arm beneath the sheet and tried to move it, but could not. She was like a block of solid ice.

"Oh, Jesus," Kirk said.

Liz looked over her shoulder. "What's wrong?"

Kirk shook his head. "I'm not sure, she's not…I can't…I think she's *frozen*."

"Is she…well, did she…die again?" Randy said.

Kirk unfastened his seatbelt and got close to Natalie, put his face in front of hers. The faint ghost of her perfume still clung to her, but there was another smell beneath that. Something... dark. "Natalie, can you hear me?"

She grunted once, but her face was frozen, a grimacing mask. Her eyes did not move in their sockets.

"She's responding," Kirk said, "but she can't move."

"Oh, my God," Liz said.

Kirk got back in his seat, fastened the belt. "What?"

"You know what this is?" she said. "It's rigor mortis."

Kirk said, "But she's not dead anymore."

Liz turned in her seat, craned her head around to look at him. "Are you sure?"

"What do you mean?"

"Did Mrs. Kobylka say she was going to bring Natalie back to *life*?" Liz said. "Or did she just say she was going to bring her *back*?"

"What the hell's the difference?" Randy said.

"Oh, shit," Kirk muttered as realization set in. "You mean she might...still be dead."

Randy raised his voice. "*What*?"

Liz began to cry again. "Oh, God, this is *so* fucked up. I can't believe this. I wanna go home."

"What the fuck're you *talking* about?" Randy said.

Wiping her eyes with a knuckle, Liz said, "There's a big difference between a living person and a dead person who's been, like, I don't know...reanimated." She laughed nervously. "Listen to me. I can't believe I just said that."

"Re*animated*?" Randy said. Eyes wide, he glanced back and forth between the road and Liz. "Fuck, man. I saw that movie."

"Pay attention to the road, Randy," Kirk said. He looked at Natalie.

She remained motionless, and made another small grunting sound, as if she were gagging.

"How long does rigor mortis last?" Kirk said.

"I hope you're not asking me," Randy said.

Liz said, "I don't know."

"Do you have your laptop?" Kirk asked.

"Yeah."

"Look it up."

"Are you insane? I'm sitting in a car with a walking dead person and you want me to surf the Web? We should be *on* the web, people would *pay* to see this shit."

"Please, Liz."

She brought her backpack up off the floorboard and into her lap. "Isn't Rigor Mortis the name of a band? I'm probably gonna find a bunch of metalhead bulletin boards."

2.

Randy killed the headlights before pulling into the circular driveway in front of the Mundy's ranch-style house. Kirk unfastened his seatbelt and bent forward.

"Did you find anything yet?" he said.

Liz snapped at him. "Gimme a break, Kirk, I just started looking a few minutes ago."

Kirk and Randy got out of the car and met at the rear door on the driver's side, Natalie's door. Kirk opened it. He and Randy whispered to each other.

"Help me carry her into the back," Kirk said.

Randy nervously rubbed his hands on the front of his denim jacket as if wiping something sticky off them. He winced and said, "Look, dude, I'm not sure I wanna...y'know...touch her."

"But she can't walk."

"I know, man, she can't walk because she's dead, which is why I don't wanna touch her."

"She walked to the car with me, you *saw* her," Kirk said.

"Come on, she's wrapped in a sheet so you don't have to touch her—oh, nevermind."

Kirk slid his right arm behind her shoulders, his left beneath her legs and lifted her out of the car. She remained frozen in a sitting position.

Randy said, "She looks like a Barcalounger." He followed as Kirk carried her past the garage and into the back yard. They walked around the covered concrete swimming pool and Kirk carried her into the small pool-house. He fumbled for the light, switched it on.

There was an old black vinyl-upholstered couch and an end-table in the pool-house's concrete-floored main room, which was icy cold. But it was used primarily to store pool equipment, and as a place for people to change clothes or shower when they used the pool in the summer. No one ever went into the pool-house during the winter months.

He went to the couch, but changed his mind—the front window provided a clear view of the couch from outside. He carried her into the bathroom and set her down on the closed lid of the toilet. The tiled, pale-green bathroom was small, with a shower to the right of the toilet, a sink to the left.

"She smells," Randy said, his voice unsteady. "I may be sick."

"Well, try not to be," Kirk said.

Randy stepped into the open doorway of the bathroom and faced Kirk. "Listen to me," he whispered. "I'm thinking we did the wrong thing tonight, Kirk. She's stiff as a board. That old woman—she was jerking us around, this is some kind of trick. She's *dead*. This is a serious crime, stealing a dead body. I mean...well, *isn't* it? It should be if it's not, it's a pretty gross thing to do, and dude, I think that's what we've done."

Kirk pointed to Natalie and said, "Randy, I saw her sit up on that table and look around. She looked at *me*. You saw her walk out of that funeral home with me. And she's still making sounds. You heard them, didn't you?"

"That was her? I thought it was you. Are you sure it wasn't, like…gas?"

"She's alive, Randy."

"But she's going to be stiff for about twenty-four hours," Liz said. She stood just outside the bathroom, arms folded across her chest. "According to the Columbia Encyclopedia online, anyway."

"She'll be safe here tonight," Kirk said as he and Randy stepped out of the bathroom. He pulled the door closed. "I'll keep checking on her tomorrow."

"You're just gonna check on her?" Liz said. "What're you gonna do if she starts moving around? Or if she starts to…you know…smell."

"She already smells," Randy said.

Kirk clenched his fists at his sides and closed his eyes a moment. He spoke quietly. "Please just…*stop*, okay? I…I'm not sure what I'm going to do."

"You okay, Kirk?" Randy said.

He took a deep breath and opened his eyes. "No. But I will be. Thanks for helping out."

Kirk walked them back to the car. As they drove away, he fumbled his keys from his pocket, but paused before unlocking the front door. He thought of Natalie sitting like a posed mannequin on the toilet in the pool-house. Leaving her there all alone made his chest ache. He put the keys back in his pocket and walked around the house.

He went to her in the small bathroom. She looked less like a human being sitting stiffly on the toilet than she had while lying dead on the stainless-steel table back at Richmond's.

"Can you hear me, Nat?" he whispered.

She made no sound this time.

"I'll come back out first thing tomorrow, I promise. To-morrow's the first day of Christmas vacation, so I won't have to worry about school. We'll be together, and we'll...work this all out." He wanted to take her in his arms and kiss her, hold her tight. But even in the cold, he could smell the odor—like meat that had been left out of the refrigerator and had gone bad. He could not bring himself to do it. Instead, he went out and got a folded-up old afghan from the couch and wrapped it around her over the sheet to keep her warm.

He left the pool-house, walked past the pool, and unlocked the back door of the house. As he passed the kitchen on his way down the hall, Dad said, "Kirk. Where have you been?"

3.

Kirk jumped at the sound of Dad's voice. The kitchen was dark. Dad sat at the small oval table with a bottle of whisky and a half-full glass in front of him. He smiled wearily with his mouth, but not with his eyes.

"Nowhere," Kirk said.

"You were nowhere?" Dad spoke just above a whisper and kept smiling in the dark. "Well, you had to be somewhere."

Kirk's voice was suddenly hoarse. "I was just riding around with Randy and Liz. We didn't go anywhere, just drove around. Just talked. You know."

"Sit down, Kirky." Dad used to call him "Kirky" when Kirk was little, and sometimes it still slipped out.

Dad was Donald Mundy, but everyone called him Don. His old friends called him Donny. He was tall and slim, completely bald on top, with graying brown hair that grew around the back of his head from ear to ear. He ran a small advertising agency with his brother, Kirk's uncle Matt. Most of the time, Dad was almost embarrassingly upbeat and cheerful. Everyone liked him. He was active in community organizations, went to church with Mom every Sunday. As far as Kirk was concerned,

Dad was a likeable geek. He had never known Dad to raise his voice in anger or say a bad word about anyone—he was able to find something good in everyone he met. Mom, on the other hand, was a little high-strung, almost as nervous and hyper as Bud and Lou, her two ferrets, which had the run of the house. Dad was the level head in the family. But there were times when he couldn't sleep well. This was not the first time Kirk had found him in the kitchen late at night sipping whisky. The first time had been when Kirk was eight years old. It happened maybe once or twice a year.

Dad wasn't a big drinker—he got cheerfully tipsy on Christmas and New Year's, but otherwise his drinking was limited to a couple beers when they barbecued in the back yard on summer weekends. The rest of the time, he drank Snapple. But on those late nights when he could not fall asleep—it went on for days, once as long as two weeks—he took the bottle out of the cupboard over the refrigerator. During those periods, Kirk noticed there was something different about Dad's eyes. They did not smile when his mouth smiled. There was a sadness to them, a darkness. By the time he was twelve, Kirk could tell when Dad wasn't sleeping simply by the detached look in his eyes when he smiled.

Kirk had wondered what it was that kept Dad from sleeping, but had never asked. He went to the table, pulled out a chair, and seated himself.

"I've told you in the past," Dad said, "that you can always talk to me about anything, anytime you've got a problem, or even when you don't. We've had some good talks, I think. I remember what it was like to be your age, and I've got no illusions about how you see me. I'm your goofy dad, maybe a little embarrassing sometimes in front of your friends. But I love you very much. I want the best for you, the best of everything. And I want you to know, Kirk, how deeply, *deeply* pained I am by what's happened. Natalie was a wonderful girl.

I know how much she meant to you."

Kirk's lips felt numb. "Thanks, Dad," he said. "I appreciate that."

"I want to make sure you're not blaming yourself for what happened. It wasn't your fault, Kirk. That drunk ran right through that stop sign, all the witnesses said so. You don't, do you? Blame yourself, I mean?"

Kirk bowed his head. "I keep thinking I should've told her to put on her seatbelt."

"Kirk, you can't think that way. It'll make you sick. The seatbelt might not have made any difference, you know. He slammed right into her. Look, I want you to promise me you won't think that way. All right?" Kirk nodded as Dad sipped his drink. "So, where were you?"

"I told you. Just driving around with Randy and Liz. We talked. About Nat. We even cried a little."

"Of course you did. You shouldn't be afraid to cry, Kirk. You've experienced a horrible loss." He turned his head slowly from side to side and looked for a moment as if *he* were about to cry. "Not the kind of loss you should have to deal with at your age."

Kirk waited for him to continue. When he didn't, Kirk began to stand.

"You haven't done anything...foolish, have you?" Dad whispered.

Kirk froze, hunched over, halfway out of his chair. He slowly sat down again. "What do you mean?"

"Just what I said. You haven't done anything foolish, have you?"

"We just...drove around. That's all."

Dad looked at him for a moment, studied him. "Okay. Look, Kirk, if you want to talk, I'm here. Promise me you'll speak up."

"Thanks, Dad. I will." Kirk stood. "How come you can't

sleep?"

Dad smiled up at Kirk and once again, his eyes remained dark and unexpressive beneath a slightly furrowed brow. He lifted his glass and took a sip. "Just can't sleep. That's all."

After a moment, Kirk nodded. "Okay. Well, I'm going to bed. Goodnight."

"Goodnight, Kirky."

- THREE -

1.

Kirk was slowly awakened the next morning by the chirping of his cell phone on the bedstand. He always left one of his windows open a few inches when he slept, and he could hear rain falling outside. He had slept little the night before. Twice he had gotten up, climbed out the window, and gone to the pool-house to check on Natalie. Her condition had not changed. He sat up on the edge of his bed and answered the phone. It was Luanne.

"Kirk, what did you *do* last night?" she hissed.

"What? Wait a sec." He rubbed his eyes and shook his head to rid it of the dregs of sleep. He looked at the clock on his bedstand; it was 8:49.

Luanne whispered, "Natalie is gone, Kirk, she's *gone*. A police officer was here, some woman. She's going to come see you."

"What? Me? The police?"

"You *took* her, didn't you?"

"Not…exactly."

"Don't bullshit me, Kirk. I left you downstairs with her, and then she was gone."

"Did you tell your dad you let me in?"

"No, I told them I don't know anything about this."

"I won't say anything."

"Where is she? Where did you take her?"

"Well, I didn't exactly *take* her."

"What the hell are you talking about?"

"Can you keep it to yourself?"

"Who am I going to tell? Do you know what my dad would do if he found out I was involved in this? He'd have *me* on the embalming table."

Kirk told her everything that had happened the night before. "She walked out with me, Luanne."

The silence on the other end of the line stretched on for a while. Then, still whispering, she said, "You're not joking, are you?"

"No." Kirk heard the doorbell ring. It cleared his sleep-fogged mind. "There's somebody here."

"It's probably that cop."

Now Kirk whispered. "Why does she want to talk to me?"

"Because you're the boyfriend."

The doorbell rang again.

"Hang on," Kirk whispered. He waited and listened. Thirty seconds passed, then he heard a car door close in front of the house. An engine started. A moment later, he heard the car drive away. "Okay, she's gone."

"Look, Kirk," Luanne said, "I'm not sure I believe you. But what*ever* happened last night...when that cop finally catches up with you, and she *will*, you can't tell her I let you in. You have to say you found the back door unlocked, because if my dad finds out—"

"Don't worry, Luanne, you're safe. I promise. I'll take the blame. But they're going to need strong evidence against me, because I plan to lie my ass off. I was with friends all evening, and then I came home."

"So...Natalie's there?"

"Not with me at the moment, no."

"And she's…alive?"

"She walked out of there with me last night, Luanne. But now she's—well, she's not moving."

"Rigor mortis."

"Yeah. But she makes sounds."

"Jesus, Kirk, what have you done?"

"To tell you the truth, I'm not sure."

Once off the phone, Kirk quickly dressed in jeans and a sweatshirt. His parents were at work—Dad at the agency in nearby Redding, Mom at a stationary store she managed there in Anderson—and his eleven-year-old brother Kevin was spending the day at Uncle Matt's and Aunt Kathy's house with their cousin Jake. That left the house to Kirk for the day—Kirk and his mother's ferrets, Bud and Lou.

In the pool-house, Natalie was still seated stiffly on the toilet, wrapped in the afghan and sheet. Her mouth was still pulled back in a rictus grin. The smell was a bit stronger than it had been the night before, but it still wasn't too bad. He made a mental note to spray the pool-house with an air freshener.

"Nat, can you hear me?" he said.

She made a small grunting sound.

All he could do was wait.

2.

Officer Pam McCready of the Anderson Police Department was built like a fire hydrant with short auburn hair and large tortoiseshell-framed glasses that kept sliding down her small round nose. "You don't know anything about this, Kirk?" she said.

Dad and Mom and Kevin stared at him, waiting for a response.

Mom had been cooking dinner and Dad and Kevin had been watching television when McCready came to the door. Kirk had been in his bedroom wondering what he was going to do once Natalie started moving around. Kevin had come to his bedroom and said, "There's a cop at the door wants to talk to you." The walk from his bedroom had been a long one as he tried to relax his face and reveal nothing.

Kirk's heart pounded in his ears as he said, "No, I don't. When did it happen?"

"Late last night," McCready said.

"You mean, somebody just broke in and...took her?" Kirk said.

McCready shook her head. "They didn't break in, but yes, someone took her."

Mom was so upset by the news that tears sprang to her eyes and she sniffled. Dad frowned silently at Kirk.

"Where were you last night?" McCready asked.

"I was out with a couple friends. We drove around awhile and talked. Then I came home."

"I was up when he got here," Dad said. "A little before midnight, I think it was."

"Where did you and your friends go, Kirk?" she asked.

He shrugged one shoulder. "Nowhere, really. We drove around, is all. We talked, listened to music. We didn't really want to go anywhere. We were pretty upset."

"Where exactly did you drive?" McCready said.

"Where? Exactly? Um, well, we drove all over the place. Into Redding and all over town, then, uh...Palo Cedro, we drove out to Palo Cedro. And then we came back into Anderson on Deschutes."

"You didn't stop anywhere?"

"No. Oh, wait." After they left the hospital, they had stopped at an AM/PM minimart so Randy could take a leak and Liz could buy a soda. Kirk told McCready about the stop.

"You were still in Redding at that point?"

"Yes."

"At what time did you stop at the minimart?"

"It was a bad night, Officer McCready. Natalie had just died. I'm not sure what time it was. Maybe nine o'clock, nine-thirty. Maybe closer to ten. I'm not sure."

"I understand. After that, you just drove around for a couple hours?"

Kirk nodded. "Till almost midnight, when Randy dropped me off at my place."

"Who's car were you in?"

"Randy's mother's car, Randy was driving."

"After you were dropped off, where did they go?"

Kirk shrugged. "As far as I know, they went home."

"I'd like to talk to both of them," she said.

He gave her their names and addresses and she wrote them down in a small notebook.

McCready nodded. "Okay. I'd appreciate it if you'd keep your eyes and ears open, Kirk. If you hear anything about this, if you suspect anyone—" She took a small card from her shirt pocket and handed it to him. "—you'll call me, won't you?"

Kirk took the card and nodded. "Sure."

After McCready left, Kirk headed back to his bedroom, but Dad caught up with him in the hall.

"Kirk," he said, "I'm going to ask you again. Did you do something foolish last night?"

"I...I don't know what you mean by foolish."

"You don't know *anything* about what happened to Natalie's body?"

Kirk's brain clenched as he tried to keep his face neutral. "No, I don't know anything about it."

Dad stared at him for a long time, frowning, then nodded once and patted his shoulder. His face relaxed and he smiled a little. "Okay. If you say so. Do you have plans tonight?"

"No. I'm tired. I think I'll go to bed early, maybe read a little."

"Well, don't skip dinner."

In his bedroom, Kirk called Randy on his cell phone. They'd spoken briefly that afternoon—Randy had wanted to come over, but Kirk had said he wanted to be alone. Now he told Randy about Officer McCready.

"Why the fuck's she wanna to talk to *me*?" he said, his voice becoming high and squeaky.

"Because you were with me last night," Kirk said. "And because you were a friend of Nat's. That makes us suspects."

"I'm a *suspect*?"

"Just calm down. Get out of the house if you don't want to see her, but make sure you call Liz and warn her. We've got to get our stories straight. After we stopped at the AM/PM, we went out driving, nothing else, we just drove around. You drove us to—are you listening? This is important. You drove us to Redding and we drove around there for a while, then we went to Palo Cedro, and then—"

"Palo *Cedro*? You said we drove out to Palo *Cedro*? You think she'll *buy* it? Even people who *live* in Palo Cedro don't drive through it after six o'clock at night."

"It was the first thing that popped into my head. We drove around in Redding, then drove out to Palo Cedro, then came back to Anderson on Deschutes. Got that?"

"I got it, I got it."

"As soon as we hang up, call Liz and tell her, okay?"

"Yeah. Then can I come over to your house?"

"Not tonight. But plan on coming over early tomorrow. I'm going to need help."

"Help doing what?"

"Deciding what to do with Natalie."

3.

After dinner, Kirk went to his room and tried to do some homework. He couldn't concentrate, so he played a computer game for a while. All he could think about was Natalie sitting alone out in the pool-house.

There was a knock at the door and Mom came in. He was seated at his desk and she went to him, hugged him. She was plump, with short, curly blonde hair, and she smelled of the stew they'd had for dinner.

"Oh, Kirk, baby, I'm *so* sorry," she said. "Who would *do* such a horrible thing?"

It took him a moment to realize she was still talking about the disappearance of Natalie's body.

"Can I get you anything, sweetheart?" she said.

"No, I'm fine, Mom."

"If there's anything you need, or if you want to talk, you know I'm always here for you. I just don't understand how someone could *do* such a thing. Can you imagine why someone would *do* such a thing?"

Kirk imagined Mom coming across Natalie in the pool-house and it gave him a chill. She would probably have to be hospitalized.

She finally left, and he went on with his game for awhile, then stretched out on his bed. Time crawled along.

He waited until he heard his parents close their bedroom door and the house became silent. He went down the hall to the bathroom and took from a shelf an aerosol can of pot-pourri-scented air-freshener. Back in his bedroom, he turned off the light. He stuffed a couple pillows under his blankets just in case someone decided to look in on him. He took a penlight from the drawer of his bedstand and climbed out his window.

The night was damp and still and cold. The rain had stopped, but clouds blocked out the light of the moon and stars. Kirk moved silently across the back yard, around the covered pool, and went into the pool-house.

The odor had grown stronger, but thanks to the cold weather, it was not as bad as Kirk had feared. He relied on his penlight instead of turning on the lights inside the pool-house.

Natalie had not moved from her place on the toilet, but as soon as he entered the bathroom, she made a quiet, high-pitched sound and moved slightly beneath the sheet and afghan. Her eyes moved a little, but a milky film had developed over them and they seemed to have sunk deeper into their sockets. He put the can of air freshener on the counter beside the sink and closed his hand on her upper arm beneath the blanket, tried to move it. It was still stiff, but there was a little more give than before.

"Nat, can you understand me?"

She made a noise that sounded like, "Uh-huh," but he wasn't sure. Once she was able to move around, would she be able to walk and talk? Would she be anything like the Natalie he knew? And what was he going to do with her?

It had seemed like such a good idea to go to Mrs. Kobylka and ask her to help him. But he hadn't thought it through—he hadn't even thought it *halfway* through.

Natalie struggled as if her body were bound. Her cheeks were hollow and her cheekbones stood out against her grayish-yellow skin.

"I'll come back a little later, okay?" he said. "I promise, I'll be back in a little while."

Before leaving, he sprayed the air freshener all around inside the pool-house.

Back in the house, he put the can of air freshener on his bedstand, then stripped down to his boxers and got into bed. He did not expect to sleep, though—he had too much on his mind, too much to think about. But he'd slept little the night before, and it wasn't long before he drifted off into a deep sleep.

4.

In his dream, Kirk was with Natalie. They were nowhere in particular. All that mattered was that they were together. They were lying down, Kirk on his back, Natalie on her side next to him, and they were kissing. She was naked and he stroked her silky skin. Her long black hair draped down and tickled his face as she threw a leg over him and straddled his hips. He moved his hands over her breasts, squeezed them, took one in his mouth. It was one of those dreams that was so vivid and immediate that he had no clue he was dreaming. He was lost in her, consumed by her—and then there was a terrible smell, the kind of smell that conjured images of dead and rotting animals on the roadside and squirming maggots. It filled his nostrils, his throat, and became bigger than the dream itself, until—

—Kirk woke up coughing. There was a weight on top of him. When he opened his eyes to the gray light of morning, he thought for a moment he was still dreaming.

Natalie was on top of him, naked and grinning, her dead eyes just inches above his face. Her puckered breasts dangled flatly from her chest. When she spoke, the odor from her mouth was vile. She said, "Kiss me, Frog Boy.

- FOUR -

1.

Kirk's erection had slipped out of his boxers and was pressed hard against something ice-cold and sticky-moist. The erection wilted immediately as Kirk struggled to get her off him. He closed his hands on her upper arms and was repulsed by what he felt—cold skin that was dry and scaly, reptilian in texture. Natalie's thighs clutched him with surprising strength, but he rolled her off and fell out of bed. He hit the floor with a thud and sprang to his feet, hoping no one else in the house had heard the sound of his fall.

As Natalie sat up on the edge of the bed, Kirk stood still a moment and listened for the sound of someone coming toward his room. He heard nothing. The clock on his bedstand read 8:57—his parents had already left for the day. He wondered if Kevin was home, or if he was spending the day with Jake again.

The sash of the window he'd left open a crack had been lifted all the way up—Natalie had climbed through it as she had in the past. He considered closing it, but thought better of it when he got another whiff of Natalie.

She stood and moved close to him. "Kiss me, Frog Boy," she said again, smiling. Her voice sounded like a boot being pulled out of thick mud.

The smell that came from her mouth was so sickening, Kirk gagged. He grabbed the can of potpourri air freshener and sprayed it around the room, then took the cell phone from the bedstand and punched in Randy's number. As soon as Randy answered, he said, "I need you and Liz to get over here right away."

"'Sup?"

Kirk looked at Natalie. She stared at him with her head cocked to one side. Her whole body was a sickly blend of gray and yellow. Her skin was striated and scaly, breasts flat, nipples puckered. Her face was taut on her skull, sunken eyes bracketed by deep-set temples. She stared at him like a slow-witted child for a long moment, then sat down heavily on the edge of the bed, as if she were exhausted and bored.

"Natalie's up, that's what," Kirk said. "Call Liz. Tell her to pick you up in her car."

"Why can't I use my mom's car?"

Natalie got up, went to Kirk, and knelt before him. "Let's do it here," she said.

"I'll tell you later," Kirk said. "Tell Liz to bring some clothes, something old that she doesn't care about. And some perfume, tell her to bring some strong perfume."

Natalie pulled his boxer shorts down with one tug and closed her other hand, cold and lizard-like, over his penis.

"No!" Kirk shouted, jumping backward. He bent down and pulled up his boxers. "Stop that, Natalie, please. Sit down. Just sit down."

She stood and went back to the bed, dropped onto the edge and stared at him.

"What's going on over there?" Randy asked.

"She tried to…she wants to…just get over here, okay?"

"What are we going to do?"

"I'll explain when you get here." He cut the connection and put the phone back on the bedstand.

Natalie lay back and leaned on her elbows, spread her knees, and said, "Let's do it here. It'll be ex…ex…" She frowned a moment as she searched for the right word. "Exciting." She pulled her dry, cracked, purple lips back in something that was supposed to be a smile. It looked, instead, like an expression of pain.

Between her legs, her vulva had turned a deep yellow and glistened with draining fluids. The smell that rose up from her vagina was rank.

Kirk had to turn away, unable to look at her anymore. He quickly put on jeans and a sweatshirt, socks and sneakers. Without looking directly at her, he said, "Natalie, you have to stay here, okay? Can you stay right here for a few minutes?"

"Kirk?" She said the name as if she'd never spoken it before and sounded scared and confused.

He turned to her as she sat up on the bed.

"I'm…" She cocked her head again and seemed to have

difficulty finding the word. "Hungry. I'm hungry."

"Just stay right here for a few minutes, okay? Don't move."

Kirk opened his bedroom door and poked his head out. He looked down the hall, listened for the sound of someone else in the house. He stepped out of the room, closed the door, and went down the hall to the living room.

"Kevin?" he called.

The house was silent. He went into the kitchen.

Apparently, his parents had decided to let him sleep instead of waking him for breakfast. His mother had left a note on the counter telling him Kevin was spending the day with Jake again. She wrote that he should not make plans for that night because Dad was bringing home a Christmas tree and they were going to decorate it.

Something rubbed up against Kirk's ankle and scared him so badly, he cried out and tossed the note into the air. He looked down to see one of the ferrets slinking around his feet. Mom had gotten them almost a year ago, but Kirk had never gotten used to their presence in the house. They made him nervous. Although Mom could somehow tell Bud and Lou apart, they were identical to Kirk's eyes. He nudged the ferret with his foot and said, "Go on, Bud. Or Lou."

The ferret skittered out of the kitchen.

Kirk opened the refrigerator to find something for Natalie to eat. He quickly made her a sandwich of turkey cold cuts and lettuce and wrapped it in a paper towel. He went back up the hall and stood at his bedroom door for almost a full minute. He did not want to go back in his bedroom and see her again. The person—the *thing*—in his bedroom was not the Natalie he had lost. It was certainly not the Natalie he had *expected* Mrs. Kobylka's spell to resurrect.

"Hungry," Natalie said in the bedroom.

Kirk wondered if she knew he was standing outside the door. Was that possible?

He went into the bedroom and found her lying on her back on the bed, staring at the ceiling, hands flat on her flat belly.

"Hungry," she said again, talking to herself. She wasn't aware he had returned.

He kicked the bedroom door closed behind him. She sat up as he went to her and handed her the sandwich.

Natalie stared at it a moment before taking it. She held it to her nose, touched the crust of the bread to her tongue, then took a bite out of it. She chewed clumsily, sloppily, as if she weren't sure what she was doing, and pieces of meat fell out of her mouth onto her thighs. She bent forward and spit the rest of it onto the floor and tossed the remainder of the sandwich aside. It landed on the corner of the bed.

"You're not hungry anymore?" Kirk said.

Natalie stood and bits of turkey lunchmeat dropped from her thighs onto the floor. She stretched out her arms and stumbled toward him.

Kirk moved backward quickly, until his back was pressed against the door. She closed in and wrapped her arms around his neck. He shuddered at the sensation of her cold, scaly skin rubbing against him. Her face filled his field of vision and the closer she got, the more Natalie opened her mouth. The odor that came out of her brought tears to Kirk's eyes and he pushed her away a second before her teeth clacked together. He reached behind him, grabbed the doorknob, opened the door and quickly backed out of the room. He pulled it closed and stood there clutching the doorknob with both hands.

He took a few deep breaths as his stomach roiled with nausea from her horrible smell. But it was her attempt to bite his face that made him realize what a horrible mistake he had made.

2.

The doorbell rang. Randy and Liz normally would walk in without ringing the bell or knocking when they knew Kirk was home alone, but Kirk's parents always locked the door when they left in the morning, even if someone was still at home.

"Natalie, listen to me," Kirk said to his bedroom door. "Stay in there and I'll be back in a few minutes, okay?"

"Hungry," she whimpered.

"Just stay there for a few minutes and I'll be right back." He hurried down the hall and opened the front door.

Liz had a satchel slung over her shoulder. She patted the satchel and said, "I assumed you wanted clothes for Nat, right?"

"Yes."

"My mom refilled her Vicodin prescription this morning," Randy said with a grin. "I brought two for each of us."

Kirk closed the door and said, "Come into the kitchen, we can have Pop Tarts, or something."

In the kitchen, Kirk took a package of Pop Tarts from the cupboard and dropped three of them into the giant toaster.

"Where is she?" Randy asked, looking all around with caution.

"In my bedroom. And she's *hungry*."

"Oh, fuck," Randy said as he handed out the Vicodin. "Hungry for what?"

"Not for Louis Rich sliced roast turkey breast, I know that. She almost took a bite out of my face."

"You were right, Liz," Randy whispered. "She's been re-animated. She's a zombie. A flesh-eater."

"Come on, Randy, could you cut that shit out," Kirk said, but without anger.

"But that's what we're dealing with, right?" Randy said. "What if she'd bitten you? Is it contagious? In all the movies, if you get bitten by a zombie you turn into one. All I'm saying is, we should think about this shit and be prepared."

"He's right, Kirk," Liz said. "We should be careful around her. A bite could be bad."

As realization set in—Mrs. Kobylka had not given him Natalie, she had given him a reanimated corpse with a twist of cannibalism—Kirk was overcome by vertigo and swayed, grabbed the edge of the kitchen counter for anchor.

"Dude," Randy said.

Liz said, "Are you okay, Kirk?"

"I'm just trying to wrap my brain around all this," Kirk said. The dizziness passed.

The Pop Tarts popped up and startled them. Kirk opened the refrigerator and handed each of them a Mountain Dew, got one for himself. They drank the pills down with the soda, then ate the Pop Tarts as they talked.

"What are we going to do?" Kirk said. "Why did you want us to come in Liz's car?"

"Because nobody else drives Liz's car but Liz, so they won't notice the smell."

"The *smell?*" Liz said. "Hey, *I'll* notice the smell."

"We'll roll down the windows, Liz. I don't have anyone else to ask, or I would. My car's totaled, remember?"

Liz thought about it a moment.

"I've got air freshener," Kirk said.

Liz was reluctant. "All right. Where we gonna go?"

"To see Mrs. Kobylka."

"*Again?*" Randy said.

"This isn't what I asked for," Kirk said.

"Are you sure, Kirk?" Liz said. "Think about it. That old lady might speak with an accent, but I bet she understands English just fine, and she's probably going to hold you to whatever you said, word for word. What did you say to her?"

While Kirk tried to remember his words, Randy said, "You

said you wanted her to bring Natalie back. That's all you said."

Kirk knew he was right. He had been no more specific than that. It hadn't occurred to him that he needed to be—he thought bringing Natalie back would result in *bringing Natalie back*, not creating that hungry, smelly, decaying thing in his bedroom.

"You're right," Kirk said. "That's all I said."

Liz nodded. "She'll probably remember that and throw it right in your face."

"But there's got to be some way of getting rid of...of..." Kirk couldn't say her name, he could not say, *But there's got to be some way of getting rid of Natalie.* He told himself that was okay, because it wasn't Natalie they were dealing with. "...of getting rid of her."

"She said there was no way to undo it," Randy said. "Remember?"

"But there's *got* to be," Kirk said. "Some spell, some potion to make her...like she was before."

"You mean, dead?" Randy said.

"Yeah."

"She's already dead, Kirk," Randy said. "You need something that'll get that through her fuckin' skull."

"Where is she?" Liz asked.

"In my bedroom," Kirk said. "We should go get her dressed. But I'm warning you. She doesn't look good. And the smell..." Kirk got an idea and turned to a tall, narrow cupboard next to the refrigerator. On the top shelf, Mom kept a variety of over-the-counter drugs: aspirin, cough syrup, antacids, Bactine, rubbing alcohol. He took down a blue jar of Vicks VapoRub and unscrewed the lid. He held the jar out to Randy and Liz. "They did this in *Silence of the Lambs*. Put a little under your nose. It'll help with the smell."

"Is it *that* bad?" Liz said.

"It wasn't as bad as I'd expected," Kirk said, "until she

opened her mouth. And her legs. If you get too close...well, it's pretty bad."

They put a little of the strong-odored ointment just beneath their noses and Kirk replaced the jar in the cupboard. They left the kitchen and walked down the hall.

"She's not all there," Kirk said quietly. "She seems to have some memories, but...it's not really Nat. She's really just a—"

Even through the Vicks, Kirk smelled Natalie in the hall just a second before Liz screamed behind him.

3.

Kirk spun around and saw Liz standing at the bathroom door staring in with a hand over her mouth. He and Randy went to her and looked into the bathroom.

Natalie was lying in the bathtub, knees hiked up, feet resting on the edges of the tub. She held one of the limp ferrets in her hands and gnawed into its belly. Blood was smeared on her face and was matted in the animal's fur. Natalie made small guttural sounds as she bit into the dead ferret, stopped to chew for a moment, then bit in again. A strand of intestine dangled from the ferret's open abdomen.

Kirk, Randy, and Liz stood frozen just outside the bathroom doorway, their jaws slack. Natalie stopped eating and slowly turned her head toward them. A tuft of bloodied fur stuck out of the corner of her black-red mouth. When she spoke, her voice sounded like a clogged drain.

"Hungry," she said. Then she buried her face in the eviscerated ferret again and continued to eat.

"Oh Jesus breakfast," Liz said. She stepped into the bathroom, lifted the toilet lid and seat, knelt before it, and vomited.

Randy stepped away from the door and leaned his back against the wall. He took a couple deep breaths and swallowed hard a few times.

Kirk rubbed the back of his neck as he paced in the hall. "What am I going to tell my mother?" he said, his voice hoarse.

After flushing the toilet and rinsing her mouth in the sink, Liz came out of the bathroom looking pale and unwell. She leaned against the wall beside Randy, then he put an arm around her and she leaned on him.

Kirk stood in the doorway again and watched as Natalie ate his mother's ferret.

That story you hear, what happen to that dog? Mrs. Kobylka had asked. *Your girlfriend...she's no dog.*

Kirk wondered what the old woman had meant. He wondered what had happened to the dog in the story passed down by children over the decades.

He scrubbed his face with both hands and said, "I've got to clean up this mess. You guys don't have to help if you don't want, but...I'd sure appreciate it."

- FIVE -

1.

As he held open a white garbage bag so Kirk could drop the gutted ferret into it, Randy winced, looked away, and muttered, "Guess what *I* did on my Christmas vacation."

Kirk and Randy began to clean up the bloody mess in the tub. Kirk had already gotten most of the blood off Natalie, and she was in his bedroom with Liz, who'd said she would try to get her dressed.

"But if she tries to fuckin' bite me," Liz had told Kirk, "you're gonna have to do it yourself."

Once the bathroom was clean, Kirk threw the bloody sponge and rags into the garbage bag with what was left of the ferret and tied it off. He carried the bag out of the bathroom and down the hall to his bedroom, and Randy followed.

Crying quietly, Liz pulled a baggy old green sweater over Natalie's raised arms. Natalie sat on the bed in a pair of blue jeans, her pale, swollen feet bare. Her feet had gotten wet when she'd left the funeral home, and again when she'd walked from the pool-house to Kirk's bedroom window, and they had not recovered from it. They had become spongy and bloated. Liz appeared to be dressing a grossly overgrown toddler as she tugged the sweater down over Natalie's head. Once the sweater was on, Liz went to Randy and pressed her face to his neck. He put his arms around her.

Liz turned her head to Kirk and said, "That's not Natalie."

"I know," Kirk said with a nod.

"It's a dead body that doesn't fucking *blink* and shouldn't be muh-moving around." She sobbed against Randy's shoulder.

Natalie looked up at Kirk with her filmy eyes and smiled. "Kiss me, Frog Boy," she said.

"This is so fucking *wrong*," Liz said. "We've got to *do* something with her."

"Did you bring some perfume?" Kirk asked.

"Oh, yeah." Liz went to her satchel on the bed and removed a bottle of perfume. "Coco. My grandma gave it to me for my birthday a couple years ago, and I don't like it. But I don't know if it's going to help." She removed the lid from the bottle. "How am I gonna put it on her, 'cause there's no fuckin'*way* I'm gonna touch her again." After a moment, she tipped the bottle over Natalie's head and sprinkled the perfume all over her. The perfume's scent was overwhelming in such quantity, but it only clashed with the smell of rotting flesh, it did not camouflage it. Liz put the perfume bottle back in the satchel.

Kirk said, "Let's get her in the car."

He found a pair of old sneakers in his closet and put them on Natalie's feet, a gray watch cap that covered most of the gash in her forehead. He went into his parents' bedroom and found an old pair of large, round sunglasses his mother used to wear. Back in his bedroom, he put the sunglasses on Natalie and said, "We need to cover as much of her face as possible, just in case someone sees her."

"Even if someone doesn't," Randy muttered.

They hurried Natalie through the house and out the front door, with Liz following and spraying air freshener along the way.

2.

"This is worse than that time you threw up in here, Randy," Liz said as she drove her gray 1996 Toyota Camry up the hill on the road that led to Mrs. Kobylka's house.

"That wasn't even *close* to this," Randy said. "Besides, I only threw up a little. I didn't cut loose till I got outta the car."

Liz said, "You're hallucinating, because I had a five-dollar scratch-off ticket on the floor and you turned it to mush by drowning it in your puke. It took me forever to get the smell out of here."

"Why the fuck're you leaving five-dollar scratch-off tickets on the floor of your car?"

"I knew where it was, didn't I?"

In the backseat, Kirk had watched Natalie throughout the ride. Looking at her did not hurt as much as it had at first, now that he was certain it was not Natalie. Sometimes she looked back at him, and sometimes she looked surprised, as if she'd forgotten he was there since the last time she'd looked at him. Once, she'd reached for him and said, "Kiss me, Frog Boy," in that horrible voice. She'd toyed with the seatbelt after Kirk had fastened it. Sometimes her hands fumbled together in her lap. A few times, she'd uttered baby-like nonsense syllables. Kirk hoped her meal would keep her that relaxed and calm for a while. He hoped she would not be getting hungry again very soon.

After leaving the house, Liz had driven to a nearby 7-Eleven. There was a garbage Dumpster against a side wall of the store. Liz had pulled up to the curb and Randy had gotten out and tossed into the Dumpster the bag containing the bloody rags and sponge, and the remains of poor Bud. Or Lou.

Bud and Lou had been trying to get out of the house since they'd gotten there. Mom had laid down strict rules—never leave any doors or windows open that the ferrets could get to, and when entering or leaving the house, *always* be very careful not to let them out. Kirk would use that. He would play dumb when he got home. It would be concluded eventually that the ferret had gotten out—quickly and stealthily, he would say, because he hadn't noticed—sometime while Kirk was home, maybe when Randy and Liz were entering or leaving. But it pained Kirk to know how upset Mom would be, how much it would hurt her to lose one of her pets. *She loves those damned things,* he thought.

Liz made a U-turn at the dead-end of Hilltop Road and stopped the car in front of Mrs. Kobylka's house, behind the old pickup truck.

"Leave the engine running," Kirk said. "I hope I won't be long."

"I'm coming with you," Randy said as he got out of the car. "I wanna get another look at that fuckin' bird."

It was not raining, but a cold wind blew that made Kirk shiver even though he wore a down jacket. Dark bulging clouds sailed across the morning sky.

Kirk went up the steps to Mrs. Kobylka's porch. His hand was poised to knock on the edge of the screen door when one of the white curtains in the front door's window jerked aside. Her wide eye peered out at him.

"What you want?" she shouted. "I do what you ask for, why you bother me now?"

"You *didn't* give me what I asked for," Kirk said. "She's still dead, Mrs. Kobylka. I wanted Natalie alive again."

"I do magic, not miracles."

"What am I going to *do* with her?" Kirk said.

"I told you she would be your responsibility."

"But she's *dead.*"

Mrs. Kobylka unlocked and opened the door and peered at Kirk through the screen, hands on her hips. "She's *your* responsibility."

"But what do I *do* with her?" Kirk said, raising his voice. "Isn't there some way to make her...like she was? I mean, dead. The way she is now, it's just not right."

"Like I told you, you asked for it. And I told you there was no undoing it, too. You didn't listen to me when I talked to you?"

"But there must be some magic, some spell—"

"Are you ready to pay the price?"

Kirk's jaw dropped. "Is that what this is? A scam? You want money now?"

"I'm not talking about *money.*" She shook her head in disgust and dismissed them with a wave of her gnarled hand. "You go away now. This is your problem, not mine." She stepped back and closed the door, locked it loudly.

"I don't have much money," Kirk said, "but I'll give you what I've—"

"Go away or I call the police!" Mrs. Kobylka shouted behind the door.

"Oh, shit, that's the last thing we need," Randy said. "Come on, let's go."

Kirk did not want to leave; he wanted to talk some sense into that infuriating old woman. But she sounded pretty serious about not talking to him anymore more.

"I'm calling the police right now, you don't go away!" she shouted.

She sounded pretty serious about that, too.

As Kirk and Randy turned on the porch and went down the steps, Liz ran up the broken path. She wore a sickened expression on her face, elbows bent, and shook her hands as if they'd been burned.

Liz said, "She's starting to say she's hungry again!"

They got in the idling car.

Natalie turned to Kirk and gave him another of those hideous smiles. "I'm hungry, Kirk," she said in that moist, strangled voice. She grabbed his arm and pulled his hand to her mouth.

Liz screamed and Randy made a frightened wailing sound.

"No!" Kirk shouted as he jerked his hand back. "No, you can't eat *us*, okay? Jesus." He scooted as far away from her as possible and fastened his seatbelt. He decided not to fasten Natalie's—what difference would it make? He said, "Let's get out of here."

Liz started the car, and her voice trembled as she said, "Where do we go now?"

"The Mt. Shasta Mall," Kirk said.

"Are you on crack?" Randy said.

"Hungry," Natalie said.

Liz suddenly pounded on the steering wheel and screamed, "She says she's hungry, dammit! She's gonna start fuckin' biting *all* of us in a minute! What are we gonna *do*? Jesus Christ, I don't wanna be a fuckin' *zombie*. I wanna go *home*."

Randy took her in his arms and held her, murmured reassurances to her as she cried. "We could leave her here on Mrs. Kobylka's porch," he said to Kirk after a while. "She'll end up doing something with her, don't you think?"

Kirk shook his head. "I'm afraid she'd send Natalie right back to me, or make trouble for us. I was serious about the mall."

Natalie leaned over and reached for his wrist. "I'm. Hungry."

Kirk pulled his hands in close and pressed himself against the side of the cab away from her. He said, "We're gonna lose her in the food court."

3.

The Mt. Shasta Mall had been refurbished a couple years ago with a new main entrance, a large food court, and new storefronts. Along with the mall's new look had come a new Christmas decoration—a gigantic reindeer that appeared to have been made of snow-white twigs stood in front of the mall covered with white lights. For the last two Christmas seasons, while under the influence of mood-and-consciousness-altering substances, Kirk, Natalie, Randy, and Liz had found the reindeer at once frightening and side-splittingly funny.

Liz drove slowly through the parking lot looking for a space. Christmas shoppers were out in force and the lot was packed.

"We're just gonna take her in there and leave?" Randy said for the third time.

"Someone will recognize her eventually," Kirk said.

"They ran a picture of her in today's *Searchlight*," Liz said. "With the article about her body being stolen."

"It was in the paper?" Kirk said.

"Yep."

"Well, there you go. Someone will recognize her."

"And they'll call the police," Liz said.

Kirk said, "Yeah."

"And they'll call an ambulance, and they'll take her to a hospital," Randy said.

Kirk said, "Yeah."

"They'll find out she's dead."

Kirk shook his head. "That won't be our problem."

"They'll wonder where she came from," Liz said.

"They'll *know* where she came from," Kirk said. "The Richmond Funeral Home. They'll know she walked out because they'll see her walking. And yeah, they'll know she's dead. So what? If they find her here alone, it won't involve us. Maybe she'll become famous. Maybe she'll get a guest spot on *Fear Factor* and they'll make guys kiss her. Whatever happens, all we have to do is sit back and pretend it's news to us, because we had nothing to do with it, right?"

Liz found a parking space so far out into the outer edge of the lot that the mall seemed to be on the distant horizon.

"You know," Randy said, "that's not a bad idea. It might work."

They got out of the car. Natalie wanted to hold Kirk's hand. He refused at first, but Randy said, "Hey, it'll help her to blend in."

Finally, Kirk took her hand and they started walking toward the mall. Kirk walked beside Randy and leaned toward him to whisper, "This is disgusting."

"What is?" Randy said.

Pale vapor puffed from their mouths in the cold when they spoke.

"Holding her hand. It feels so…I don't know, so…" Kirk started laughing.

Randy laughed with him.

The Vicodin had kicked in.

"What're you guys laughing at?" Liz said on the other side of Randy.

They were too busy trying to stop laughing to tell her.

Inside, the mall was busy and noisy. They wandered past the food court, which was to the left of the entrance, and soaked in the atmosphere. Christmas music played over the sound system and there were bright holiday decorations everywhere. Santa sat in an enormous red-and-gold throne in the center of the mall surrounded by toys and children stood in line to sit on his knee.

Kirk had almost forgotten it was the Christmas season. Losing Natalie had knocked all the holiday spirit out of him. But suddenly, there in the mall surrounded by decorated trees and garlands of plastic holly, with the Christmas music playing and the lights blinking, in the company of his two best friends, holding the hand of Natalie's walking corpse, it somehow felt like Christmas.

Kirk turned around and said they should head back to the food court. They were almost there when Liz said, "Oh, let's go into Hot Topic!"

Hot Topic was a popular store, but it was very small and cramped with merchandise. It was crowded with teenagers, as always, and Randy, Liz, Kirk, and Natalie had to shoulder their way through the store. They were browsing the t-shirt selection when they began to hear the comments.

"What the fuck is that smell?" someone said.

"Jesus Christ, what *is* that?" someone else said.

They heard someone gag.

Kirk realized Natalie was stinking the place up fast. He met Randy's eyes and Kirk jerked his head toward the front of the store. He turned to Natalie. She was staring at her right hand. He tugged on her left and said, "Come on."

"Hungry," she said, and Kirk felt panic blossom in his chest.

On their way out of the store, moving as quickly as they could, they heard other remarks mixed with laughter.

"Shit, did you see that chick?"

"She looked dead!"

"What was I thinking?" Kirk said once they were out. "We

never should've gone in there."

"That was close," Randy said.

They went across to the food court. It was a cathedral of fast food in which voices echoed off the cavernously high ceiling. It was a clash of aromas: Chinese food, Italian food, Mexican food, Greek food, hamburgers, hotdogs, donuts, Coco, and rotting flesh, all in one place.

"I want an apple fritter," Liz said.

"Okay," Randy said. He turned to Kirk. "You want a donut?"

Kirk shook his head.

"Uh…does she?" He nodded toward Natalie, who was staring at the ceiling.

Kirk rolled his eyes. "That's *not* what she eats."

Randy's eyes widened and his cheeks paled. "Oh, yeah. I almost forgot. Fuck. I was gonna have a donut, but now I'm not so sure."

"Well, go get mine and we'll find a table," Liz said.

All the tables in the food court were occupied. Liz spotted two women and three kids leaving one of the tables near the front, by the tall windows, and they quickly claimed it.

Once they were seated, Liz said, "Jesus, I can really smell her, Kirk. The Vicks worked pretty well for awhile, but I think mine's worn out, because she's really getting to me."

"Don't worry, we'll go as soon as Randy comes back."

"Where'd he go?"

"To get your apple fritter."

"I can't eat an apple fritter now. She's making me sick to my stomach."

"But," Kirk said, "thanks to the Vicodin, you don't really care, do you?"

Liz grinned. "No shit."

Natalie was staring out the window looking more stoned than the three of them combined when Randy came to the table with a white bag. Kirk stood and nodded at Liz, who got to her feet. Together, they walked away from the table and left Natalie alone in the food court.

- SIX -

1.

It's not Natalie. It's only her body. Kirk had to keep telling himself that as he walked away from Natalie. He looked over his shoulder. She was looking around slowly now. She looked confused, but she did not look confused in the way Natalie used to when she looked confused—there was no resemblance. This Natalie looked confused the way a mentally handicapped child might.

Outside the food court, Kirk led them to one of the banks of plastic molded chairs. Kirk and Randy sat down with Liz between them and they both sat forward with forearms on thighs.

"She's nothing like Natalie, is she?" Kirk said.

Randy shook his head and Liz said, "No, she's not. But there were times...I don't know, like, for a split second, there were a couple times when it was Natalie. But it happened so fast, it could've been my imagination."

"Why are we still here?" Randy said.

Kirk shrugged. "I don't know. We should probably go."

But they did not leave their seats. They liked sitting there, and they felt *so* good. All three of them wished Natalie could be there with them. The smelly, purple-lipped corpse in the sunglasses and watch cap was a small piece of Natalie, and they were reluctant to leave her behind. They sat there and watched her.

Natalie scooted her chair away from the table and stood, looked around. She did not seem to notice that they were gone—if she did, it did not appear to matter to her. Her lips moved. She was talking to herself.

"What's she saying?" Randy whispered.

Kirk said, "I think she's saying, 'I'm hungry,' over and over."

"Oh, shit," Liz said.

Natalie struck with the speed of a snake. She threw herself on a very fat woman in her thirties carrying shopping bags in both hands on her way out of the food court. Kirk, Liz, and Randy shot from their chairs and ran through the crowd toward her as the fat woman shrieked. Fortunately, the fat woman dropped the bags and struggled while Natalie took great bites out of the air in the general area of the fat woman's neck. When she screamed the second time, there was horror in the sound, and Kirk realized she must have gotten a good look at Natalie, or maybe a whiff of her, or both.

Kirk and Randy each grabbed one of Natalie's elbows from behind and pulled her off the fat woman.

"Let's get out of here fast," Kirk said, and they turned and hurried out with Liz in the lead and Natalie stumbling between them, her sunglasses askew.

2.

"Are you sure nobody's looking?" Kirk said.

"I don't even *see* anybody at this end of the parking lot," Liz said.

They stood at the rear of the Camry with the trunk open.

"Okay," Kirk said to Natalie, "get in there. Go on, get in."

Natalie clumsily got into the trunk.

"Head down," Kirk said. As soon as her head was down, he slammed the trunk.

Before they got into the car, Liz sprayed the cab with the air freshener. Instead of masking the smell of Natalie's decay, the potpourri aroma simply combined with it to create a new odor that was no less offensive. Inside, Kirk sat forward in the backseat with his head between the two front seats, and they looked at each other in silence for a long moment. Liz started laughing first, but Kirk and Randy caught it almost immediately, and it took a few minutes for them to stop.

"Fuck, I love Vicodin," Randy said.

"Where do we go next?" Liz asked.

Kirk frowned. "I don't know. That was my back-up plan. I don't have any more ideas. I can't just...turn her *loose* on people. Not if she's going to try to eat them."

"And what if it's contagious, like in the movies?" Randy said. "We'd have a zombie plague on our hands."

"I have a plan," Liz said. She started the car, backed out of the parking slot, and started driving.

"What's the plan?" Kirk said.

"You'll see."

She drove them to Baskin & Robbins. "I've got an ice cream craving," she said.

"That's your plan?" Randy said.

"Hey, as long as we're high, we might as well enjoy it."

They went inside and ordered bowls of ice cream. They sat at a table in the back corner.

"We need ideas," Kirk said.

They ate in silence for several minutes.

"Oh, shit," Randy whispered.

"What?" Kirk said.

"What if Natalie's banging on the trunk and calling for help? If somebody hears her, they'll call the police."

Kirk sighed. "I almost wish someone would call the police. I'd like to get it over with."

Liz said, "I say take her back to your place and let her eat the other weasel."

"Ferret."

"Whatever. Those fuckin' things give me the willies."

"Maybe I can keep her in the pool-house one more night. If I can feed her. But what do I feed her?"

"Raw meat," Randy said. "Got any steaks at home?"

"Yeah, probably. But will she want that? She seems to like her food a little more…well, alive."

When they were done with their ice cream, they went back out to the car to find that Natalie was making no noise at all.

"The Vicodin's wearing off," Randy said.

"I've got twenty bucks," Liz said. "You guys got any money?" They said they did. She said, "Let's go see Dicky."

Kirk and Randy agreed a visit to Dicky Parks was in order. Dicky had gone to Anderson High School a couple years ago. He'd gone through his junior year twice when he finally dropped out. Everyone they knew got their drugs from Dicky, or from Dicky's father Wyatt, with whom he lived.

Kirk had known Dicky and Wyatt as long as he'd known Natalie, or most of his other friends at school. Natalie had tried to help him find a job after he dropped out of high school, but he had no ambition, and the fact was, Dicky wasn't very bright. Then they learned why he wasn't interested in a job—Dicky was selling drugs with his dad, and making good money at it. He always gave them a discount. Dicky had once told Natalie that they were the only people from school who treated him like a human being. "Most of 'em," he'd said, "they'll buy my shit, but they won't even look at me to say hi at the mall."

Natalie had a way with people, all kinds of people. She was friendly to everyone and anyone. She belonged to no particular clique at school, but was accepted by all of them. She hated the way everyone grouped up socially at school and turned their backs on others, and she refused to participate. Thinking of her made Kirk's chest ache. He thought of the stumbling creature in the trunk and missed Natalie all the more.

Dicky and Wyatt lived on a spot of land at the end of a long road—it was paved, but far too narrow for more than one vehicle at a time—in an area known as Churn Creek Bottom just north of Anderson. They lived in a couple double-wide mobile homes that had been patched together. Their nearest neighbor was three-quarters of a mile away. Wyatt's shiny white 1965 Mustang was parked under a rickety-looking carport. The Mustang was Wyatt's most prized possession—sometimes it was a little creepy how much he loved that car. But Dicky's pickup truck was not there.

Wyatt came to the sliding glass door and smiled. "Hey, you guys. Come on in. Dicky's not here. I don't know when he'll be back. Could be any minute, could be midnight."

Wyatt was in his forties. He kept his head smoothly shaved and wore a goatee of black and white hair. He had a gut, but his tattooed arms were muscular. His voice was coarse and loud, which some people interpreted as anger—it was just the way he talked. He wore a white T-shirt, a pair of baggy blue sweatpants and sandals.

Kirk was surprised when Wyatt gave him a hug and slapped him on the back a few times. "Man, I am so fuckin' sorry about Natalie. I've been sick about it since I heard. She was a hell of a girl and I'm gonna miss her."

"Thanks, Wyatt," Kirk said.

"Now, here's what I wanna do." Wyatt disappeared down a short hall for a moment and came back with a baggie filled with marijuana. "You know how, when somebody dies, all their friends bring gifts of food to the house? They bring casseroles and spaghetti and fried chicken and macaroni and cheese and potato salad and pies. Well, I can't fuckin'cook, so here's what I'm bringin'." He handed the baggy to Kirk. "That's a gift from Dicky an'me for all three a ya, so be sure to divide it up evenly, no favorites. That's the premium Wyattweed, too. Enjoy it in good health."

"Wow, Wyatt," Kirk said as he took the baggy taut with buds.

They spent the next ten minutes thanking him. They decided to have some, so Kirk opened the baggie and they smoked a little in one of Wyatt's bongs. Liz declined and said, "I'm driving, and I can't drive if I'm smoke weed. Got any Vicodin?" Wyatt said he did, and gave her two with a diet Coke.

"Have they found Natalie's body yet?" Wyatt asked. "I read it got stole."

Kirk said, "I don't know."

"Neither do I," Randy said.

"Me, neither," Liz said.

"We didn't have anything to do with that," Kirk said.

"Well, course ya didn't," Wyatt said. "I's just wonderin'if they'd found her yet. That's a terrible thing, her gettin'stole like that."

Kirk nodded. "Yeah, we think it's pretty...sick."

They talked with Wyatt awhile longer, but Dicky never showed up. Kirk said they were planning to see a movie.

"Good idea," Wyatt said. "Get your mind off it all. Have a toke with your popcorn."

They spent another five minutes thanking him for the pot, then he walked them out to their car. They were just getting in when they heard the thumping.

"Hungry! Hungry!" The word was muffled, but Kirk recognized it.

Wyatt said, "What the fuck was that?"

3.

Liz dropped into her seat, pulled the door closed, slipped the key into the ignition, and started the car. Wyatt knocked a knuckle on Liz's window. She pressed the switch and sent the glass humming down.

"Who's in your trunk?" he said. Kirk started to get into the back seat on the other side of the car, but froze when Wyatt shouted, "*Kirk*, Goddammit, who ya got in that fuckin'trunk?"

Kirk stepped away from the car and ran a hand through his hair.

"Tell him," Randy said. "Wyat'll keep it to himself."

"Keep *what* to myself?"

Liz rested her forehead on the backs of her hands on the steering wheel and said, "I wanna go home."

"What the fuck's goin'on here, guys?" Wyatt said. "Is Dicky involved in this, whatever the fuck it is?"

"No, no," Kirk said, shaking his head. He went to the rear of the car and said, "Okay, come on, Liz, open the trunk."

Thump-thump. Thump-thump-thump. "Hungry! I'm hungry!"

Liz killed the engine, got out, and joined Kirk. She unlocked the trunk and it popped open.

"Natalie wasn't stolen from the funeral home, Wyatt," Kirk said. "She walked out."

Natalie swayed a moment, then stood straight, her sunglasses crooked. Kirk took the sunglasses off her face and revealed her milky eyes sunken deep in their sockets.

Wyatt's reaction was almost comical. He slapped his right hand to his chest and staggered backward. He coughed for awhile, then laughed, then he stood still and stared with naked horror and disgust at Natalie, who kept tugging on Kirk's arm and saying, "Hungry. I'm hungry."

Kirk began to tell Wyatt the whole story. As Kirk spoke, Wyatt slowly came closer to them, a step or two at a time. Kirk was explaining what had happened to one of Mom's ferrets when Natalie pounced like a jungle cat.

She hit Wyatt and wrapped her arms and legs around him, and he stumbled backward. He fell hard on the rough lawn that grew in patches around the mobile home. Wyatt grunted when his back hit the ground, then gurgled and kicked and tried to pry Natalie off his body. A bright arterial spray arced in the air and spattered over the clumps of grass. Again and again and again.

It all happened so fast, but when Kirk moved to react, he felt as if he were moving slow, so slow. The blood continued to spurt from Wyatt's throat. His kicks slowed down until his legs were barely moving, and his arms fell still at his sides.

Kirk and Randy and Liz were rushing toward Wyatt and Natalie, but Kirk stopped suddenly and said, "No, wait. We shouldn't go near the body."

"What if he's not dead?"

The spray of blood had stopped. So had any movement. Natalie made sloppy chewing sounds as she buried her face in Wyatt's throat.

"Don't go near the body. Let's go back to the car and just…wait."

"*Wait?*" Randy said. "What the fuck are we waiting for?"

"For Natalie to finish eating."

4.

Liz got back in the car, put her elbows on the steering wheel and her hands over her ears. Kirk and Randy paced slowly together and avoided looking in Natalie's direction. But they could still hear her.

She had ripped off Wyatt's T-shirt and chewed into his belly. Now she was smacking her lips sloppily as she ate, but they did not want to know what she was eating, so they did not look.

"God, I hope Dicky doesn't get here before we leave," Kirk said.

"I can't believe we let her do this," Randy said. His voice was hoarse with emotion. "I really liked Wyatt."

"You think I didn't? There was nothing we could do, Randy. If you're spurting blood three or four feet into the air from your neck, it's over. It didn't take long, either. She tore his throat out. She just bit down and—"

"Stop, I know, I was there, remember? Look, I've been thinking. What if we bury her?"

"Alive?"

"You can't bury her alive, Kirk, she's dead."

"Yeah, I know, but...the way she is?"

"What do *you* wanna do, load her up with NyQuil?"

"I don't know, I...I-I-I..." Kirk stopped pacing and took a deep breath. "Do you realize we're talking about a girl who, at this very moment, is eating the guts out of a friend of ours? I liked Wyatt, too. What are we going to—"

"No, she's not," Randy said.

"What?"

"Listen. She's not eating anymore."

They turned to her slowly. Natalie was lying on her back on the grass a few feet away from Wyatt's gutted corpse.

"Natalie?" Kirk said. "Are you ready to go home?"

An enormous farting sound came from her direction. Several seconds later, she sat up. "Home," she said as she got to her feet. She walked unsteadily toward them.

"Wait a second," Kirk said. "She can't get in the car like that. She's covered with blood."

"What? You want her to wash up?"

Kirk looked around until he spotted a garden hose curled up at a front corner of the mobile home. A green spray-nozzle was attached to the end of the hose. He went to Natalie and said, "Hold it, stand right there. Don't move." He got the hose.

As he hosed her off, Natalie did not make a sound, but wore an expression of shock—eyes clenched shut, mouth yawning open. When he tried to wash the blood off her face, the water's pressure was strong enough to completely collapse Natalie's nose.

5.

"That wasn't very nice," Randy said as Liz drove them back up Churn Creek Road.

"What do you mean, not very *nice*," Kirk said. "It's not Natalie, Randy. I was just trying to get all that blood off her."

"She won't be able to wear those sunglasses anymore," Randy said.

Kirk sighed. "We've established that, Randy."

Kirk had tried putting the sunglasses on Natalie just before they left the Parks house. The glasses had fallen off her face each time because there was no longer anything there to hold them up.

"It's like a belly button," Liz said. Every few seconds, she glanced in the rearview mirror at Natalie. "It went from being an outie to an innie."

Her nose had collapsed into her face. Natalie said it hurt. She kept saying, "Ow." Something about the fact that she felt pain disturbed Kirk. How could she still feel pain if she were nothing more than a reanimated corpse?

They could hear her in the trunk of the car. Every time Natalie said, "Ow," it was difficult not to laugh—because of her collapsed nose, she sounded a little like a duck, and they found that hilarious. They'd been futilely fighting the laughter since Natalie had first spoken after her nose collapsed. "Ow."

"Where am I going?" Liz said.

"My place," Kirk said.

- SEVEN -

1.

Natalie seemed to remember the pool-house well enough—she went into the bathroom and sat on the toilet seat.

"Maybe she'll stay in there," Kirk said.

Randy and Liz sat on the couch and she snuggled into the crook of his arm.

Kirk paced. "I should probably give her a shower."

"A shower?" Randy said. "What the fuck are you talking about, like a *baby* shower?"

"No, you dink, a *shower*, to get the rest of that blood off her."

"Yeah, but what else is gonna come off?" Randy said. "Is she in any shape to take a shower?"

Kirk shrugged his shoulders. "I don't know. For all I know, it might make her smell better."

"Then do it," Liz said.

Kirk did not relish the thought of bathing Natalie's corpse. He decided he only wanted to get the blood off her face. The rest could be covered up with clothes. He did not want to draw attention when they took her back to Mrs. Kobylka, which Kirk intended to do. If necessary, he would threaten to burn down her house with her in it unless she helped him. But he never got the chance.

He got Natalie undressed and into the shower. "Wash your face, Natalie."

She said, "Let's do it here. It'll be exciting."

"No, we won't be doing it. Just wash your face, okay? Can you remember how to wash your face?"

"Too...hot."

"The water's too hot?"

She nodded once and stepped back away from the stream.

Kirk leaned into the shower and adjusted the temperature a

little. Once again, he was disturbed to know that she could feel pain. He grabbed a washcloth off the shelf over the toilet, got it wet, soaped it up, then put one foot in the shower and said, "Okay, turn around, face me." He had to tug on her shoulder to get her to turn around. He put the other foot in the shower––so what if he got a little wet?––and put his left hand on the back of her head. He pressed the soapy washcloth to her left cheek, and Natalie's face collapsed beneath the weight of his hand with a breathy crunch, like a delicate mask. Kirk gasped when he realized what he'd done. He cried out and pushed her away when he saw the maggots crawling out of her destroyed nose. He tripped out of the shower backward, nearly fell, but steadied himself with a hand on the edge of the sink.

"She's coming apart," he said.

"What?" Liz said in the other room.

Kirk left the bathroom. "I said she's––"

The pool-house door opened and Dad came in. He stopped just inside the door and stood there in his suit, with a copy of the *Sacramento Bee* tucked under his left arm. "What is that God-awful smell? Kirk, what's going on in here?"

2.

Kirk's mind froze up. He could think of no fictitious explanation, but would Dad believe the truth?

"Let's do it in here, Kirk!" Natalie called from the bathroom.

"Oh, Jesus, no," Dad said as he crossed the room and stepped through the open bathroom door. "Oh, no!" Kirk had never heard Dad sound as emotional as he did when he cried out those two words in the pool-house bathroom. He sounded at once angry and afraid. He turned and came out of the bathroom, looked pleadingly at Kirk. "I asked you if you'd done anything foolish, Kirky. I asked if you knew anything about her disappearance. You lied to me."

Kirk nodded. "I'm sorry, Dad. But you don't know the whole story. When you hear it, you'll understand why—"

"I told you to stay away from her, didn't I?" Dad said. "How many times did I tell you to stay away from that old woman, to leave her alone? Why didn't you?" He stepped over to Kirk and let his newspaper drop to the floor as he put his hands on Kirk's shoulders and shook him violently a few times. "Why *didn't* you, Goddammit?"

The bottom fell out of Kirk's stomach. Dad knew what he had done, he knew about Mrs. Kobylka. But Kirk could not imagine how.

"How did you know?" Kirk said.

"How do you think? I guessed as soon as I saw her." He pointed at the bathroom doorway, where Natalie stood naked, the left side of her face crushed. What looked from that short distance like a couple small globs of mayonnaise on her face were actually clumps of maggots coming out of her left inverted nostril.

Kirk said, "But how did you know about Mrs. Kobylka?"

"You think you and your friends discovered her?" Dad said. "She's been around a long time. My dad used to say she looked old when *he* was a kid. When I was a kid, my friends and I used to make up stories about her to tell each other. We used to scare the crap out of ourselves. So did all the other kids. Creepy old Mrs. Kobylka on Witch's Hill."

"Did you ever hear the one about the dog?" Kirk said. "Some say it was a Doberman, others say it was a German shepherd."

Randy said, "I heard one version where it was a St. Bernard, like Cujo."

"It was a German shepherd," Dad said. "His name was Duke, and he was the best dog in the world. He was smart, and funny, and loyal. One day, he just stopped playing. We took him to the vet, and he had cancer. We had to have him put to sleep. I didn't want to. I begged my mother to let me take him home and take good care of him so he could get well. I was only ten at the time. All I knew was, I wanted my dog. But I couldn't have him. Mom explained that if we did not have Duke put down, he would die soon anyway, and in a lot of pain, which would be cruel. But I couldn't accept it. I got the idea maybe thirty or forty minutes after we buried Duke in the back yard—if Mrs. Kobylka is really a witch, why not enlist her services? See, when I was a kid, the story was that she had brought back some kid's dead cat. So, why not my dog?"

"It was *your* dog?" Kirk said, his voice an awed whisper. He exchanged a stunned glance with Randy.

Dad said, "I rode my bike over to her house and knocked on her door and asked her right up front, 'Are you a witch?'"

Kirk nodded. "That's pretty much what I did."

"Well, it was a mistake, Kirk," Dad said with quiet intensity. "It was a big mistake. It still keeps me up some nights, and that was a dog. This is a person, this is...*Natalie*."

"What keeps you up some nights?" Kirk asked.

"I should've been more specific," Dad said. "I should've told you the truth early on, maybe you would've stayed away from her then."

"*What* keeps you up?" Kirk asked again.

"Nightmares. The memory of what I had to do. There's a price to pay for what you've done, Kirk."

Mrs. Kobylka had asked him if he was ready to pay the price, but it had sounded like bullshit coming from her. Coming from Dad, it sounded ominous.

"What's happened since you brought her back?" Dad asked. "Has anyone been hurt?"

Kirk looked at Randy and Liz for a moment. He saw no point in lying to Dad—he'd hear about it sooner or later, and he would know. Kirk told him about Mom's ferret, and then about Wyatt Parks.

"What the hell were you doing at Wyatt Parks' house?" Dad asked.

Kirk gulped. He thought a moment about the baggie of pot—he was relieved when he remembered it was still in the glovebox in Liz's car where Dad couldn't see it. "We stopped by to see Dicky. But he wasn't home."

"Jesus Christ," Dad said, shaking his head. He took his cell phone from the right pocket of his suitcoat and punched in a number. He waited a moment, then said, "This is Donald Mundy, could I speak to Bob Brentwood, please?"

Bob Brentwood was an old friend of Dad's, one of his oldest. They'd grown up together. Bob was a Sheriff's deputy. A few months ago, he'd broken his arm in a fall while hiking and he was stuck at a desk at the Sheriff's station in Anderson until his arm was out of its cast.

"Hi, Bobby," Dad said. "Can you get away for a little bit? Something's come up. Something...urgent. I can't explain on the phone. Meet me in ten minutes in front of Mrs. Kobylka's house." He paused a moment. "Yes, Mrs. Kobylka's, you heard me right. See you there." He closed the phone and dropped it back in his pocket. He nodded toward the bathroom and said, "Wrap her up in something. We're going to see Mrs. Kobylka."

"We already saw her," Kirk said. "She wouldn't help us."

"That's because you didn't know what to ask for, and we don't have time for you to figure it out for yourself. Let's go."

3.

They put Natalie, wrapped in the sheet and afghan and wearing Kirk's old sneakers, into the back of Dad's Dodge Durango. Liz was horrified by the maggots crawling out of Natalie's crushed face and started crying again as she said, "That is so fucking wrong." Kirk sat in the front seat with Dad, Randy and Liz in the seat behind them. They rolled down all the windows because of the smell.

"Why are you home so early, Dad?" Kirk asked.

"I took half the day off. I was going to have some lunch and then spend the afternoon Christmas tree shopping." Dad was a perfectionist when it came to finding the right Christmas tree and could shop for one all day long until he was satisfied.

From the rear of the SUV, Natalie said, "Hungry," as Dad started the engine.

"Oh, Jesus, she's hungry again," Liz said. "She's gonna put on weight."

"Dad, why is Natalie like that? Why does she want to eat... people?"

"She's craving what used to flow through her body—blood, energy, life. Eating the living gives her a taste of that. But it's never enough."

"How do you know?"

"It's not something I know, but I've had a lot of time to think about it and that's what I believe. You'll think about this a lot, too, Kirk. There will be nights when *you* won't be able to sleep."

"What happened with your dog?" Randy asked.

"We lived over by the river when I was a kid, near the park," Dad said. "My dad had built a fort in the back yard for me. It was a thing of beauty, like a miniature log cabin. I kept Duke in there. But it was summer, and a hot one, and he started to stink pretty fast. And all he did was howl miserably. There was a patch of woods between our back yard and the Sacramento River and I took Duke down there and tied him to a tree close enough to the river to get a drink. He was howling when I left, he howled all night, and he was howling the next morning when I went to him. He smelled bad, and he didn't look good, but I thought if I took him for a walk, he might stop howling. He did, while we walked. I took him over to the edge of the park. There were a few women there with several small children, a couple babies, and a few dogs. We were walking along the edge of the park, and Duke just took off. He caught me off guard and the leash slipped right out of my hand. He didn't make a sound. He snatched up a little terrier and ran off to the bushes and ate it. We were out of there before anyone missed the dog. Duke had blood all over his muzzle and he licked his chops all the way back to his tree. I washed his muzzle off at the river, and then he curled up as if to take a nap. He'd stopped howling. He didn't make a sound until the next morning."

In the backseat, Randy and Liz leaned forward and listened closely. Behind them, Natalie said, "Hungry."

Dad said, "I took Duke walking along the edge of the park again the next morning. The women and all their children and babies and dogs were back. They had their blankets spread out and a large picnic basket open. They were looking for the dog. They were walking all around that area of the park calling his name. Rufus, they called him. I figured Duke would go after another of the little dogs. Keeping him fed was the only way to keep him from howling until I figured out what I was going to do with him. I unhooked the leash from his collar and he took off without a sound. But he snatched up one of the babies and took it into the bushes. And ate it. The baby never made a sound. Everyone was looking for the dog, and again, we were out of there before anyone knew what had happened." He said nothing for several seconds, then muttered, "A baby."

"Is that what keeps you awake some nights?" Kirk asked.

"That's part of it," Dad said. "In my nightmares, I always see Duke eating the baby. And in some of them, I'm eating the baby. Because it was my fault. Just as if I'd done it myself. But I stayed in those bushes, out of sight, while my dog did that.

My blood-thirsty dog that, because of me, had been risen from the dead." He looked at Kirk a moment, then at Randy and Liz in the rearview, back at Kirk, then at the road again. "That's how you've got to think of this. I don't know whose idea it was, or how deeply you're involved, Randy and Liz, but—"

"It was my idea, and I did it," Kirk said. "They were there, but they didn't participate. I'm the one who brought Natalie back."

"Then all this is your responsibility. The ferret, and Wyatt Parks...anyone she hurts. And you're responsible for what's going to happen to her."

"What's going to happen to her?" Kirk asked.

"Mrs. Kobylka will tell you."

"Why does something have to *happen* to her?" Kirk said. "Besides, it's not Natalie. It's just her body. Like Duke—he was different, right? Not the same dog after you brought him back? It wasn't Duke, right?"

"He didn't know how to play anymore," Dad said. "He gave it a try, but he was very uncoordinated afterward. But it was still Duke. It was like he was sick, or something." He pointed a thumb over his shoulder. "That's Natalie back there. Imagine if she were in an accident and sustained severe brain damage and was never the same again. She'd still be Natalie, wouldn't she? Well...that's Natalie. It's all that's left of her, anyway. The difference is that she's dead. So naturally, she's not going to behave the same way. She's...not all there anymore, Kirk. But she's still Natalie."

Kirk felt a wave of nausea. That *was* Natalie—and she felt pain, and she was walking around with a crushed face and maggots crawling around in her head because of him. Kirk's vision was fractured by hot tears as he thought about what he had done to her in his blind and frantic eagerness to have her back.

"When we get to Mrs. Kobylka's," Dad said, "let me do the

talking. Speak only if you're spoken to. I don't think you realize exactly how dangerous that old woman is. If you did, you never would have gone to her."

Kirk looked over his shoulder at Randy and Liz. Randy mouthed the words, *Holy shit.*

"We're never going to get that smell out of this car," Dad said. "I don't know what we're going to tell your mother. By the way, about the ferret...we're going to say nothing, okay? Say nothing, and we'll assume it slipped out the door when someone was coming in or going out, okay?"

"Yeah, that was my plan," Kirk said.

Dad said, "You cleaned up the mess in the bathroom?"

Kirk nodded. "Randy and I scrubbed it down."

"Good. How bad does the house smell?"

"I don't know."

Dad shook his head. "Your mom's going to flip over that odor. The pool-house is awful."

"What are we going to do?"

"I don't know yet. We may have to tell her the truth."

"Tell *mom* the truth?"

"I know. We may have to resuscitate her, but we may have to tell her the truth anyway. Don't worry, she grew up with the same stories about Mrs. Kobylka that I did. She probably won't take much convincing."

"What about Kevin?"

"Kevin can be dealt with. If we have to, we can tell him a stray cat died under the pool-house, or something."

"So, it'll be our secret?" Kirk said.

Dad nodded. "Every family has its secrets, Kirk. They're usually kept for the good of someone else. It would be for your mother's own good if we could come up with a way of keeping this from her. Because if we have to tell her the truth, she's really going to freak."

Kirk found himself laughing. He was still feeling the

residual effects of the pot and was unusually relaxed considering the circumstances.

Dad smiled. "Maybe I can get a couple Xanax into her before we tell her. That might make a little difference."

Dad drove up Witch's Hill. At the top, Kirk saw a Sheriff's cruiser parked at the road's dead-end.

"Bobby beat me here," Dad said as he parked beside the cruiser. "You guys stay in here, I'm going to go talk to Bobby."

"Why do you have to talk to Bobby?" Kirk asked.

"He's the only one who knows about what happened with Duke. He came here with me to talk to Mrs. Kobylka the night I brought Duke back. He'll understand all this. He's also a cop, so he'll know what we should do next. Natalie killed someone, Kirk, and there's a good chance you could get blamed for that. I don't know if we should take her to Mrs. Kobylka, or if we should go to the cops with this whole story. So I'm going to ask Bobby."

Dad got out of the SUV, closed the door, and got into the cruiser with Bobby.

4.

Randy said, "You think we could get in trouble, too? 'Cause we were there when she killed him? We didn't do anything about it."

"There was nothing we could do," Kirk said. "As soon as she got out of the trunk, it was out of our hands."

"She moved so fast," Liz said.

"Hungry," Natalie said in back. "I'm hungry."

"Wait just a little bit longer, okay, Nat?" Kirk said.

She turned and looked him. "Longer?"

"Just a little longer, honey." His voice broke on the last word and he turned away from her. Staring at the dashboard, he whispered, "I can't believe I've done this to her."

"You didn't know it was going to be like this," Liz said. "If you'd known, you wouldn't have done it."

A noise in the back made them all turn toward Natalie. She was starting to climb toward them over the seats. She tried to smile, but it only made her broken face look more horrific.

"No, Nat, stay there, okay?" Kirk said. "Just for a little while longer, okay? Please?"

She slowly moved back to the rear compartment of the SUV without taking her eyes from Kirk. He could not look at her collapsed face long. It made him feel like dying.

- EIGHT -

1.

A few minutes later, Dad and Bobby got out of the cruiser.

Bobby was tall and beefy with short-cropped black hair speckled with gray and wire-framed glasses that looked small on his large face. His right arm was in a blue fiberglass cast. He and Dad came to the driver's side of the Durango and Dad opened the door. They moved in close. Bobby wrinkled his nose and recoiled at the smell at first.

"Bobby needs to ask you a few questions, Kirk," Dad said.

Bobby had a high, scratchy voice. "What happened with Wyatt Parks?"

"We went over to see Dicky, but he wasn't home. We had Natalie in the trunk, and when we—"

"In the *trunk*?" Dad said. "How could you do that, Kirk?"

Kirk closed his eyes a moment. "I didn't think it was Natalie. I thought it was just her body, not *her*. If she'd complained or made any noise, I would've taken her out, but she didn't. Not until Wyatt walked us out to our car. Then she pounded on the trunk and started talking. Wyatt got upset and wanted to know who was in our trunk. So we showed him. And she attacked him."

"She didn't just attack him," Liz said, "she was *on* him in a second."

"What did she do to him?" Bobby asked.

Kirk said, "She ripped his throat out with her teeth. He didn't...last long."

"And then she ate him," Dad said. "Right?"

Kirk nodded.

"Jesus," Bobby said. "Well, it hasn't been reported yet, so I'm guessing nobody's found him. Did you touch the body, any of you?"

"We didn't go near the body," Kirk said. "We went to the car."

"And you let her eat him?" Bobby said.

"We didn't know what else to *do*," Kirk said. "I knew if we went over there, we'd have to pull her off him, and we could leave something."

"Leave something?" Bobby said.

"I watch *CSI*. We could leave hairs, fibers, maybe even fingerprints. I figured she'd come to us eventually, when she was done, and if we stayed away from the body, there'd be nothing to connect us to it."

Bobby nodded. "That was good thinking, Kirk. But you were in the house. Do you go there often?"

"Sometimes we stop by to see Dicky. Every few weeks or so."

"Are you aware," Bobby said, "that Wyatt Parks is a convicted drug dealer and that his son Dicky has been in trouble with the law for drugs as well?"

Kirk widened his eyes and said, "You're kidding. Really?" He turned to Randy.

"Dicky? He didn't say anything about that." Randy turned to Liz. "Did you know anything about that?"

"It's news to me," Liz said.

"That wouldn't happen to have anything to do with your visits, would it?" Bobby said.

"We grew up with Dicky, we know him from school. We stop and see him once in awhile, that's all."

"You say Natalie bit Wyatt?" Bobby asked Kirk.

"A lot, yeah."

"Well, even if you become a suspect, the teeth marks won't match. But to tell you the truth, Natalie should be given a medal. I don't know if anybody's going to look too hard to find the killer of Wyatt Parks. He sold drugs to kids, did some time. He was probably doing it again; we just hadn't caught him yet. My guess is, you'll be safe. But if you're smart, you'll stay clear of Dicky Parks from now on. He's nothing but trouble, just like his old man."

Kirk, Randy, and Liz nodded their agreement.

To Kirk, Dad said, "We'll have a talk about that later." To Bobby, he said, "So what do you think we should do?"

Bobby chewed on his lower lip a moment, then said, "You come forward with a story like this, I don't know *what* would happen. I think your best bet is to get rid of her and lay low. Get rid of her before she does it again and you've got too much trouble to lay low from, if you get my meaning."

"I get your meaning," Dad said. "Thanks, Bobby."

"No problem, Donny. Sorry you have to go through this again."

"Go through what again?" Kirk asked.

"I've gotta run," Bobby said. He turned to Kirk. "You stay away from that Parks kid, Kirk."

"He will," Dad said. "Thanks for coming out, Bobby."

He got in the cruiser, started the engine, and backed out of his parking place at the road's dead-end, then headed back down the hill.

Dad said, "Okay, everybody out. We're going in to see Mrs.

Kobylka."

"I'm not going in there," Liz said.

"Oh, yes you are," Dad said. "All of you. It might not have been your idea, but you were involved. Let's go."

2.

Mrs. Kobylka opened her door and came out on the porch while they were making their way through the front gate.

"What you want?" she said. "Why you don't leave me alone?"

"Mrs. Kobylka," Dad said. "My son is ready to pay the price for what he's done."

"Is that so?" She turned to Kirk, stepped over and stood in front of him. She smiled. "You learn anything, boy?"

"You mean, like, be careful what you wish for?" Kirk said.

The corners of her mouth turned downward and her eyebrows rose high as she wobbled her head back and forth. "Mm, that could be, that could be. Learn anything else?"

"Well...I learned not to fuck with you," Kirk said.

"Kirk!" Dad said.

But Mrs. Kobylka laughed hard enough to have a brief coughing fit. Smiling, she patted Kirk on the shoulder and said, "That's my boy." She waggled her fingers at Natalie and said, "Bring her around back of the house."

They all turned and went back out the front gate, around the fenced front yard and along the side of the house to the back. There was nothing there but weeds and a rickety old clothesline. The yard became the large empty field that spread beyond it.

There was a spacious screened-in porch on the back of the house. Mrs. Kobylka came out with a hammer in one hand and a cloth bag in the other. She went to Kirk and handed them to him.

"In the bag," she said, "are stakes that are attached to manacles. You are to undress the girl, put her on the ground, drive in the stakes, and put the manacles on her wrists and ankles."

"I will not," Kirk said.

"Kirk, you'll do as you're told," Dad said.

"Dad, I won't do anything to hurt her."

Mrs. Kobylka said, "You will do it, or I will make you do it, it is your choice."

Kirk said, "There's no way I'm going to stake Natalie to the—"

Mrs. Kobylka raised her hand, palm out, and passed it in front of Kirk's face as she muttered something under her breath.

Kirk stopped talking and put the hammer and cloth bag on the ground. He turned to Natalie and said, "Let's get you out of these things." He took the blanket off first and handed it to Dad, then the sheet.

"I'm hungry," Natalie said.

"Just wait a little while longer," Kirk said as he tugged on her elbow. "Get down here on the ground for now, just lie down."

Once she was flat on her back, he began to position her properly, although inside, all he wanted to do was scream at the top of his lungs, "Stop!" Arms raised, legs spread. He hammered the barbed stakes into the hard, rocky ground and fastened the manacles to Natalie's wrists and ankles. Then he stood over her and surveyed his work.

"Hungry, Kirk," Natalie said. "I'm hungry."

Suddenly, Kirk was in control of himself once again and he turned to Mrs. Kobylka. "Why...did I just do that?"

She smiled. "Because I made you do it. You will wait here." She turned and went back into the house.

Kirk got down on his knees and tried to pull one of the

stakes out, but he could not. Each time he tried, his hands became limp.

The back door opened and Mrs. Kobylka returned with Baltazar, her enormous black-and-red bird, on her right arm. The bird immediately took flight and Kirk watched it soar into the air. Gooseflesh crawled across the back of his neck. The bird's wings *were* like a bat's, just as he'd suspected when he'd seen Baltazar in his cage the first time. They were like a bat's wings, but enormous in span. The bird circled a few times high above them, a black crescent against the gray clouds, then dove. The sound Baltazar made was a mixture of a hawk's piercing cry and the squealing of a piglet. It landed in a flutter of its vast wings on the ground beside Natalie.

Mrs. Kobylka stepped in front of Kirk. "You will watch."

"Watch what?" Kirk said, although he had a sickening feeling he knew what was about to happen. "Don't tell me you're going to let that bird—"

Mrs. Kobylka passed her hand in front of his face again and mumbled something, then stepped aside, saying again, "You will watch."

3.

Baltazar hopped onto Natalie's abdomen and began eating her genitals first. Her scream was shrill and child-like and she struggled against her manacles.

Kirk could not move or speak. He could not even move his eyes in their sockets. He was frozen in place, able to do no more than breathe, and watch as Baltazar ate Natalie.

Kirk's eyes, out of his control, followed every move Baltazar's head made. The bird consumed Natalie's flesh with surprising speed, although each second seemed an eternity to Kirk. Baltazar had a mouth that opened beyond the beak. Small razor-like teeth rimmed the beak and mouth. The bird also used its tongue to pull meat into its mouth—the tongue was long and narrow and black, forked at the end, prehensile, with three rows of curved red barbs. Baltazar made guttural cooing sounds as he ate.

Kirk could not close his eyes or look away as the bird ate the flesh off Natalie's bones, and he could not cover his ears to block out her horrible screams. Sometimes she called his name pleadingly, and a couple times, she cried out, "Frog Boy! Frog Boy!" Baltazar tore into her flesh continuously with talons, tongue, beak, and teeth. Her energy slowly decreased, but she still struggled weakly with her arms and shoulders, and turned her head back and forth.

Kirk wanted to help her, to pull that filthy bird off her and tear it apart with his bare hands. But he could not even move a single finger. As he watched the bird eat its way to the bone down one leg and up the other, Kirk felt as if his heart were being crushed in an enormous fist, squeezed into mush. He wanted to die. He prayed that God would end his life, strike him dead.

Baltazar took to the air for a break and flew in a few circles in the sky. While he was gone, what was left of Natalie lay there crying and babbling.

"Momma, please let me help," she said, "I can baste the turkey." She cried for awhile, lying there even more naked than before—clean bones from the waist down—then said, "Santa brought me the new Barbie!" She laughed a little, then screamed and cried, "Kirk! Kirk! I'm hungry!"

Baltazar returned and went back to his meal.

Above the dark clouds, the sun moved west in the sky. Natalie's screams became hoarse as Baltazar dined on her internal organs.

Inside his head, Kirk was screaming, too. He kept hearing Dad say, *That's Natalie. It's all that's left of her, anyway. The difference is that she's dead. So naturally, she's not going to behave the same way. She's...not all there anymore, Kirk. But she's still Natalie...still Natalie...still Natalie...*

He thought of Natalie as she had been—beautiful and smart and funny and so sexy. And she had trusted him. If she hadn't trusted him, then why would she call his name now? She expected him to help her. He was, after all, standing right there—she could *see* him. It tore him up inside. He was afraid he would lose his mind before this was finished.

It went on forever, and Kirk saw each and every piece of Natalie's flesh go down the bird's gullet. He watched as there was less and less of Natalie, more and more clean bone.

Natalie became silent once Baltazar got to her throat.

The dark sky grew darker. Mrs. Kobylka turned on the lights in her back porch, then a bright light over the porch door that cast a pool of illumination on Natalie and Baltazar once night fell.

Kirk was cold and nauseated. He vomited and it dribbled down his chin and spattered onto his denim jacket because he could not bend over.

After peeling off and eating her eyelids, the bird seemed to linger over the eyeballs.

Kirk watched as Baltazar broke open her skull with many patient but fierce blows of its beak to get to Natalie's brain. He picked off the maggots one at a time with rapid-fire precision, using both beak and tongue.

When it was over and he was released from the spell of mute immobility, Kirk collapsed to the ground and lost consciousness.

- NINE -

1.

Kirk was out no more than a few seconds, but was momentarily confused when he regained consciousness. Was he dreaming? Having a nightmare? A few feet away, beside Natalie's clean skeleton, Baltazar released a squealing shriek and fluttered his fleshy wings, and Kirk knew he had not been dreaming.

Dad helped him to his feet. "You're going to be okay," Dad said.

Kirk felt as if his brain had been run through a meat-grinder. He ached all over, especially in his chest, where the ache felt bad enough to kill him. But he knew, with regret, that it would not.

"Can...can I go home now?" Kirk said.

"Not yet," Mrs. Kobylka said. "You have work to do."

"Come on, Dad," Kirk said, "can't I go home?"

"I'm afraid not, Kirky. You're not finished here yet."

Kirk looked around but did not see his friends. "Where are Randy and Liz?"

"They went to the car," Dad said. "They couldn't watch anymore. I'm going to take them back to Liz's car at our place. I'll need to have a talk with your mother. Then I'll come back here."

"You're *leaving* me here?" Kirk said.

"The worst part is over, Kirky. Just do what Mrs. Kobylka tells you, and put it behind you as quickly as you can." Dad turned and walked around the corner of the house.

Mrs. Kobylka stepped in front of him and smiled. "You finish up now, eh? Come." She turned and headed for the back porch. She called, "Balty, come!" and the hideous bird followed her in. Kirk followed the bird.

"Wait here," she said on the porch. She and the bird went

inside the house.

The porch was well lighted. There was a rocking chair and a table with magazines on it at the far end. There were no throw-rugs or mats, the concrete floor was bare. Near the door leading out to the back yard was a large mortar and pestle next to a bright blue plastic bucket with a small matching blue plastic shovel, a child's beach toy. Nearby on the floor was a small sledgehammer. Next to that, a gunnysack lay in a heap.

Mrs. Kobylka shuffled back out on the porch. "Come into the kitchen and wash up."

He went inside, washed his hands and face at the sink, then went back out on the porch with her. She pointed at the back yard. "You take the sack out there and bring all the bones and the hammer in here. You use the two hammers to break the bones up into small pieces here on the floor. Then you use that—" She pointed to the mortar and pestle. "—to crush the bones up. It will make a sticky paste. You put the paste in the bucket and bring it in to me. One bucket at a time. You don't stop until the bones are gone."

Speaking more to himself than to Mrs. Kobylka, Kirk said, "That'll take all night."

"It will take as long as it takes."

"I'm hungry and thirsty. Could I have something to—"

"I bring you a drink. You will eat soon." She went back in the house. She came back out a couple minutes later with a tall cold glass of lemonade.

Kirk drained the glass with a few gulps, then did as he was told.

2.

When Kirk went in the back door with the first bucket of pale-pink gravelly paste made of Natalie's ground-up bones, Mrs.

Kobylka directed him to the dining area attached to the kitchen. A rectangular table had been covered with newspapers and a large cookie sheet had been set out. Waiting at the empty cookie sheet was Baltazar.

"Put it on the sheet for Balty," Mrs. Kobylka said. She sat in the kitchen, in front of the oven, on a chair from the dinette set. She had the television on the TV tray in front of her and she was crocheting.

Newspaper crackled beneath Baltazar's talons as the bird paced near the cookie sheet. The bird watched Kirk carefully while pacing. Baltazar stopped for a moment, shifted weight back and forth from one foot to the other, then started pacing again. As soon as Kirk started scooping the paste out of the bucket with the small plastic shovel, Baltazar moved in close. As much as he had eaten already, the bird was anxious to get started on the crunchy paste. When the bucket was empty, Kirk went back out on the porch.

It was messy work. Bone marrow splattered, and Kirk had it all over his shirt, and on his face and arms. The only thing that allowed him to do it was his newfound ability not to think about what he was doing. He thought about the pot Wyatt had given them and looked forward to getting his third of it and getting hugely stoned. He thought of Christmas and wondered what he would be getting this year, and of school starting again, and he thought about whether or not he wanted to go to college after he graduated from high school, what he wanted to study. Liz planned to go to Humboldt to study speech therapy, but Kirk and Randy hadn't decided yet. He thought of anything, anything at all—except what he was doing, what he had been doing, what he had done.

The next time he walked through the back door he was greeted by a pleasant aroma. Mrs. Kobylka was baking something.

Kirk went to the cookie sheet on the dining table. It had

been licked clean. He scooped more of the crunchy goo out onto the sheet.

"You like oatmeal cookies?" Mrs. Kobylka asked as he was on his way out.

His stomach gurgled with hunger. "Yes, I do."

"They will be ready soon. Mrs. Kobylka makes delicious brown-sugar oatmeal cookies."

As he went back to work breaking up and crushing Natalie's bones, Kirk could think of nothing but Mrs. Kobylka's cookies. Did she really think he'd fall for it? It was so *obvious*. He was supposed to think Baltazar was eating the bonepaste, when in fact Mrs. Kobylka had been making cookies out of it. Why would she want him to eat Natalie's bones? Was it part of her magic?

I don't think you realize exactly how dangerous that old woman is, Dad had said. *If you did, you never would have gone to her.*

Kirk worked as fast as he could, and as soon as he had another full bucket, he went into the house. Cookies were piled on a plate on the counter, and another batch was in the oven.

Before emptying the bucket, Kirk stood beside Mrs. Kobylka as she crocheted and watched television, and he said, "There's no fucking *way* I'm going to eat Natalie's bones."

Startled, she looked up at him and said, "You are a lunatic, you know that? You're all crazy, *all* of you. You watch too much TV, that's what it is. TV has made you all crazy. Go put it in on the cookie sheet for Balty."

Once again, Baltazar paced anxiously, waiting for the next serving.

"Bring a chair over here," Mrs. Kobylka said as she went to the refrigerator. She got a carton of milk out, poured some in a glass. She put the carton back, closed the refrigerator. When he was done, Kirk carried a chair over from the table and set it next to hers. He put the bucket down on the floor. "Sit," she said. Once he was seated, she handed him the glass of milk and offered the plate of cookies. "You think I make your girl-friend's bones into cookies for you to eat? Don't be stupid. Too much TV."

A horrible sound rose up from the dining table—a slurping, sucking, snorting, snarling sound. Disgusted, Kirk looked over at Baltazar as the bird ate. He did not look long.

He took one of the cookies and sniffed it. It smelled like oatmeal and brown sugar. "These are real cookies?"

She frowned. "Of *course* they're real cookies, dammit. *Take* some; *eat* them. You said you were hungry, that's why I baked them. Who makes cookies out of bones, you don't even know how stupid that sounds. You break your teeth on those things."

Kirk bit into the cookie. It was delicious. So was the cold milk. He took two more cookies from the plate before Mrs. Kobylka put it back on the counter.

Kirk's knees and back ached from kneeling on the concrete floor. He was so tired, he came close to nodding off while sitting there eating cookies. He had no idea what time it was, only that the night was wearing on. He did not want to know--knowing what time it was would only make the time pass slower.

Mrs. Kobylka picked up her crocheting from the chair, sat down, and went back to it. There was a game show on the small black-and-white television. Baltazar continued to make nauseating sounds while eating, and Kirk avoided looking at the bird.

"What kind of bird is Baltazar?" Kirk asked.

"No kind of bird you ever heard of before."

"Well, I'm no expert on birds—these cookies are delicious, by the way—but as far as I know, Baltazar doesn't exist. I think I would've caught Baltazar on the Discovery Channel or Animal Planet by now."

She stopped crocheting and looked at him. "You did not

believe I could raise your girlfriend until it happened, did you? No. You thought, she's a crazy old woman, and there's no such thing as magic. But now, I'm not so crazy, eh? And you've seen my magic work, so you know there *is* such a thing. You see Balty right over there. How can you say he does not exist?"

Mrs. Kobylka put her crocheting in her lap and took the plate of cookies off the counter, offered it to Kirk again, and he took a couple more. They were delicious, and he was ravenous.

"There are worlds that exist all around us that most people will never *imagine*, to say nothing of *seeing*," Mrs. Kobylka said. "You've seen a little bit of that. A glimpse. Are you going to deny it to yourself now? Bury it?"

Kirk was too busy eating cookies to respond, but he was listening carefully.

"Why not let it open your mind," she said, "change your perspective? Eh? But...no. You're all alike. You prefer your Martha Stewart dreams to the wonders that are all around you."

Kirk gulped some milk and she offered him the plate again. He took a couple more cookies.

"Eat those, then go back to work," she said. She sounded impatient with him.

3.

It had rained during the night, but the porch was dry. When Kirk was finished, he knew something was not right. Something was missing. There were no more bones on the concrete floor of the back porch, but he was missing one. He had not taken either of the hammers to the skull, had not even seen it. He flipped on the outdoor light and went out and searched the patch of ground where Natalie had been staked.

She had been staked there, spread out naked and helpless.

She had screamed as that bird had eaten her, and Kirk had watched every second of it.

Kirk had so successfully preoccupied his mind all night long that he'd rid it, for a while, of the awful memory of what had happened earlier. It all rushed back and Kirk's knees gave way beneath him. On his knees in the rain, his hands in the mud, he sobbed and asked Natalie to forgive him. He clutched at his stomach with one hand, but the pain was too deep to reach. It was much deeper than his stomach. His soul was ripped open and hemorrhaging.

"Get out of the mud!" Mrs. Kobylka shouted from the porch door.

Kirk slowly got to his feet and went into the porch, collected himself. "I can't find the skull."

"It's on top of the microwave," Mrs. Kobylka said as she went into the house. "Wash the mud off your hands."

Kirk followed her in and sure enough, the skull was sitting upright on top of the microwave oven. Kirk washed his hands in the kitchen sink.

"Take it down the hall to the room at the end," she said. "Keep walking straight across the room to what looks like a cabinet. There is a key in the lock. Turn it and open it. Go in and put the skull on a shelf."

Kirk carried the skull on his left hand down the hall and into the room at the end. He groped for a light switch and found it, turned on the light. It was a small, impossibly cluttered room, and directly across from him was what appeared to be a double-doored cabinet of shiny dark wood. A small brass key was in the lock above the handle on the door on the right. Kirk turned the key, pulled on the handle. Both doors opened outward and revealed a walk-in closet. Inside, the walls were covered with shelves, and on the shelves were skulls, two rows on each shelf: human skulls, dog skulls, cat skulls, tiny baby skulls, bird skulls, even what looked like a monkey skull. There had to be a couple hundred of them at least. He could not tell how deep the closet was because the shelves disappeared into darkness on the far side. Kirk felt like the skulls were staring directly at him, each one of them. He quickly squeezed Natalie's skull onto a shelf between two dog skulls, turned and got out of the closet. He closed the doors, turned the key, and noticed his hands trembling. He turned the light off on his way out of the room and hurried back up the dark hall.

Mrs. Kobylka was waiting for him. She stood at the end of the hall with hands on her hips. "You saw my collection, yes?"

Why did she want me to see that? Kirk wondered. He did not have the answer, but the question gave him the creeps.

"That is so you'll know," she said.

"Know? Know...what?"

"When you came to me and told me your name, I knew exactly who you were, who your father was. I remembered his dog, Duke. I remembered your father's father. And all their wives. You think when you come to me, you were doing something no one had ever done before, yes? Well, now you know better. I know everyone in this town. I know their secrets. They come to me for my magic, but when they see me on the street, they look the other way. And they all think *they* are the only one to think of coming to me. Now...*you* are a part of my big family. You've seen my secret collection, something I show no one." She moved closer to him. "You will tell no one what you saw in there. Ever. If you do, I will know. The second you tell someone, the instant the words leave your mouth, I will know, and I will take from you whatever happiness you have. And you know now that I can do this, yes?"

Kirk did not take a moment to think about it, did not hesitate for a second. He nodded and said, "Yes, I do."

"Good. And now that I have done this for you, maybe someday I ask you for a favor." Her mouth curled into a sneer as she looked him up and down. "But I doubt it." Mrs. Kobylka went over to the table and held out her arm. Baltazar hopped up on it and she carried him to his cage in the corner of the living room. "You can go home now, Kirk Mundy."

Baltazar got into the large black cage and she closed the door.

"I can?" Kirk said.

"Your father is parked outside, waiting for you."

Kirk hurried out to the back porch and snatched up his down jacket, then hurried back through the house. He stopped in front of the old woman. He did not know what to say. "Thank you" did not seem entirely appropriate.

"I don't know what to say," he said.

"Say goodbye," she said.

He slipped on his jacket and headed for the front door. Daggers of ice stabbed into his chest when he heard Natalie's loud, bouncy laughter behind him. Kirk spun around and faced Baltazar's cage in the corner of the living room.

"Kiss me, Frog Boy," the bird said in Natalie's voice.

Kirk clenched his fists and groaned.

"Let's do it here, it'll be exciting."

Mrs. Kobylka went to him, put a hand on his shoulder and turned him around. "Go," she said.

"Kirk! Kirk!" Baltazar cried in Natalie's voice.

Kirk threw himself at the front door, fumbled with the knob, threw it open, and stumbled through the screen door. He could not get out of the house fast enough. He heard Natalie laughing again, until Mrs. Kobylka closed the front door.

The Durango was parked in front of the house, and when he saw it, Kirk broke into a run.

- TEN -

1.

Officer McCready never returned with further questions for Kirk, Randy, or Liz about the disappearance of Natalie's body. The *Record Searchlight* hinted at a connection between the brutal murder of convicted drug dealer Wyatt Parks and Natalie's disappearance, but gave no details.

Dad called Bobby and learned that the Sheriff's Department was baffled. At first, they'd sweated Dicky Parks, but he had a solid alibi. Forensic technicians found on Wyatt Parks' mutilated body necrotic tissue specimens foreign to his DNA. The tissue was found to have come from a decaying human corpse. Because Natalie's body had been stolen from the Richmond Funeral Home recently, the tissue was checked against DNA material taken from Natalie Gilbert's hairbrush, and there was a match. Natalie Gilbert's corpse had been on Wyatt Parks, or Wyatt Parks had been on the corpse, on or around the time of his death. When questioned about it, Dicky was able to account for every second of his time the night Natalie Gilbert's body had disappeared, and he had witnesses. Someone in forensics got the bright idea of checking the bite marks on Parks with Natalie Gilbert's dental records. Another match, but this time it made no sense at all. Natalie Gilbert was already dead—she could not have bitten Wyatt Parks. Had someone manipulated her body to make it appear she had?

They did not have the answers yet, but they had plenty of questions, and a deputy came by one day to ask a few. He asked Kirk if Natalie had been friends with Dicky or Wyatt Parks. Kirk said he and Natalie knew them, but weren't close. He said Natalie had tried to help Dicky get a job when he dropped out of high school, but he hadn't been interested.

Randy and Liz told the deputy the same thing.

After that, the Sheriff's Department lost interest in them.

2.

Mom worked miracles with the house, particularly Kirk's bedroom, and the pool-house. It took her a few days—she even took a couple days off work to do it—but she got rid of the smell. She never mentioned it to Kirk, or anyone else. For Mom, that took considerable effort—she loved nothing more than having a good cleaning-disaster story to tell.

Dad said he'd told her "a version of the truth." He said he would be surprised if she ever brought it up.

By the end of the week, the Christmas tree was up and the house smelled of the silvertip pine.

3.

Kirk and Randy and Liz continued to spend time together, although that time slowly decreased. They enjoyed the Wyatt-weed, usually before going to a movie together. In the car, they played music. They didn't talk much anymore. Or maybe they simply said more when they talked, and talked less.

June came, and they graduated, and suddenly they were no longer students for the first time in twelve years.

They slowly grew apart that summer. Randy got a job at a large hardware store and lumberyard. Liz went to Eureka early and found an apartment with a roommate—she'd decided to take a couple classes at Humboldt during the summer to familiarize herself with the campus. Kirk did not do much of anything that summer.

Kirk saw Randy now and then and he was worried about him because he was drinking a lot. Too much. They saw Liz in early August and were surprised by how skinny she was—she had lost at least twenty pounds she could not afford to lose, because Liz was a very slender girl. Kirk suspected she had developed an eating disorder, but it never came up in their brief conversation.

Kirk did not sleep much. When he did sleep, he heard Baltazar's shrieking, piglet-like squeal and Natalie's endless screams. He saw the bird tearing her puckered nipples from her deflated breasts, eating her filmy eyeballs. The Wyattweed helped, while it lasted.

One evening in early August, while Kirk was playing a game on his computer, Dad came to his room.

"Have you decided what you want to do with yourself, Kirky?" he asked. "You can take some classes at Shasta College, or get a job—whatever you want."

"I want to be able to sleep again."

"You will. It'll just take time. Meanwhile, you've got to get back on your feet. You'll be living with this the rest of your life."

"Randy's drinking a lot. I think Liz is bulimic, or something. I'm just…numb."

"Then you've got to snap out of it now while you still can," Dad said. "Mom and I are worried about you. Even Kevin has noticed something is wrong."

"I keep thinking…what else is going on out there that I don't know about?"

Dad frowned. "What do you mean?"

"Mrs. Kobylka really *is* a witch who can raise the dead. Zombies *are* real. So what *else* is true that I've been laughing at my whole life? Are there space aliens? Werewolves? Vampires?"

"Kirk, you can't think that way. It'll make you sick. You've got your future to think about. Whatever Mrs. Kobylka did, whatever that was, it was…wrong, unnatural. If it weren't, we'd *all* be doing it. It's not a part of our lives, it has nothing to do with our world, so there's no reason for you even to *think* about it. What happened…just think of it as a bad dream. Put

it behind you. And do it quickly. Because if this keeps up...
well, you won't be able to get any counseling, because you can't
tell anyone what's bothering you. You have to snap out of this,
Kirk, because you don't have a choice."

The next day, Kirk went to Rite-Aid and bought a picture
frame. At home, he put on some music he and Natalie had
liked. He found a picture of himself and Natalie taken at a
spring dance. He put the picture in the frame and placed it on
his bedstand.

He started looking for a job. He got a catalog of the classes
being offered at Shasta College and browsed through it.

He went to bed every night hoping he would be able to
sleep. But he did one thing differently.

He closed and locked his window every night, the window
Natalie used to climb through to come to bed with him. Kirk
could not help wondering how many dead pets were wandering
through the night, how many dead loved ones were shuffling
around with an insatiable hunger to feed. It did not feel safe to
leave the window open anymore. He no longer knew what was
out there.

Feeding Frenzy
MATT HULTS

THE RESTAURANT STOOD less than forty feet away, small and unimpressive in comparison to the encompassing forest landscape, but also the blackest thing in sight on an otherwise bright and sunny day.

Ron parked the rental car just outside the entrance to the parking lot, pulling to a stop amid a small pile of animal bones that crunched beneath the tires.

He switched off the engine. "Not exactly the first impression I was hoping for," he said.

Beside him, Greg seemed undeterred. Minus his beer-gut and his rapidly receding hairline, the older man looked like a six-year-old kid on a jackpot Christmas morning. "Don't worry about it," he replied. "They told me the property was a little messy. Look at the building, though! Are you sure this is the right address?"

Ron nodded to the realty sign standing to the left. "This is the place, all right."

"Jeez... It's in great shape!"

Maybe, maybe not, Ron thought, but he decided to hold his tongue. They were already falling into their usual mode of operation, Greg seeking out the sweet deal while Ron remained ever-watchful for the lemon that could sour it.

They got out of the car.

Outside, the smell of dry oak leaves instantly enveloped them. Ron drew in a long breath of it, cleansing the stink of the rental company's pine-scented air freshener from his sinuses. He glanced behind them, to the dirt lane that tethered the old restaurant to the highway, frowning at the distance. It couldn't have measured more than fifty yards in length—he spotted traffic blinking between the trees—but the silence here made it seem immeasurably farther than it looked.

"It's kind of out-of-the-way, don't you think?" he asked.

Greg had already reached the building and was tugging at the locked doors. He glanced over his shoulder. "Are you kidding? This is a prime location. We're surrounded by farmland and national forest. We'll get all the traffic between Brainerd and Clearwater Creek. Cut down some of those trees and we can put up a sign that'll practically be on the highway!"

Farmland and forest, Ron thought, but again he kept his comments to himself.

"The realtor must be running late, huh?" Greg asked. He cupped both hands over his face and leaned forward, trying to find a chink in the plywood armor that covered the building's windows.

Ron strolled across the lot. He studied the dimensions of the restaurant, guessing that the original owner had attempted to emulate the layout of a traditional fast-food business but with a slightly higher-scale motif, to set it apart from the larger chains that dominated North America's roadways.

He'd never seen a fast-food joint with a black slate-shingled roof and widow's walk. Or wrought iron lampposts shaped to resemble a cluster of entwined tentacles. Still, despite its unorthodox appearance, Ron thought the building looked good and sturdy. That, coupled with the rock-bottom price tag, opened a world of possibilities for improvements. Nevertheless, he didn't want to get too excited too fast.

Greg joined him as he made his way around the side of the building to get a look at the back.

"You said this was a fixer-upper, right?" Ron asked.

Greg nodded. "The ad mentioned 'extensive fire-damage' but this looks a lot better than I imagined."

Ron stopped walking.

"Oh, hey, a takeout window!" Greg said, pointing. "This is great! That'll save us even more money on the renovation!"

But Ron wasn't looking at the takeout window. "What's that?" he asked.

Focused as he was on the drive-thru, Greg had failed to notice the giant hole in the wall of trees beyond the restaurant, or the enormous four-lane road that extended off the parking lot, stretching to a pinpoint in the far depths of the surrounding forest.

Greg gaped at the sight. "Holy, shit!" he laughed. "And you were worried about being too far from the highway!"

Ron ignored the comment and approached the road. A gust of wind ushered a group of dead leaves across the concrete, but, other than that, the vast avenue appeared as vacant as a desert wasteland.

No cars.

No people.

Just a wide lane of unbroken grey cement that receded into the distant shadows.

"You don't think this is a bit strange?" he asked.

Greg shrugged. "Could be under construction… Maybe it's a new expansion to the Interstate?"

"Leading to a restaurant?" Ron replied. "There's no median, no streetlights—"

The sound of wheels crunching over gravel broke into the conversation, and they both looked toward the parking lot.

"That must be the realtor," Greg remarked. "We can ask her about it."

They headed back toward the car. Ron let Greg lead the way, lingering behind just long enough to cast one last glance at the unusual forest road. They'd walked only a short distance, but from his new perspective he noted how the trees shielded it from sight, the branches interlacing overhead, enclosing it like a tunnel.

Greg threw a hand against his chest, halting him in his tracks.

"God bless the locals!" his friend said. Then, before Ron had a chance to get his meaning, the man resumed walking, stealthily adding, "Be a pal and let the single guy do the talking…"

Ron followed his line of sight to where he spotted the realtor exiting her vehicle.

Dwarfed by the SUV she'd arrived in, the petite young woman looked in need of a climbing harness to get from the driver's seat to the ground. On the contrary, she moved with an athletic grace, seeming to flow from one position to the next. Out in the open, her long blonde hair caught the full radiance of the sun, contrasting with the black material of her pants and jacket, which hugged the trim contours of her body.

He thought of Diane back home, so far away, knowing that if they did indeed buy the restaurant he'd become a local himself for the first several months of operation, overseeing the renovation and training all the staff.

Ahead of him Greg looked back, twitched his eyebrows.

Ron shook his head and followed.

This is business, he opened his mouth to say before the other man was out of earshot, but stopped short when his gaze once again shifted to the girl. She still stood next to the open door of her sport utility, a blatant expression of perplexity creasing the skin across her brow. Her full attention remained focused straight ahead, staring at the restaurant, and she didn't even notice Greg approaching until he'd closed within the last ten feet of her.

She spun to face him as if suddenly realizing she was in the shadow of a grizzly bear.

"We'll take it!" Greg declared before she had a chance to say anything.

Ron watched the look of fear mix with another fleeting flash of bewilderment, and then she was laughing with embarrassment. Her voice sounded melodic in the open woodland air.

"You must be Mr. Brunik," the woman said, offering Greg her hand. "Wendy Thomas. We spoke on the phone."

"It's nice to finally meet the woman the beautiful voice belongs to," he said.

Her smile stiffened at the corners, becoming more perfunctory than genuine.

A moment later Ron stepped up to join them, trying to think of something that would downplay Greg's excitement until they'd viewed the entire property, and when the realtor faced him there was no mistaking the way their eyes locked. Her smile of sincerity returned and she instantly dropped Greg's hand.

"And you're Mr. Caldmond, correct?"

In her business-minded clothing, she looked like an office intern who's college diploma was still a year or two away.

"Pleased to meet you, Mrs. Thomas," Ron replied, purposely emphasizing the prefix.

Her hand slipped neatly into his, smooth and dainty, but slightly chilled. It lingered there a heartbeat longer than what might've been considered professionally courteous.

"*Miss*, actually," she corrected.

Behind her, Greg placed his hands together and mouthed 'thank you' to the sky.

Ron pretended not to see. He acknowledged the realtor's smile with a polite one of his own, then pivoted away from both of them in an attempt to get things back on course.

He gestured to the restaurant. "So the bank is only asking for payment of the back taxes, is that right?"

The girl looked up at it. "Yes. Due to the fire…"

They started walking toward the building. "Greg mentioned that. May I ask what happened?"

"Arson," she said, glancing between the both of them. "The previous owner tried to burn it down, possibly as an insurance scam. It was the biggest news story the town paper has reported in ages."

"Nice," Greg commented. "Free publicity!"

At the door, Wendy entered her security code on the digital lock that secured the two door handles together and the device unclasped.

Ron and Greg both took a handle.

Together, they pulled the twin doors open.

Their eager shadows leapt inside the room ahead of them, a trio of jet-black explorers in an even blacker realm of darkness. Having all the other windows covered, the spacious main chamber exuded the ambiance of an empty mausoleum. The predominant smell of smoke hung wraithlike in the air.

"Oh, I forgot," Wendy said, then reached to extract a small—

Greg flipped a switch on the wall and the overhead lights clicked on.

—flashlight from her jacket pocket.

She glanced around.

"Juice works!" Greg cheered.

They stood before the main dining area.

Dozens of heaped tables and chairs lined the walls to either side, no doubt pushed aside by the responding firemen on the night of the blaze, but all the permanent structures remained in place—booths, condiment counter, waste bins—and Ron immediately recognized the familiar floor plan typical of any fast-food restaurant, one designed with the intent of facilitating an easy flow from the ordering counter to the seating area, thus maximizing turn over at the registers.

Wendy cleared her throat. "As you can see, all the related equipment is included. Everything from the kitchen appliances, to whatever toilet paper is left hanging in the bathrooms. Let me show you the work area…"

With a tap of his shoe, Ron set the rubber door-stoppers in place and proceeded inside. They crossed the tiled floor and passed through a partition in the far right side of the main service counter, moving behind the bank of cash registers.

"Feed the Customer… Obey the Rules!" Greg said.

Ron and Wendy both halted in their tracks and faced him.

"What?" Ron asked.

Greg pointed to a sign affixed to the wall beside the counter. "Must be a mission statement or something, huh?"

Resuming the tour, they migrated to the kitchen.

There, several overhead lights flickered in erratic bursts, their plastic diffusers hanging open. Rows of various stainless steel appliances lined the walls, veiled in streaks of soot and grease that reminded Ron of sunken ships overcome by rust.

Wendy pointed out the coolers, mixers, meat-slicers, microwaves, gas ovens, deep-fryers, hot-plates, and heat-lamps. The grill alone looked as long as one of the preparation tables, housing an amazing twenty burners, with a flattop fry-station at the far end. Overhead, all sizes of spatulas, ladles, whisks, colanders, pots, and pans hung from a ceiling rack. In the back, the door to the walk-in freezer hung ajar, emitting a smell that would make a health inspector's head spin.

"This is great stuff," Greg said, checking a giant mixer that stood tall enough to come level with his chest. "A little work and a few gallons of degreaser and it'll be as good as new!"

Ron nodded his agreement, but remained silent. He spied the black residue of ash and cinders, still smelled the cloying stink of smoke—if anything, it was stronger here—but he had yet to see any real fire damage.

They moved along, visiting the dry-goods storeroom in the back—which seemed to contain all the original provisions that had been present at the restaurant's closure—as well as the adjacent offices.

The manager's office was crammed with all manner of clutter, from broken chairs that must've come from the dining room, to boxes overflowing with charred kitchen accessories and half-burnt legal papers.

Through the clutter, Ron spotted a large painting of The Last Supper hanging askew on the far wall. It seemed an odd choice of artwork to decorate a business office, and the peculiarity of it only magnified when he looked closer.

In the picture, behind Christ and his disciples, loomed the massive forest highway he'd seen outside. The sight produced a tingle of mixed puzzlement and unease, and he suddenly realized that somewhere during their round of introductions with Wendy he'd forgot to inquire about the road.

Now he opened his mouth to do just that when something banged deeper in the building.

They all jumped.

"What the hell?" Greg asked.

Then it came again, the noise of something crashing in the dining room.

"That sounded like the door," Ron said.

He edged past Greg and Wendy, striding down the hall, to the front of the restaurant—

Where a man stood before one of the registers as if waiting to place an order.

All three of them jerked to a stop at the surprise.

The newcomer stood glaring at them from under a whirlwind of white hair, his eyes locked on them like gun sights. He wore a brown stain-splotched trench coat that looked as though it had seen a lifetime of squatting in abandon houses and sleeping under bridges. Although Ron had just laid eyes on him, the deep scowl of anger on the stranger's face told him they were in for trouble. Across the room, the restaurant doors were closed.

"Food," the derelict demanded.

Greg smirked. "Does this place look open to you, pal?"

The man hefted a double-bladed ax into view as his answer. It had been concealed by the counter, but now he brought it up fast, swinging it over his head and slamming it down into the register. The huge blade cleaved the machine in two. Sparks jumped into the air.

Greg flinched so hard he collapsed backwards on his ass.

"Food!" the crazed customer shouted. "Give me a burger!"

Ron stepped forward, shaking with adrenaline. The ax-wielder spotted him and readied another swing.

"We'll get it right away," he said, the words coming out of his mouth on autopilot. "How would you like that prepared, sir?"

It seemed surreal given the insane situation, letting his managerial instincts take over, hearing his voice adopt the familiar apologetic tone an angry customer always wants to hear, but amazingly it worked. The maniac relaxed, releasing his grip on the ax to scratch the stubble of his chin.

"Rare, I reckon," he said in an almost-normal voice. "With, ah…fries and a sody-pop."

Ron forced a smile. "Rare burger with fries and a drink. That'll be just one moment, sir." He backed up as he spoke, urging the others to follow. Greg shuffled rearward on the floor.

"No *goddamn* onions, though!" the man roared after them.

"Hold the onions!" Ron repeated.

They retreated to the back of the building, all moving in reverse to keep and eye on the entry to the hallway. Ron expected the madman to come rushing after them at any second, but they reached the storeroom unmolested.

"Jesus!" Greg gasped. Sweat glistened on his brow. "What the fuck was that about?"

Ron didn't bother speculating on an answer. Instead, he charged to the storeroom's rear wall, heaving aside a hill of empty boxes and other useless scrap. There, hidden behind the heap, he uncovered the set of loading doors he'd been hoping he would find.

To his dismay, a padlocked chain secured the push-bars to the frame.

"Wendy, do you have a key for this?" he asked, trying to keep his voice steady.

The girl shook her head. "Just the code for the one up front."

"Shit!" Greg cried.

Ron dug into his pockets. Found his cell phone. "Look for something we can use as weapons!" he said, then glanced to the empty hallway, wondering how long they had before their disgruntled guest came to file a complaint.

He looked to the phone, but it didn't even light up.

"My phone's dead," he said. "Anyone else—"

"In the car," Wendy replied.

Greg shook his head.

Ron held back the avalanche of obscenities that almost rolled off his tongue and sat down on a stack of milk crates to mentally scrutinize his options.

No phone. No windows. And no key to the only door. Which leaves trying to get past the psychotic hobo with the ax.

Just then, he spotted several boxes of press-paper dinner-ware and plastic utensils on the other side of the room.

Back on his feet, he crossed the floor and grabbed a package of paper cups, tearing it open.

"What are you doing?" Greg asked.

"I'm getting him his drink."

"Are you nuts?"

"Would you prefer he come back here and look for it, where we don't have any way to escape?"

The idea seemed to sink in, and the man sagged into silence.

Ron cracked open a container of plastic lids for the cups. "Look, you saw how he eased off when I said we'd feed him, right? So let's keep it up. We'll pretend to fill his order, and when we go back up front, we can try getting out the drive-thru window."

"I don't think I'll fit!" Greg replied. "Jesus, man, you can't leave me!"

"We'll help Wendy out, then. She can go for help, and I'll stay here with you...unless either of you have a better idea?"

They made a quick detour through the kitchen, rummaging through the equipment for whatever they could use. In the far corner, Ron discovered a ten-inch butcher knife in a plastic crate beside the wash-station. All three of them stared at it, seeing its horrible potential, but said nothing as Ron slipped it into his belt and covered it with his shirt.

"Let's go," he said.

He led them toward the registers, finding the wild-eyed derelict exactly where they'd left him—

But now there were six more people lined up behind him.

Ron's stride faltered when he saw them, and Wendy and Greg almost ran into his back.

He saw a slack-jawed boy in tattered overalls holding a shotgun.

A grossly overweight woman sucking a pacifier.

A blindfolded girl with a badly bruised neck—

Greg gave him a shove, prodding him onward.

"Just one minute folks," he mumbled, and then they were at the end of the counter, where they slipped into the drive-thru station alcove and mercifully out of sight of the patrons.

"What hell is going on?" Greg asked.

"Did you see their faces?" Wendy whispered. "My, God, did you see them?"

Ron nodded. He looked down and realized he'd crushed the paper cup into a wad. Now he tossed it away and moved to the window, sliding it aside. He stepped back and kicked out the plywood board covering the frame.

Static suddenly hissed out of the nearby intercom.

Ron jumped at the sound of it, facing the small metal box as an unearthly voice issued from the speaker. "...ausage ...muffin...an...two sma...ingers wit...side...f brai...s."

Ron gaped at it. Beside him, Greg pushed past him and stuck his face to the glass.

"There's a car!" he cried. "Hey! Help us! We're trapped in here!"

Ron heard the growl of an engine. A cough of exhaust.

A second later the car pulled parallel with the takeout area––it looked like a fusion of a hearse and a 1950's Buick—and the driver's window rolled down, revealing nothing but a solid, impenetrable darkness.

"Get us out of here!" Greg pleaded.

But before he could say another word, a hand extended out of the void inside the car, a green sore-speckle thing that stretched impossibly long, bridging the gap between the vehicle and the building to reach through the takeout window and grab Greg's shirt.

"Get off me!" he bellowed.

Both Ron and Wendy seized his arms, yanking him free to the sound of tearing fabric.

The arm withdrew, taking a scrap of cloth with it.

"Fuck this!" Greg screamed.

Ron's grip on him had loosened as he watched the elongated appendage vanish back into the inky darkness of the car, and the other man broke free, twisting away, running for the front.

"Greg!" Wendy cried.

Her voice snapped Ron back to attention, and he bolted after his friend, rounding the corner in time to see Greg vault the counter, half-leaping, half-falling off the other side.

Where now over *thirty* customers shuffled about the main room, falling into lines before each of the registers!

Ron watched with paralytic wonder as they turned on Greg in unison.

Before the man even managed to regain his balance, the customers tackled him to the ground, dropping over him like bloodthirsty monsters in a zombie film. Ron stepped forward, about to lunge after him, but several of the closest patrons turned on him, each holding something sharp.

He froze in place behind the counter, covering his mouth as he heard what sounded like ripping carpet arise from beneath the pile.

Followed by a piercing scream.

He watched the things tear and gnash and snarl, and finally spun away when he saw the creatures begin passing around severed limbs and handfuls of dripping crimson gore. Fresh blood drooled from their mouths.

Wendy shrieked the entire time, crying out so powerfully that Ron's ears rang with each new exhalation. Without looking to the feasting masses, he clutched her to his chest and guided her to the kitchen.

"Oh, God!" she sobbed. "They're crazy! They're going to kill us! What do we do?"

Ron peered through one of the heat lamp stations, looking at the motley collection of customers now churning shoulder-to-shoulder in the dining room. Those who hadn't attacked Greg clustered at the counter, no longer content to stand in orderly lines. They pressed forward, leaning over the edge, searching the cashier area.

A wrinkled old man crawling with bugs jabbed a pitchfork at a register. A one-armed lady whose eyes glared through a net of bandages threw a rock at the menu. Behind her, a pair of suit-clad young men wrestled over a dead rat.

But none of them followed us, he thought. *Why not?*

"Because customers aren't allowed behind the counter," he whispered to himself.

Wendy's sobbing slowed. She gazed at him as though a third eye had opened on his forehead. Ron met her eyes, thinking of the green hand that had tried to seize Greg, stretching out to reach him like something from a nightmare. He sensed a revelation teetering at the edge of his understanding.

"We have to get cooking," he said. "Before they eat us, too."

A small smile ticked at the corner of the girl's mouth, like a seam about to come undone.

"Cook…" she echoed in a tone of disbelief. "*For them?*"

Ron nodded, eyeing the sign over her shoulder, the one Greg had spotted earlier.

Feed the Customer… Obey the Rules!

He looked to the crowd once again, his gaze drifting over a dozen ghastly sights: a man with no eyes; a woman half-enshrouded by mold; a pale sexless figure covered in ants.

They were something else, he realized, something supernatural, and he and Greg and Wendy had somehow become trapped here, held specifically for their servitude.

But Greg had broken the rules…

Wendy was already shaking her head, fresh tears brimming in her eyes. "You're crazy!"

Before he could explain himself, a chair from the seating area smashed against the opposite side of the wall, shattering two of the heat lamps, pelting them with hot glass. He looked up and saw the crowd massing before the registers like rioters lined up against a barricade. A hundred voices hollered, "Food!"

"Trust me," he said, hauling Wendy to her feet. "We need to feed them! Start looking for anything we can use!"

Together they attacked the kitchen, clawing open cabinets, searching shelves, rummaging through the detritus scattered throughout the room. Ron had no idea what eatables they could possibly find—if any—but as they searched the building, they discovered hidden caches of all imaginable ingredients: buns, condiments, spices, vegetables, canned fillings, pre-made mixes that declared: *Just add water!*

Ron went to the walk-in freezer, certain that there couldn't be anything salvageable inside—not with that horrid smell seeping from the door—but when he looked, he found row after row of plastic-wrapped hamburger patties waiting for the grill. The temperature inside the freezer easily rivaled that of the kitchen, and though Ron knew the patties had to be rancid, he snatched up a bag in each hand and called for Wendy to come help him.

Something growled.

The sound made him jerk with fear, dropping the bags of hamburger as he drew the butcher knife from his belt.

Wendy ran to his side, reaching him in time to witness a cloudy white eyeball pop open on the gigantic pile of reeking meat heaped against the freezer's far wall.

Her scream ripped across his eardrums at the very moment a lopsided mouth tore a hole in the huge mound of ground beef staring back at them. The meat-pile yawned as they looked on, displaying teeth made from broken bones and disgorging a huge bovine organ that must've been its tongue. Five smaller eyes surfaced at various points around the first one.

The thing's attention focused on the knife in Ron's hand. Its eyes narrowed.

A second later it coughed up a watery stream of red-brown liquid that struck Ron dead-center in the chest, soaking his shirt and hair, spraying in all directions.

He slammed the door and threw the locking pin in place, looking at Wendy, meat juice dripping off his face. Her mascara traced the paths of her tears down both cheeks.

"Co...come on," he said, picking up the bags of patties. "We need to hurry."

At the stove, he fired up the burners, switched on the deep fryer. Overhead, the malfunctioning lights had ceased flickering and now glowed bright and steady. Readout LEDs flashed to life on almost all the other appliances.

They completed sixty orders at an average rate of four minutes per meal, a miracle time born of high-pressure stress and good ol' fashion terror. The customers came, ordered, and paid whatever they felt like paying. Currencies from around the world disappeared into the cash drawers, along with shells and stones, bones and teeth. At one point, a skinny girl with blue-grey skin dressed only in fishnet stockings and a frayed leather dog collar offered Ron a "freebee" in exchange for her chocolate milkshake, to which he politely replied, "It's on the house."

Wendy refused to follow him to the counter, opting instead to watch the grill while he dealt with the horde of unearthly customers up front.

"We're out of hamburger patties," she said when he rushed to change the baskets in the deep fryer. She cast a furtive glance at where they'd stacked a dozen canisters of soft drink mix in front of the freezer door.

Ron sighed. "There's something that looks like meat hanging in the janitor's closet...I'll go cut some slabs off that in a minute."

He reloaded the fryers and returned to the registers, delivering a tray of fish sticks. Ahead of him, a sea of pale-skinned patrons waited their turn at the counter.

A teenage girl dripping mud and seaweed stepped forward.

"How…" he began, then had to stop, trying to work up saliva. He wiped sweat off his face. "How may I…"

But he pivoted away without finishing, leaning against the ice cream machine, which currently churned a mixture of vanilla soft-server and black sludge.

"Screw this!" he cried. "I can't. I can't do it anymore—"

"Hello, sir," a voice said at his back.

Ron flinched and spun around, recoiling at the sight of a tall gaunt figure dressed in a paper hat and apron. Behind it stood a trio of men with wads of bloody gauze taped over their eyes.

"We're here about the jobs," the tall one said. He handed Ron a quartet of papers labeled 'Application for Employment.'

Ron blinked, stammering a string of unintelligible sounds before finally saying the one thing that seemed the most appropriate. "You're hired."

"Thank you, sir," the emaciated creature answered. It immediately took up a position near the deep fryer, causing Wendy to scream when she saw it coming. The thing reached into the bubbling oil with its bare hands, transferring the cooked food to the proper containers. The other men each manned a register, two up front and one at the drive-thru alcove.

Wendy hurried to Ron's side. "What…" she started, but then trailed off, perhaps knowing he'd have no rational answer for her question.

The hours passed. Customers continued to arrive, flooding the dining room far beyond what would normally be acceptable by state safety regulations—yet the restaurant managed to accommodate them. More employees showed up, as well. They no longer approached Ron, acting out the formalities of regular job applicants as the first few had, but just turned up and went to work.

The rhythm of the restaurant filled the air. Pots clanking, registers buzzing, voices calling out the orders. From the dining room came the constant slavering sounds of snapping teeth and chewing jaws while the patrons devoured meal after meal after meal.

And they were getting stranger, too. As were their orders.

Ron glimpsed a walking jumpsuit with a mass of purple vines sprouting from the neckline; a mound of black fur whose hidden claws clicked against the tile; a skinless beast that reminded him of the malevolent mound of sentient beef in the freezer.

He avoided the front line as much as possible now, busying himself by stocking mundane supplies that mysteriously showed up in the storeroom: plastic forks; paper cups; napkins; straws. Occasionally he'd come across a box labeled 'Dried Monkey Heads' or an economy-size can of 'Powdered Semen', but at least those items were contained and out of sight. It was when he'd encounter a worker delivering some hideous tray of ingredients to the kitchen that he felt his stomach somersault inside him. Twice he'd vomited on the floor, not having time to find the restroom. The first time a dutiful employee appeared with a mop and bucket; the second time they brought a carryout bag.

He was more concerned about Wendy than himself, though. She followed him like his shadow, crying out each time one of the malformed workers came within arm's reach of her—which had become a regular occurrence given the cramped conditions. More than once he'd needed to lift her from the floor after she'd slumped into a corner.

Now he looked up as he deposited a fresh container of salt and pepper packets at the counter, shocked to see a normal-looking gentleman in glasses approach the register. He had a nervous, sheepish way about him that reminded Ron of the acting style of Woody Allen, and he almost screamed at the guy to run and find help.

Then the man smiled a mouth full of razor-pointed teeth. "Do you happen to have any live children?" he asked.

Ron stood frozen. "Fresh out," he replied, praying it was the first and only time such a request had come in.

The gentleman snapped his fingers. He pushed his glasses up. "I guess I'll just have a chicken sandwich, then."

Ron keyed in the order and fled back toward the kitchen—

Where he noticed Wendy had disappeared.

"Wendy!" he shouted. He hurried through the kitchen, pushing past the workers as they went about their chores, but couldn't find her. He dashed past the freezer. "Fucker!" the thing inside barked—and rushed down the back hall.

He found her in the manager's office, tucked into the corner beside a plastic potted plant. The small room appeared immaculate, a far cry from when he'd first viewed it. The furniture all looked new now, as did the various office-related supplies and corporate-themed decor. Behind the desk, the picture of the Last Supper gleamed as if just painted.

"It's my fault," Wendy wailed when she saw him. "I knew something was wrong when I drove up. The place was fixed! When I first toured it last month, the building was just a burnt out shell. But today...I should've said something, anything, but I needed the commission..."

Her confession deteriorated into a sorrowful moan.

He sat down beside her. Took her hands in his.

"We'll be all right. We just need to feed the customers and obey the rules."

"But what does that mean?"

"I don't know," he said. "It's like we've skipped the Twilight Zone and gone straight to Hell. All I know is that we're still alive, and if we can stay that way long enough, we'll find a way out of here...this place seems to need us."

"Which is why we'll never get out," she said. Despite her tears, the words came out soft and calm, sounding frighteningly like acceptance.

He opened his mouth, not yet sure what he planned to say, only knowing that he had to get her back to work before whatever force controlled this place decided she was slacking.

"Look we—" he started, but stopped when he spotted something lying forgotten under the desk. He let go of Wendy's hands and crawled over to it.

He picked it up and hope instantly charged his nerves.

"Look at this!" he said. "It's the ID badge of the previous manager."

When she didn't move, he returned to her side, holding the badge forward. He tapped the headshot under the laminate. "Wendy, do you recognize this guy?"

She stared at it for a moment, eyes blank, but then a look of understanding enlivened her features. "Al Tolbec," she whispered, reading the signature on the badge. "Yes! He's the owner, the one who tried to burn this place down."

Ron could see a fresh glint of resolve in her eyes, a growing excitement he felt himself.

"And where is Tolbec now?" he asked knowingly.

"A mental hospital," she replied. "That's why the insurance company dropped the arson suit and ownership of the property reverted to the bank, because the courts found him insane!"

"Of course they did!" Ron laughed. "Imagine trying to tell a judge you built a restaurant that caters exclusively to the dead!"

He got up, helping Wendy to her feet. "That's not the important part, though. What matters is that Tolbec got out. He got out and tried to destroy this place. And if he found a way to escape—"

"So can we!" Wendy finished for him.

Ron nodded.

From the hallway came the background noise of the workers laboring in the kitchen, along with the constant undertone of the feasting creatures in the dining room.

Ron crossed the office and checked the hall, finding it vacant. He eased the door closed, wiping a layer of nervous sweat off his forehead.

"Okay..." he said, pacing back and forth. "For whatever reason this place seems to function on the same principles as an average fast-food business. Maybe we can use that somehow?"

Wendy pondered the problem, chewing her lower lip.

"We seem to be integral to servicing the customers," Ron thought aloud. "Which would make us employees, I guess... But we can't just quit and walk out..."

Suddenly Wendy's face brightened. "You could fire me!" she said.

"What?"

She stepped around the desk to stand before him. "Listen, the workers—those ghosts, or corpses, or whatever they are—they all listen to you! They came to you to get hired. They act like you run the place! If what you're saying is true, that makes you the manager. I'm just another employee to them. If you fired me, I'd have to leave!"

Ron mulled it over for a moment, seeing her reasoning, but finally shook his head no.

"I can't let you risk yourself like that," he said. "I have a feeling that in this place you don't get fired; you get terminated."

Her expression of optimism dissolved into a shudder.

"We have to try something simple," he said. Then, after a second of contemplation, he grabbed her hand. "Follow me!"

Ron raced out of the office, towing Wendy along with him, heading for the storeroom—

But slid to a halt after only a few feet, stopped by the sight of one of the skeletonized workers in the hall, blocking their path. It leaned against the wall, glaring at them like a back-alley thug.

Ron forced a commanding tone. "Afraid that wall will fall over if you don't hold it up?"

The thing straightened. Its sneer vanished from its shrink-wrapped head, replaced by a definite look of unease.

"Get your bony ass back to work!" Ron boomed.

To his surprise, the figure spun away and hot-tailed it back to the kitchen.

He looked to Wendy. "Let's move!"

They hurried to the storeroom, to where three waste barrels sat to the right of the chained doors. Each overflowed with stuffed trash bags.

He hefted a bag in each hand and turned to the doors. He took a deep breath.

"This place is a goddamn disgrace!" he said, voicing his words to the entire room. "Do I have to do everything around here?"

He looked to Wendy. "I'm taking the trash out."

He knew it was a long-shot, an outright absurdity given the fact new supplies seemed to arrive out of thin air whenever needed, but when he looked back to the door, the padlock fell open.

Wendy gasped.

Ron pulled the chains away, dropping them to the floor. When he depressed the push-bar, he heard the beautiful sound of the latching mechanism release.

He faced Wendy. "Stay here," he said.

She grabbed the sleeve of his shirt. "No—"

"I'll make sure it's safe first," he rushed on. "Obey the rules, remember?"

She held his stare, her eyes wide with fright, but her grip slid away from his arm and she nodded her understanding.

He pushed the door open.

Outside, darkness surrounded the restaurant. Ron hadn't worn his watch and couldn't recall seeing any clocks in the building, but he had the distinct feeling that the black air outside wasn't a result of the passage of time. There was a substance to the abysmal depths that went beyond his full understanding, a presence that seemed to loom in at all sides, and after only several steps out the door, his exposed flesh had gone as cold as the plastic skin of a body bag.

He walked forward, forcing himself to ignore it.

Fifty feet away, a single lamppost stood in the gloom. It spotlighted a grime-splashed dumpster in a yellow cone of light, looking like two props on a vast empty stage.

He saw no stars overhead. No silhouettes of the trees that bordered the parking lot.

Thirty-some feet from the restaurant, he looked to the left, to where he should've been able to spot the concrete of the expansive four-lane highway, but again saw only the all-encompassing darkness.

He quickened his pace, finally stepping into the lamp's circle of light. He glanced up to see its wooden post waver, as if not entirely solid.

He lifted the lid of the dumpster.

A hot breath pushed past his arm when he did, and his mouth fell open as he found himself staring into a massive tooth-lined throat that descended into a hazy orange oblivion of fire.

He stumbled away, shaking.

There was a heart-stopping moment when he felt the trash bags begin to fall from his grasp, and it only came out of the sheer terror of not knowing what might happen if he didn't finish the task that he found the strength to heave them into the dumpster from a distance.

He turned and started back toward the restaurant at a fast walk.

From here, all he saw of the building was the white rectangle of light that marked the open back door. Wendy's silhouette stood at the threshold, eagerly awaiting his signal to join him.

He shook his head as he neared, praying she saw it.

Don't come out! he wanted to scream. *Whatever you do, don't come out here!*

He'd closed to within sight of her when he spotted a new employee enter the room behind her.

"Wendy!" he cried, voicing her name far louder than intended. He'd meant to warn her that his plan had failed, that she should stay put, but she must've misread the horror on his face and thought he was reacting to the thing approaching behind her.

"Phone call for you, sir," the worker announced.

She spun to face the man, and when she did Ron had a clear view of the creature.

It was Greg.

Though torn limb from limb just hours ago, the man appeared whole, pieced back together like some horrific jigsaw puzzle. Thick black sutures followed the bloody lines of his wounds like a network of interconnected rivers, crisscrossing the visible parts of his body. He had on the same type of grease-stained apron worn by the kitchen staff—which bowed inward over his stomach, as if covering a huge hole—as well as a creased paper hat.

Wendy ran.

She charged forward without a sound, bolting into the unknown.

Ron lunged for her as she ran past, but only grazed the soft skin of her hand.

"No! Don't!" he cried.

He turned around to see the darkness flow forward, coming at them like a wave. Wendy froze at the sight of it, watching as it swallowed the dumpster and lamppost, racing toward her.

Ron grabbed her. Pulled her back to the doors.

But then something had her.

Both of them screamed as her feet got yanked out from under her, and Ron swung around to see her legs lift off the ground, immersed up to her knees in the darkness.

"Ron!" she cried.

He held her with one hand, seized the push-bar of the door with the other.

Greg's corpse watched them indifferently.

"Ron! Oh, God! Help, me!" she screamed.

The darkness consumed her up to the waist, pulling her higher, until Ron was looking *up* at her as he fought the pull her inside.

Grunting, he held on with all of his might, feeling his muscle fibers stretch to their limit. The veins of his arms stood out like lightning bolts. But he wasn't only fighting the brute strength of the entity outside, he discovered; he was straining against uncounted hours of sweating over a hot grill, handling food drenched in oil.

Skin slid over skin.

First he had her whole hand.

Then just her palm.

Then only her fingers.

He looked into her face as he felt her nails reach the edge of his grip, knowing that in the next second he'd lose her. With tears slipping from his eyes, he tried the only thing left that might save her.

"Wendy!" he shouted.

The terrified girl looked down, meeting his eyes.

"You're *fired!*" he yelled.

Her screams cut off, replaced by stunned silence.

"Effective immediately," he added. "Get off the property!"

She held his stare even as the darkness seeped over her face.

And then she was gone, pulled out of his hands.

The doors flew shut. Ron collapsed to his knees.

He sat on the floor in the aftermath of his actions, doubling over as a flood of emotions washed over him. "Oh, Christ," he cried. "What've I done?"

Behind him, the thing that was once his friend repeated its message. "Phone for you, sir."

Ron faced it, finding no hint of compassion.

He pushed to his feet, wiping tears from his face. "Where?" he asked. "There's no phone in the office?"

"Up front, sir."

He pushed past the thing, striding down the hall, trying not to dwell on the fact he'd just lost his last tether to the rational world.

Please, God, let her have made it out…

He didn't look at the swarm of customers as he rounded the corner. Instead, he focused on the black rotary-dial phone mounted beside the notorious sign that outlined the rest-aurant's enigmatic rules.

He snatched up the handset, expecting some disgusting slurping noise or something requesting an order of flame-broiled afterbirths.

"Hello?"

"Finally!" Diane's voice spoke from the receiver. "You've had me worried sick for hours!"

Ron's heart convulsed at the sound of his wife's words. He almost dropped the handset as his whole body went weak. "Diane!"

"What's going on up there? I thought you'd be back by now. Do you know how long it took to track down this number—?"

"Diane, listen," he cut in, unable to suppress his desperate tone. "I need help! Call the police, or—"

Ron fell silent as he saw a fresh batch of customers enter the restaurant. It was the first time he'd seen the doors open since setting foot inside, and his eyes boggled at the warm yellow sunlight glowing outside.

Where he spotted a van sitting in the parking lot.

Cartoon letters announced "We Deliver!" across the vehicle's side.

Ron licked his lips, thinking fast. Four feet away, a decomposing cashier turned from his register to face him.

"Place an order!" Ron whispered into the phone.

"An order?" his wife echoed. "But I thought—"

"I know, I know," Ron said. "Just do it. Whatever you want! Please!"

"You know I don't like the kids eating that stuff."

"Please!" Ron nearly screamed.

"All right..." his wife answered. "Just bring home some hamburgers, I guess. But no pop! You know how Eric reacts to sugar."

"Four hamburgers to go!" Ron called to the kitchen, almost laughing. "Right away, ma'am! Thank you for ordering! I love you!"

"Are you sure you're—"

Ron hung up the phone.

"Let's go!" he shouted. "I got a VIP order to deliver, pronto!"

He moved through the kitchen, spurring the workers faster, simultaneously searching for keys. Miraculously, he found a set on a pegboard not far from the phone.

"Are we ready?" he called.

Four burgers were passed to the front, boxed for delivery.

He placed the keys on top of the stack, scooped them into his arms.

And turned around to meet the cadaverous face of a young man sporting a mouthful of worms. A glossy tag pinned to his shirt identified him as a "Deliveryman."

"I'll get that for you, sir," he said, taking the boxes.

And before Ron could react, the thing was walking away, vanishing into the throng of inhuman customers.

Ron stared after him, numb. He spun to reach for the phone, but now the wall showed no sign of ever having had one installed.

Thoughts clashed in his mind, from the question of whether or not Wendy had returned to the real world and was even now trying to find help, to the idea that a reanimated corpse was driving cross-country with four boxes of god-knew-what, bound for his family.

In the end, he pushed those mind-shattering contemplations aside.

He'd wait, bide his time. But he had to remain sane.

At the counter, he slipped on an apron, faced the masses waiting to order, and stepped up to a register.

He cleared his throat.

"Next."

Wings
JESSICA BROWN

I WAS SITTING ON MY PORCH enjoying an unusually frosty September sunrise, coffee in hand, when the dead came back to life. At least I think it was then. I hadn't noticed the weird stuff before those few minutes before the sun came up, but it was dark and I could be mistaken.

I don't think I am, though.

The first thing I noticed was a rustling in the leaves under my half-dead apple tree. There were a few jerky movements and suddenly a head peeked up from under a wet brown clump of fallen foliage. It was a bird. I watched as it stretched out, clumsily regained its balance, and tried to fly. It couldn't, its wings being nothing more than the hollowed quill-ends of feathers stuck precariously to fragile bone, and it soon fell over on its side in the exact same place it had reanimated. Only, at the time, I didn't know it was a moving corpse. I just thought it was sick.

That's why I jumped off the porch and went running to it, thinking my mind was playing tricks on me in the near dark. Maybe it had just fallen from a branch before I woke up, or had dropped out of the sky mid-flight. I found it quickly by following the wheezing gasps it made, its mouth open like a starving chick. I scooped it up and held it, cupped in the palms of my hands. No, there was no mistaking it. I could see bone in its wings and on its chest and half of its skull was showing. I screamed and went to drop it, but it clasped my fingers in its beak and held on tighter than I thought it should have been able to.

It broke the skin.

I shook it off and went flying back into the house, running my hands under hot water and scrubbing them god knows how many times. As I pressed a paper towel to the open cut I looked out the kitchen window. Shadow, my neighbor's black Labrador, was walking down the street on her way to their house. Shadow had been dead since the early summer, hit by a carload of drunken college kids. Their daughter had screamed and thrown rocks at the disappearing car, and tried to half carry, half drag the dog home, but she'd died out there on the street. She'd been buried at the pet cemetery down the road. And now, here she was, most of her face worn down to the bone, and all the vertebrae of her tail exposed.

I saw the Stevensons' front door open and their kid, Susie, come running out to see her dog. She was only five, and I doubt she even knew Shadow had been dead. I remember my mother telling me my hamster had "gone to heaven" when I was about that age and I can still recall the feeling of utter confusion I'd had since I hadn't known where this place she was telling me about even *was*. Was it in Ohio, near Grandma's house?

She was down by the end of the driveway before her parents got out the door and started following her, Shadow running around the corner of their yard. She was laughing and smiling and opened her arms wide, when the dog jumped up in a giant puppy hug-

And tore a chunk out of her shoulder. He got a bit of her neck too.

I grabbed some duct tape out of the junk drawer and wrapped it around the paper towel, sealing it off, and ran out the front door. Janet Stevenson was holding her daughter, screaming, kicking at the dog that was still howling and snapping its jaws. By the time I got across the lawn to them David, her husband, had come running around the garage with a shotgun under his arm. "Get away! Move back!" He raised the gun and fired and Shadow's head came off. He fired a second time, and then a third, and finally a fourth until there wasn't much left of the dog but pieces of fur and bits of bone and decomposing flesh. "Janet, get Susie in the house and call an ambulance!" He looked at first at my face, then my finger, which was seeping blood out from under the tape, and then back up to my face again. "You okay?"

I nodded.

"All right, help me out here then."

I took a hose to the mess in front of his house, washing all the blood and junk down the street and into the drain at the corner. Once I was satisfied all traces of the dog were gone I rolled up the hose and walked into their house. God, my finger was aching. Susie was laying on the kitchen table in her underoos and a Doodlebops t-shirt, her bloody clothes in a pile beneath a chair. Janet was pressing a towel to the open wound across her shoulder. She was swearing quietly into the phone and her fingers were trembling. "David, it's still busy."

"What the hell? They have multiple lines for this kind of shit!"

Susie started to cry. "Mommy, it hurts. It hurts so bad..."

Janet's lip trembled. "I know, honey. I know. Just try to hold on for a little bit longer while we get you to a hospital, okay?" She was trying to sound reassuring but I could see she was holding back tears of her own.

David took the phone from her. "I'll keep trying them. Get some good clothes on her and lay her down or something." He looked at me. "Can you help her out? Thanks."

I held Susie while Janet ran to get some clothes for her. I was cradling her, her eyes barely even open, when I noticed a strange feeling in my arm. Something was poking me. I turned her over slightly and noticed a strange bump on the back of her underpants. It was like something was growing out of her tailbone. "What the hell are you doing?" David hollered at me.

"Uh, nothing really." His eyes were accusatory, burning holes into me as he glared. "I just—"

Janet came running down the hallway. "What's going on?"

"Nothing, nothing. Shit! It's still busy! It's been busy for fifteen minutes straight. Honey, get her dressed and ready, we're driving to the hospital."

I left their house and went running down the street, my legs moving faster than they'd ever moved in my entire life. I slammed my front door behind me and locked it, then dead bolted it. I locked and secured every other door and window I had. I peeked out the window to the porch and saw a half-decomposed butterfly perched atop the coffee cup I'd left outside. It was missing an antenna and its wings were thin and transparent as tissue in places, nothing more than fragile colorless framework in others.

Scampering up my trees were a half dozen nearly skeletal squirrels, their bushy tails connected to bleached hipbones. Most of them didn't have eyes left and I stood there, shocked, wondering how in the hell they could even make it up and around the boughs in the condition they were in. The worst part of all was the howling noise that came from the road up above my house. It was like a pack of wild dogs starving to death, prowling for food.

No, that's exactly what it was. Little dogs, big dogs, the newly dead, the long-since-buried—they all came walking down my street. The pet cemetery had yielded up its charges and they were heading my way.

I watched the Stevensons' car go flying out onto the highway and wondered if they'd seen the dogs that would no doubt be rounding my corner any moment now. I peeked through the window on my heavy front door and saw them, twenty or so, stop and look up at my house. I kept stock still, not even blinking, until they started walking again. Then I grabbed my little portable TV, my cell phone, and my laptop, and headed for my Panic Room.

It's not really a Panic Room, to be honest. It's just one of those attics accessible by yanking a cord in the ceiling of my walk-in closet, but I can remove the cord and lock it from the inside and nobody can get to me. It's air-conditioned up there and I have a couch and some power outlets if I need them.

I've been holed up here for two days now. This is where I turned on the little TV and found that it wasn't just the pet cemetery that had expelled its residents. It was *every* cemetery, every morgue. I saw footage of a half-burnt body walking from a crematorium on some late night show. People who haven't evacuated to somewhere else (wherever that may be) have all been barricading themselves inside their homes, hoping to avoid contact with the dead.

They brought in a scientist on one of those shows, a molecular biologist I think they called her. She had some long-winded theory about viruses and saliva and mutating DNA and some other stuff. It seems a lot of people who came into contact with the dead have been changing, usually people who came into contact with non-human dead. Apparently whatever is causing the dead to move might also be causing bitten people's DNA to change its structure to match the original host body. That would mean that little Susie, if she's even still alive, probably has a tail by now. We're all fucked.

I'm turning off the TV and I'm going to try to sleep now. I've been up for over forty-eight straight hours, living off ramen noodles, caffeine, and fear. I need to lie down. I don't know if I'll be able to sleep, though. My finger's throbbing and my body is a mass of aches. I think I might have some sort of fever, and my shoulder blades hurt like hell.

The Man Who Breaks the Bad News
KEALAN PATRICK BURKE

"SAMUEL! ANSWER THE DOOR!" Linda shrieks and Sam levers himself out of the easy chair with a moan. The simplest of movements are beginning to feel too much like hard work these days and he longs for some peace, or at least a place where he can get some.

He opens the door and gives the well-dressed stranger on the stoop a suspicious glance. In this neighborhood, and with Sam's increasing financial concerns, a man in a suit can only be the bearer of bad tidings.

"What is it?" he asks the stranger, his suspicion exacerbated by the omnipresent toothy smile on the man's long ashen face.

"Good morning, Mr. Bradley. My name is Thomas Wilder. I wondered if I might have a word?"

Sam's knuckles whiten on the door. "What about?"

"About last Friday."

Sam raises an eyebrow and flips through a mental index. Friday? What happened three days ago to warrant the interest of this dapper visitor? Nothing, he decides, unless it was some meager traffic violation—perhaps changing lanes where he shouldn't or clipping a curb. But wouldn't that have summoned the police? The man on the porch doesn't look much like a cop. In fact, if anything he looks more like a mortician, dressed in a black three-piece suit and blue silk tie. His silver hair is pasted down on both sides of his gaunt skull, enhancing the impression of things funereal. Coral blue eyes glimmer with intelligence.

Definitely not a cop.

"I don't know what you're talking about, Thomas," Sam says indignantly, hoping that his use of the man's first name will be enough to offend him.

Wilder's smile broadens. "I understand completely. Perhaps if I could come in we could discuss this further."

"I don't think that's such a great idea. My wife is in there."

Wilder raises an eyebrow.

"She's not feeling well," Sam splutters. "Besides, who are you anyway?"

Wilder fishes a black leather wallet from his inside pocket and Sam has the terrible feeling he's dealing with someone far more important than a cop.

F.B.I? C.I.A? I.R.S? Uh-oh.

Wilder flips open the wallet, exposing his identification. Sam's squints at the miniature rendition of the man's face, a grim smile beneath a stern black acronym. "U.S.S.R.D? What the hell is *that*? You a Russian?"

The other man gives a patient sigh. "Mr. Bradley, let me put your mind at ease. I'm not here to arrest you or to issue any papers. You're not in trouble, but it is important that we speak immediately and iron out a few...um...details."

"What kind of details?"

Wilder's eyes narrow as if he has to summon great concentration to deliver his words. "About your death, sir."

"My death? What, like life insurance? If that's what you're here for—"

"No," Wilder interrupts. "About your death last Friday on Route 32."

Sam slams the door.

~

Sam opens the door. He isn't surprised to see Wilder still standing there.

"What does U.S.S.R.D stand for? And before you get cocky, I'm only asking so I know what to tell the cops when they ask for specifics."

"United States Special Retrieval Division. And calling the police wouldn't do you any good. They are well aware of our operation and support it one hundred per cent."

Sam sneers. "I'm sure, well if it's all the same I think I'll try them anyway."

Wilder doesn't respond. Once again, Sam shuts him outside and hurries to the phone.

"Samuel? Who's at the door?" Linda roars from the kitchen, startling him.

"Some nut," he calls back and picks up the phone. He dials and waits patiently to be put through to the Harperville Police. Eventually a bored voice answers: "Sergeant Stapler speaking. How can I help you?"

"Sergeant Stapler. Hi, this is Sam Bradley on Oak Street."

"Right," Stapler says, sounding as if he has no idea who Sam is and doesn't much care. "How can I help you, Sam?"

"Well, there's a guy at my door harassing me. He's an old guy, dressed in black. Says he's from something called the United States Recuperation Department or something."

"Yes?"

Sam frowns. "He says I'm dead!"

There is a long pause, sufficient time to bring beads of perspiration to Sam's brow and then Stapler causally replies: "*Are* you dead?"

"Well, I...*what?*"

Stapler clears his throat. "If someone from the U.S.S.R.D is at your door then I suspect you might have expired, Sam. Sorry."

Sam feels his brain itch. "Has the whole bloody world gone nuts?"

"My advice is to cooperate fully with them. There'll be less hassle that way."

"But I…"

"Be sure to give my condolences to your wife."

"What?"

"You have a wife, right?"

"I…yes! But you don't understand! I—"

"Tough break, buddy."

"Hey, wait!" Sam says but finds himself pleading with a dead line.

∞∞∞Ⓗ∞∞∞

"Is there somewhere we can go to talk?"

Sam stares at Wilder, envious of his unfettered patience. "What kind of scam is this?"

Wilder sighs. "Please, just come with me for a chat and I'll explain everything. It shouldn't take too long."

Sam steps outside, closes the door behind him. "It better not. My wife is making steak."

Wilder nods and turns away, Sam plodding unsteadily along behind him.

∞∞∞Ⓗ∞∞∞

Back in the seventies, Greta's Diner was a hot spot for local teens—the place to hang out in Harperville. The passing of time and modern technology however have stolen the appeal and now it caters only to those who don't care about its crumbling façade, peeling paint or ever-present smell of old shoes.

The raucous laughter of youth has long been driven from the air by the ghostly smoke from the pipes of old men, who sit and grumble to themselves while watching the world outside their haven move much too fast for their liking.

Wilder takes a seat by the grimy window and looks out at the cracked concrete parking lot, deserted but for a rusted pea-green Volkswagen with a flat tire. With a grimace, Sam lowers himself into the seat on the opposite side of the Formica table and glances at Wilder. "So?"

Wilder raises a hand. "Would you like something to eat?"

"No, I told you Linda's making dinner."

"Right. Coffee?"

"Water."

Wilder seems content to wait on a waitress that isn't coming.

Meanwhile Sam's impatience is burning holes in the back of his eyes. "So?" he repeats, "what's the deal?"

"The deal is, Sam, you're dead. You died Friday at around midday—or eleven fifty-one if you want specifics—while stuck in traffic on Route 32. Do you remember anything about that?"

Sam doesn't want to think about it but feels an obligation to prove this madman wrong. When he casts his mind back, he sees himself sitting in his Oldsmobile, smoking a cigarette and swearing loudly at the driver of the Taurus who has cut him off. The heat is fierce and he is suddenly finding it difficult to breathe. The cigarette of course, isn't helping but it's the only thing keeping him relatively calm. He remembers honking his horn and...

"Hmm."

Wilder leans forward on his elbows. "Yes?"

"I had a pain in my chest. Nothing special, I get them all the time."

"Do you get them now?"

Sam hasn't realized it until now but…he *hasn't* suffered chest pains in a while.

"Do you even smoke now?"

Sam shrugs. "The chest pains were particularly bad that day. I thought it might be a heart attack and vowed to quit smoking if it turned out to be nothing. It was nothing so I didn't smoke again."

Wilder gives a slight sad shake of his head. "I'm afraid it wasn't nothing, Sam. It was a heart attack. A fatal one. The reason you don't smoke anymore is because the dead rarely feel the need."

Sam slams a hand down on the table. "Will you stop saying that! I'm not d—"

They both watch the small fingernail skid across the table between them. Sam's eyes widen, his gaze dropping to the little finger on his right hand.

The nail has come off, leaving a mottled indentation in its wake.

He stares at it a moment longer, mouth open, a moan sounding from somewhere deep in his throat. "That's not right," he says eventually and looks at Wilder, who doesn't seem at all surprised.

"It is if you've passed away," Wilder responds calmly. "You shouldn't let it alarm you too much. This condition, this *reanimation*, isn't unique to you. An explosion of this type of phenomenon has appeared all over the country in the past six months."

Sam looks back at his finger, at the ugly warped space where his nail once sat. "Phenomenon?"

Wilder looks over his shoulder and, satisfied that the old man near the counter is paying them no attention, he says in a low voice: "We call them 'walking dead'. People who've died but for some inexplicable reason get up and walk around as if nothing happened, seemingly oblivious to their own passing."

Sam scoffs. "That's crazy. I saw a movie like that. Zombies, staggering around a farmhouse, munching on human flesh. It made me sick. Are you trying to tell me that's what I am? A zombie?"

Wilder waves away the notion. "I assure you, Sam. You won't find yourself strangely enamored by human flesh and although I detest the use of the word 'zombie', it is probably the closest description of what you are. Not a monster, we don't think of cases like yours as being akin to demonic resurrection, rather a sickness or a virus that leaves its victims in a state of confusion."

"But…" Sam continues to shake his head, waiting for the punchline so he can go home to Linda. "That's insane. I'm not dead. Dead people stay dead, don't they?"

"They used to," Wilder says in a grave tone. "Until that meteor crashed in New Mexico. Since then it's been as you so succinctly put it 'insane.' I wish I had an explanation to offer you as to why you're sitting here listening to a stranger telling you you're dead, but I don't."

Sam's eyes narrow. "You could be pulling some kind of con on me. How do I know you're not?"

Wilder surveys the room again. "Put out your hand."

"What for?"

"Please, just do it."

Reluctantly, Sam slides his wounded hand across the table until it's close to Wilder. Wilder reaches into his pocket and withdraws a small black cylinder.

"What's that for?"

He hears a click and a six-inch metal blade springs from the top of the cylinder. He flinches and prepares to pull away but Wilder clamps a hand on his wrist and in an instant brings the blade down like a guillotine, severing the tops of four of his fingers, only the thumb remaining intact. The fingertips hop and scatter across the Formica.

"Oh sssshhhit!" Sam moans and inhales enough breath to power the scream barreling up his throat.

Wilder raises a finger to his lips and Sam catches the scream behind his teeth.

The old folks at the head of the diner look in their direction, shrug and go back to complaining.

"Look," Wilder says and points at Sam's ruined fingers. "Do you see any blood?"

He's right. Sam watches them for a moment. No blood, just dry stumps. More significant still is the fact that he feels no pain at all. Nothing. Not even the slightest ache.

I'm in shock, he tells himself but knows it not to be true.

He looks at Wilder who is busy collecting the fingertips and wrapping them in a pristine white handkerchief. "I'm dead?"

Wilder nods. "I'm afraid so."

Sam's face droops and he begins to blubber, Wilder's hand suddenly appearing on his shoulder. "I'm here to help you Sam."

Sam looks up; eyes dry because there are no tears available. "This *sucks*."

∞∞∞⊙∞∞∞

"What happens now?"

They are standing outside Sam's house, Wilder looking the picture of dignity, Sam looking dejected, shoulders hunched and head low.

"A car will come for you at dawn. There's no need to pack, anything you need will be provided for you at the clinic."

"Clinic?"

"Yes, consider it a rest home for the undead. You'll be taken care of there."

Sam frowns. "What will happen to me?"

"We'll monitor the progress of your...decomposition and do our best to compensate for it. You'll be made to feel at home."

"You mean I'll...rot?" Sam asks, voice brittle.

Wilder nods solemnly. "As all dead folk do. The only consolation is you won't feel it. There will be no pain whatsoever and you'll be doing science a favor."

"How?"

"By studying your post-mortem brain functions, we can try to determine the cause of this most peculiar phenomenon and perhaps attempt to find a cure."

"What do I tell Linda?"

Wilder looks at the house and back to Sam. "As little as possible. If you were to stay with her, she'd be forced to watch bits and pieces of you dropping off until you were nothing but a talking skeleton. That would be a lot more traumatic for her than your sudden 'disappearance', don't you think?"

"I guess."

"I guarantee it would."

Sam shuffles toward the steps leading to his front door. He stops, turns.

"What happens when the study is over?"

But Wilder is already walking away.

∞∞∞⊙∞∞∞

At the dinner table, Sam finds himself completely repelled by the sight of the bloody sirloin swimming in his plate and turning his potatoes a dark maroon. The longer he looks at it the less human he feels.

But I'm not human, am I? According to Wilder, I'm a zombie.

The thought makes his undead stomach turn.

As he scrapes his chair back from the table, Linda fixes him with a puzzled look. "Something wrong with the meat?"

"Uh…" Sam begins, struggling to think of a convincing excuse. "No, it looks delicious. I'm just not feeling very well this evening."

"What happened to your fingers?" she asks, pointing at his bandaged fist.

"I…"

"What have you been up to Samuel? You have that look in your eyes that tells me you've been up to something."

"Nothing. Some idiot at the diner slammed the door on my hand. It was an accident."

"What were you doing at the diner?"

"What?"

"You never go there anymore. Why today?"

"Just felt like it, that's all. Jesus, what's with the third degree? I can't go for a coffee anymore?"

"We have plenty of coffee here."

"So I wanted to get out of the house for a while, okay?"

She levels him with a gaze brimful of suspicion. "I see. So you go to a diner you haven't been to in years, hurt your hand and now you won't eat your dinner. Would you not be at least a little suspicious?"

Sam shrugs.

Linda clasps her hands beneath her chin. "Who was that man today?"

"What man?"

"The one you were talking to outside."

"Nobody."

"He certainly seemed to upset you."

Sam looks at her, incredulous. "You were listening?"

"I thought it might be important."

"It was nothing. Life insurance."

"I see." Linda says, but it is clear she doesn't buy into his stuttered explanation. She recommences her assault on the meat before her; filling her mouth with the almost raw sirloin, blood trickling from the corner of her mouth. Sam looks away in disgust.

"I'm off to bingo in about a half hour. Want me to put your dinner in the oven until you feel up to it?" she asks when she's finished.

A butterfly of panic flutters against Sam's chest. "Bingo? Tonight? Do you have to go? I thought..."

She gets up from the table. "Thought what?"

He shrugs, defeated and gets to his feet, wincing inwardly at the crack of his knees as he does so. "Nothing. I...maybe you can skip it just for tonight, eh? We'll have a quiet night at home."

"I never miss bingo," Linda says, frowning.

"Well, one night wouldn't kill you would it?"

"Just what is wrong with you, Sam? You look like death warmed over. Is something the matter?"

Wilder's voice fills his head like Muzak on an elevator descending into the darkness: *If you were to stay with her, she'd be forced to watch bits and pieces of you dropping off until you were nothing but a talking skeleton. That would be a hell of a lot more traumatic for her than your sudden 'disappearance', don't you think?*

"No. Nothing wrong," he mutters and wrenches himself away from the table.

He shuffles into the dark living room, propelled forth by his wife's exasperated sigh, and thumbs on the television. The white noise fills his head like angry wasps.

With trembling hands he slides open the cabinet beneath the television and squints to make out the titles of the videos stacked atop one another in uneven piles. At last he finds the one he's looking for and, trying his best to ignore the gruesome pictures on the cover, shoves the tape into the gaping maw of the VCR.

Swallowing dryly, he clicks the button on the remote and eases himself into a recliner. His bones feel like kindling as he struggles to get comfortable.

On the screen, in gloomy black and white, he watches a black car winding its way toward a graveyard and wonders if that's really where he should be. A graveyard.

Dead.

Buried.

Worm food.

He shudders, his chest tightening at the thought of that black car waiting outside his house in the morning like a patient vulture.

They're coming to get you Barb'raaaaaa.

He switches off the television and sighs, coughs, hacks up bits of brown papery matter. Winces at the sight of them coiled atop his bandaged hand.

He forces himself to swallow a knot of fear.

They can't hurt me, can they? I'm dead.

The thought offers him little comfort as he sits there alone, cloaked in shadow.

∞∞∞⊙∞∞∞

Dawn creeps silently through the world and Sam jerks himself from non-sleep with a stifled cry. The room glows with hazy orange light that might, under any other circumstances have seemed warm, comforting, but now looks like the reflected light of a funeral pyre.

Damn Wilder, he thinks miserably, *I should stay with Linda. God knows she's a tyrant at the best of times but...I still love her!* This rare admission makes him sure he has felt his rotten heart kick but it might have been nothing more than a memory.

He slowly, carefully gets to his feet to a chorus of snaps and cracks and walks stiff-legged into the kitchen. Thankfully, Linda is still sleeping. He remembers hearing her come home, the feel of her lips brushing against the taut dead skin on his forehead. Rather than wake him, she opted to leave him sleep in the living room and now he aches for her for the first time in years. The ache becomes an almost physical pain, sparking doubts in his mind about the validity of Wilder's claims. If he can feel sorrow, loss, love...doesn't that make him alive?

No. He looks at his bandaged hand, the discoloration on the gauze. He thinks about his severed fingers, discarded like nail clippings with not an ounce of pain. His nerves are dead, of that there can be no doubt and soon he will shed his skin like a snake, sloughing off his identity to become nothing more than a cadaver exposed for all the world to see and study. The thought frightens him. Just how long will he remain aware of what they are doing to him? Once his eyes shrivel in their sockets and he can see no more, how long will his emotions, his loneliness take to die? If he has to lie on a cold table knowing what they are doing to him despite being spared the sensations that come with their needles and hooks, he does not want to be capable of thought.

Will they take care of that too?

I can't do this.

And yet he knows he has to. There are no other options available for him now that he knows the truth. All he can do is accept his fate as it has been written and go blindly into the jaws of science. He can only hope that when he finally abandons this crumbling vessel that sags on his bones like an over-worn suit, something infinitely better awaits him on the other side of somewhere.

He trudges up the stairs, head low, spine crackling and makes his way toward the bedroom.

Easing open the door, he looks at Linda; her hands curled slightly as if to maintain their grasp on sleep, graying hair splayed out around her head in a steel corona, chest rising and falling...

Breathing.

Sam puts a frail hand over his own mouth and exhales. Perhaps a slight chill brushes his scabrous palm but nothing more. He swallows. "Linda..."

Breathing.

His eyes widen.

The sheets rise and fall in soft whispers...

A small sad smile pinches the skin of Sam's mouth.

∞∞⊖∞∞

The car is waiting just as Wilder promised; a swollen cockroach nestled against the curb with black eyes for windows that stare vapidly back at Sam as he descends the steps of his home with deliberate slowness. He is appalled at the lack of mobility that has suddenly overtaken his joints and muscles, almost as if rigor mortis has been waiting for just this moment to take hold of him.

It hurts, but only his pride.

The car window hums down and he looks up to see a familiar face smiling out at him. "Good morning Mr. Bradley!"

Sam nods and forces his leg down the last step. With a sigh of relief that emerges more like a croak, he approaches the car in a stoop, like a man balancing a stack of fine china on his head.

"You're looking splendid!" Wilder proclaims and Sam summons the memory of a smile. "Thank you. I wasn't expecting to see you here."

Wilder purses his lips. "Well I think we both know why my presence is necessary, don't we?" His eyes drop to the fresh bloodstains on Sam's hands.

The driver door clicks open and Sam is surprised to see a chauffeur coming around to his side of the car. With a polite nod, the young man opens the door for him. Wilder scoots over in his seat to make room. "Hop in!"

Sam's bones click like castanets as he maneuvers himself into the vehicle. Once he is as comfortable as he can get, he looks at Wilder. "I couldn't do it you know. I couldn't do it alone."

Wilder smiles. "I know. You'd be surprised how often that happens. That's why it was important that I be here. After all," he says with a wink. "I'm the man who breaks the bad news."

Sam stares for a moment. "How do you think she'll take it?" he asks but Wilder doesn't answer.

They both turn to look back at the house.

And wait.

Immunity
JEFF STRAND

BELIEVE ME, I *HOWLED* WHEN THAT CORPSE—putrid meat dangling from its bones—sunk its teeth into the underside of my right arm. I won't say the pain was indescribable, since there are plenty of good descriptive words: excruciating, agonizing, unbearable, and so on. I'd seen friends, family, and strangers get bit, and even while they shrieked I'd never imagined it could hurt this much.

I pulled my arm away, leaving a strip of flesh in the zombie's jaws, and cried out for help. Not that it was necessary; my traveling companion Allen was right there. He shot the zombie in the head and it dropped. Then he looked at me sadly. "You know what has to be done."

No. No way. I'd been on the other side many times, but I wasn't going to let Allen murder me. I could fight off the infection. I knew I could. So before he had a chance to get over his moment of melancholy, I dove at him, tackled him to the ground and pulled the gun out of his hand. Then I blew his brains out.

Heh. You didn't often see zombies shooting humans in the head.

Stop that. I wasn't a zombie. I'd never be a zombie. The others were weak. They succumbed to the infection because they believed what everybody said—you can't fight it. Well, I could fight it. I'd fight it and be stronger for the experience. I'd be an inspiration to The Bitten. A hero.

166

∞∞∞ⓗ∞∞∞

Not dead yet, so that was a promising sign. I'd been bit twelve hours ago, according to my watch, and I was the furthest thing from a shambling, mindless creature. The average time from bite to death? Two hours. But not me. Still alive and kicking, thank you very much. I was awesome.

∞∞∞ⓗ∞∞∞

Twenty-four hours. I didn't sleep during that time because that might've allowed the infection to overpower me, but I felt fine. My arm didn't even hurt.

I was immune.

Immune!

I was the key to humanity's survival! Whether it was something in my blood or my brain or whatever, I possessed the ability to withstand a bite from one of those things and not become one myself.

I needed to find people. There were scientists studying what was happening, and I could be the link to a cure. The zombies would eventually lose their spot at the top of the food chain, and life would return to normal. They'd build statues in my honor. Write songs. Name cathedrals.

I slowly walked through the forest, feeling pretty darn legendary.

∞∞∞ⓗ∞∞∞

The little girl screamed when she saw me. So did her mother.

IMMUNITY

I tried to tell her that I was okay, that I was immune, that I was humanity's savior, but my voice didn't work—it was merely a soft groan.

I wanted to weep as I fed upon the little girl's flesh, but there were no tears, just hunger.

In the Land of the Blind
ROBERT SWARTWOOD

LIKE EVERYONE ELSE HE KNEW, Steven's heart did not
beat. Instead it lay dead in his chest, as docile as his brain and
his lungs and his soul. So when he first heard the faint beating
sound coming from outside his bedroom window, he didn't
know what to think.

He considered telling his parents. He'd been hearing the
beating for almost a week now. Somewhere in the trees and
bushes beyond their backyard. Its continuous thump-thumping
sounded not outside of his head, but rather in.

When his friend Jimmy came over to the house one day,
Steven took him out back.

"Do you hear that?"

"Hear what?"

"Nothing."

If Jimmy couldn't hear the beating, Steven knew his parents
wouldn't either. They'd just stare down at him with dead eyes
and say, *Oh Steven, don't make things up. You know what will happen
if you do.*

He knew. It dealt with something only the zombies had,
something called imagination. It was dangerous and evil and
those who had it were hunted down and put out of their
misery.

But one night the beating became too much for Steven. He
snuck outside with a shovel—why the shovel, he didn't know,
except that he would need it—and followed the sound until he

came to a spot beneath a willow tree. He placed his hand on the dirt where the thump-thumping was the loudest and felt the earth vibrating. He began to dig.

An hour later, his body wearing down, the shovel clinked against something solid. He glanced up and noticed an owl watching him from one of the willow tree's branches. It stared back at him with lifeless eyes.

What Steven pulled from the earth was a strange rock. It was shaped like a perfect cube, five inches wide, five inches long, and five inches thick. Something inside the rock pulsed, causing it to shake in his hands.

A voice behind him asked, "Do you know what's inside?"

The rock fell to the ground. Steven, his small hands shaking, quickly turned.

The thing standing there was a crime against nature. Menacingly tall, its hair dark, its eyes full of life, it was one of the zombies he'd learned to fear. A thing that shouldn't exist. A thing that had imagination, a soul, life.

"Don't be afraid." The zombie's voice carried none of the roughness that Steven was accustomed to hearing. "I'm not going to hurt you."

Steven opened his mouth but could not speak.

The zombie smiled. "Though even if I were to hurt you, you wouldn't actually *feel* anything."

The owl in the trees hooted twice, flew away.

"That was meant as a joke," the zombie said, his smile fading. "A poor joke, I know, but a joke nonetheless. Please, say something. I'm risking my life talking to you, the least you could do is say hello."

Steven didn't want to say hello. He wanted to run away. But he knew that if he did the zombie would chase after him and tear him apart limb by limb, so he stayed motionless.

The zombie said, "You're about ten years old, aren't you."

Steven nodded.

"You came out here because you heard it calling you." The zombie motioned with his head at the rock cube on the ground just behind Steven. "Am I right?"

Steven found his voice. "Please don't hurt me."

"Didn't you hear what I said before? I'm not going to hurt you."

"What do you want?" Steven said, and took a step back, looked around at all the trees, searching for the quickest escape.

The zombie sighed. "I don't even know what I want anymore. A long time ago I used to think it was possible for the living and the dead to exist side by side. But now…" He shrugged. "Now this is the land of the dead, and it will always be the land of the dead."

Steven took another step back, the heel of his sneaker bumping the rock. He looked down at it, looked back up at the zombie. Hesitantly he asked, "What's inside there?"

"What do you think? It's your heart."

"My…heart? But that can't be. My heart"—he pointed at his chest—"is right here."

"Okay," the zombie said, smiling again, "it's not really your heart. But inside that cube is life. The thing that will make you just like me."

"I don't want to be just like you. You…you…you're a monster. You don't deserve to exist."

"You really have no idea, do you? Say, how many colors are there?"

Steven hesitated again, looking every which way, wishing his parents were here with him right now, wishing Hunters would come to his rescue.

"Colors?" he said. "There are…three. Black, white, and gray."

The smile had faded completely from the zombie's face, his expression now somber. "I really do pity your kind. You miss out on all the little things. Like actually feeling the sun when it's shining down on you. Or the wind against your face. Smelling the honeysuckles in the spring and tasting even a pinch of sugar." The zombie shook his head. "Do you realize the rest of the earth hasn't moved on? It's just mankind and all the animals. You've all moved on, decayed, become what you are. You've all become blind, and those like me, the living, are one-eyed men. We're kings."

"Please," Steven said, and this time his voice cracked even more. He wanted to cry but didn't know how, and his lower lip trembled, his hands still shook, and without thinking he bent down and grabbed the cube-shaped rock, held it close to him as if it offered some form of protection. "Please, I just want to go home. I don't...I don't want to expire."

"If I were you," the zombie said, "I wouldn't want to expire either. Not until I experienced everything this world has to offer. Because to see the true color of the sky, and the shade it takes when the sun sets...to experience that for even a second is worth all the fear of being hunted down and destroyed."

"Please," Steven said again, holding the pulsing cube in his hands, and it was at that moment the Hunters came out of the shadows.

They wore black uniforms and masks and carried broadswords. The zombie heard them coming—their heavy boots striking the earth sounded like thunder—but he made no effort to escape. He simply stood there, staring back at Steven, and said, "Don't accept your existence for what it is. Question it. Question everything."

One of the six Hunters stepped forward. He raised his broadsword and swung it.

Some kind of liquid splattered Steven's face as the zombie's head was severed from the rest of its body. He'd heard about living blood but had never known it to exist until now.

The Hunters took the zombie's body away. Steven was taken back home, where his parents scolded him. His father said some very mean things. His mother cried but shed no tears. They sent him up to his room and told him he wasn't to come out until they said so.

Sitting on his bed, the cube in his lap (he'd managed to hide it from the Hunters and his parents), Steven stared out his window at the rising sun. It was gray just like the sky. Just like the trees. Just like everything.

The cube-shaped rock in his lap continued to pulse. The sound was so loud it almost drowned out parents' arguing downstairs.

He placed his hands on the cube and held it tight. The cube pulsed even more. And slowly, so very slowly, the cube began to dissolve until there was nothing left at all.

Steven closed his eyes. None of it made sense. The sound was gone but still he felt the beating, which now came from within his chest.

∞∞∞⊖∞∞∞

He opened his bedroom door with caution and tiptoed the length of the hallway toward the steps. Somewhere downstairs his parents continued arguing, and though he only caught a few words, he knew their dispute involved him. They were worried —not only had their son tried to run away tonight, but he had almost been expired by a zombie—and they wanted to protect him but weren't sure just how to do it.

He stood at the top of the stairs much longer than he'd intended, staring at the pictures on the walls, at the carpet, even the boarder that ran near the ceiling. Each was a different color, a different shade. Nothing like the gray he'd become accustomed to his entire existence.

Everything had changed the moment he realized his heart had started beating. His body had somehow absorbed the life inside the cube. A warm tingling in his chest had spread throughout his entire body, down his legs to his toes, down his arms to his fingertips, and when he opened his eyes again he had watched with a kind of wonder as the black and white and gray of the world began receding around him, until the floor, the walls, the ceiling, *everything* was painted with color.

He had fallen back onto the bed then, his body shutting down for a couple of seconds, the muscles and tendons which had never really been used before having to recharge. Even his lungs had begun to work, and he breathed oxygen for the first time, taking large gulps of air until he became acquainted with this new function and began breathing regularly.

As he lay there he sniffed the stale air, could smell what he somehow knew internally was a mixture of dust and decayed skin and hair and laundry detergent. He knew other things internally now too, as if a door to new information in his brain had just been opened.

Somewhere below him now, probably in the kitchen, his parents continued their argument, though there was less intensity now, less gargled and guttural shouting. He knew what they were arguing about. His father wanted to send Steven away for psychiatric help, while his mother wanted to just ignore it, pretend like the entire thing hadn't happened. Eventually they would arrive to a decision and come to see him. And when they did, what would they find?

Their son—a monstrosity, a crime against nature.

A zombie.

He shuddered at the thought, feeling a chill race through his soul, and found it both terrifying and exhilarating at the same time. It was a feeling he'd never experienced before, and he wanted to feel it again. How many more feelings were there? How many more colors? He remembered the zombie mentioning something about smells and tastes. How many of those were there?

A gasp pulled him away from his thoughts.

He glanced down the stairs to find his parents standing at the bottom. Unlike Steven's skin, which had become pale and smooth, theirs was decayed and brownish gray, their eyes and hair pitch black.

Steven's mother had been the one who gasped. She held her hand to her mouth and stared up at him with wide black eyes. His father stood beside her, slowly shaking his head.

"I'm very disappointed in you," he said, his voice scratchy and rough. The sound of his words caused another shudder to pass through Steven's body, though this one wasn't as pleasing.

"Oh sweetie," his mother said. "What have you done?"

When Steven didn't respond, his father said, "I have no choice. I have to call them."

He turned away and disappeared from Steven's sight, leaving only his mother to stand there with her hand still to her mouth. She shook her head, her dull eyes expressing no emotion—though Steven thought that if she were alive they'd show sadness, maybe even tears.

She opened her mouth to speak. Steven expected to hear her gargled voice again, but nothing came out. She shook her head and waved him toward her.

He started down the steps, taking them one at a time, finding the sound his sneakers made on the wood pleasant in a strange sort of way. When he reached the landing his mother fell to her knees. She gripped his shoulders, wrapped her arms around him. Her body reeked of rot and decay and Steven tried to step out of the dead embrace.

"I'm so sorry," she said, holding onto him tightly. Her breath, he knew internally, smelled of rancid fish. "Your father's calling the Hunters. They'll be here any minute. Why would you do this? Didn't we raise you properly? Didn't we give you everything you ever needed? Why, Steven? *Why?*"

He stared into her dead eyes and tried to find something there, some kind of life. He had no answer for her and simply shook his head.

His father returned.

"They'll be here soon, Steven. Make it easy on yourself and don't try to fight them."

Body now trembling, he felt wetness underneath his arms and something churning in the pit of his stomach. His mother's dead hands squeezed his shoulders briefly once more and he glanced back into her dry colorless face, into her black depthless eyes.

Her cracked lips moved, forming just one word, and though she didn't use her damaged voice, he heard the word clearly in his mind: *Run.*

Steven hesitated. He glanced at his father and saw that his father had seen what just passed between mother and son. His father's black eyes became impossibly large. "No," he said, and started forward, and Steven backed out of his mother's embrace, bolted for the door.

∞∞∞◉∞∞∞

The first thing that struck him outside was the sunlight, and he had to pause, had to allow his eyes to adjust to the sudden brilliance. He lifted his face to the sky, closed his eyes, enjoyed the warmth for only an instant before he remembered he should be running. Opening his eyes, he saw that indeed the sky wasn't gray but blue, lighter than his tee-shirt, speckled with white puffs of clouds, and all around him was green—in the trees, in the grass, even on some houses.

Scents wafted through the air, mixed scents his new internal mind picked out and pieced apart and gave names to: fresh grass, motor oil, dog shit, dandelions.

Across the street, two dead children played in a front lawn. Steven had once known their names but they, much like his own parents, were now strangers to him. They'd been running around, using large plastic broadswords to play Henry the Hunter, neither noticing him until one paused and stared across the street, then said something to the other and pointed.

Two sets of wide dead eyes stared back at him.

The door behind him opened. He heard his mother's voice, begging his father to stop, to please let her baby go. His father told her to shut up, that he would deal with her later. Then there was the sound of his father's heavy footsteps on the porch, his father yelling at him to stop.

Steven ran.

The two children across the street saw him coming and screamed, their voices harsh and flat as they scrambled away.

He reached the street and paused, uncertain where to go next. He thought about the zombie from last night. It had been old, about Steven's father's age. How had it survived so many years?

Sunlight glinted off of something shiny down the street. It was an SUV, one that he had seen only hours before when it had brought him home. The Hunters were coming.

He turned and sprinted in the other direction, hearing shouts from houses where the dead inside saw him and cried out. Sweat ran down his face, as did tears, tears he now shed because he knew it was hopeless, that he wouldn't outrun the Hunters, that he could never outrun them.

The street came to an end, a bright red stop sign signaling that the driver must either turn left or right. Beyond the bisecting street were trees and bushes and tall grass.

Steven continued forward.

He glanced back after he'd passed a couple dozen trees, saw the Hunters back there, all spread out, all heading in his direction. Before him the woods stretched on for miles, seemingly endless, taunting him with the promise of freedom. He tried keeping his focus on what lay before him but he kept glancing back over his shoulder, each time finding the Hunters gaining more and more ground.

Steven ran, tears and sweat in his eyes, until suddenly there was no ground beneath him. A rut, a simple hole, and it twisted his ankle, caused him to fall.

He tried getting up but fell back down, his ankle denying him any support. He glanced back, saw that the Hunters were even closer.

Fresh tears came, forced by the pain—by *real* pain—by the realization that he was soon going to die, but also forced by a surreal form of happiness. He didn't know how many minutes had passed since his body had absorbed the life inside that cube, but he wouldn't change it for anything, even if given the chance.

The sound of thunder grew stronger as the Hunters neared.

Steven tried getting up once more before falling back down. He looked around him for some kind of help but only saw the grass, the trees…and he noticed a bush he hadn't seen before, a green bush covered with many small white and yellow flowers. Something inside him whispered they were honey-suckles, and without thinking he crawled the few yards to the bush and reached out, took one of the flowers from its branch and brought it to his nose, to his tongue.

The Hunters surrounded him, their broadswords drawn and ready. The lead Hunter—the one that had taken the zombie's head only hours before—stepped forward.

Steven hardly noticed. The sweet pure scent and taste of the flower was more than anything he had ever wished for. Despite the pain, despite the tears, despite the knowledge of his impending death, he closed his eyes and tried to keep this moment fresh in his mind, tried to keep it with him forever.

Nowhere People
GARY McMAHON

THE NIGHT SEEMED TO PRESS against my windscreen like a thick fluid as I drove towards the town centre, one eye on the radio recessed into the dashboard as I attempted to tune it to an all-night Jazz and Blues station. Charlie Parker's horn pierced the bubble of stale air inside the cab, and I let myself lean back into the driver's seat, the music washing over me and bringing calm to my mind.

I was tired: dog-tired. As the Beatles once said, it had been a hard day's night. I was at the back end of a ten-hour shift, and my lower back was singing like a chorus of crippled choirboys from being locked into the same position for so long. These suicide shifts were killing me, but it was the only way to make any serious cash in the taxi game. And I needed real money more than ever now: after Jude's birth, Tanya had gone part-time to enable her to look after our baby daughter, so I was the only major wage earner in the household.

Streetlights flashed past, blinking like sodium strobes before my weary eyes, and the night folk prowled the avenues looking for mischief. Low rent prostitutes paraded the footpath outside the Mecca bingo hall; tired, overweight beat coppers watched them from shop doorways and ate chips from greasy bunched newspapers. Clubbers and pubbers staggered like somnambulists towards generic fast food outlets, craving empty calories to help them sleep the sleep of the pissed.

The two-way radio in the cab belched static, then Claire's deep growling voice cut in: 'Karl...Karl, where are you? Number 27? Karl, dammit, *come back!*'

I smiled, lifted the plastic mouthpiece from its perch, and told her that I'd be picking up in ten minutes. This seemed to placate her, and she even told me the latest asylum seeker joke that was doing the rounds back at the depot. It was un-surprisingly crude—vulgar, even—and I couldn't be bothered to force a laugh. Claire called me a humorless bastard, then hopped off the line, leaving more of that empty ululating static to take her place.

Two girls who looked far too young to be out this late crossed the road without looking on the zebra crossing that suddenly appeared before me, causing me to slam on the car's brakes. Their thin anemic faces slowly turned to look at me without really registering my presence, and I glimpsed a profound emptiness in their blank, lusterless eyes. One of them was mechanically pushing pieces of rolled up kebab into her lipstick-smeared mouth; the other was chain-smoking cheap cigarettes. Both of them looked lost, half dead before the age of twenty. I thought of my own newborn daughter, and made a silent promise to myself that she would never end up like that, walking the streets at two a.m., cruising for randy drunks with money in their pockets. In less than an hour these two girls would be bending over in some grimy back alley, or sucking dick in a cheap B&B along the Coast Road. It was just too damned depressing. I felt ice lock around my heart in a sculpted fist.

The girls reached the other side of the road, and a big Mercedes cruised up to the curb, the driver leaning out of the side window to whisper sour nothings from behind a cupped hand. The girls smiled dead smiles and climbed into the back seat, too-short skirts riding up over pallid thighs bereft of muscle tone. All that remained on the footpath when the car pulled away was the discarded kebab wrapper and some pale, dry scraps of meat.

There was a huge advertising hoarding stapled to the wall at the corner of Mylton Road and O'Reilly Street, selling rampant consumers some new brand of alcopop. Graffiti had been daubed across it in thick red dripping lines; I glanced at the slogan as I drove past it.

ARSEYLUM SEEKERS OUT! KILL EM ALL!

The viciously droll message was unequivocal, fuelled by impotent rage and directionless tabloid-driven jingoism. The hatred behind the words was terrifying, bland and unfocused, ready to turn on anyone different from what was considered the norm. The people who had written the words operated under the assumption that all immigrants were money grabbing scam artists, even the honest ones. It was at once sickening and heartbreaking.

I thought of Jude once more, fearing for her future. I prayed that I was strong enough to educate her to the dangers of such narrow, uninformed thinking. Hoped that I was man enough for the daunting task that lay ahead. It dawned on me yet again that raising a child was the most difficult and risky undertaking of all: if you screwed it up, you were just adding to the dumb herd, producing another mindless follower. The enormity of it all made me want to stop the car and run into the night, screaming until my throat burned. But I drove on, heading towards my last pick-up of this harrowing shift. My final few quid before going home to flop lifelessly into bed alongside my sleeping wife.

The man was waiting by the curb outside the Pound Shop when I drew up, shifting his weight from one foot to the other. He seemed nervous, but I assumed that he was just riled at me for being late. He lifted a small brown hand and twitched a little half smile as I stopped the car, then jumped into the back seat, slamming the door behind him as if in an attempt to keep out the night.

'Sorry I'm late, pal. Bit of confusion back at base camp.'

'S'okay, my friend. No problem.' His accent was certainly foreign, but I couldn't place where in the world he could be from. Asia? The Far East? My ignorance of such things truly knows no bounds.

'Where to, boss?'

'Wishwell, please. Palm Tree Way.

Shit. I could've done without a trip to that part of town at this hour. Wishwell was the worst estate in the borough, and the vermin who were housed there would still be up and about, fighting with each other, playing loud music on stolen stereos, smoking weed and drinking illegally imported French booze.

'Good night out?' I asked, making small talk.

'No, no. I've been working. Cleaning offices. I go home now, tend to family. Sleep.'

So he worked the graveyard shift cleaning town centre offices: doing the jobs nobody else would do, just like so many other immigrants in this country. Oiling the hidden wheels of commerce. Paid shitty wages under the counter—tax-free, but with no additional benefits—just to enable him to feed and clothe his family. This hardworking man was exactly the type of person the graffiti on the hoarding had been aimed at: a man just trying to get by, to do right by his family. I had more in common with him than I did the scum who had painted the vitriol. I pitied him for living in Wishwell, but it was probably the only housing the council had offered.

'Tough shift, eh?' I glanced at him in the rearview mirror: small face, ever-blinking eyes, creased brown skin.

'Yes, mister. Just like you, I work hard to make something of myself and my family.'

I took the quick route in an effort to save him a quid on the fare-down by the river, past the dark and abandoned shipyard and the flat-roofed clothing warehouses. The man had lapsed into silence. He sat staring out of the side window with those nervous blinking eyes, his thoughtful features bathed in a wash of sodium light from the lamps that lined the curb along the riverbank. I wondered again where he had come from, what he had given up to come here and feel safe. But was he really safe? I didn't think so. Persecution comes in many forms.

I dropped him at the outskirts of Wishwell, refusing his offer of a tip and bidding him goodnight. He smiled at me, shook my hand and wished my family well. I watched him as he darted across the road, ducking into a narrow alley lined with battered green wheelybins behind a low block of flats. Tom Waits croaked near-tunelessly from the radio, and I reached down to let off the handbrake.

Long shadows detached themselves from some ragged bushes that overhung the mouth of the alley, slow moving but purposeful: three stooped figures, nothing more than dense silhouettes, drifted into the alley, following the man who'd just left my car.

There was something not quite right about the figures, and my internal alarm bell started ringing. They moved clumsily, without natural rhythm, and their limbs looked too slack, as if lacking any proper working joints. I opened the car door, set my foot on the curb. Listened. But there was only silence, underlain by the dry rustling of dead leaves and empty crisp packets in the gutters, and the usual distant estate sounds of bass heavy dance music, crying kids, shouting spouses.

I waited for roughly thirty seconds, and when nothing happened I closed the door and drove off into the night towards a promise of warmth and safety that could only be realized when at last I curled into my sleeping wife's soft and welcoming back.

∞∞⊙∞∞

It was only when I saw the television news two days later that I realized I'd been expecting the report. A local asylum seeker, Jalal al-hakim, from Iraq, had gone missing. He had last been seen leaving the city centre offices he cleaned as part of a five-man crew at one-thirty a.m. on Saturday morning. Police were treating his disappearance as suspicious; Mister al-hakim had only been in England for eight months, after fleeing persecution and torture in his own country. He was an outgoing, friendly, family man, liked by both his workmates and his employers, and had no known enemies.

Al-hakim's face flashed up at me from the screen. It was a recent photograph, probably taken by his wife, in which he played with his two young daughters. He was laughing; he looked happy. But still a shadow seemed to loom over his small frame, shading his features.

My insides churned as if I had an ulcer, and my skin prickled as if stung by nettles. I had been the last person to see this man before he'd vanished; I was a potential witness. So I rang the police without finishing my morning coffee and told them what little I knew, agreeing to go down to the station to make a statement later that morning. But still my conscience wasn't clear: I had driven away after watching those shambling figures follow him down the alley. I felt ashamed, cowardly in an almost abstract kind of way, and desperate to make amends.

I left the house without telling Tanya about what had happened. She couldn't help but notice my reticence, along with the fact that I was more withdrawn than usual, and stared a silent question at me as I kissed Jude goodbye. I shook my head, smiled sadly. She brushed her dry lips against my forehead, blew hot stale morning-breathe against my hairline, winked at me as I drew away and opened the front door.

I went to the police station in my lunch hour, not expecting much and receiving even less than that. It was fruitless. I informed a disinterested uniformed officer of what had happened that night, and about the shadowy figures I'd seen slinking into the alley; then I left, feeling utterly disillusioned. Nobody cared about these people, not the public, the police, or the politicians. All they were was an election tool, a way of faking interest in the community. Local councilors would bleat on about asylum seekers and their attendant problems all day long, but when it came to caring—actually *doing something*—they suddenly clammed up and found some more pressing business. It seemed that nobody wanted to get their hands dirty.

There was more graffiti visible on the flyover abutment behind the High Street on my way back to the depot:

GET SHOT OF IMMIGRINT SHIT!

Charming. And these people thought they were so much better than everyone else? They couldn't even spell in their own language, while the people they despised so much could speak it if not better then certainly more politely than these restless natives.

By the time I got back to the depot Claire was on a break. She was pouring herself a coffee as I walked in, and made me one with an air of faked irritation so I didn't feel like I was getting special treatment. We sat at the chipped Formica table in the cramped office at the rear of the tiny building, and I told her about my visit to the police station.

'Are you really that surprised?' she asked me in a tone of mock incredulity, that broken glass growl of hers coming from somewhere down near her boots. 'C'mon, Karl, nobody gives a shit about anybody these days. It's dog eat dog out there, and if you aren't a consumer you just get consumed.' She sipped at the awful coffee, her large bland face forming a grimace around the rim of the mug.

'I s'ppose you're right,' I relented, then blew on my own drink, watching with a faint nausea as the skin that the milk had formed on its surface rippled like an oil slick on a park pond. 'I was just hoping for more, y'know?'

'And that's what I like about you: you're different. You give a shit. But don't let it go to your head, because I'll deny ever saying it if it comes out.' She smiled one of her rare sunny-day smiles, then went back to the coffee. I felt numb, empty. Ghost-like.

'Anyway,' said Claire, disrupting my bleak thoughts and attempting to change the subject. 'You heard the latest?'

I hadn't, but knew that I was about to; Claire was the woman to see if you wanted to know what was going on in Scarbridge. She was better than the local news—more up-to-date, and her sources never failed her.

'Which is what?' I asked, wondering if I'd soon regret it.

'Well, it seems that about four months ago half a dozen corpses went missing from the town morgue. Those kids who died from smoke inhalation in that warehouse fire down by the old Dock Road...the silly sods who set it alight while they were trying to rob it? Them. Their bodies. Stolen.'

I glanced up at her, looking for any sign that this was one of her morbid little jokes. Her face was rigid, blank; she was telling the truth.

'Fuck,' I said quietly, placing my mug on the scarred tabletop. 'Some people will steal anything.'

She smiled; a sad, tired expression. 'It was all hushed up by the authorities, of course. Too embarrassing to let into the public domain. People are finding out though; they always do. Nothing stays buried for very long round here. Someone spoke to someone else after a few too many pints, and the news is breaking out like little fires all round the estates. Just like always.'

Four months ago. Just about the same time that the attacks on immigrants had begun: foreign families being burned out of their low rent council housing, kids spat on at school, a pregnant woman pelted with fruit in the local supermarket, one or two people even going missing, just like al-hakim…there had even been a picket line outside one of the town's three primary schools, the parents in the area refusing to allow a couple of Turkish children into the building. One of their fathers had been hospitalized when someone had thrown an engineering brick at his head. It was all so wrong…such a fucking mess.

I wondered if the incidents were linked: whether some right wing group was about to implicate the immigrant community in the theft of those boy's bodies, laying claims to all kinds of voodoo and necrophilia. Breeding even more fear. More violence.

I didn't want to think about where it all might end.

∞∞∞◉∞∞∞

The chill early hours again; midweek in Scarbridge, when all the smart folk are tucked up in their beds, wrapped in sleeping yoga poses around their loved ones. I was returning to the depot from a drop-off in Newcastle—a nice little earner—and decided on impulse to take a detour.

The urge to return to Wishwell came upon me un-announced. Now, with the aid of hindsight, I can put it down to shame, guilt, the need to do something—to do *anything*. I didn't know what I would do when I got there, but I did know that I had to go back to the mouth of that alley. To inspect the place where I'd dropped off al-hakim for his final truncated journey home.

Winter was closing in like a gloved hand around a warm neck, choking the life out of the world: trees had shed their blossoms long ago, the sky looked brittle as a sheet of glass, and a sharp chill had crept into the air. Yet still I saw young women dressed in nothing more than artfully placed scraps of wispy material and tottering about on four-inch heels, displaying their goose pimples to whoever cared to look. I shook my head in amazement at these people. Once more, I vowed that my child would be raised differently, brought up with intelligence and thought for the future.

Wishwell dominated the skyline to the east, three and a half miles out of town, it's run down tower blocks blocking out the stars. The four central ragged concrete towers were surrounded by a maze of estate blocks—cramped terraced houses, cheap purpose-built flats: the estate was a riot of contrasting architectural styles, and had been continually added to since the early 1960s. I drove to the perimeter of the estate and parked up by the alley; I turned off the radio and sat in silence behind the wheel, remembering those lumbering loose-limbed figures and their odd disjointed movements. How they'd seemed to detach themselves from the darkness like smoke.

Was there really some extremist neo-fascist group operating out of Wishwell? Some militant offshoot of one of the local right wing political parties, whose aim was to clear the immigrant population out of the district, starting with this grubby, downtrodden estate? The thought terrified me, but made complete sense. There had been an intense paranoia and distrust of the asylum seekers who had been shipped into the area for quite some time now, and such reactionary groups feed off negative emotions like hyenas at a rotting cadaver.

I left the car, making sure I locked it up, and headed towards the black maw of the alley. Straggly bushes, like clasping skeletal fingers, had stretched across the entrance, forming a natural barrier that I was forced to duck beneath. It was dark in there, the solitary streetlamp shedding no light. Had it been sabotaged, or was I just tapping into that vein of paranoia and distrust? I stepped gently along the length of the alley, expecting dark shapes to jump out in front of me, their slack limbs waving at me, blanched hands grabbing for my throat...

But I reached the other end without incident, and found myself in a small square surrounded by shabby box-like cluster homes that had probably been grafted onto the estate in the mid 1970s. I registered movement at the periphery of my vision, and spun around to face whatever had caused it; a dark blur slipped away into another narrow alley, followed by two more. It was them, the same lurching figures I'd seen that night.

I followed, keeping to the edge of the square, hugging the rough outlines of privet bushes and lopsided garden walls. The figures were turning right at the other end of the alley, and I waited until they were out of sight before following any further. My heart beat double-time and my mouth went very dry; I felt afraid yet exhilarated. *I was doing something.*

I stalked the men through the estate—I could now tell that they were male by the clothing that I glimpsed beneath the muted orange glow cast by the few working sodium lights: hooded sweatshirts, baseball caps, gaudy tracksuits. They shambled through labyrinthine passages and beneath arched stone walkways, never speaking, not even glancing at one another. I treaded oh so softly, but still the crumbling concrete beneath my feet seemed to mock me: shifting like tectonic plates as I walked and crunching loudly in the heavy silence of deep night. The men didn't hear me; the forces of good seemed to be on my side.

The vast night sky pressed down on me like a huge sheet of black ice, threatening to trap me in the moment until I could be discovered shivering in the pale dawn. Stars blinked out one by one, like heavenly lamps being switched off. The men entered a boxy flat somewhere near the heart of the estate, not far from those glowering grey tower blocks that watched dispassionately from so many broken and boarded windows far above. I hid in a garden in sight of the flat, and waited for inspiration.

Much later I woke without even realizing that I'd nodded off. I was cold and my lips were beginning to chap. The estate was in total darkness, and I estimated the time to be well into the ungodly early hours. The sky was still pitch-black, but the stars had turned themselves back on. I let go of the hedge that I'd been cuddling, and climbed over the low garden wall, making no sound and feeling justifiably proud of my stealth. Not once did I stop to ask myself what I was doing; I didn't even pause to think of what might happen to Tanya and Jude if any foul deed befell me. I was focused, determined to do what was right.

I inched across to the building the men had entered. It was a ground floor flat, with dirty net curtains barely visible through the crudely whitewashed windows. The small front garden was weed-choked and littered with empty beer cans, takeaway wrappers, clots of old food. I spotted a thin strip of flagstone walkway along one side of the building, and followed it round to the back. The rear door stood ajar, hanging from rusty hinges. Obviously security wasn't a priority here; but, saying that, they were safe on their own ground, surrounded by their own people, so probably felt no need to lock doors and bolt windows.

I pushed open the door, and waited for the squeal of those hinges. It didn't come; the door swung silently open on a vaporous cloud of dust to reveal a messy galley kitchen that led onto a cluttered hallway with mildewed cardboard boxes stacked against the walls. To the right of this hallway was another door, this one a homemade affair constructed from thick lengths of timber and painted a dull yellow. I rode my luck, expecting this door to be unlocked too. It was, so I opened it.

A steep concrete staircase led down into a fathomless darkness; as I stepped down I briefly questioned my actions then pushed the thought away. I was acting on pure impulse now, shutting off my mind and going with my gut instinct. If I stopped, I would panic: if I panicked, I would bolt—probably drawing attention to my presence in the process. All I needed was one look, a single glimpse into what I knew must be the control room of this sinister organization. Then I could go to the police armed with proof, and bolstered by the knowledge that I wasn't imagining some convoluted conspiracy and these people actually existed.

The stairs led into a large basement, and it was blacker than night down there; there was no natural illumination, and I doubted that I would find a light switch even if I were foolish enough to try. So I walked into the gloom, so afraid by now that I couldn't halt my momentum, like a man running full-tilt down a very steep incline. I was simply a series of actions, with little thought behind them.

Soon I was lost in the dark, unable to even guess at which direction was out. After a while I began to see shapes form out of the darkness: sketchy figures propped against the seeping black walls. There was no sound in there but that of my own ragged breathing, so I knew that the figures were corpses; immediately after this realization, I became certain that they were the bodies stolen from the morgue. I slowly counted the outlines that sat slumped against the bowing brickwork: there were six of them. *Half a dozen.*

My feet slipped on the slimy earthen floor as I advanced further into the room, looking for an object to take away with me as solid evidence. Something crunched loudly underfoot, and I pitched sideways in a clumsy fall. As I went down my right hand pushed against, then slid off some vaguely familiar shape on the floor. My fingers poked into moist holes, and I felt teeth rattle against my wedding ring. A face. There was a face on the floor.

I looked down, unable to help myself. Blind eyes stared back at me, an open mouth yawning emptily into the chill air of the room. It was only then that I realized I'd been walking on the dead all along; mutilated bodies lay in a thick carpet of decay on the basement floor, and as my eyes at last became accustomed to the darkness I realized that not one of them was Caucasian. I was lying on a crust of murdered immigrants.

And that was when I saw al-hakim. Or rather what was left of him. The top half of his torso stood upright amid a heap of severed limbs to my immediate left, his torn face sporting what were obviously teeth marks. Bleached bone showed through like plastic where hungry mouths had scooped out hunks of his wrinkled golden brown cheeks.

I looked again at those six immobile figures that leaned against the wall, at their lurid sports casuals and stained Burberry baseball caps. Something strained at the centre of my mind, a thought that couldn't quite escape its cage. And then they moved. The bodies. All six of them, twitching and jerking like marionettes as they attempted to get to their feet. But *still not breathing*, not any of them. They were dead; but they moved. Towards me.

It was only then that I managed to regain control of my senses, and ran blindly across the corpse-layered floor, looking for an exit. The figures reached for me as I fled, loose white fingers groping for my living flesh, but I kicked them away, screaming now and not caring who heard. It was only through blind luck that I stumbled upon the stairs, my flailing hands bashing against the chipped concrete and three fingers breaking against the jagged treads. I climbed them in a blind frenzy, wanting only to get out. To be away from that place and those things...

Nobody accosted me on my way back to the car; it was as if I didn't matter, they didn't care what I'd seen because nobody would believe me anyway. I sat behind the wheel for an hour, just waiting and watching the greasy sun struggle up from the eastern rim of the world. If they wanted to silence me, they had only to come for me. As I sat there attempting to set my broken fingers I thought about how easy it would be to steal a few corpses, especially if the authorities were in on it. And I thought about what it might take to raise the resentful dead. To focus all the rage and the bitterness, the hostility and xenophobia that exists at street level to something higher, something darker. Call it urban magic, ghetto voodoo.

If you could bring back the dead you could do anything, even use the undead puppets at your command to cleanse your town, your country, and whip up even more crude bigotry and warped nationalism along the way. Dress them up in England shirts and tracksuit bottoms, and send them out to feast on the foreign invaders, to *consume before we are consumed*.

When I finally started the engine a watercolor dawn was smearing itself across the steel-grey sky. Curtains were opening in windows on the estate—early risers getting ready to face the new day. As I drove back to my family, to my own imperfect little world, I knew that I wouldn't ever fully understand what I'd seen. But what exactly had I seen? Even now, eighteen months later, I cannot be fully sure. But I'm certain that it's still out there, in some form or another, perhaps biding its time in some fetid basement darkness, growing angry and hungry and waiting to be unleashed.

It was only when I arrived home that I realized they—whoever *they* are—had known about me all along. They must have been monitoring me, waiting to see how much I would learn. Someone must have tipped them off about my interest in the disappearance of al-hakim. Perhaps it was Claire, consuming before she herself was consumed by whatever the fuck stalks in darkness. I just don't know. I'm not sure of anything anymore; I don't even know what is real and what exists only in my mind.

The front door was ajar, and as I walked into the hallway my heart stopped beating. I felt dead; as dead as those things that must have come lurching through the twilight towards everything that I held dear.

Tanya was lying face down on the stairs, her left arm stretched out before her as if she'd been reaching towards something upstairs. The nursery. The back of her head was red and matted, the ivory bone of her skull showing through in patches. I didn't turn her over; didn't want to see the expression on her face. I looked up, towards the upstairs landing. The bathroom door had been kicked in; it hung from its hinges like a bomb had gone through it. I felt my body move, taking each stair as if it were a mile high. I knew what I would find when I walked into the nursery, and I wanted to delay the sight as long as I could; forever, if that was possible.

Tears streaked my face, but my throat was too constricted to release any sound. I didn't want to know, didn't want to see, but still I had to ascend and acknowledge what had happened. As I stepped onto the landing carpet, I imagined Tanya moving behind me, raising her head and opening her mouth to reveal a gaping darkness at the centre of her. Lifting herself to her feet and shambling up after me.

But that didn't happen; not yet. Hopefully, it never will.

By the time the police found me cradling Jude's cold, cold body in my warm hands, the tears had finally stopped. The world spun around me like some mad, gaudy carousel, and I could sense things hiding in the shadows of the world. I looked up at the uniformed officers, and had a vague recollection of summoning them with the mobile phone that now lay on the floor under Jude's crib. I looked at my daughter's pale face, smiled at her and wished her pleasant dreams and prayed to God that her sleep would last forever.

I told the police officers about the house in Wishwell—of course I did; but it was no use. They didn't see what I had. The apocalypse in the cellar was still there, although nothing else remained but the images in my mind. Their colleagues had probably been there first, hastily shepherding those un-breathing things into the back of a van and relocating them to somewhere else in the depths of the estate.

I didn't do it: I didn't kill my all of those people. But nobody will believe me, not the police, the psychologists, or the friends that have deserted me since my arrest. I miss my family, my babies. They would have believed me.

And somewhere out there—in the shithole squalor of a broken-down housing estate—it's still happening. I read the newspapers with interest, specifically the stories of attacks on foreigners. Last week, an Asian child went missing. The week before that, it was a Serbian mother of three. It's started again.

It's getting dark outside, and nights are the worst. That's when I hear uneven shuffling footsteps in the corridor outside my cell, and hear my name whispered, as if by the wind.

Muddy Waters
BRIAN KNIGHT

THE BIG MAN WAS NOT PHOTOGENIC; he was a conglomeration of sun burnt scalp, greasy red facial hair, and sallow, liver spotted skin. Mona watched the tape, listening to her questions and his grunted, mumbled replies with a mixture of awe and disgust. After the interview he had grabbed her ass and asked her out.

She would use the footage anyway, it leant her piece the rustic roughness it needed. It was only a five minute story, and net even a lead, but she meant to upstage KLUTV's star reporter, the bitch Susan Potter, every chance she got until the producers either promoted her for her efforts, or she got a better offer.

Her crude interviewee, a saw shop owner named Harris Baugh, stood beside the seldom traveled highway outside the little town of Pierce, Idaho, next to the narrow dirt side road and a sign that said *Campbell's Pond - 5 Miles.* All around them was the green of Spruce and Pine, supported by a thick base of Huckleberry bushes and other underbrush. The narrow road to Campbell's Pond was like a dim corridor into no-where. Above them the sky was gray with clouds, it had rained only minutes after the conclusion of her interview with Baugh, who was returning from a fishing trip at the pond when they talked him into the interview.

"It ain't a natural pond," he said. "I don't think anybody knows for sure how it got there, but legend has it old

Preacher Campbell did it in the early eighteen hundreds when Pierce was called Oro-fino City." Baugh turned from the camera, stared down the shaded pond road, eyes narrowed and beard bristling. "His old church house is still out in the woods, there's a trail that goes to it, but folks around here mostly leave it alone."

"How did Preacher Campbell create Campbell's Pond, and why."

"He didn't create it lady, he was one of God's preachers, not God himself." Baugh smiled at his wit, and continued, "There's a creek that feeds it, Oro-fino Creek. Campbell diverted it into the valley where the pond is now, then spent the last few months of his life damming the other end up with dead fallen trees, rocks, and dirt. The department of lands dumped their own load of rock on it about ten years ago when they built the road to the campground over it. It leaks a little, but stays full with the creek still feeding it.

"Why," he said with a far off look that wanted to be thoughtful but came across as dimwitted. "God only knows."

The camera paned back to Mona, looking out of her element in her crisp KLUTV wardrobe. "It was at Campbell's Pond Camping Ground where little Timothy Walker was last seen. Timmy Walker, seven years old last January, was last seen around the shore of Campbell's Pond and is presumed drowned." She wore her solemn face like a mask, could exchange it with any of her many camera faces without an effort. She was convincing. "Mr. Baugh, could you detail the search for Timmy Walker."

The camera paned back to Baugh, who seconds before was fixated on Mona's breasts. He looked up just before the camera can catch his drooling stare. "Well, me and some other fellows from town," he poked a thumb back in the direction of Pierce, "we searched the woods all around here. We searched the old church house and fished around the shores of the pond."

"Why didn't the Search and Rescue search the pond more thoroughly? Campbell's Pond isn't large, or deep."

Baugh's stance became defensive at that question, as if she had called him a coward. "Lady, only a fool would go out in that water. There are almost two hundred years of rotten trees, pondweed, and lilies at the bottom of that puddle. The waters so muddy a man would be stuck fast down there before he knew it." Then, like an afterthought, "I've fished here since I was a kid, bit I've never like that pond."

He cameraman panned back to Mona on cue. "You mean you've come here all these years and never once went into the water."

Again, Baugh's wide face filed the screen. He paused, seemed to be in deep thought. Probably for dramatic effect, then concluded. "Lady, not on a dare."

∞∞∞⊙∞∞∞

Mona stopped the tape and grinned, satisfied. The station gave her shit stories and she turned them into gold.

"Kiss my ass, Susan," she said, sliding the news van's side door open and stepping out into the quiet campground. She knew that it would be full again by on Saturday, drowning or no drowning these locales loved their fishing, but on that Wednesday afternoon, it was deserted. Her only company was a lone moose, as big as a horse and with a monstrous spread of antlers. It trod lazily in the shallow water at the far end of the pond, eating strings of slimy weed and lilies from the surface.

She decided to wander around for a bit, take in the scenery and find some good angles for filler footage while the cameraman was back in town with her car picking up food and picnic supplies. Since there were no campers out today, and no crackling campfires to take pictures of, she decided they would create their own. Roast a few hotdogs and marshmallows like campers do. Mike, the cameraman, was pretty good looking and not too dumb, so maybe when they got back to the station she'd talk him into buying her a drink or two. She'd thought of trying him out while they were up here all alone, but she wanted to get promoted, not fired.

The campground consisted of several interconnected clearings, some pond side and others farther away. Each boasted a picnic table, fire pit, and concrete barriers to mark a parking spot. There were a handful of public restrooms, little more than glorified port-a-potties which Mona didn't care to explore, and three fishing docks that reached into the pond's muddy waters like slimy wooden fingers. It was all too quaint, too typical. Your average Idaho mountain campground. She wanted something more distinct, a memorable parting shot for her story.

Mona walked to a camp spot on the perimeter of the campground, farthest from the road out to the highway, spotted a trail into the forest beyond, and followed it. She didn't know where Preacher Campbell's old church house was, or even if it still existed as Baugh claimed, but if it was out there she meant to get footage of it.

Much of the wood out here was dead. She didn't know who owned the land, but whoever it was had chosen not to log or thin the area. The last few years had been dry ones, so all it would take is a touch of lightning, or a carelessly flung cigarette but to burn this wilderness up. As she got deeper into the woods the trail forked and branched.

She continued on the straightest path, noticing how it became rougher and less hospitable the farther she walked. Deadwood littered the stony, uneven path. Wild shrub, thistle, and what looked like nightshade crowded in. Low hanging limbs, which were trimmed away from the trail farther back, became an increasing annoyance, and she had to duck and twist around them every few feet. Mona knew she was working on assumption, but right now assumption was all she had to work with. It made sense that if the locals who frequented the campground left the old church house alone, the trail there would not be maintained. Finally the trail ended, swallowed up by the woods, a dead end. She cursed her luck, and the wasted time, when a sound in the distance caught her ears. Probably a dear or something, breaking through the brush as it fled her presence. She didn't see it, but when she looked she did see an old weather worn building, brooding in the darkness of a tightly packed clearing.

If the trail had been neglected, then the old wood plank structure had been blighted. The walls were a warped mess, the windows, which might have once held glass, were ugly moss lined sockets. There was no front door, just an old flap of burlap nailed over the entrance, caked with moss and filth. Someone had spray painted the legend *God Damned This Place* on it in bright hunter orange letters. Even the bit of rural graffiti was old, dull. That the place still stood was a wonder of the ages, or at least the past two centuries. Standing, somewhat crookedly, atop the square, two-story structure was a bell tower, minus the bell.

Mona approached the building with some trepidation. She wasn't bothered by the morbid legend painted on the rotting cloth door, or even the utter decrepitude of the place, but by the thought that some large, perhaps dangerous animal might have a den in the deserted church. She knew that these woods supported bears and mountain lions, maybe even a few wolves, and though most simply ran at the sight of a human, that hungry or hurt animals were very likely to attack a lone traveler.

She stepped to the door, almost screaming as her foot struck something small and furry. A large squirrel, laying on its side, staring up at her with eyes the pale color of curdled milk. It was quite dead, its matted fir crawling with flies and not a few maggots. The tail twitched slightly, the work of undead nerves, or maybe an imperceptible breeze. She watched it closely for a few moments, but it remained dead. The tail did not move.

She stepped around the small corpse and grabbed the edge of the rotting burlap and pulled it slowly to the side. No animals were in evidence, what she could see in the darkness within were a few old wooden chairs, rotting in neat rows on either side of a short, filth cakes isle, and a primitive looking pulpit, the sign on the cross was carved into its graying wood.

A dry rustle, the sound of breaking limbs and disturbed brush, made her jump, dropping the cloth back into place. She breathed deeply, cursed herself for being so damned spooked, but could not bring herself to open up the burlap flap again. Maybe later, with Mike at her side and the camera rolling, but not now.

She stepped away, not yet daring to turn her back on the place, and shrieked aloud as she bumped into something else. She turned around in time to see a small boy running down the path back to Campbell's Pond. She couldn't see his face, just the back of his head, his dirty short-cropped hair, but his clothes fit the description of Timothy Walker, the missing boy.

Slowly, her heart settled and her breathing eased, and a smile spread across her face.

Local KLUTV reporter Mona Hobbs turns hero, rescuing a lost child from the wilderness of northern Idaho. Story tonight at seven.

She saw this all perfectly in her minds eye, the same way she saw her own stories, shot by shot and word by word before they were even started. It was why she was good at her job, her power of visualization.

"*Timothy, wait!*"

He ran without looking back, likely scared by her scream. He was probably weak though, lost for days in the woods without food, so she knew she could catch him.

She decided as she gave chase down the rough trail, that she would ask the Susan Potter, the bitch, to do her interview.

∞∞∞⊖∞∞∞

The boy, not as weak as Mona figured, put on a good chase, but she kept him in sight. He turned sharply on several forks in the long trail, leading her into unexplored territory. She was afraid her would get her lost as well. Then she saw the end of the trail, it opened up into a camp spot beside the pond. The boy ran through the camp, to the edge of the pond, and onto one of the fishing docks, not stopping until he reached the end. She slowed as he turned to face her, not wanting to spook him again, and stepped onto the dock. It tilted slightly, moving under her feet, making her a little sea sick.

"Don't be afraid, Timmy," she said in the most soothing voice she could muster "You're found now. I'm not going to hurt you. I just want to get you out of here and back with your parents.

He watched her intensely as she approached slowly, not saying a word. If the run had tired him as it had her he didn't show it. Where she was huffing for breath, her heart pounding under her blouse, he seemed to barely breath at all. He looked sick, skin pail, eyes sunken and sallow, mouth drooping at the corners. As she closed in on him his eyes narrowed slightly. Only the whites showed, and he simply fell over backward into the water.

"No!" She ran the last few steps to the edge, but when she looked down into the water he was gone, the only sign of his passing a growing wave of ripples that moved the dock ever so slightly. If he was close to the dock she couldn't see him, the water around the dock was suddenly muddier than the rest of the pond, as if stirred up at the bottom. A dead, bloated fish floated only feet away, its eyes the same curdled milk color as the squirrel's had been. It's swollen belly a floating restraint for flies.

Then the flies scattered, and the fish rolled over in the water. With a splash of its yellowing tail it slipped into the muddy water and vanished

"What the hell?" She was no outdoorswoman, but that fish had been dead. *Dead!* A floating maggot buffet one second, and swimming off the next.

She was still watching the rippling wake of the fish when she heard the loud, menacing grunt behind her. It echoed across the green-brown waters of Campbell's Pond, not the grunt of a harassed animal, but something else entirely. It was guttural, a moaning, gurgling sound, like something coughing through a mouthful of mud, and the voice itself was almost human. Almost.

She turned and saw the moose she'd spied earlier watching her from the shore. Muddy fir hung in dark clumps from it's strangely elongated face; its massive antlers were pitted like sheets of twisted, rusty metal. It looked thinner than before, gaunt. When it opened its mouth, too wide it seemed to Mona, and bellowed at her again in its strange, slightly human voice, the smell of rotten meat washed over her, making her feel nauseous.

It stepped forward, head down and waving back and forth, then stopped, placing a pitted and misshapen hoof on the edge of the dock.

Mona stood perfectly still, arms out like a circus wirewalker, trying to keep her balance. The heels of her feet hung just over the edge of the wood, above the water.

The moose snorted again, and stomped its hoof against the edge of the dock with a loud crack that echoed like a gunshot. The dock rocked violently. Mona fought desperately for balance.

The moose raised its hoof again, brought it down with another loud report, and the plank beneath it splintered. Then it did it a third time, and a fourth. Mona lost her fight for balance, and fell face forward onto the shaking dock, her scream cut short by a grunt of pain. She felt water splash her ankles, which hung in the air over the water, and a pair of cold, wrinkly hands closed around them. She dug madly for purchase as they slowly drug her over the edge.

The moose raised its antlered head to the sky and howled laughter.

"No!" She dug at the splintered wood, screaming as one of her nails tore free, then finally found the crack between two boards and held fast. The fingers dug savagely into her flesh, tugging insistently, but she held.

"*Let go*," she screamed, and began thrashing her feet. She felt her heel connect with something soft. The hands loosened. She kicked again with all her strength, and broke free, scrambling back onto the dock.

The moose snorted, it's milky eyes glowering at her, and began stomping again.

She held firmly to the dock. "*Go away!*" she cried. "*Please, go away!*"

Instead, the moose advanced, and the narrow dock began to sink under its weight. Water washed around her, splashed into her mouth, up her nose. It tasted like a combination of piss and death. She felt the cold hands fumble for her feet again as the dock went under. The moose toppled over with a grunt as the dock turned sideways beneath it, and slid sideways into the water. The dock popped from the surface of the water like a cork. Mona was bucked off into the water.

For a second all was dark as the muddy waters washed over her, and she felt something old, rotten, and evil digging at her head. It was like being mind raped. Her feet found the soft bottom and she broke the surface of the water. As she struggled to the shore through grasping weeds and mud that sucked the shoes from her feet, the raping presence fell away. She heaved herself ashore, then stood and ran, barefoot and shrieking in the direction of her van.

The high cackling laughter of a child, and the heavy crushing lope of the moose followed her. Rocks dug and cut the bottoms of her feet, limbs slapped at her face. As she drew closer to the van her legs began to cramp, threatening to drop her, and she knew she wouldn't make it. Somehow she did.

She leapt through the open sliding door and turned in time to see the moose charging, Timmy Walker riding its twisted back like a demented cowboy. She grabbed the door handle and yanked it shut with the last of her strength. It latched home just as the moose rammed it.

Mona was thrown back against the van's complex of recording and broadcasting equipment, and when she fell forward onto the van's carpeted floor she was out cold.

Outside the moose rammed the van again buckling the side and twisting the door in its tracks. The boy howled laughter, screamed his approval in the language of the dead. After several minutes the moose stopped it's assault, and the van stilled.

∞∞⊖∞∞

Mona awoke, head pounding, every muscle in her body tight to the point of cramp, her torn feet throbbing. She wiped sticky blood from her face. Her cloths, still wet with the foul pond water, clung to her like a second diseased skin.

It was night. She saw the lazy water of Campbell's Pond reflecting moonlight through the cracked windshield. She also saw headlights.

"Mike," she whispered. She tried the side door, but it wouldn't budge. The back door was untouched, she pushed it open and stepped out fearfully into the night. It was raining again, lightly. A stroke of lightning lit the sky above, and several seconds later the boom of thunder followed. She found the KLUTV station wagon, motor still running, lights pointed into the deep woods. The driver's door was open. The side and hood of the white station wagon was smeared with blood, a crimson trail led away from the car, toward the pond. She followed it with her eyes and saw Timmy Walker dragging Mike's crushed and mutilated corps into the water.

Somewhere in the dark campground, unseen but close, the moose snorted.

The station wagon's running motor, open door beckoned, and she ran to it. As she climbed in, shutting the door behind her, the boy screamed howled into the night. The moose answered with a grunt, and charged out of the darkness.

Mona put the station wagon in drive and whipped around toward the camp's exit, tearing the passenger side mirror off as she scraped the side of an ancient and warped cedar.

Mona sped away, the dam that Preacher Campbell had built two hundred years ago of deadwood, rocks, and dirt came into view. She saw the moose just before it hit. With a strength she couldn't fathom, the animal pushed her off the road. The moose collapsed in the dirt. Its neck was twisted and bowed horribly, snapped into an S shape. The station wagon slid sideways down the steep embankment and came to a crashing halt against the trees at the edge of the forest.

By the time Timmy Walker stood at the edge of the road,

looking down at the wreck with a twisted, rotting smile, she was already gone.

∞∞⊙∞∞

Mona ran through the dark forest without thought, barely conscious in her terror. The trees and shrubs seemed to impede her willfully, slapping and cutting her, tangling her arms and legs. Making her fall painfully to the rough forest floor times without number. At some unremembered point she stumbled onto a trail and collapsed on a bed of dried pine needles, leafs, and moss.

She lay there for a while, watching the moon as it crested the trees to her left, glided across the weeping sky, and disappeared behind the trees to her right. At length she awoke to her surroundings, and recalled her last image of the psychotic moose; lying in a heap on the road, it's neck snapped from the force of its attack on her car.

If the moose was dead she might have a chance of getting out.

On the heal of that, as if she had called down a curse with her optimistic thoughts, came the steady thump, thump, thump, of a heavy hoofed animal advancing on the trail.

Probably a deer, she thought, pulling herself up with the help of a low hanging limb. She knew it wasn't, those steps were too solid, like the beating of some gruesome underground heart. She saw its dark shape advancing on her, the boy riding its back like some demented junior range rider.

Its neck broke, she thought, a new wave of panic rising within. *It can't be alive—its neck is broke!*

It stepped out of the darkness, into a patch of moon glow only feet away from her. Its neck was broken; its head flopped uselessly between its advancing forelegs. The large pitted antlers drug ground between them, digging a long divot down the center of the trail. Its tongue hung from the parted mouth like a piece of drying leather. It stopped a few feet away from her, lifted a hoof, and stomped the ground.

"Hey lady, wanna ride?" The boy leaned forward; laying belly first on the beast's matted back, and beckoned to her with an outstretched hand. There were two voices, the one on top was a child's voice, high pitched, amused. The one below was something else, a low moan that seemed to come from the earth itself, from the trees, the nightshade, the midnight sky, and the rain.

"What do you want?" She backed away, clutching at the foliage for support as she fumbled blindly over the uneven path.

The boy sat up, grabbing two fistfuls of fir, and tugged on them. The moose's dangling head let out a snort, blowing up dried pine needles and twigs in a miniature dust devil. Then it advanced again. The boy leaned back on his perch and laughed with his two mingled voices.

Mona backed away quicker, moaning in horror. "*What do you want?*"

"We want you." The boys twisting, bloated lips didn't move. Only the low voice spoke this time. "*Ride with us!*"

"Leave me alone!" She turned to run, and felt something clamp down on her ankle. Small sharp teeth tore through skin and dug into meat. She felt a tendon snap like a worn rubber band, the pain like cold fire under her skin. She tumbled to her side, felt the wind forced from her lungs by the impact, saw the dead squirrel she'd found by the church earlier as it ran up her leg and disappeared under the folds of her skirt.

Then a blanket of shaggy brown fur and falling hooves, and the thick smell of carrion, blotted out the world. The last sounds Mona heard were the deep moaning from somewhere within the earth, the sound of stomping hooves and cracking bones, and her own pained screams.

MUDDY WATERS

∞∞∞Ⓗ∞∞∞

Beneath the surface of Campbell's Pond all was still, the muddy waters had settled, and through slimy green fingers of pondweed Mona saw what Preacher Campbell had diverted the stream to cover up those two centuries ago.

The graveyard had been small, dug in rocky, soured earth. Some of the primitive headstones still stood, but most had tipped and were covered by vegetation and silt. Many of them were open; a few were empty. She felt the deep pulsing in the earth beneath her, like a heartbeat.

She lay, belly down and still, like a fish on the bottom, her fingers dug into the soft mud. Her head was tilted up, and she watched with wide milky eyes as the sun rose in the world above, turning the surface from onyx to sapphire, to glowing, foggy crystal. Then the people came, as they often did.

She could hear them talking, laughing, yelling in surprise or frustration as they reeled in or lost their latest catch. She heard the splashes from above and around as the people above cast their baited hooks and lures, felt the ripple of disturbed water. She watched a bright silver can float lazily above her, reflecting sunlight on the water around it like fire.

At a nearby dock something broke the surface of the water, small bare feet. They kicked back and forth, stirring up weeds, scaring the fish away. She could smell them, the pleasant odor of vital flesh. She wanted to reach out and touch them.

There was a sting in her neck as a barbed hook pierced her skin and a pulling sensation as someone from above tried to pull her up. She struggled against it briefly. Then she felt the tension disappear as the line snapped.

Mona crawled across the bottom of Campbell's Pond,

toward the thickest concentration of the green aquatic vines, and slipped down into one of the empty graves.

There she watched, and waited.

Darkness Comprehended
HARRY SHANNON &
GORD ROLLO

"And the light shineth in darkness
Yet the darkness comprehended it not."
The Gospel According to St. John 1:5

"SHE'S TURNING ZOM!" Kendall whispered. He had the reddened, richly veined nose of a heavy, lifelong drinker, even thought he was still a few years shy of his thirtieth birthday. Zack Pitt stepped forward, heavy work boots crunching through the broken glass, and leaned down to have a look. Kendall raised his shotgun with trembling hands and pointed it at the dead woman.

"Put that thing down before you blow your dick off," Pitt said. "Maybe she won't make it all the way. Some don't."

They had entered the deserted supermarket in search of supplies. Pitt hadn't seen her at first. The blonde, half-naked corpse lay beneath a huge pile of shelving and masonry, near some usable, if dented canned goods. Her breasts had flattened in death; the neck was broken, head lolling at an odd angle. At one time she'd been quite pretty. Pitt ordered the younger men to search for food while he guarded the entrance. He'd left Kendall to guard the body. Everything had been fine until she'd started moving again.

"Bart! Jon! You guys almost done back there?"

Muffled acknowledgements from the storeroom: *Almost done, boss.* Pitt wrinkled his nose. "Stinks in here,"

"Maybe it's a fucking nest," Kendall whispered.

Pitt grimaced and rubbed his face. The thought had crossed his mind. "Jesus, let's hope not." His vision swam out of focus, bursting into white dots before darkening. He lost his balance and stumbled a step forward.

"You okay, boss? You don't look so good."

Pitt shrugged and grabbed a plastic bottle from the shelf. He opened it and sipped some tepid water. "I'm just tired. I can't seem to sleep through the night."

Kendall's eyes widened and he raised his weapon. "Damn!"

The dead woman was writhing in the rubble now, making eerily erotic sounds. Some plaster fell away, exposing her face. Rats had eaten away her nose and one blue eye was missing. Her teeth pulled back in an involuntary snarl. Her dress was ripped and shredded. She was wearing sexy, pink thong underwear.

Bart, a skinny teenager with long black hair that contrasted sharply with his pale white skin, came out of the back offices. He was lugging a canvas sack. Back before the world went to hell he would have been labeled a Goth, but now people belonged to only one of two groups: *Us* or *Them.* Bart said: "Scored some boxes of ammo, Mr. Pitt." Then he saw the dead woman and cringed. "Shit, she's turning."

Kendall looked panicked. He started edging toward the door. "She's almost all the way back, Pitt. For Chrissakes, do her!"

"No, the noise could bring more," Pitt said. "Let's just get the hell out."

Just then the woman sat up, arms stiff at her sides. Her one remaining eye was spider-webbed with reddened veins. Her mouth opened impossibly wide and sound like the distant shriek of a hurricane filled the market. Time seemed to elongate and slow. Pitt found himself frozen, wondering: *I wonder what she's feeling? Thinking?*

Jon, a muscular black kid in his early twenties, came running into the market. He tripped over a box of cat food, regained his footing and closed the gap. "Shut her up!"

Kendall's finger twitched. The shotgun roared. The top of the woman's head vanished in a spray of blood, tissue and bone. Her body collapsed again and the room went silent. The four men froze in place and held their breath, listening with a desperation that transcended the senses. Their eyes met like football players in a huddle. They waited.

Bart was the first to speak. He brushed back his long dark hair and grinned. "I think we're cool," he said. He moved toward the plate glass window and peered out into the street. "Nothing happening outside."

"It'll be dark soon," Kendall said. His face was pale; voice hoarse and crackled with tension. "We got a pretty good haul today, why push our luck?"

Pitt nodded, and decided Kendall would be replaced on the next run. *His nerves are shot. He's losing it.* "You're right," he said, soothingly. "Jon, Bart, you move those boxes. I'll take point. Kendall, just cover the rear."

Each man dropped into position, Kendall visibly relieved to not have point. Pitt turned too rapidly and endured another wave of dizziness. He stepped out into the middle of the street, rifle at port arms. *Keep it together.* He searched the alleys for movement and trotted away through the trash and debris. Jon followed, wobbling along with a wheelbarrow full of dented soup cans; then Bart with three crates of powdered milk and a twelve-pack of cheap beer.

Kendall, still inside the nearly deserted market, turned his back to the street. He backed carefully towards the front door. He found himself humming tunelessly, some pop tune from the Twentieth Century, *baby, baby I think I love you...* He froze as two things struck him simultaneously. First, that he had not reloaded the shotgun.

Second that a nearby pile of trash nearby had just...*moved*.

"Pitt?"

Pitt, across the street, stopped in his tracks and turned just in time to have another long, slow black-hole experience: Kendall fumbling through his suddenly bottomless pants pocket for some cold, tubular shells; meanwhile, a figure coming up and out of a huge stack of garbage, something that had once been a rent-a-cop. It still wore tattered strips of grey uniform and an absurdly comic hat with a shiny black bill. Then Kendall cracking open the weapon; the Zom on its feet and lurching forward while making that high keening a Zom makes when he's starving; Kendall trying to load those shells with shaking fingers, dropping the first but getting the second; the Zom snarling and extending bloody fingers with yellowed and cracked nails, hungrily closing the gap.

"Get out of the way!" Pitt called.

They all wanted to shoot but couldn't without hitting Kendall, and by the time the man tried to run he was toast. The Zom grabbed Kendall's right arm and twisted it around and up so that it made a hideous *craaaaking* sound. Kendall grunted and spewed out a mouthful of thick, syrupy vomit. The Zom clawed at his guts with those Fu Manchu nails, trying to open his soft lower belly. Kendall dropped his hands to protect himself. It closed with him in an obscene parody of a slow dance and bit deeply into his neck, severing the carotid artery. Dark blood spurted with each desperate pump of his weakening heart, arcing high and away. Kendall kicked his legs like a man on the gallows and his eyes rolled back as he died.

Pitt crossed the deserted street, closed the distance. He watched as it fed. His skin tingled as he looked deep into the creature's empty eyes for a long, dark moment. *Where has your soul gone? Do you hate what you're doing right now...or lust for it? Is it both at once? What the fuck is going on in your head?* Pitt shuddered, shook the cobwebs from his head.

"Mr. Pitt?"

It was his crew, awaiting orders. Pitt crossed himself, raised his weapon and barked. "Waste them both."

The others came out of their trance to fire. The three continued firing, the barrage going on and on until the red, white and purple pieces that had been Kendall were indistinguishable from the remnants of the Zom. Silence, and the fading stench of cordite. "Their heads, too," Pitt said sadly. "Make sure you destroy the brains."

They jogged back to camp. Not for the first time, Pitt found it difficult to keep up. At forty, he was by far the oldest of the twenty-three rag tag survivors, many of whom were half his age. They followed him because he'd managed to keep them alive for the last few years. During that time, Pitt had lost his right eye to a Zom who got too close and his hair had gone completely white. He wondered if his leadership went un-challenged because the others were afraid of him. In his own mind he was just a football player gone to seed; an ex-marine turned ex-bouncer.

They paused near some trashcans at the entrance and whistled sharply. The sun was sinking into the bloody red skyline, and time was short. The guard whistled back and they jogged up to the next level of the airport parking lot with-out incident. The women greeted their men warmly and took the food to storage. Pitt went alone to the railing and looked down. The undead were already coming out to howl at the moon. Pitt shivered, although it was not yet cold, his weary mind still obsessed with questions. *What are they thinking? Feeling? What would it have been like for Kendall, if I had left him there, let him turn?*

The others had posted guards, opened the beer and begun to celebrate. Pitt slid further into the shadows. He reached into his jacket, removed a tattered leather wallet and took out his last remaining picture of Maria. His features softened. It was a shot from their honeymoon. Maria was standing on the hotel steps. She had her hands on her skirted hips and was smiling sweetly into the camera; long black hair swept out to one side, held aloft by a sudden gust of wind. Pitt stared at the photograph for a very long time. He did not cry, not any more. His tears had dried, turned to dust and blown away. In a way, the picture calmed him; reminded him of other lives in other times and places.

...Down at Waterfront Park walking hand in hand, because even with the trash and floating human waste it is their place, and they need to talk about the baby. Pitt scolds her, forces himself to ignore the hurt in her deep, brown eyes. "How could you have been so stupid, Maria? We can't bring a poor innocent child into this crazy fucked-up world."

She states her case, and it is for life even in the face of death. Pitt weakens. Soon they are sitting on a wobbly bench on the outer edge of the park. Pitt is rubbing his hand over Maria's swollen belly, feeling his child's feeble kicks, when the group of undead swarms out of the old public washroom building. There are too many of them, no time to reload the rifle. The bench rests against a concrete wall. Pitt stands on the seat and scurries up for a quick drop to safety on the far side. He reaches, starts pulling Maria up out of harms way, but her hands are slippery from sweat. He loses her. She looks up at him, both terror and forgiveness in her beautiful eyes.

Zom's are on her, scratching, clawing, pulling his beloved Maria away from his outstretched, shaking hands. Pitt screams and without hesitation jumps back down to try help her, pulling his back-up, a 9mm Glock, from his pants. He fires the moment his feet hit the grass. "Take me!" he cries. But they have no interest in him. They are rapidly backing away; content to protect the prize they already have in their filthy clutches.

Pitt uses all fifteen rounds, but only drops the Zom's on the outer fringes of the group. They are gone in a heartbeat, disappearing back into the bathroom, locking and barring the entrance behind them, Pitt still outside pounding on the door all alone with his tears and screams of hopeless rage as he hears Maria pleading…

"Mr. Pitt?"

Hands grabbed Pitt by the shoulders. He reacted violently, jumped to his feet ready to lash out. But it was only young Jon. "Sorry, we all know you need your rest, but you were screaming in your sleep. Keene asked me to check if you were okay."

Wake me? Pitt tried to get the world to stop spinning. *Was I dreaming?* He'd dozed off. "Fuck! What time is it? How long was I out?"

"It's nearly midnight," Jon said, gently. "You need more than five hours. Why don't you try to go back to sleep?"

"I have to go," Pitt said matter-of-factly. He gathered up his gun and ammo belt, headed for the door.

Jon followed, shifting from one foot to another, building up his nerve, finally saying: "You've got to stop doing this, Mr. Pitt. It's killing you. You can search for her forever, but it won't do any good. Accept it and get on with your life. The Zom's took her and she's gone!"

Pitt turned in a flash. He tossed Jon against the concrete wall, clutched his throat, screamed into the ebony face just inches away, "Fuck you, you little punk. You don't have the slightest clue what you're talking about, so stay out of this, you hear me? Stay the fuck out of it!"

"Yes, sir," Jon croaked. Pitt saw his own spittle on the boy's cheek and felt a wave of shame heat his belly. But he could not bring himself to apologize.

Pitt released the young man and bolted out the door into the parking lot stairwell. He knew no one would follow, but he ran down the stairs two at a time anyway, not slowing his pace until he was out on the street and several blocks back into the dark, rotting belly of the city. Only then did he slow to a walk; raggedy breath sucking in and out of clenched, chipped teeth, heart pounding in its bone cage, pulse loud enough that he was sure any Zom within a mile radius could hear it. He could picture one suddenly sitting up, rotting ears turned to the wind, picking up the tiny *thump-thumps,* then lurching to its feet, greedily searching for him.

Bring it on, Pitt thought. *I don't care any more.*

He held up his lantern. As if his thoughts had given substance to reality, three decaying females moved out of the shadows across the street, running in their broken high heeled shoes and tattered fancy dresses. Pitt drew the Glock and put a blue-tinged hole in the center of the first two foreheads. They dropped instantly. But the third ducked at the right time and was on top of him before he could aim again.

She hissed and spat but she was weak, likely starving. Pitt was able to throw her roughly to the ground. He pinned her beneath his weight. She tried to claw and bite, but he used his knees to keep her helpless. He wanted to shoot her and get on with things, but he paused anyway. He needed to look into those wild, bloodshot eyes and ask her something very important.

"Do you remember your name?"

The Zom snarled and hawked an unmentionable fluid. Pitt slapped her, tried to hold her gaze. "Can you remember who you were? I need to know."

She hissed again, spat a mouthful of blood at his face and started thrashing with all her might. Pitt felt an almost unbearable sadness take him. He jammed his gun into her gaping maw and pulled the trigger three times. The top of her skull exploded into a jigsaw puzzle; tiny pieces scattered across the cluttered street.

Pitt climbed to his feet and walked away. He moved further into the city. Three blocks later, vision blurred and equilibrium doing cartwheels again, he collapsed in a heap against the front window of a boarded up Dry Cleaning company. His consciousness drifted into a fugue state. He rested for several minutes, stomach queasy, until his head suddenly cleared again. He got to his feet.

Pitt pressed on. He was tired, angry and confused yet knew that he was only delaying the inevitable. He paused in a doorway, took a series of deep breaths to steel his nerves then picked up his pace. He headed straight for the old warehouse on the corner of Columbia and Market Streets, determined to finish things.

The warehouse was a plain old rectangular box, three stories high, spread out covering most of a city block. Pitt had no idea who had once owned the property. There was no logo anywhere on the building; the only paint the sprayed graffiti of long-dead gang members. The warehouse belonged to Pitt now. He had claimed it weeks ago by chaining the rusty door shut and applying a sturdy lock.

Pitt unlocked the door, slipped quietly inside. He locked it behind him.

It was still inside the building and much chillier than out on the street. Pitt stood, weaving in the darkness; eyes closed and fingers tightly gripping his gun. He listened for any movements in the gloom. *Nothing. Wait…no, nothing.*

Then he heard the scrape of a chain dragging across cold concrete. A nervous smile touched the corners of his mouth.

Thank God!

Pitt started the backup generator. He clicked the light switch. The dust-covered fluorescents cast a dull but adequate amount of light. Maria stood exactly where he'd left her, inside what had once been a small storage room. The walls, floor and ceiling were solid concrete. Pitt had hurriedly constructed a set of bars to seal off the front of the small room. She wasn't going anywhere, but for safety he'd also fashioned a chain around her ankle and attached it to the rusty bed frame.

Pitt walked nearer to the bars. Maria hissed at him and tried to claw through the gate, but it was something of a reflexive gesture, with little real effort behind it. Pitt took that as a very good sign. *She remembers me. She knows who I am! God, even turned, she's still beautiful.*

It had taken two seemingly endless, bloody nights to find her again—to battle his way into the tunnels under Waterfront Park where they were keeping Maria for extra food. She'd already been bitten several times and was well on her way to turning Zom, but Pitt hadn't been able to shoot her. So he had brought her here, to this abandoned warehouse. He'd kept her existence secret from the group and continued the charade of searching for her night after night.

Pitt removed his coat and shirt. Maria growled and shuffled. Saliva drooled from her shattered lower teeth.

"I know, sweetheart," Pitt said, kindly. "It won't be long, now."

He started to prepare the needle. Maria paced back and forth like an impatient panther. Pitt jabbed the large wooden needle into his left forearm, successfully hitting the vein on the first try. He quickly attached the hollow rubber flex-tube. He didn't want to waste a precious drop. Maria grabbed the end of the tube that protruded into her cell. She sucked hungrily. Pitt groaned, from a mixture of emotional pleasure and physical pain. She started to drain his life away and once again the loss of blood made his vision blur and his ears ring. Pitt clenched his jaw and pinched himself to stay conscious.

It's for the baby. The baby.

Maria's distended belly was huge, now. Joy raced through Pitt as he imagined the baby as it kicked inside of her. *I'll make it up to you, honey*, he thought. *Thank God our baby's still alive.*

Pitt finally yanked the needle from his arm. He heard Maria growl at the abrupt end of her feast. Pitt debated returning to the parking garage, but sank to his knees. *It's over,* he thought.

I'm staying here with my family. Before he could change his mind, Pitt unbolted the door leading into the small concrete cell. He opened the door and collapsed.

Screaming...

A horrible keening sound made Pitt bolt upright; fireworks exploded in front of his eyes and a white-hot knife of pain shot down his spine. He nearly lost consciousness again but fought his way back. After a long moment, he remembered what he had done and adrenaline flooded his veins. He knew he was as good as dead. After a long moment, there came another shriek. Pitt opened his eyes.

The door to Maria's cell was yawning open. She was no longer inside. A trail of clotted blood led out the door and past where he sat on the floor. With a supreme effort, Pitt managed to get to his feet to see where Maria had gone.

He found her curled in a ball over on the far side of the building. She was slowly rocking back and forth, keeping a watchful eye on her surroundings. It was early morning now, and pale light filtered through the skylights. Pitt could see that Maria was holding something in her arms. Something small, that writhed.

Pitt staggered over. He simply had to see. Maria lurched to her feet and tentatively offered up the child. It was a dirty, blood-smeared, oddly deformed little boy; a darkling who was half-living, half-dead.

Pitt had never seen anything so beautiful.

Maria yanked on his left arm, pointing first to his many scabs and then to the baby's mouth. *She wants me to feed him.* And Pitt fully comprehended the darkness at last. He closed his eyes, crossed himself and prayed. When he opened them again, Maria was snarling in hunger.

Zack Pitt looked down at where the needle lay on the filthy, concrete floor. He startled Maria by kicking it away toward the empty cell. He looked deep into her feral eyes, turned his head to the side and offered the baby his throat. The elongated, preternaturally sharp teeth quickly broke the skin...

And their child began to suckle.

Connections
SIMON McCAFFERY

TODAY ANDREW TIED HIS SNEAKERS without my help, and I cried. The last time I shed tears in front of my son was nine years ago, on the morning I stood beside Shelly in a baggy blue hospital gown and watched the obstetrician lift him, naked and glistening and beautiful, into the light. Later, when his condition was finally diagnosed, Shelly cried on and off for weeks. Not me. One of the psychiatric counselors had the gall to tell me I had difficulty *externalizing my emotions*, and it was all I could do not to strangle the son of a bitch right there in his two-hundred-dollar-an-hour office.

There are new things, little things, each day now.

I try to remain objective, to not become too hopeful, to maintain my professional distance. But when I see the floppy loops of the bowknots on Andrew's scuffed Reeboks I sweep his little body into my arms in a crushing hug. Tears collect in my beard like raindrops. He tries to kiss me through the leather muzzle and I wish for the thousandth time that Shelly was alive to share these moments.

For the rest of the afternoon we concentrate on flash cards and bits of the Wechsler scale for children. Andrew fiddles with the colored blocks and simple wooden puzzles, but I can tell he is growing distracted. It's been hours since lunch, so I finally put the blocks and cards away for the day. There was a time not long ago when I made it home from my office in time for dinner two, maybe three nights a week. Now, with Shelly gone and the world turned into a grotesque *Tales From The Crypt* script, it's up to me to care for our son. To be there for him.

The coffin-like freezer in the basement (supplied with juice from a gasoline-powered generator during the sporadic power "interruptions") is empty. That means a trip into town.

"Okay, little man, Dad's going out for a bit. Can you hold down the fort for me?"

I give Andrew another hug—positive reinforcement is so crucial—and leave his toy-cluttered room, locking the door behind me.

Downstairs, the lawn looks empty through the distorting, fish-eye lens of the garage door's peephole. I thumb the switch that raises the large two-car bay's segmented door and it clatters up with a familiar hum. Naturally, nothing lurches into sight, though you can never be too careful. I slip into the Taurus wagon and back it out quickly, hitting the button on the remote to close the garage door. The days haven't begun to shorten yet, but every expedition is dangerous and Andrew prefers if I return before sundown. Or am I simply projecting that emotion?

The knot of armed men at the tall iron subdivision gates parts to let me through. I recognize two of tonight's sentries: Allan Sprouse, formerly one of the city's most successful dermatologists, and Richard McCaslin, the balding lawyer who lives behind us in an imitation Colonial with jutting redwood Jacuzzi deck. Both men are dressed for the muggy August air in jogging shorts and bright Nike T-shirts. Both heft pump shotguns as casually as they once held golf clubs. Sawed-off barrels, like Citizen Patrol Squads, are now perfectly legal. 'Just Do It' is now a gruesomely apt slogan to have emblazoned on your chest.

They wave, I wave and the iron gates rattle shut behind the station wagon with a clang that makes you think of war films. The men turn back to their discussion.

The Oakbriar subdivision—refuge for affluent doctors, lawyers, certified public accountants, and yes, private-practice psychologists—has faired better than most surrounding enclaves of Kansas City suburbia. Over the past six months we have quickly evolved into a tiny feudal state, a fortress of upper-class sanity in this new Dark Age. The high stone walls and ebony faux-iron metal gates erected for a sense of exclusivity now serve a more practical purpose.

As always, the sight of my neighbors carrying those ugly truncated weapons with such cool indifference persists in my mind's eye. How would good old Al and Richie react to Andrew if they showed up for a friendly Friday night poker game? I have to suppress the rage and horror that squeezes my heart.

But Andrew is safe inside his room, with its boarded-up windows and disabled light switch to prevent anyone from seeing his tiny face peering out.

I take the expressway that cuts across Overland Park. Nine miles away the neighborhoods begin to deteriorate significantly.

Giggles automatically start to build in my throat and I nearly drift into a stalled dump truck. *Deteriorate significantly.* Oh man, we shrinks—exalted plumbers of the psyche—are chock full of smooth, politically correct euphemisms.

In the reddening light the endless rows of abandoned or razed tract homes resemble a huge, hellish graveyard. Every boarded-up house is a testament to the horrifying siege that still isn't over. Out near the airport, a roiling column of tar-black smoke rises from the pyres that burn day and night as the remnants of the Kansas City National Guard and Army Corps of Engineers dispose of citizens who have succumbed to *post-viability outplacement.* The legion of suicides and twice-dead plague victims.

I exit on Riverside Avenue, skirting the warning signs and makeshift barricades, and begin cruising the desolate side streets. Unlike most expeditions, it doesn't take long to find what I'm looking for.

A figure shambles almost directly into the path of the Taurus. A woman, young and alone. I hit the brakes, swing open the driver's door and scan all directions quickly. First, to make sure she's alone; some of them hunt in instinctive packs, using decoys. And if a band of undead doesn't creep up on you, a passing caravan of trigger-happy Guardsmen can always punch your ticket for free.

The street is empty. I step out, leaving the Taurus' engine running.

The woman immediately turns clumsily in my direction, as if directed by a crude organic radar or tropism. Her skin is pale but uncorrupted and her gait is not the stiff, robot-jerk that comes with time and decay. She has only recently started her night-walk. She will do.

I step toward her, trying to look in all directions at once. But the dead woman and I are alone.

I scan her body for the killing wound with a clinician's eye. The only visible injury is a discolored, shallow crater of flesh missing on her left arm below the elbow—probably a bite-mark. That's really all it takes; once the plague virus enters the bloodstream it goes to work fast. There's no such thing as a non-lethal wound or antidote. She was probably fighting off one or more of them and got careless, or just unlucky. She escaped, only to succumb to the virus six to twelve hours later. Of course death wouldn't stop her from infecting others. Laughably christened PAP by the Centers For Disease Control, Postmortem Ambulant Plague makes HIV look like the snifffles. The word *zombie* is taboo, mucho politically incorrect, mentioned only in the sleaziest of checkout counter tabloids.

They are slow and without intellect, driven by a single prime instinct: to feed. I walk right up to her, drawing the nine-millimeter handgun from inside my jacket. Her green eyes are fixed and dilated. Flat, like a doll's. The rose-colored sunset behind us ignites her disheveled blonde hair like copper.

I place the muzzle of the gun against her forehead just as her outstretched arms close around me in an eager Venus-flytrap embrace. I try not to think of Shelly as I squeeze the trigger.

∞∞⊙∞∞

What I do—the horrors I conceal from my neighbors—I do for the love of my son.

We suspected something was seriously wrong with Andrew before he celebrated his first birthday. By the age of two the diagnosis of his condition had been changed from "developmentally disabled" to Early Infantile Autism. Not long after he began displaying traces of Savant Syndrome, which I now know is commonly linked to EIA.

Physically, Andrew is perfectly formed, with the delicate facial features of Shelly and my dark eyes and hair. Autism doesn't make itself known with the recognizable deformities of Down's syndrome and other genetic errors.

Endless EEGs and other scans found no physical abnormalities in his brain. He wasn't retarded or a deaf-mute. He didn't display the rocking, swaying and head-banging of the schizophrenic. He didn't curl up in the corner in a fetal ball or bray "Five minutes to Wapner!" every afternoon like a fractured chronometer. The damage was deep inside his brain, where billions of neurons make uncountable synaptic connections.

"For all practical purposes, Andrew exists inside his own personal universe," explained a bland young specialist named, of all things, Graves. "He doesn't perceive—doesn't *process*— reality the same way we do."

It was like being dropped into a Richard Matheson Twilight Zone script. *You can hold your son, sing him a lullaby, whisper your love in his tiny pink ear, but he is trapped in the Andrew Dimension.*

The neural pathways inside our son's brain had been crossed or scrambled in some unfathomable way, and all the things we assumed we'd experience with him—summer Little League games, teaching him to ride a bicycle, sending him off to a good private grammar school in anticipation of an ivy-league education—were over. That's what Shelly kept muttering on the shell-shocked drive home, endlessly. *It's over for him.* No more Kodak moments for the Strickland family.

I made up my mind on that terrible ride home that nothing was over. Wasn't it within my power to rescue our son? To break through the barriers and make a connection?

∞∞∞⊙∞∞∞

Loading the woman in the back of the Taurus takes longer than I'd like.

My hands are sweat-slick and her body won't cooperate. The fresher ones are like huge, floppy rag dolls. I'm certain that at any second an olive-drab patrol truck will rumble around the corner, aiming high-powered searchlights like probing fingers. Night rules these streets after sundown; no sodium-arc lights flicker to life on this dead grid of the city. And they shoot on sight after curfew; aim for the head and ask questions later.

Finally, I shove the woman's feet underneath the humped bedspread and slam down the hatchback. It doesn't click shut. I reinsert the key and free the swatch of trapped cloth from the lock, then shut it firmly.

I turn to get in the car and there's one standing right behind me.

There's no time to wonder where it came from or how it approached so silently. Blackened, fetid claws reach for my jacket and face. Unlike the body stuffed under the bedspread, this advanced plague victim looks like an exhumed mummy and smells like it died the same year as Elvis. No hair, eyes or nose, but plenty of yellow, leaning teeth. It must have evaded hundreds of cleanup patrols.

I grasp its cool leathery neck with my right hand and grope for the handgun with my left. We do a clumsy half-waltz turn and slam into the side of the car. Despite the gallon of adrenaline singing in my blood I'm pinned against the flank of the Taurus, fumbling for the damn gun. The reanimated corpse snags a handful of my hair and pulls me closer to that lipless, picket-fence grin. The smell of carrion envelopes me in a sickening cloud.

I free the gun from the folds of my jacket with a terror-driven burst of strength and wedge it underneath the creature's snapping jaw. The slug rockets up into the cranial cavity and the creepshow thing's skull explodes like a cherry bomb inside a rotted pumpkin.

∞∞∞⊙∞∞∞

The power is still on when I return, shaken but reasonably cleaned up, and that makes preparing dinner for Andrew in the basement a lot easier.

In the cold light of six overhead fluorescent bars, I change into some old clothes and tie on a butcher's apron. A pair of electrician's thick rubber gloves protect my hands. My nostrils are held shut with one of those little clamps swimmers use. I pick up the Black & Decker jigsaw and depress the red plastic trigger; the compact saw whines and its single metal tooth blurs.

Before I make the first incision, my mind has already slipped into a familiar numbness. It's amazing what you can condition yourself to do if you have no other choice. In high school biology I had to have a classmate—Wanda Petersen—prick my finger to take a blood sample. Even then, watching bright blood well up on my fingertip, I had to sit down and bend forward to stop the grayness creeping into my vision and the roaring in my ears.

I fill an aluminum pan with enough meat for Andrew's supper. The rest is quickly wrapped in white butcher's paper and deposited in the freezer. The bony, inedible parts are scraped in a couple of Glad Heavy Duty trash bags with the drawstring top. Hefty, hefty, hefty! These will be dumped into one of the city-sponsored pyres with the rest of the garbage.

The remaining ritual is a hundred times worse.

I set the pan of flesh in front of Andrew, who is seated against the far wall in his harness. He struggles to grasp the pan, which is just beyond his reach.

"What do we say, Andrew?"

Andrew's dry little mouth moves. His body wriggles against the nylon harness straps.

"One word, Andrew. You can do it. Say 'Daddy.'"

Andrew begins to make a low mewling noise.

"One word, son. *One word*, little guy."

Andrew's eyes never leave the pan. His mouth snaps open and shut like a suffocating fish.

"Say 'Daddy.' I *know* you can do it."

Andrew thrashes harder against his harness and one of the straps presses into his throat. His head jerks up for a moment and he utters a sound like *Aaad*.

"That's my boy! That's wonderful, Andrew!" I slide the pan toward him.

231

While he eats I remove the stained apron and strip off the gore-streaked gloves, tossing them into the bone-bag. Holding a can of Glade air freshener, I fan the air until the room reeks of lemons. I step toward the stairs, more than ready for a scalding hot shower, when the doorbell chimes.

I freeze at the bottom of the steps, listening.

The bell rings again.

"You stay right here," I needlessly tell Andrew. I hurry up the steps, wondering who the hell it could be. It's not my evening to stand sentry at the subdivision gates—

The bell rings again as I hurry through the kitchen and across the carpeted expanse of the living room to the foyer. I flick on the porch light and peer out through the peephole.

Allan Sprouse and Richie McCaslin's distorted faces stare back. For a moment, a freezing terror envelopes me. *Some-body's finally seen Andrew while I was away,* my mind yammers, *and they've come to take him.*

But instead of returning to the kitchen for the gun, I open the door.

We stare at each other for a second that seems to stretch out, and Al and Richie glance at each other.

"Hey, Frank, you mind if we come in?" Richie says.

"If you're busy we can come back later," Al adds.

They're both staring at me. For a crazy moment I'm sure I'll look down and see the dripping butcher's apron still tied around my waist.

"No, no. Come on in, guys. You both just come off shift?"

"Yeah," Richie says, "Bert and Hal drew the graveyard this week."

"They'll probably blow each other's heads off," adds Al cheerfully. "Those two couldn't find their asses in the dark with both hands."

"So what's up?" I ask.

Al and Richie glance at each other again.

"We just stopped by to bum a couple of beers," Al says with a grin. "Maybe catch a game on TV."

We all laugh dutifully at this joke.

I fetch three bottles of beer—chilled, no less—and we sit on the teal sectional couch that Shelly damn near crucified herself picking out. Nobody turns on the thirty-five-inch Sony to watch the Emergency Broadcast messages and laughable Center For Disease Control warnings that play endlessly on two of the three networks. Good old TBS, however, is still serving up Eastwood westerns, Cary Grant thrillers and Shirley Temple.

"You know, buddy, you should move in with Claire and the kids," Al ventures softly. "It's not good, you knocking around by yourself in this big house."

"That's kind of you to offer," I smile, "but I'm okay. Really." I can imagine watching Andrew playing with Brad and Al Jr., can imagine Al striding toward them across the grass, shouting and waving them away, leveling the sawed-off shot-gun—

"Really."

They finally leave an hour later; the most unbearable, nerve-shattering hour of my life. Sitting on my dead wife's sofa, making macho small talk and waiting to hear Andrew start moaning or banging his pan against the concrete basement floor—

If good old Al and Richie had stayed ten minutes longer I think I would have walked calmly into the kitchen, removed the gun from the counter drawer and shot them both.

I lean against the door for several moments, counting backward from one hundred, until my stomach settles. Then I hurry to the basement.

∞∞∞⊖∞∞∞

Later I sit in Andrew's room, a Scotch in hand, watching him draw pictures. Besides the other obvious differences, the plague has apparently accomplished what a platoon of high-paid specialists could not; the Savant Syndrome no longer guides his chunky little hands.

A fraction of all autistic children exhibit an island of stunning, inexplicable talent. Andrew isn't—wasn't—a lightning calculator or calendar savant. He couldn't play an opera score after hearing it once. He didn't build painstaking scale-models of nineteenth-century sailing ships like James Henry Pullen, the celebrated idiot-genius of Earlswood Asylum.

Instead, he would sit hunched over a child's drawing table for hours, sketching impossibly detailed, dynamic pictures. Trees, horses, a Greyhound bus. Some fantastic imaging system inside his mind required only the briefest glimpse of an object to imprint it forever in his memory. The horse gallops from view, the smoke-farting city bus grinds away into traffic, but not to Andrew. These images persisted in a three-dimensional freeze-frame of time, to be accessed in full clarity a day, a month, a year later.

Then the plague virus escaped from some lab, or hitched a ride on a shuttle flight, or simply mutated on its own. Shelly never made it home from Andrew's routine doctor's appointment, probably sacrificed herself to save him. She had driven him because, as always, *I* had a full roster of patients to see and couldn't escape from the office. And somehow he found his way home with nothing worse that the tip of one finger missing.

"May I look at this, Andrew?"

Three vaguely human figures with balloon-heads and disproportionate limbs stand on a crayola-green lawn. The sun is a crude mandala with radiating beams of light. A month ago the people would have been rendered in near-photographic detail and perspective, every anatomical detail exact.

"This is *wonderful*, Andrew."

He doesn't acknowledge this praise, but continues to squint at the paper and slow-moving point of his crayon. From the looks of it, he's trying to sketch a deer, but his hand, stripped of its unearthly deftness, is producing what more resembles a mutated, horned dog.

"Who are these people in your picture?"

Andrew continues his tortuous rendering of the dog-deer. The crayon—burnt sienna—suddenly snaps in two. For a moment Andrew stares at the stump of crayola in his clenched fist, and I see (or imagine I see) an expression of confusion, loss and fear cross his solemn gray face.

Only it's not my imagination. You don't have to be a neurologist to see that the virus hasn't had the same effect on Andrew it has on people whose brain chemistry functioned normally in life. The little boy once irretrievably lost is emerging from his inner world, a bit more each day. *My son.* All I need is a little more time.

After I strap Andrew in bed I shuffle down the hall to the bathroom. Too tired for even a shower, I reach for the Extra Strength Tylenol behind the mirrored cabinet. I see my drawn, haggard reflection and stop.

During the hot, unspeakable hour it took me to butcher the undead woman in the basement, I must have absently wiped away a drop of sweat. Smeared across my right eyebrow is a thin comma of dried blood.

∞∞∞⦿∞∞∞

I awake in bed from a torch-lit nightmare, hearing a terrible pounding and angry, shouting voices.

Except it isn't a dream. No polite doorbell this time. Downstairs, I hear fists battering against the front door.

"Open the door, Frank!"

I slip on a robe and hurry downstairs, splinters of ice lodged in my chest. Idiot! Of course they'd seen the blood!

"Don't make this any harder than it has to be, Frank. Open the goddamned door!"

I pad up to the door and peer through the tiny lens. Al Sprouse's face glares back, eyes gleaming with hatred and fear, lips pulled back in a feral grimace. The lawn is filled with men carrying high-powered flashlights and weapons.

"We know what you're feeding in the basement," Al bellows, only inches away. "That thing isn't your kid. Not anymore. You know the law, Frank."

I back up, trembling uncontrollably.

"It's not natural," Richie chimes in. "And by harboring it you're endangering all of us. We all signed the agreement."

So sue me, you chicken-shit asshole. My son's not dead.

I blink, realizing I've spoken the words aloud, angrily. "If I could just show you," I add, ashamed of the waver in my voice, "you'd understand. He's not like the others."

"Okay, okay," Al's voice drops to a soothing, diplomatic tone. "Unlock the door and we'll take a look at your boy. If what you say is true, he needs to be checked out by doctors. You have my word on that, Frank."

Shaking now from anguish and rage instead of fear, I step back toward the door. Al and his mob believe my son is a mindless monster deserving of nothing more than a bullet through the brain. And like all the so-called specialists and CDC witch doctors, he doesn't even have the guts to come out and say it.

I remove the handgun from my robe pocket and cock it. On the other side of the door, I hear Al grab the doorknob eagerly, thinking the *click* is the door's deadbolt being retracted.

I fire once, point-blank. Al screams and I hear a body fall. Shouts follow. A shadow crosses the picture window and I fire twice, shattering glass. Richie screams and falls.

Someone opens fire on the house. Splinters of wood explode from the door. A bullet drones past my right ear and an invisible hand tugs at the hem of my bathrobe. A flaming bottle pinwheels through the gaping hole in the window. It smashes against the coffee table and sprays liquid fire across the sofa and carpet. From beyond the kitchen, a hollow booming and metal screech as the garage door is breached with ball-peen hammers and axes.

I turn and flee up the stairs, hearing more shouts and gunfire. At least they've stopped beating against the door.

Upstairs I burst into Andrew's room and bolt the door shut, breathing in great huffs of air like an asthma victim having an attack. Andrew is struggling to sit up, his eyes wide and alarmed. I can't begin to imagine what my face looks like. I unstrap him and set him on the floor behind me.

Grunting with the effort, I pry loose the plywood panel covering his window and peer out. The lawn below is a sea of bobbing lights. A shout goes up and pale faces stare up at me. I duck, but no one fires. After a minute I peer down again.

Several men are lighting crude torches and tossing them through the shattered living room window. They're not going to drag us from the house and chance eating a bullet. They're simply going to burn it to the ground.

For God knows how long I can only stare out at the milling people on the lawn, hypnotized by fear.

Then the smell of smoke begins to fill the small room. I strip the sheet off Andrew's bed and stuff it into the crack below the door. Still, it isn't long before the air turns acrid and I start coughing.

For a moment I entertain a fantasy: *I see myself pluck Andrew up from the floor and tuck him under one arm like a Hollywood firefighter. I unlock his bedroom door, ignoring the searing heat lapping at the other side, and force it open. Dodging crackling walls of flame, I carry him down the steps and navigate the fire-engulfed house to the garage. We pile into the Taurus, Andrew curled in the back seat and me behind the wheel. I key the engine and we rocket through the remains of the garage door in an explosion of plastic and metal, scattering men like bowling pins as we roar off into the night—*

But that's strictly Ambrose Bierce "Incident at Owl Creek" bullshit. The house is going up like a Roman candle and a mob of armed men surround it.

Suddenly the exhaustion hits me and all the strength drains out of my legs like water. I feel a deceptive, defeated calm. There are five shots left in the pistol. Better a quick bullet than the agony of fire.

I can hear the inferno below us, consuming the house and the last remnants of our old life. The floor is growing hotter, beginning to smoke.

I sit beside Andrew and draw him into my arms, resting his head against my shoulder. My hand is shaking so bad I almost drop the gun. Then my son's expression registers and it falls to the floor with a clatter.

Andrew is looking at me. Not *through* me. His small, sad eyes are filled with confusion, like those of a child that has just awoken from a long, fitful sleep. In that galvanizing instant every atom of my being cries out with joy that the long-awaited connection has finally been made.

"Daddy?"

And in the next, the house collapses around us.

Sign of the Times
JOHN GROVER

Monroe Massachusetts Daily Gazette
Excerpt from page 5B:
Public Awareness Editorial

TODAY MARKS the one-year anniversary since the horrible accident at the Brickner Laboratories that unleashed the plague. This airborne virus spread wildly across the United States bringing the recently dead back to life. The undead stalked and killed many citizens creating even more victims like themselves.

With official orders from the President, the National Guard, along with armed swat teams, contained this unholy threat, ridding the country of most of the walking dead. Some managed to escape the martial efforts but were seen as little threat as public awareness of the epidemic grew and Americans took the necessary precautions to protect themselves.

Today very few of these walking threats have been spotted but undoubtedly there are a few that remain among us. Although the virus is no longer spreading, the dead still rise. Anyone who dies presently rises and attacks the living. For this reason it has become common practice to see brick fireplaces or cremation fires in the backyards of most American homes.

A new law has been formed that states any human being in the United States, be they friend, relative or family member, who passes on must be burned and cremated within the hour. This is of the utmost importance, citing the hazardous implications that may occur. Government and church officials have bestowed the right of family to give their loved ones the last

239

rites in the case of death and properly dispose of the body.

Funerals as we know them have become non-existent. It is now commonplace to witness a family quietly praying in their backyard as they place a white sheet wrapped form into a fiery resting place.

Today, as of nine am, restoration of the Brickner Laboratories has begun. The first layer of foundation has been poured as the work crews ready to frame the new building.

∞∞∞⊖∞∞∞

Virginia sighed before crumbling the newspaper and tossing it into the kitchen trash bucket. Standing in front of the sink, the faucet dripping sporadically, she stared out into the backyard. Her eyes traced the brick structure that loomed at the far end of the yard, poised just before the wheat fields that seemed to stretch on forever.

Richard had it built six months after the plague-virus struck the country. Just in case, he said. You never knew when it would be necessary. Better to be prepared than be stupid. Was that movement in the field? Had there been a glimpse of something, a shape, a shadow, sluggishly pushing through the wheat? Perhaps one of them, searching mindlessly, lumbering with primal response, propelled by basic motor functions with a single desire; destroy anything alive.

Virginia wasn't sure and honestly, she didn't care. To her right a strainer full of stainless steel pots sat drying. She caught her reflection in them as she turned to leave the sink. Her auburn hair was streaked with gray and the bun she tied it back with was becoming unraveled. Strands sprung from every side of her head and most times she would be aghast with this but now, it wasn't worth the effort.

Bags wore heavy beneath her blue eyes and there was a sadness in them, that of a life gone by, of a world gone to hell. She was tired, tired of it all.

Her thin hands took hold of the yellow apron she wore and rubbed it swiftly. Removing the apron, she threw it over the pots and pans, hiding the image of herself she could no longer bear to see.

"Ginny!" Richard called from the parlor.

His voice grated right through her and she shuddered slightly when she heard it.

"Where's my iced tea, babe?" he bellowed. "You know I need one with my shows."

Shaking her head, she walked to the fridge and retrieved the pitcher of iced tea; the sound of the ice cubes jingling around in it annoyed her.

Handing him a tall cold glass, she sat in the rocking chair across from him. Taking a sip he grinned widely at her. "Thanks babe."

She hated that grin. Even more, she hated when he called her babe.

Twenty-two years of cooking meals, scrubbing floors, cleaning toilets, sewing torn trousers and loose buttons, bringing glasses of iced tea and hearing the words "thanks babe" in return and what did she have to show for it?

Nothing. Not a shred of fulfillment, her entire life had simply passed her by and she was tired, oh so tired. *My soul is empty*, she thought. *I am so drained. I might as well be one of them out there.*

It wasn't as if Richard was a bad man. He had never laid a hand on her or even raised his voice. There again, that was part of the problem. He was so nonchalant about everything, never growing angry, never getting riled up, never getting depressed. It was as if there was no emotion at all. Show something Goddamn it, anything! Show that you're moved by something.

If only he had wanted children. She craved to be a part of something bigger, to give a part of herself to something that would grow and bloom rather than remain in servitude to someone so occupied with themselves.

Children were out of the question. For God's sake, they might have taken some of the attention away from him. A wife's duty was to her husband he believed firmly. The subject was closed.

For another hour she sat mute in her chair, rocking steadily as Richard remained fixated on his shows. Even they were all the same, pointless and dull.

How did I marry such a boring man?

Virginia could barely stand to look at him now as her eyes tried to find something, anything else in the room to stare at.

"Babe, could I get another iced tea?"

The rocking chair stopped in mid rock, the voice drilled through her and she crinkled her nose with disdain. She had had about enough.

Getting up, she walked over to his outstretched hand and took the glass without saying a word.

Virginia stood in front of the kitchen window again and stared at the bricked furnace in the backyard. The bricks seemed to wiggle about as she watched them. She wasn't sure how long she stood there but the call finally jarred her out of her trance.

"Ginny, where's my tea?"

"Oh, it's coming," she mumbled.

She left the kitchen and walked down the hall. Into her bathroom she strolled and opened the vanity mirror before her. She avoided looking at her own reflection.

She grasped the prescription sleeping pills in her palm. She'd been using them for months now. Along with everything else she was having trouble sleeping as well.

She dropped the white powder into the tall glass, watching it dissolve. Grinding the pills actually took effort and this surprised her. Had she really grown so weak?

Handing Richard the glass she watched him grin that

sickening, mocking grin of his and returned to her chair. She waited, studying his face, his hands, every line and wrinkle on him.

The moments passed and she watched as his eyes grew heavy and his head bobbed slightly.

Her chair rocked back and forth rhythmically, it seemed like an eternity before the pills took full affect but eventually they did.

The glass tumbled to the floor, half melted ice cubes rolling across the rug. His body slumped down in the chair, his head lobbing to one side.

She smiled. For the first time in so long she smiled. For a few minutes she sat there, without saying a word. She stopped rocking and stared at her slumbering husband. Even in his sleep he was totally aggravating.

Getting up she walked back to the kitchen, catching the backyard furnace in the corner of her eye, and stepped out onto the back porch. There was time now.

She basked in the gentle breeze that stirred, watching the wheat ripple. No rush, take everything slow. "Now it's my turn to live," she said. "No one will ever know. All I have to do is drag him over to it."

Returning to the kitchen she searched the junk drawer in the far corner, finally discovering the box of long matches she'd been looking for.

She made her way towards the fireplace, clutching the matches tightly and looked down, its sooty opening like an ashen mouth yawning at her. They had only used it once, Richard insisted on roasting hotdogs in it. Just to see what it would be like. "No more orders, no more demands. It's my time now."

Bending, she began tossing pieces of wood into the furnace from the pile on the ground. From the indented shelf at waist level she grabbed the small can of charcoal fluid and squirt it generously over the wood.

With one strike the match ignited and without hesitation she launched it into the furnace.

A dull poof resounded in her ears. "I'll just say he had a heart attack. Died in his sleep. Of course officer, you know the law. I had to get him into the fire as soon as possible... No one will ever know."

Another smile drew on her face. It felt good. "My life again. Mine." The fatigue was not as bad as before. Hope was returning. She could not wait to begin her new life. For the first time in years she was actually excited about something.

As the fire roared to its start, the scent of rot drifted in the breeze, filling her nostrils.

Virginia watched the hot ash sail past her face as she heard the thrashing of the grass behind her. She turned ever so slowly—

And an undead man lunged on top of her! The two hit the ground hard.

A scream escaped as she struggled to get out from under the undead stranger. His cold hands reached around her throat, the flesh hanging off in leathery ribbons as he gnashed at her with yellow and black teeth.

Many times he tried to bite into her throat or face but she had managed to swerve away from his snapping jaws, his torn lips twisted in some perverse smile. Bracing one arm against his head, she searched the ground. She eyed the woodpile beside her and with some luck felt one slip into her hand.

With one hard swing she connected with his head, splinters shattering, fragments of flesh with them. Managing to roll him off she stood up as he squirmed on the ground.

Her breath heavy, pulse racing, she tried to regain her composure while searching for something to aid her. A single pitchfork stood on the left side of the furnace. Grabbing it with both hands she waited for him to get up. She couldn't believe it; she was actually fighting to stay alive. It felt wonderful.

The undead man stumbled to his feet, a low moan rising from him. Stammering for her, he raised his arms, his fingers wiggling like an infant begging for food.

The pitchfork plunged into his stomach, dark blood soaking his already torn clothes.

With one thrust she hurled him into the fire, letting the pitchfork fall to the ground. She ran her jittery fingers through her hair and untied it, letting it caress her shoulders.

Utterly proud of herself, Virginia began her trip back to the house. "It's time Richard, time for things to begin again, fresh and new."

The TV still buzzed in the distance as if nothing had changed. Leaning against the counter for a moment, she caught her breath. Pulling open the fridge she poured herself a glass of iced tea. Taking hearty gulps, she sighed. "Would you like some tea babe," she mocked then laughed aloud. Her palm quickly covered her lips. "Shame on you, Ginny," she giggled.

She stood in front of the bathroom mirror, after having taken a good hot shower, drying the beads of water from her flesh. This was going to be difficult. Richard outweighed her and was taller too. Physically and mentally she needed to prepare herself.

"Don't wait too long," she said. "Those pills won't last forever."

After dressing and pacing for a bit she decided to get it over with. The first thing she did when she walked into the parlor was turn the freaking TV off. What a TV junkie he was, day and night—my shows, my shows!

"Well Richard, thanks for all the years of boredom and misery. Don't worry about me; I'll be just fine. Don't be concerned with the shell of a woman that you created." *Just keep watching your shows and thinking about yourself. Yes, and thank you too for opting not to have kids, so thoughtful of you. I'm so glad I could be your drone all these years.*

"You shit," she gave him one quick slap across the face. How liberating that was. "This isn't going to be easy."

She took hold of his feet and prepared to pull when she noticed something. Virginia gazed at his chest. Why wasn't it rising?

Richard seemed not to be breathing. She knew he was a very heavy sleeper but this was ridiculous.

She let his feet drop to the floor with a thud and drew herself up to his face. She placed her hands on his chest and felt nothing. Moving to his face she noticed that it was slightly cold.

Did it really happen? No, it wasn't the right time. I must have overdosed him or something, she thought. "I don't believe it. Richard, are you really dead?" She leaned her face down onto his chest and listened for a heart beat.

Nothing.

I really did it. She thought with triumph, her ear still to his chest. *Well no matter, I still have to get you in the fire. Then it's done. How long ago did you die? Wait, Oh God, how long—*

She glanced up at the clock to see how much time had passed since his death and just then Richard's eyes opened. There was a glassy look in them, a lifelessness that permeated them as he lifted his head and bit into his wife's throat.

Her warm blood splattered his face, gushing into his mouth. Virginia's wails filled the house until dwindling away to silence.

The two tumbled out of the chair and to the floor, Richard scrambled over her body, devouring bits and pieces of her and pulling her innards out like a kid playing in the mud.

Moments later Richard shuffled out onto the back porch. His dead eyes glanced at the fire burning in the furnace at the end of the yard. Moaning softly, he turned and started towards the main street away from his home.

After an hour the quiet of the house was broken by the stirrings of clumsy movement. The porch door flung open and the undead Virginia stepped out. Finally she was able to start her new life, even if it was in death.

After, Life
JEFF PARISH

DEATH. DARKNESS. Ralph's entire world revolved around those two things. It had always been so, and he saw no reason to believe it would ever be otherwise. And yet, he expected more. He needed more. There had to be something beyond the corpse stench, the eternal night filling everything. Hadn't there been more, once…before?

Before what? He shook his head. If this had always been, how could there be a before? Ralph hammered a fist in frustration. A muffled thud answered. *Shouldn't that hurt?* But what did it mean to hurt? Memory stirred, rose and sank beneath dark waves, offering only a bright glimpse of a brown-haired woman weeping at his side. He clutched his chest and nodded. That flare of remembered agony. That was pain.

Who was the woman?

He growled and tried to lash out. Questions provided their own pain. They droned and needled incessantly, but nothing he did could drive them away.

Something kept him from venting his anger. Every blow landed on a soft, yielding surface that boxed him in on every side. His hard-soled shoes drummed top and bottom. His fists beat a steady tattoo to either side. Even his head knocked on something when he tried to sit up. No matter how hard he struck, it failed to yield more than a soft thud. He tried to weep, but no tears came.

Vanessa cried enough for us both.

248

He twitched at the thought. Vanessa…was that the woman? It felt right. Another memory surfaced. The woman—Vanessa—sobbing and begging: "Don't leave me, Ralph. Never leave me."

He could hear his own voice, frail and barely audible: "I won't."

That vow burned through him. It spoke of a world beyond the darkness. It promised him more. If only he could reach her. Roaring, Ralph rammed both feet against the top of his prison. It refused to budge. He struck it again. Again. Again. The wall creaked. He rained blow after blow until wood splintered and shattered. Flesh tore under the onslaught, but he didn't care. He felt no pain. Indeed, he felt little beyond a growing need to be out in whatever world existed beyond this box. And underneath the panic, hunger.

He found dirt. It poured inside. He clawed his way through thick, gooey earth, frantic to climb free. Hunger and alarm grew with every stroke. Vanessa's tear-streaked face filled his vision. She begged him over and over again not to leave her. She needed him. He'd promised. So he dug.

His right hand broke through first, followed by his left. He emerged and looked around. He had never dreamed of such space. A bright circle overhead spread silver light over an otherwise darkened world. Stone crucifixes and other markers surrounded him. Ralph climbed unsteadily to his feet. Now freed, hunger gnawed at him, driving him forward. His steps hurried. He stumbled over tree roots and headstones, but he had to keep moving.

Vanessa needed him. And he needed her.

Paradise Denied
JOHN L. FRENCH

THE APOCALYPSE was a big disappointment. No trumpets, no Second Coming. Maybe somewhere the forces of Good were preparing to do battle with the armies of Satan, but not in Baltimore.

All the signs had been there. Astronomers were suddenly unable to find stars that had always been in the sky. And some quasar that had been 40 million light years distant was now only 39.9 million light years from us. The scientists tried to explain it away by talking of dark matter and refinements in measurements. But the next month that quasar was just a little bit closer and more stars were gone. And then the Righteous disappeared.

It wasn't like the Fundamentalists predicted. Planes didn't fall from the sky and cars didn't crash into buildings as their operators suddenly vanished. It was more gradual. One by one, a few more each day, people just disappeared. A husband and wife would fall asleep together. One would wake up to find only the pajamas the other had slept in. A family out camping would go for a hike. They'd come to a bend in the trail with the children out of sight for just a second. The parents would be left alone. Or a man would leave his house, go back in for his umbrella and would not be seen again.

Police Missing Persons Units were so busy that they stopped taking reports. Terrorists were blamed, then aliens. The religious right had an answer, but no one listened to them. That is, not until all the children disappeared.

By the time everybody figured out just what was going on, the world's population had been reduced by twenty percent, and all children who had not reached puberty were gone. The Pope, the Archbishop of Canterbury and the chief rabbi of Jerusalem (all three newly elected) made a joint announcement declaring The End of Days was upon us.

What surprised most people was not that Judgment had occurred, but that so many had been Taken. Twenty percent? Who would have thought there were that many truly good people in the world? And they were from all walks of life, although there was a sudden and acute shortage of nurses, teachers and religious ministers. Yeah, I know, the last surprised me too. Maybe dedicating your life to God and the service of others pays off.

More poor people were Taken than rich. I guess having money gives you more time and opportunity to commit the really big sins. Prisons were emptier, by about ten percent. Says something about the legal system.

Who stayed behind? Well, let's just say there weren't that many special elections on local, state or federal levels. And those groups that had preached about and looked forward to the Rapture were more than a bit disheartened that no more of them got taken up than anybody else.

After the initial shock went away, a feeling of despair swept through the survivors. We had fought the good fight, we had run the race, and we had lost. Our souls had been weighed and found wanting. We were just not good enough.

Church attendance fell. For who could trust a minister whom God had rejected? Crime went up as the police slacked off. Why bother arresting some when all had been judged guilty? And charities collapsed as donations dried up and most of the remaining do-gooders left to do something for themselves.

The party started shortly after that, one big party that lasted for weeks. When you know that Heaven has been denied you, when there is no hope of a reward after death, why not grab all the pleasure you can? Drugs, alcohol, sex—why abstain? Adultery, theft, even murder—if you wanted to, why not? Do What Thou Will became the first and only commandment for far too many people.

Gradually, though, some sanity returned. A general religious council was called. All were invited—Catholic, Protestant, Jew, Muslim, Hindu, whatever—it didn't matter, every denomination, every faith was invited. There was a God, and He didn't play favorites. By mutual consent it was held in Jerusalem. There, Hope was again found at the bottom of the chest.

God has not abandoned us, it was decided. Those that had been Taken were the ones who at that time had found favor with Him. And they had been Taken for a purpose—to warn the rest of us that the end of the world was approaching. It was a test, to see if we could overcome our faults and weakness, to see if we could make ourselves worthy of Heaven.

We had not gotten off to a very good start. But slowly, things got better. Churches filled up again, and charities found even more donors and volunteers. And people went back to work mindful of the fact that each word said in anger, each lie told about a co-worker, each customer cheated, was a step away from Paradise.

That didn't last, either. Humanity being what it is, things soon leveled off. There were good people, better people, worse people. Mostly, there were just average people, content to live out the days they had left. With all the children gone, and no babies being born, the story of man on earth was coming to a close.

Then the dead returned.

We were ready for them. With the Taken gone and the universe growing a bit smaller every time you looked up, it didn't take a divinity degree to figure out what was going to happen next. So when the first of the undead crawled out of his grave, there were people there to meet him.

Granted, some of those people had flamethrowers, just in case. No one knew just what we'd be dealing with. Too many late night movies had everyone thinking 'flesh-eating zombies.'

No one got napalmed. The dead who emerged were more like frightened children—unsure of what was going on, unable to remember what just happened and willing to go anywhere and do anything they were told.

Camps had been set up, and those who returned were led to them. There they were photographed and fingerprinted, their identities checked against the names over the graves out of which they had crawled.

One thing we didn't know was how many would return. Would all the dead rise, or just some? Would there be centurions wandering Europe, wondering just what the Hell had happened to their perfect world and the Pax Romana? Would legions of soldiers rise up and resume fighting the wars that killed them?

It turned out that not everyone came back, just those who had died in the past ten years or so. When a final count was finally made, about the same number returned as had been Taken. Some kind of balance had been made.

It was commonly believed that the recent dead who didn't return were those who, if they'd been alive, would have been among the Taken. The ones who returned hadn't earned Heaven in their lifetime, and were sent back to try again.

One thing that no one thought of at the time was the legal issue. What rights did the Returned have? I guess that's why so many lawyers were left behind, to argue that point. In the end, a heavily conservative Supreme Court ruled that precedent held—that most rights of citizen ended at death, and unless Congress acted, it didn't matter if the dead had come back or not.

Congress didn't act. Mindful of the fact that their living constituents, the survivors and (more importantly) heirs of the deceased could vote and those Returned could not (except in Chicago, where the dead had been voting for over a century), the House and Senate did nothing.

The camps closed. Most of the Returned were taken in by family. Some just wandered from place to place. Still others found their way into the cities, where they took shelter in the poorest of dwellings and did the work no one else wanted to do.

All this had been a year ago. Back then I was cop, a good cop. At least, I thought I'd been a good cop. I guess I was, by the standards of the day. Sure, I'd planted evidence, but only when I knew my guy was guilty. And maybe at times a suspect got roughed up, but he wouldn't have talked any other way. And if somebody ran from me and I caught up to him, well, he had to get a beat down, just to teach him some respect. But I did my job—catching the bad guys and protecting the average citizen. And I never took more than I deserved, and then only when it was offered.

It was back when the big party ended. A lot of people started taking a good long look at themselves, trying to figure out why others had left and they had stayed behind. I was one of them. I remember sitting home alone. My wife and I had split and my son, well, he would have been eight this year. I remember looking at my badge and for the first time seeing the tarnish on it.

I almost quit. For a long time I wondered if the kind of cop I was could give way to the kind of man I had to become. What could I do—go private? Same job, same environment, less pay and no pension. I could give it all up and do the 9-5 bit, but that would leave me too much free time to find trouble and get in it. So I'd kept the badge, and did what I could to polish it up.

The first thing was to get out of narcotics and vice. Too many temptations. My record was good, so I was able to wangle a transfer to the Northeast Station as a district investigator. It wasn't a high crime area. A few shootings in the trouble spots, the occasional B&E in the residential areas and hold-ups along the Belair Rd. and Harford Rd. corridors.

The District Investigation Section office was set up in the old courtroom. When they moved the district courts to a central location the judge's box and prisoner benches went with them, leaving a large empty space to fill. Some cheap drywall and spackle, second hand desks and chairs from city surplus and a few computers with obsolete operating systems and it was office space.

Being the new guy, I got the desk closest to the door. That meant I'd be the person anyone coming in and looking for help would see. I got the cranks, the complainers and the kooks. I also got the people who came in with real problems, the ones who had no one else to turn to, the ones I needed to help.

I was reading reports about a B&E suspect called the Spider for his ability to get into otherwise inaccessible second floor windows when I heard laughter out in the hall. It wasn't the hale and hearty kind that comes from a shared joke told well, but rather the hard-edged laughter that comes at someone's expense. Then I heard, "Dead man walking." More laughter. After it died down, a slow, deliberate voice asked something. "Through that door, freak," the desk sergeant answered. "Office on your left. And don't touch anything. Hey, somebody hold the door for this corpse." Funny that, fear of contamination leading to a basic human courtesy.

I turned in my chair and watched as the zombie came in. He had the same deliberate gait they all did, moving a limb at a time as his conscious mind gave the orders that once came automatically. They might be up and about, but fully alive they weren't.

I stood up and waited while he shuffled over. As he did I took mental notes. He dressed well, a suit with a clean, white shirt and knotted tie. That must of taken some time, given the undead's usual lack of hand-eye coordination. He carried a briefcase, and if it wasn't for his shambling walk and grey going to white pallor, he could have been any businessman coming in to file a complaint.

When he finally got close enough, I held out my hand in greeting. His face showed what little surprise it could, then he brought up his hand and we shook, me trying not to flinch at the touch of his cold grip, him pretending not to notice. Civilities over, I invited him to sit down with a wave of my hand.

"How can I help you, Mister...?"

"Foreman," he said, his speech slow and deliberate as his mouth formed one syllable at a time. "Terry Foreman."

"I'm Detective John Scott. What can I do for you?"

"I would like you to investigate a murder."

I was ready for anything but that. Sometimes the undead will come in and try to file a theft or assault complaint. I'd have to explain to them that, being dead, they had no legal standing under the law, so technically, whatever anyone did to them was not considered a crime. Then I'd find out what happened and try to find a way to charge their assailants. Desecrating a corpse is a misdemeanor, so is robbing one. One of those charges generally sticks if brought before a liberal enough judge.

Murder was a different story, and I told Foreman that. "Not my division, Mr. Foreman. If you witnessed a murder or know of one that's been committed, I can call a Homicide detective for you."

He sat there unmoving, not saying a thing. Maybe he was forming his words. Maybe he was waiting to be told to leave.

"Give me the details," I finally said, breaking the uncomfortable silence. "I'll look into it and call Homicide myself. Now whose murder are we talking about, Mr. Foreman?"

"Mine."

This was new. I'd talked to many a murder suspect, but never a victim. And it suddenly occurred to me that a lot of cold cases could be cleared up if we could only locate the victims and ask them what I asked Foreman, "Who killed you?"

He shook his head. "If I knew I wouldn't be here."

I'd forgotten. In the post-resurrection interviews it turned out many of the Returned didn't remember their deaths, especially the sudden violent ones. And none of them remembered what happened between death and resurrection.

"What do you remember?"

"Not much of that last day. I know I had a meeting with my business partner. After that, a young National Guardsman with a nasty looking weapon was saying something about crispy critters."

I wanted to go further, but then I realized that I might be dealing with a closed case. His murder might already have been solved.

"Mr. Foreman, I am going to look into this, but first I'm going to have to pull the report. Give me you number and…"

While I was talking he reached into his briefcase and pulled out a folder. He handed it to me. It was a BPD case file, complaint number 06-4G97810. Under the number was the heading "Homicide – Foreman, Terrence."

"Where did you get this?"

He smiled, "It's one of the few rights we have left."

Of course. The Victim's Rights Bill of '03. When the City Council passed it zombie rights weren't a consideration. The bill specified that crime *victims* had the right to review their case folders. And while Foreman might not be a citizen under the law, there was no doubt he was a victim.

I opened the case folder and took a quick glance. On the first page, stamped in red, was the word "Open." That meant it hadn't been solved or otherwise disposed of. I leafed through the rest of it—police and crime scene reports, lab results, witness interviews—it looked like it was all there. I put it on my desk to read later.

"Who wanted to kill you, Mr. Foreman?"

"I can't think of anyone."

The trouble with questioning zombies is that they show little emotion. Their faces generally don't move much unless they want them to. And with a near expressionless voice it's hard to tell if one of them is lying. I fell back on one of the givens in detective work—everybody lies.

"Mr. Foreman, when I look through that folder I'm going to find two or three people with a reason to have wanted you dead. Why not save me the trouble and tell me yourself. Let's start with the obvious—wife, girlfriend?"

"Wife, we were married five years."

"And how did you two get along."

"Fine."

The answer came too quickly. I started tapping the case folder with one finger. If he were telling me the truth he'd see the tapping as a nervous gesture. If not...

"She'd been having an affair." Something showed on his face that time, a sorrow so deep it had to come out. A sadness that death couldn't ease.

"When did you find out?"

"A few days before I...you know."

"Who wanted the divorce, you or her?"

"No, we were trying to work things out."

That could be true or not. Either way, his wife was now suspect number one.

"You mentioned a meeting with your partner. How was business?" I started tapping again.

"Not good, bad actually. I'd gotten the result of an independent audit and…"

"Your partner was cheating you."

Foreman nodded. Suspect number two.

"Your partner and your wife, were they…together?"

"No, it wasn't him. She wouldn't tell me who, but it wasn't him, I'm sure."

Unknown boyfriend, number three.

I stood up with the folder and made copies. When I came back he was standing. He took his originals with his left and offered me his right. I took it, asking as I did, "your wife, ex-wife, is she…" I fumbled for the right term. Words like "alive" and "dead" are losing their meaning.

Foreman forced a smile. "She's alive, not a zombie like me."

My face must have shown my surprise, the undead don't usually use "Z" word. Foreman kept his smile. "I am what I am, Detective. Thank you for your help."

I walked him out, hoping my presence would prevent any more harassment from the desk sergeant.

It did, sort of. The uniformed Buddha behind the desk saved his comments for me.

"You were with that cadav a mighty long time, Scott. What are you, some kinda necro or somethin?"

There was a lot I could have said back. Comments about his large size, small IQ or doubtful parentage came to mind. I even thought about the ever popular "He wanted directions to your mother's house. I told him to expect at least an hour's wait and have his two dollars ready." Instead I turned the other cheek, took the laughter that came my way and went back to my desk.

I called Homicide and told them what I had.

"Foreman, Foreman," muttered the harried detective as he searched through a year's worth of computer entries. "Oh yeah, here it is. It's been dropped into the Cold Case bin. No one's really working it right now, but if you want to bring him down I can see him," I heard him paging through a calendar, "Tuesday a week."

"So soon?" I asked, not trying to disguise the sarcasm.

"Listen, Scott, I don't know what it's like up in the great Northeast, but down here in the real world we're swamped. The murder rate's been going up ever since the dead returned. Word on the street is that it ain't murder if they come back after you kill them. And you try getting a homicide conviction after the so-called victim walks into the courtroom. Baltimore juries never were the brightest, and there's always one of the twelve who can't tell the difference between alive and undead."

He rambled for another few minutes. When he paused to breathe, I made my offer. "Look, if it's that busy how about I look into it? If I get any where I'll give you a call, say, Tuesday next."

I got a "Yeah, you do that," and then he hung up.

I slipped a CYA memo into the case folder noting the date and time that I had been given permission by the Homicide Unit to investigate one of their cold cases then sat back and started reading reports.

Ten months and three days before the Righteous started leaving us, Terry Foreman was found dead in his car. The car was parked in his driveway, the motor running. Foreman was slumped over in the driver's seat, having died from a close-contact gunshot wound to the head.

Foreman's body was discovered by a curious neighbor who noticed the car idling for about twenty minutes before going over to investigate. According to his wife, Debbie (nee Lochlear), Foreman had left the house forty minutes prior to the discovery of his body.

No gun, casings or bullets were found on the scene. The Medical Examiner did recover a .38 bullet from the inside of Foreman's head. The bullet was suitable for comparison should a suspect weapon be recovered. The Crime Lab did a nice job of photographing and diagramming the scene. The lab techs also dusted Foreman's car, recovering quite a few latent prints, all of which were matched with Foreman, his wife, the neighbor and the first officer on the scene.

The area was canvassed and of course, no one heard or saw anything. Foreman's wife and business partner were both questioned, routinely it seems, with no mention of either infidelity or embezzlement. But then, that's not the sort of thing one brags about to police investigating a murder.

Updates filed one, two, three and six months after the murder reported little progress in the case. The last update listed "solvability" as "poor," and recommended that the case be placed in the "Pending" file to wait further developments.

There were none, not until the dead returned and one of them walked into my office.

I started with the wife, the ex Mrs. Foreman and now Debbie Lochlear. She'd moved out of the Hamilton duplex she'd shared with her husband into a pricier Perry Hall condo. Perry Hall was in Baltimore County and out of city jurisdiction, but I was only going there to chat, this time at least.

I'd called ahead and she was expecting me. So when I rang the bell she buzzed me in right away.

"Ms. Lochlear," I said when she opened the apartment door, "I'm Detective Scott." She let me in and offered coffee. I took a cup and we sat at the kitchen table and talked.

"You said you had some information about my husband's death?"

"Yes, Ma'am. I've been asked to reopen the case."

"By who?"

"Your husband."

"But I'm not married... Terry's back?"

She was genuinely surprised. I looked at her hard, trying to find some guilt or fear but came up empty.

"He's back," I told her. "You didn't know?"

She shook her head. "I knew it was possible, but thought maybe he'd call. When he didn't, I thought that he'd been one of those that...didn't come back."

"How did you and Terry get along?"

It must have been the way I asked the question, because right away she said, "He told you, didn't he—about the affair?" I nodded and let her continue. "It was one of those things. Terry was a good man, the best. He loved me dearly, gave me everything. But he wasn't—exciting. One day I decided that I needed some excitement and went out and found it. Terry was never supposed to find out."

"But he did."

Her "Yeah," came out like a curse, and her following words grew bitter as she came near tears. "Someone who knew us, a 'good friend' of ours, saw me with my boyfriend one day. I guess we were being a bit obvious. Anyway, he thought Terry should know, so he told him. That night he when came home, Terry asked me about it. I never was a good liar."

"How did he take it?"

"Sat there and cried like a baby. Blamed himself for not being what I needed. We talked and I said all the right things, the things he needed to hear. Told him I'd end the affair, that I'd make it right between us again."

I halfway believed her. She might have just been someone who made a mistake. We all make them. But then she might just be telling me "all the right things" hoping I'd believe her like her husband did. "Did you make it right?" I asked.

"I would have tried, but Terry was killed a few days later."

We sipped our coffees for a few minutes, then Debbie asked, "When you talked to Terry, what did he say happened that night?"

"He doesn't remember." Did a look of relief pass across her face? It was time to play bad cop.

"Ms. Lochlear, what was your lover's name?"

"I don't think Frank had anything to do with it?"

"Frank?"

"Chavis." She gave me the address she had for him. "But he didn't do it."

"Why not? You were his. You might have told him you loved him. He didn't want to lose you. With Terry out of the way..." I let that hang and changed direction. "When your husband died, you got the house, the bank account, everything. Right?"

"Yes, but..."

I interrupted. "And Terry was well insured, he was that kind of person, double indemnity for 'accidents' like murder."

She caught on. "I did not kill my husband." No tears now. The eyes that glared at me were clear and hard.

"Someone did. Somebody put a gun to his head and pulled the trigger. Why not you or Chavis? You both got something out of it. He got you and you got," I looked around the room, "a condo in Perry Hall."

She called me a name, one I'd been called before. "I did not kill my husband," she repeated. "You want someone with a reason to kill Terry, talk to his partner. Talk to Ronald Morrison. That bastard stole from Terry, then was going to leave the firm and take most of their clients with him. Terry was going to sue. He wanted to give Morrison one last chance to make it right. He had a meeting with him the night he died. He never got there. Go see Morrison, and get out of my house."

I thanked her for her time. On the way out I stopped at the door. "You never asked, you know."

"Asked what?" she said icily, wanting me gone.

"About Terry—how he was, what he was doing, that sort of thing."

For a moment she softened. "Terry's dead," she said quietly, then she closed the door without saying another word.

It was the weekend before I could do any follow-up work. A rash of B&E's in the Glenham area combined with a string of armed robberies along Harford Rd. kept us all busy. Then I got picked for a special detail.

Friday, City Hall. The first Zombie Rights rally here in Baltimore. Anyone who didn't expect something like it sooner or later hasn't been paying attention to the last 100 years of American history.

I got "volunteered" as part of the security taskforce, to make sure the prominent undead brought here from other cities weren't killed—again. It had happened in other places, one speaker shot by a sniper, two more blown up in a car. It didn't stop the cause, only slowed it down while everyone waited for the deceased to come back from wherever the newly dead go these days. The terrorism backfired. Nothing feeds a cause like martyrs, and having living (sort of) martyrs makes the cause stronger still.

There was the usual rhetoric—Zombies should give up their old identities and adopt "post-existence" names. There was a call for a Zombie Nation, where the undead could dwell in peace. Even the name "Zombie" was attacked as insulting, a slur based on beliefs fostered by horror fiction and the movies. "Revenant" and "Non-breathing American" were the best replacements offered.

Scattered among the above were some ideas about basic human rights—freedom from harassment, fair housing and employment, the right to vote and own property. Petitions were passed around asking the State of Maryland to grant citizenship to the undead. I signed one. As one living speaker pointed out, zombie rights were in everyone's interest. You may not benefit now, but when you die and come back you will.

The rally broke up about eight. We were released at nine, after the last of the stragglers left City Hall Plaza and any threats of violence were reduced to the normal dangers a Baltimore night has to offer.

Since I was already downtown, I decided to do some work on the Foreman case. Debbie had given me an address for Frank Chavis. A phone call when I go back to my desk the day I talked to her told me that Chavis had moved on. A few calls later I had traced him to his last official place of residence—111 Penn St, the City Morgue. He had died almost six months to the day after Foreman passed on. Drinking had killed him. That and the tree he hit doing sixty with a 0.24 blood alcohol content.

Chavis didn't have a fixed address. According to government records, he was among the last to leave the containment camps set up to welcome the dead back to this world. When no one came for him, they asked him his city of origin, and when he said "Baltimore," they gave him twenty dollars and put him on a bus headed for the Trailways Travel Plaza. In life Chavis had a history of alcohol-related arrests and problems. Figuring that old habits die hard, and that some come back with you, I decided to check out the zombie bars.

It says something about Baltimore that it's only a short walk from City Hall to the notorious Block. Back in the Fifties and before, the Block was Baltimore's only tourist attraction, the only reason for a businessman to stop in the city on his way north or south. Back then, the Block was really three or four blocks long, and its strip joints and burlesque houses were famous nationwide. Blaze Starr's Two O'Clock Club was on the Block, and at the Gayety one could watch the legendary Ann Corio and Irma the Body take most of it off.

It changed in the sixties, with "free" love and increasing nudity in the movies. Fashion changed too, and by the Eighties one could see more female flesh on the beach at Ocean City than Miss Starr ever showed on stage. Videotapes and DVD's brought adult movies into the home, and camcorders let people make their own. By the Nineties the Block matched its name, having being reduced to that size, the once proud theaters now cut up into liquor stores, small video shops and strip clubs where under-aged girls dance listlessly on stage and middle-aged hookers hustled drinks to a tired disco beat.

Nothing happens in this world that someone doesn't try to make money from it. The Block had revived since the return of the dead. It was still the same size, but the entertainment had changed.

The strip clubs were still there, but now the banners out front proclaimed "Dead Girls Live!" and "The Naked and the Dead!" The bars were a mixed lot—some were for still breathing patrons, who paid for the novelty of having shuffling deadmen bring them their drinks. (And where every night some drunk loudly proclaimed, "Hey, I didn't order a Zombie," then laughs like he was the first to tell the joke.) Other bars catered to the undead crowd, where the Returned could be among their own kind. When one of the breathing mistakenly enters these places, they're stared at by pairs of cold, unblinking eyes until they feel uncomfortable and leave. It was in one of these that I found Frank Chavis.

It was called The Horseshoe Lounge. If there was a reason for the name it was lost three owners ago. The bar wasn't on The Block proper, but rather halfway down on Gay St. It was the third place I tried that night and I was tired. If Chavis wasn't there I'd give it up and start again Monday. I stood in the doorway to let my eyes adjust to the dim lighting then walked over to the bar.

Unlike his customers, the bartender was still breathing. No surprise there. These days almost any skilled profession requires a license, one of the requirements for which is that you have to be alive.

"Beer, please," I ordered once he decided to pay me some attention.

"No beer," he replied mechanically, 'Just the hard stuff."

"Ginger ale then." I knew how hard they served it in these places.

He put a small glass in front of me. "Five bucks."

"For soda?"

"A drink's a drink, and drinks here are five bucks." I put a bill on the bar. "No tip?" he asked.

"Maybe," I showed him a photo of Chavis. "Know this guy?"

He knew him. I could that by the look on his face as soon as he saw the picture. Would he tell me? That was the question.

"Maybe. Why should I tell you?"

I flashed my badge. "Because I said please." I was hoping the power of the badge would be enough. It was too late and I was too tired to think of any believable threats.

I didn't have to. He nodded toward a corner. "First booth. What about my tip?"

"Don't charge so much for drinks." I went over to where Chavis was sitting and stood by the booth until he looked up at me.

"Detective John Scott." I showed the badge. "Frank Chavis?"

"I used to be." He waved me to the opposite seat. "Chavis was my warm name. I'm Frank Thanos now. How can I help you, Officer?"

"I'm investigating the murder of Terry Foreman. I believe you knew his wife."

He filled a glass from a bottle of the hard stuff, then offered to cut my ginger ale. I declined. He took a drink, filling his mouth then pausing to swallow.

"Debbie," he said, putting his glass down. Whatever he thought of her was lost in the flatness of his voice. "They say you always remember your first. Debbie was my last. Not everything rises from the dead. I'm a stiff in everyway but the one that matters." He looked down at the bottle. "The only vice I have left, and it has to be at least 180 proof before I feel any kick." He looked back up at me. "You think I killed Foreman?"

"Did you?" I asked. I had a feeling he'd tell me if he did. It wasn't like I could do anything about it. The courts had ruled that crimes committed before a person's death were not punishable if he returned.

Thanos gave me a slow shake of his head. "No, Debbie was a nice piece, but not worth killing over. When she told me it was over, it was over. Plenty more out there. Of course, after Foreman died I did comfort her for a while. That ended about a week before I did."

"Debbie ever talk about it, say who might have wanted him dead?"

"Just that scum of a partner of his. Other than that, old Terry wasn't the type to have enemies. From what Debbie said afterwards, he was an all around nice guy, a church-going Christian sort. He'd have to be some kind of saint to take back a woman who did him wrong like she did."

"For the record, where were you when Foreman was killed?"

Thanos made the effort to shrug. "Nowhere near Debbie's place. Other than that, you find out, then we'll both know. There's parts of my warm life that just haven't come back yet. Anything else?"

I pointed to the bottle. "Just one, who's paying for that? You got a job?"

"Government handout, it's not much but all us cold ones get something to keep us out of trouble. Plus I got a few friends left."

"One of those friends named Debbie?"

He didn't answer, just stared straight ahead. When I got up he was still staring. I left him to his liquor and memories of warmer days.

Despite his denials, Thanos still could be the killer. He did wind up with Debbie. And she wound up with a nice insurance settlement, some of which she could be sharing to keep him quiet. Or she could have killed Foreman herself, with Thanos knowing and not saying. I'd see about getting a court order to look into her financial records. Right after I got back from seeing Morrison on Tuesday.

"Everything I did was legal," Ronald Morrison told me once I finally got into see him. He'd been tied up in a meeting, he said, explaining the hour he kept me waiting. That hour gave me time to review what I'd learned about Morrison & Associates.

The business grew from the remains of Foreman & Morrison. The two partners had run an advertising firm, not the biggest, but it had its share of regional and local accounts. Morrison was the idea man, the outgoing glad-hander who met and woed the clients. Foreman worked behind the scenes, running the business end of things. It came apart when Morrison emptied the corporate account and filed to dissolve the partnership. He planned to start his own firm, taking most of F&M's clients with him, leaving Foreman broke and looking for a job.

"I wasn't my fault Terry made the mistake of trusting me. We each had equal access to the money. He could have cleaned me out first if he had thought of it."

"From what I heard, Foreman wasn't that kind of man."

Morrison let out a hearty laugh, the kind that comes from enjoying a good joke. "No, he wasn't. He was a good and decent fellow, the poor fool. Honest to a fault, considerate to the employees, fair with the clients. Definitely not meant for the business world."

"You used him," I said, my tone accusing him of a crime akin to murder, "to build the business, to get everything running smooth, then you screwed him over. The night he was killed he was coming to see you, to give you a chance to do the right thing."

"And I was waiting for him," Morrison said calmly. "Was surprised when he didn't show. Terry never, ever missed an appointment. Didn't hear about his death until the next day."

"Unless you arranged it."

Morrison took the accusation of murder lightly. "Detective Scott," he smiled, "I'll admit that over the last year of our partnership I slowly drained the corporate account. Terry kept the books and he wasn't a hard man to fool. However, according to my attorney I had a legal right to do so. Terry's attorneys would no doubt see things differently and he was free to sue me. He might even have won, if he had any money left to hire attorneys. So you see, I had no motive to want him dead. In fact, he had a better reason to kill me."

Morrison was so gleefully venal and proud of the way that he'd cheated Foreman that I doubted he'd killed the man. He'd want his victim alive. He would have gloated over the remains of Foreman's shattered career then thrown the man a bone, offering him a job with the new firm. If he had no other prospects, Foreman may have swallowed his pride taken it. I got the feeling that when the Lord called the next batch of us up, Morrison wasn't going to make the cut.

A week went by. In between doing the work the Department paid me to do I managed to get Debbie Lochlear's bank statements. She showed a regular pattern of deposits from her job and withdrawals from both savings and checking. She could have been giving money to Thanos, but there was no way to be sure except to follow her. I also checked on the bullet that had been dug out of Foreman's head. It had yet to be matched to a gun, nor had the Firearms Unit's computer paired it to bullets recovered from other crime scenes.

There comes a time with some investigations when you look at what you've got and realize that you're not going to get anymore. That's when you know it's time to close the case folder for good. I was at that point with the Foreman murder. I suspected that Debbie, Thanos or both knew more than they were telling, but suspicions aren't proof. Maybe it was time to admit defeat and call the real homicide detectives. I'd give them what I had and maybe they could close things out. For me, there were just too many questions I couldn't answer.

I was going over these questions yet again, looking for answers, not really wanting someone else to break this case when I thought of the big question, the one nobody had asked. I signed out a car and drove to Perry Hall.

After the last time I didn't think Debbie would let me in, so I sat in my car and waited for someone else to enter and went in behind them.

I knocked on her apartment door. When Debbie answered and saw who it was she tried to slam it shut. I was a bit faster and had my foot and shoulder past the door before she could close it. "Get out," she told me, "I don't have to talk to you."

"Just one question," I said quietly, not wanting to rouse any helpful neighbors who might call the county police. "What did you do with the gun?"

"I didn't..." she started to deny it, then looked at my face. "You know, don't you?" I nodded and she let me in.

She gave it all up—what she did, what happened to the gun, all of it. "What happens now?" she asked when she was through.

"I honestly don't know," I told her before leaving.

Foreman lived with his sister in a housing development on 33rd St, near where Memorial Stadium used to be before Baltimore's sports teams moved downtown. On the way there from the station I stopped at Lake Montibello. How, I thought, looking at the placid waters of the lake, did she get the gun past the police? They would have searched her, the cars, the house. Where did she hide it? No matter, every house has a dozen hiding places known only to its occupants. It didn't matter either that the gun was now resting somewhere at the bottom of the lake. Let it lay there. No one needed it.

Foreman was waiting for me. "You have news?" he asked, as excited as his kind can get.

"I know who killed you," I told him. We sat down. I took out a sealed envelope. "Before I give you this, what are you going to do after you open it?"

He thought a moment. "I, I don't know."

"No 'Revenge of the Zombie' plans?"

"No. I think that I just want to know."

"Good, because there's nothing the Department can do."

"Statute of Limitations?" he asked.

"Something like that. Listen, Mr. Foreman, before you open that envelope, ask yourself how badly you need to know the name, and how willing you are to forgive the person who killed you." I stood up, offered my hand. "Good luck to you," I said, meaning every word.

The big question in this case hadn't been who killed Terry Foreman. It wasn't whether or not Debbie was paying for Thanos to keep his dead mouth shut. And it wasn't why she hadn't told the police about Morrison cheating her husband. No, it was more basic than that. This is a world where the sky is falling, where the truly good have been taken away and the dead walk among us. So why in this world did Terry Foreman, a man everyone agrees was a good man, return after death? Was it because he had some secret sin, some vice no one knew about? Or was it because in a moment of weakness and despair, having lost his wife, job and future, he got a gun, put it to his head and pulled the trigger?

Debbie told me she had heard the shot and ran out to find Foreman slumped over in the front seat, gun near his hand. Even in her shock and grief, she realized that suicide cancelled Foreman's insurance. So she took the gun, hid it well and waited for the police to ring her doorbell. Later she dropped it in the lake. When the police decided it was probably a robbery gone bad, she let them think it, rather than tell the truth or trying to place the blame on Morrison.

I closed the case out as a suicide. One day someone might read the file and contact the insurance company. If so, Debbie might be in some trouble, but it's not likely.

I never saw Terry Foreman again so I don't know if he ever opened the envelope. If he did, I hope he found the strength to forgive himself, to take the second chance we've all been given to make up for the weakness that had denied us Paradise.

On the Usefulness of old Books
KIM PAFFENROTH

HE SCANNED THE BINOCULARS along and counted them again. On the length of fence they were responsible for watching this morning, there were only twenty-seven. Four years after the initial outbreak, their clothes were faded and shredded, and the owners weren't in much better shape—digits and ears and eyes missing, toothless mouths hanging open, barely able to moan anymore. In the summers there would be hundreds outside, and they'd have to go up to the fence and shove spears through, stabbing the dead in the foreheads and eyes in order to thin them out, lest they break through the fence with their sheer weight. But now it was autumn, and the nighttime cold was slowing the dead down, so that fewer and fewer new ones showed up at the fence each day. Soon it would be cold during the day as well, and the dead would stop arriving at the fence entirely, so the living could venture outside their compound again to gather supplies. They would also take the killing past the fence and catch the dead out anywhere they could find them. He couldn't say he exactly enjoyed it, for it was hard and dirty work, but he did smile at the prospect of going outside the fence. His smile had the slight downturn of a sneer at the irony that the living were now most active during the night and the winter, times when people used to huddle inside and hear tales of the undead and other monsters.

"What are they, dad?" The man looked over at his son, eleven years old, who had again asked this rather obvious and wholly unnecessary question. The man's smile softened to the quizzical and bemused one he usually turned on his son at times of such pointless questioning. The boy looked exactly like him—same hair and eye color, same nose and chin, same gaunt build. But the boy would always have his mother's mind, a mind insatiable for questions, especially ones that seemed to have an obvious answer, but which both of them would always push further and further, never ceasing to look for what they were so certain was there—the hidden, truer meaning under the obvious, surface answer. As much as he had loved both of them, it was maddening at times, for he had long since learned that some questions were better left unasked, and many more were better left unanswered. He'd learned that long before the dead rose, and that particular phenomenon had only driven the point home in the most vivid way imaginable to him.

His remembrance of the boy's mother wiped the smile from his face, but he kept his reaction just to that, as he almost always kept his emotions under control in front of the child. At the beginning of the outbreak they had fled north, as far as they could go. Given what they heard on the radio, it hadn't been the worst choice of action. It had prolonged their lives past the initial, universal, and unimaginable carnage of cities being overrun by the living dead. But "not worst" and "good" were two totally different things, and that first winter had nearly killed all three of them anyway. The boy's mother had died in March, even as things were beginning to thaw and melt; she had been so painfully, so maddeningly close to surviving. He'd tried to cut their rations to the point where they'd last until the spring, but it had left them all too weak and susceptible to disease and she had died. He had been pretty sure at that point—and was now completely convinced—that there was no hell worse than the one they were in now. Nonetheless, he was equally sure that there were still some things that one simply never did, no matter what—if not for fear of hellfire, then just out of some sense of primal, ineradicable pollution. He therefore had decided that he would feed the boy only the remaining, regular rations, while he would take upon himself the internal torment and sickness of eating the other sustenance that had become available with her death. The two of them had survived that way, but he had known there was no way they'd make it through another winter like that on their own, so in the spring they had started moving southwards until they arrived at this community of survivors.

That other unpleasant remembrance he wiped from his mind as quickly and cleanly as he had the smile from his face, and he finally replied, "Son, I keep telling you: they're just dead people."

The boy's eyes were defiant, and he knew that, although exactly like his own, they would always sparkle with a fierce intellect that he had never had. Like any parent would, he often wondered what the boy would've become, if things hadn't changed, and he had tried out all the usual answers that proud parents would've given in that other world—doctor, scientist, president, Academy Award-winning director. But today a different answer came to him, and with an unnerving, breathless clarity that few other than religious mystics ever experience: the man knew—not wondered or hoped, but *knew*—that the boy would've been a prophet, though the man barely knew what that meant in any world other than a made up one of gods and priests. But he knew, somehow that the boy would've railed against injustice, and ignorance, and hate: the fire in the boy's eyes and the vehemence with which he now spat out his words left no doubt.

"I know that, Dad, but why do they walk around? Why do they try to kill us? Why do we have to go out and kill them? The books we have, that we read in class, they don't talk about that. I remember when Grandpa died, when I was really little, and he didn't become one of…them. When someone dies, they lie down and they stop moving. It isn't right."

The man drew his breath in slowly and deeply through his nose and felt the cold tingle, while the boy was practically panting in frustration and rage. He thought to himself how the boy would, in just a few more years, have spent more time in the world of the undead than he had in the previous one. It would be his "normal," his "regular," in a way that it could never be for his father or any of the older people. As sad as it seemed—to grow up and live in such a world—the man was almost happy for that, because he thought it might make it easier for the boy.

"I don't know, son. It just started happening one day. No one knows why. But they're still just dead people."

The boy drew himself up and back, and calmed a little. His eyes narrowed. "Mr. Grosvenor says it's because God is angry with us. He says the people out there are damned, and we will be too if we don't believe in God and do what He says."

Now it was the man's turn to spit out words. "What God says, or what Grosvenor says?" Yes, the boy was just like his mother, all right. He knew just how to push his buttons. Get your Dad to admit he doesn't know the answer to something, then tell him that someone else does. Oh, and the someone else who does know the answer—he's someone you know your Dad doesn't like. Hates, is more like it. The kid was a real button pusher. "Grosvenor is a sanctimonious asshole," the man growled as he shook his head.

Now it was the boy's turn to sneer. "A sanctified…a what kind of asshole?"

There was a certain amount of reconciliation and satisfaction that could now be gained by father and son laughing together, and the man was glad for that. "It means he doesn't know what he's talking about, and he judges other people too much."

"So, does that mean that God isn't angry?"

The man kept looking at him. "No, I guess I'd say that He is. What do you think?"

They started walking back towards the edge of the roof, away from the enclosure they had been in—a kind of blind made out of cubicle partitions that had been built on the roof of one of the perimeter buildings of their compound. The area had been an industrial park, so the buildings were sturdy and defensible—many without windows—and surrounded by a cyclone fence. The man had been told how, before they had gotten there, the battles with the dead had been fierce. But now they lived a fairly stable existence, with the outer fence secure and covered over with paper or fabric, so that the dead couldn't see them moving around within the compound. The roofs of some of the buildings had these little blinds, so they could observe the dead outside the fence and monitor their numbers and activity.

"Yeah," his son agreed, "I think He probably is." He looked sideways at his father and smiled a little more. "But I still think you're right about Mr. Grosvenor."

The man grinned and playfully punched the boy's shoulder. They climbed down the aluminum ladder to the ground. "You looking forward to going outside?" When things froze hard in a few weeks, the boy would go outside the compound with him for the first time.

"Not really. I don't know. I guess. I want some more books."

More questions needed more books, that raised more questions, that needed more books; it seemed as though it would never end. On the whole, however, he deemed it a worthier goal than booze, candles, and matches, which were what he'd be looking for.

∞∞⊙∞∞

Spiking Day arrived early that year. It was the only holiday on their rather circumscribed and grim yearly cycle, and it had no set date. It was simply declared after a week had passed in which no new zombies showed up at the fence that surrounded their little compound. Then the people of this little outpost could go outside and kill all the dead who were pressed up against the fence. The celebration of the holiday was exactly as its name implied: they would walk up to the more or less helpless dead, who could still flail about clumsily but defenselessly, and drive a spike through each of their heads. They couldn't afford to waste bullets. Any dead who were still slightly more active could be spiked at a safer distance using spears, as were any who blocked the gates. They would then drag the bodies some distance away, dump them in a pit— which was now the same one, used over and over at the beginning of each winter—and set them ablaze. Any who looked like they might have more fat would go on top, so the grease would drip down and help the fire: again, no waste was possible, and fuel was as important as ammunition. Not since the days of human sacrifice on Incan step-pyramids and Celtic moors, thousands of years past, had there been among humans a more horrible and dichotomous celebration, as the people celebrated the beginning of the season in which they would be relatively safe from attack and would be able to gather food and eat with much greater abundance than they could during the lean months of summer and autumn. It was the equivalent, in their world, of what Easter or Passover or any springtime celebration had once been in saner times. But their celebratory acts were not hiding eggs or dancing around a maypole. Instead, they built the unholy, obscene edifice of an enormous pile of burning human bodies, a hideous inferno that went on for hours, accompanied by the sickening sizzle of fat, the pop of eyeballs and various vesicles, and the oppressive stench of the smoke that roiled over them, hanging low like a shroud to hide their shame and joy from a God who could neither understand or lessen their pain.

Even in their world, however, there was some sense of decency, and the smallest children were shielded from the details or the full and personal experience of Spiking Day. This winter, that would change for his son. The man didn't really think that it'd be that big of a deal: the boy had seen the fire from a distance and had smelled the awful smoke. There were certain details, however, that he still dreaded explaining to the boy, all because he knew his rapacious intellect and the un-answerable and never-ending barrage of questions that would ensue. But as they prepared to go outside, he looked at his son in profile, and the boy's resolute features—looking today in the bright autumn sun much more like his dead mother's than they usually did—together with his calm, pierc-ing, hazel eyes, somewhat reassured the man that it would be all right.

Some of the men speared enough of the dead to allow the gates to be opened and everyone tumbled out to begin the horrible work of their joyous celebration. The first round of spiking was done with care and speed, without a sound on either side—neither a shout of triumph from the living, nor the usual moan from the dead, as though the dead were as willing and content to die as the living were eager and resigned to kill. As the bodies piled up and the writhing and tottering dead were driven further back, some people began dragging the bodies to the pit. The man and his son began this work, and he watched the boy carefully, as he knew this was actually the more horrible and unnerving part, because this was usually when one made the more graphic and nauseating observations of ravaged human anatomy. It was bad enough to drive a rusty spike into the head of what looked like a little girl. It was far worse to go to pick her up, as gently and respectfully as one could now, and have her arm tear off in your hands and her head roll away on the ground. That was guaranteed to have a two-fold effect, one bodily, one spiritual. First one would usually vomit uncontrollably—for this reason, Spiking Day was also the only fast day on their calendar, in a year with little enough eating. And then one slowly, fully, and forever after realized the full weight of how much one had violated and victimized a monster that somehow remained partially and painfully human.

One also noticed little details that were normally overlooked when fighting and killing them—the fine features still recognizable on a woman or girl, the remnants of pretty jewelry or clothes, bespeaking happier times. Finally motionless and without the horrible spasming of their minds and muscles that drove them on to fight and struggle like rabid animals possessed by every demon from hell, even their flesh seemed to look more natural, less decayed, and even, perhaps, as though it might once have been beautiful. But, of course, the irony was that when they stopped moving and they looked the most human and vulnerable and potentially beautiful, then it was time to throw them on to the fire like pieces of rotten trash. The man stifled a grim smile at this thought, out of some residual respect for the dead and not just concern for the boy, who couldn't see most of his face under the kerchief he was wearing over his nose and mouth, like everyone else that day.

It was not quite time for their immolation, however. There was one last rite to be performed, one last indignity to be committed. The dead were to be searched and anything of value still on them was thrown in a cart, to be sorted and distributed later. Four years of wandering around outdoors had left the dead at this point with very little that could be of use to the living, but even now there were enough useful surprises that the tradition stood. There was still the occasional tool, knife, pair of eyeglasses, or even handgun to be found, so that they couldn't risk throwing it all to the fire. There was little room for sentimentality or reverence in their lives in general, and Spiking Day could be no different. He watched his son go through a dead man's pockets, producing a small screwdriver and pocket-knife and tossing them into the cart.

"Good boy," the man said. Then he and the boy grabbed the corpse's wrists and ankles, dragged it over to the pit, and tossed it into the flames below.

As they walked back to do the same to another, they went past the cart full of found objects. "That's why they call it Canada, huh?" the boy asked matter-of-factly.

"What?" At first, the man could make no connection with what the boy was saying. The boy was standing next to the cart, and he looked back and forth between the objects and the flames a few yards away. The man followed his gaze and understood what the boy had realized. Before he was allowed to come out on Spiking Day, the boy would've done his part inside the compound, sorting the things that came there in the carts, and putting the objects into the storage area they called "Canada." Some wag had named it that, and the man was more grateful for the kerchief, as it concealed his crimson blush at his son's discovery of this cruel and insensitive joke. But what could they do? Black humor was the only kind they had.

"You were reading a history book?" he said, very quietly.

"Yes," the boy hissed, barely audible over the roar of the fire, as his gaze turned defiant. The man had noticed this was his more frequent reaction to such horrors; he suspected it was better, in the long run, than sorrow or confusion. The boy must have read that "Canada" was the nickname of the area in Auschwitz where they gathered all the goods confiscated from the millions of people murdered there. "Mr. Grosvenor says the Jews deserved to die, that's why the Germans did it." Mr. Grosvenor taught the kids history and social studies, since he had been a schoolteacher before the dead rose. The man tightened his fists when he thought how they had now perpetuated Grosvenor's evil foolishness far beyond the death of the old world. He hoped that their punishment for such lack of wisdom and foresight did not go beyond inconvenient conversations like the one he was now forced to have.

The boy was baiting him, daring him to come up with a better, saner explanation. The man's eyes narrowed. "Oh, they did? So, did these people deserve to die and be thrown in a fire, too?"

"Mr. Grosvenor says so. He says the zombies are Satan's army and they killed all the Jews and Muslims and atheists first, and if they ever break in here, it'll be to kill all the bad Christians we have in here, and anyone who tries to protect them." The boy had a disconcerting ability not to blink at times.

"Satan's army" was vintage, Grosvenor foolishness, as if this poor band of rotting imbeciles qualified as such a thing. The rest of the analysis also sounded like the kind of idiotic, insane thing he would come up with. Of all the people not to get killed and eaten, he'd never understand why Grosvenor should be one of them. But that wasn't his choice, and even to contemplate the justice or injustice of Grosvenor's life and these people's undeath was a recipe for frustrated, impotent madness. The man also knew he couldn't just put Grosvenor down, or demand that the boy disregard his inanities. The boy had to choose. With his great intellect came great power—but far more importantly, great responsibility.

"Is that what you say?"

The boy stared past the man's left shoulder at the flames. His eyes narrowed to the point where it seemed they were shut. His jaw relaxed slightly as he said clearly, "No."

The man relaxed a little as well. He tilted his head slightly as he eyed the boy and thought how terrible it must be to have such an over-reaching intellect, one capable of grasping and being confounded at every irony and paradox—how terrible, and at the same time, how wonderful. It would be boy's burden and his gift, all his life. The man drew himself up, equally from pride as from a feeling of being humbled. "Let's finish, son," he said quietly.

They performed the rest of their duties in silence that day, and the man thought it was good that Spiking Day had come early that year.

∞∞∞⊝∞∞∞

Less than a week after Spiking Day, people started going out again for supplies and game. The nights were consistently below freezing, and there would only be a few hours in the middle of the day when any of the dead might thaw enough to pose a threat. The man and his son prepared early one morning to go to a town that had not been investigated before. The town was right at the edge of how far they could travel to and back from in one day, so they left while the eastern horizon was just glowing, peddling their bikes down the road between old wrecked cars, their breath trailing off behind them in the damp, freezing air. The man let the boy pull ahead of him and smiled at how they looked. He had always thought whenever pairs left the compound on bikes that they looked like Mormons or Jehovah's Witnesses, slowly peddling out into the cruel and uncaring world, eager and optimistic even though hopelessly outnumbered by the unbelievers. Or, as things stood now, by those who literally believed nothing at all, because they could no longer think, or feel, or believe anything ever again. And there would be no conversions on any of their trips now, just a few miserable calories gathered for the living, or a few more spikes in the heads of the unthinking dead. Still, it always struck him as funny looking.

They peddled for hours, silently and steadily. They were both panting and exhausted from their first hard exertion in months when they stopped for water and food late in the morning. They stood next to their bikes on a long stretch of road with pine forest on either side, about fifty feet back from the road surface. The grass nearer the road was less than knee high, still frosted in some places, though most had thawed in the warm sun this morning. The man ate one of the hard boiled eggs they had brought; the chickens that had been brought to the compound were one of the greatest, most life-giving of their finds. He pulled out a handful of acorns and hickory nuts from his pocket and started breaking them with a pair of pliers and handing the insides to his son. At this point in the season, most had a little white larva in them, and he wasn't quite hungry enough today to eat those—though he had done so often enough in the last four years—so he threw those on the ground. This time of year one could afford such extra-vagances, as they'd be gathering tons of nuts before the snow fell and got too deep.

They both heard the rustling at the same time, for it was distinct and nearby. They crouched and looked toward where it had come from, as the man shoved the pliers and nuts back in his pocket. There was a stand of cattails and other reeds and tall grasses right at the edge of the forest. A very light breeze was blowing over the road and toward the little marsh, so it must have smelled them. Now they could hear the moan, as the grasses swayed from side to side, more and more violently. The man pulled the aluminum baseball bat from its holder next to the bicycle's front wheel. "Stay here," he said to his son as he started to walk toward the moving grass.

The boy grabbed his sleeve. "Let me come," he said, not exactly fearfully, as he would've just the previous year. "I want to see."

The man took a step back, still eyeing the grass. "You want to see? What? You've seen them killed before. And you don't know what's in the grass between here and there. Could be one lying down. You know that's happened to people before."

"The grass isn't that tall. We'll both just keep an eye out. I've got boots on. I'll be careful."

The man hesitated again. After Spiking Day, the boy had seen pretty much every indignity that could be inflicted on the human body, so he didn't see what harm there could be in him witnessing another brutal slaying. It bothered him that the boy actually wanted to see it, but there was no telling with him what exactly was going through his head. "Okay, but stay close, and keep watching the ground and checking behind us."

As they made their way towards the marsh, they could see the arms flailing about in the grasses, and then the zombie had torn enough stalks out of the way that they could see it. The sun had warmed it enough that it could move its torso and arms, and it could moan, but its feet were stuck in the frozen mud of the marsh. It stared at them, slack-jawed, and stopped tearing at the grass so that it could reach out towards them. It had been male, but it was now impossibly emaciated from decay, with only a few shreds of clothing hanging off its pitiful frame. It looked more like a scarecrow than anything else. But, unfortunately for it and them, it was still deadly. And human. Its eyes were locked on them, and its moans grew to a crescendo as it tried to tear itself loose from its earthly shackles. The man and boy stopped and watched as it leaned to the right and every one of its stringy muscles strained to lift its left foot, but it didn't budge. The zombie went slack and mysteriously stopped moaning, as it tilted its head back and looked at the sun. Then, while still focused on the sun, it renewed its pulling on its left foot, though it didn't moan or make a sound this time, but just strained with all its strength.

As often happened when watching the dead from a safe distance, the whole loathsome, pathetic display was mesmerizing. "It's like he's worshiping the sun," the boy whispered.

"People used to," the man said without thinking. "I guess now they do." For some reason, the role reversal between living and dead seemed less ironic this time, and somehow more pleasant and even comforting.

There was a slow, quiet, ripping sound, and they watched as the zombie ripped its left leg off from its ankle and foot, which remained stuck in the mud. It tilted its head back down and tried now to lunge for them, but tottering on one foot, it just fell forward on its face, its right leg suffering the same fate as its left. "Oh, God," the man muttered as the mangled body now lifted itself up on its hands and knees and started crawling towards them and away from its own feet. He looked over at the boy, who watched with seemingly no emotion whatsoever. The man realized again the difference between the older and younger generations: the man would never get used to seeing a human body mutilated in such ways without the owner making the slightest sound or reaction, while for the boy, it was completely normal.

The zombie was covered in mud, and its hands crunched through the thin layer of ice on some puddles as it struggled towards them. "It's like in the book you gave me," the boy said.

The man was again confused. "What? What book?" He couldn't conceive of any book, anywhere, that would contain something as horrible as what they now saw, let alone anything he might have given his son or let him read.

"The one where the guy goes through hell and he sees all the dead people. Some of them are in ice, and one of them is eating someone, like they do." The man suddenly remembered that he had found a copy of Dante's *Inferno* during a foraging raid last year, and he had given it to his son, because he remembered liking the book in college. But he had assumed that the boy wouldn't read it for years.

287

The man went to raise the bat to finish it. "Wait," his son said softly. As he always did, the man waited for whatever it was the boy needed to see or think before proceeding. "He doesn't know he's in hell. He should, so he won't fight so much to stay here." The boy took a step to the left, and the figure on the ground continued to watch and crawl towards him, as the man raised the bat. "You shouldn't fight," the boy said clearly, with a tone of compassion and calm, to the thing at their feet. "It's going to be all right." The man could feel tears welling up, not for the present situation, but because his son sounded just like he had years before when he had sat at his own father's hospital bed. The dead would always be objects of revulsion to him, but he could see that his son regarded them quite rightly as objects of sympathy and concern. His son turned to him. "It's going to be all right."

He nodded, then the bat came down once, hard, and there was no way to tell if the boy's words had made the slightest difference to the one who now lay motionless before them. It would be nice to think that its final expression was one of peace and acceptance, but it could more easily and plausibly have been interpreted as defiance, or rage, or mere incomprehension. But the man knew the comfort that his son's words hard brought to him, at least, if not to his victim. "Let's go get you some more books," he said as they got back on their bikes. "I think you get more out of them than I ever did."

The Revelations of Dr. Maitland
CHARLES BLACK

"OKAY, SO YOU DON'T BELIEVE IN GHOSTS?"

Dr. Andrew Maitland stood at the window, looking at the moonlit grounds of Amicus House while his host, Roger Hilton, a businessman, sat in a comfortable leather armchair.

"Correct."

"Well, what do you think happens after we die?" Maitland asked, drawing the burgundy-colored velvet curtains closed.

"Either we get put in a box in the ground and we rot, or our bodies get cremated."

"Hmm." Dr. Maitland turned his attention to one of the paintings that adorned the study walls and shuddered. Yet, "Remarkable," was his verdict.

"What's that?" asked his friend.

"This painting." Maitland indicated the picture in question.

Hilton rose from his seat and joined his friend. "Dear God."

The painting was a nighttime scene of four figures in a cemetery. At a glance, it appeared they were grave robbers. Closer inspection revealed that the charnel defilers were something less than human; they were bestial, and disturbingly obscene. By the light of a gibbous moon the hideous creatures engaged in acts far fouler than the theft of a corpse.

"It's a remarkable piece of work, and a remarkable likeness."

Hilton grunted. "Damned grotesque, if you ask me. Do you

think it's worth anything?"

Hilton had recently inherited the house and its contents and this was his first visit to the property. Much of what he had become heir to, he had found not to his taste.

"I don't know." Maitland looked closer. "I can't quite make it out, but I think its signed 'Pickman.'"

Hilton shrugged. "Doesn't mean anything to me. You like it?

"No, I don't. I find it terrifying," Maitland paused. "And yet, I also find a certain comfort in it."

"What are those creatures, anyway?"

"Ghouls, I should think."

"Ghouls? When did you become an expert about the *Children of the Night*?" Hilton said, doing his best to mimic Bela Lugosi.

Despite his serious mood, Maitland had to laugh.

"Come on, Andrew. My impression wasn't that bad, was it?"

"Roger, the *Children of the Night* are wolves."

"Ah well...ghosts and ghouls. Vampires and werewolves." Hilton snorted in disgust. "Load of rubbish, if you ask me."

"You think so?"

"Of course I do." The businessman resumed his seat. "The undead. Is that what this is all about?"

Maitland remained contemplating the painting. "Hmm?"

"You asked me what I thought happened after we die."

"It was the fate of the soul, I had in mind."

"Oh, you mean *Heaven and Hell.*"

"There are other possibilities," Maitland said.

"Heaven or Hell?" mused Hilton. "That's a big question," he said, lighting a cigarette. "Build up the fire, would you Andrew?"

Dr. Maitland added some coal to the flames, then occupied the other armchair.

Apart from the ticking of the clock and the roar of the fire, the two men sat in silence. Hilton smoked, considering the question, whilst his friend gazed deep into the heart of the fire's flames.

Eventually Hilton delivered his verdict: "Nope. Don't believe in either."

"How about reincarnation?"

Hilton frowned. "What? The belief that we've lived previous lives?"

"Yes, that's it. The rebirth of the soul. The cyclical return of a soul to live another life in a new body."

"No, I most certainly do not." Hilton threw the remains of his cigarette into the fire. "Reincarnation, ghosts and ghoulies…all rubbish. I can't believe we're having this conversation, Andrew. Either we've had too much to drink or not enough." The businessman reached for the decanter. "How about another?"

"Um, yes, please." Maitland held out his glass for a refill.

"So, where's all this leading?" Hilton topped up their glasses.

"I've been doing some research—" Maitland began.

Hilton interrupted with a groan. "Oh, for goodness sake, Andrew, don't tell me you've been dabbling with some sort of spiritualism."

"No, not spiritualism as such."

"A world of charlatans and fools. I don't know which I despise more."

Maitland's smile was brief. "Ah, like you, there was a time when I'd scoff at such things. But that was before—"

Hilton interrupted, "Come on Andrew; it's nonsense. It must be. I mean, haven't you noticed that everyone who claimed reincarnation was someone famous? How many were Cleopatra, or a Roman emperor? Without exception, all those previous lives were glamorous or important. They've been kings and queens, or at the very least a Red Indian princess."

Maitland smiled again. "You're exaggerating Roger. But as I said, I was skeptical myself. Then a colleague told me about a patient of his who claimed to have lived previous lives."

"I don't suppose this was a *mental* patient. Was it, old boy?"

Maitland sighed. "As a matter of fact, it was."

"There you are, then." Hilton grinned.

"I would have put it down to a delusion myself, but the patient was so convincing, and quite lucid…well most of the time. He was a scientist who specialized in recondite matters." Maitland shrugged. "I was curious and looked into the matter a bit further."

"A lot further, by the sound of it."

"I read some strange books."

"Undoubtedly written by a bunch of cranks."

"Then I began to experiment with a drug called Liao."

"Liao? I've never heard of it. And I'm surprised that you have. I never had you pegged for someone who'd be seduced by this new age counter-culture. You've not been seeing some-one behind Barbara's back, have you? Having an affair with some young hippie girl?"

"No, of course not. Barbara and I are very happy together."

Hilton hastily apologized. "Of course you are. Sorry Andrew." He poured fresh drinks. "Well, tell me about this Liao stuff."

"It's an Oriental concoction known to occultists and alchemists."

"Ah, the mystic East." Hilton smirked. "So, what's it do?"

"It enables the user to travel in time—"

"Travel in time?" roared Hilton.

"Not physically of course." Dr. Maitland sighed. "It's rather difficult to explain the effect."

"Try."

"Well, I suppose the best analogy would be it's a form of

astral projection." Maitland held up a hand to forestall the comment his friend was about to make. "Roger, the how is not the important thing. The important thing is, it works. And I've found that I lived many other lives."

Hilton was about to say something about Indian princesses, but Maitland's serious expression changed his mind. He decided it was best to humor his friend. "All right, suppose I said, prove it to me? Did you bring any of this Liao down here with you?"

"No." Maitland shook his head. "You'd take it if I had?"

"Maybe, maybe not." Hilton lit up another cigarette. "You took it, and came through it unharmed, didn't you?"

"Maybe, maybe not," Maitland echoed Hilton's own words.

Hilton frowned. "Okay, so how are you going to convince me?" He cut his question short; the rest of it—the words: *you haven't gone mad*—remained unspoken.

"I'm going to tell you about an occurrence that happened when I was not Dr. Andrew Maitland, but George Prendergast, a soldier…"

∞∞∞⊙∞∞∞

Before putting it back in his jacket pocket, Private George Prendergast kissed the picture of his sweetheart Sally-Ann, wondering if he would he ever see her again.

He took out his cigarette case and lit a woodbine, then returned the case to the same pocket as the photograph, over his heart. Prendergast had never smoked before the war. But had taken up the habit after hearing how Tommy Morsan had escaped death, when a bullet meant for his heart had struck the cigarette case he carried.

Around him, his fellow soldiers were going through similar rituals, checking weapons and equipment, saying prayers. The bombardment of enemy lines had been going on for some time; it would not be long before the signal would come and they would attack.

The signal eventually came; too soon for some, not soon enough for others, and over the top they went. Charging the enemy. Charging Death itself.

A charge across a patch of muddy, rutted ground. Shell holes filled with scummy water. A desolate wasteland where nothing grew except the number of corpses. A quagmire of death. Machine guns spitting bullets. A charge into tangles of barbed wire—except it couldn't really be called a charge. The weight of the equipment the men carried combined with the treacherousness of the mud meant they moved little faster than a walking pace.

Into No Man's Land, the zone of death. Soldiers scythed down by the hail of enemy bullets. Shells exploding, hurling men hither and thither. Prendergast was unsure whether the shells were theirs, or those of the enemy. It no longer mattered to the dead men.

"Please God, don't let me die for nothing," Prendergast prayed, convinced his death was a certainty.

Prendergast repeated the mantra as he progressed towards the enemy.

An orange cloud was drifting towards the advancing troops. "Gas!" Prendergast shouted, struggling to put on his gas mask. Before he had, the force of a nearby explosion threw him to the ground. He remained unmoving, and the battle raged on.

In the distance the guns rumbled and explosions flashed, lighting the grey sky. But that was far off, the battle had moved on.

Private Prendergast realized he was still alive. He wiped his face with his sleeve, but did not notice the blood. Instead he looked around, and was sick, adding the meager contents of his stomach to the detritus of human waste that surrounded him. Bodies and body parts lay everywhere.

He recognized the mangled remains of friends and comrades. There was Private Bobby Owens, or at least his upper half. The rest of the young soldier had been blown to kingdom come. At least the lad would not be complaining about trench-foot anymore.

Others were beyond recognition.

He heard a groan—someone else was alive. *Friend or foe?* he wondered. Unsteady on his feet, Prendergast rose.

"What the bleedin' hell...!" he muttered.

He could have sworn that he saw a severed arm move, its grasping hand pulling it along.

He shook his head, rubbed his eyes, and laughed nervously.

The arm moved again, the hand clawing the mud, dragging the limb behind it.

Prendergast licked his parched lips. His *Enfield* rifle was near at hand; he wondered whether that was what the limb was aiming to reach. Prendergast crouched down and grabbed his weapon. He pounced, bayoneting the arm. The hand jerked, clawing spasmodically, then was still.

There was more groaning now. Prendergast pulled the blade free and backed away, almost falling over another body. The soldier moaned. Prendergast recognized a comrade: Dennis Trotter.

"Thank God you're alive!"

Trotter groaned; his hand reached for Prendergast.

Prendergast bent over the wounded man, shrugging off his army pack. He would not be able to carry that and Trotter back to their own lines.

"Are you hurt badly?" he asked.

Trotter's blood soaked jacket answered that question. Prendergast opened the jacket, reeled back, retching again. There was no way Trotter could still be alive with that gaping stomach wound.

Yet Trotter raised a hand and grasped Prendergast by the

throat; he began to squeeze and pull the Private down towards him.

Shock kept Prendergast momentarily frozen; then realization that a dead friend was choking the life out of him spurred the Private into action. He struggled free, and smashed the butt of his rifle into Trotter's face.

Around him, men of both sides, including Trotter, were rising slowly—men with terrible wounds, dead men. Private Prendergast began to back away.

They were closing in on him, staggering and shambling. Men that no longer breathed groaned and moaned. Some missing limbs, others with gaping wounds were spilling entrails. Staring with sightless eyes, ruined faces, one corpse entirely headless.

Prendergast watched dazed and amazed. "This can't be happening," he muttered. Hands reached out for him, but not all of them.

A Hun with his guts hanging out, grabbed, and pulled free, some of his intestines, intent on using them as a garrote.

Prendergast fired. His bullet hit the living corpse in the eye. Prendergast was amazed for two reasons. Normally he would not have achieved such accuracy even if he had aimed for the eye. Secondly, the shot had little effect—the walking dead man staggered at the impact, paused a moment, then continued its shambling advance.

"I'll be damned if I let a bunch of dead men kill me!" he shouted, stabbing and slashing his bayonet wildly.

Though bullets had little effect, his blade proved more effective.

Prendergast fought as if possessed by the spirit of a Viking berserker. Thankfully, whatever perversion of nature had caused these dead men to rise had only affected this small corner of the battlefield. Hacking and slashing, Prendergast was able to fight his way free.

The zombies continued to pursue him, moving slowly.

Despite his wounds, and the treacherous conditions of the battlefield, the Private was able to outdistance them. He would be safe in the trenches, he told himself. Realizing this he began to laugh.

But Prendergast had become disorientated in the fog of war. He did not find his way back to the safety of his own lines.

A group scoured the battlefield, perhaps searching for the wounded. They looked up at his approach.

"God almighty!" Prendergast gasped.

There was something wrong with them.

They stood hunched, lean, and grey. Whilst some wore blood-drenched uniforms, others were dressed in tattered rags, the remnants of charnel shrouds. Skin discolored, faces misshapen, snout like. Creatures of nightmare, they did not carry rifles in their hands, the talons of these scavengers held gobbets of bloody flesh. They grinned, exposing stained canine teeth.

Private Prendergast began to scream.

And then the ghouls pounced.

∞∞∞Ⓗ∞∞∞

"…And my last memory is of the charnel stench of the foul creatures, the agonizing pain as their fangs bit into me, and their claws tearing the flesh from my still-living body. My body rent apart, and the internal organs ripped free. Thankfully oblivion overcame me and I found myself Andrew Maitland once again, back in London, in the here and now of 1972."

"Good God! I've heard of the horrors of World War One, but zombies, and ghouls!" Hilton brought his fist down on the arm of his chair. "This Liao, it sounds like it took you on a particularly wild trip. Had you been watching too many damned horror films?"

Dr. Maitland ignored the question. "I can understand your skepticism, Roger...and I might too accept your verdict of drug induced fantasy. But tell me, how would you explain this?" Maitland rose from his chair.

"Explain what?"

Maitland took off his jacket. Lately he had taken to wearing black polo neck shirts, and he pulled off the one he now wore, revealing a body covered with an innumerable number of horrific scars.

Hilton gasped and stood up, a shocked expression upon his face. "Andrew, I don't know what to say. How on earth is it possible?"

"That I cannot explain. They are not self-inflicted. The bite marks do not match my dental records, and indeed, how on earth would I have been able to bite myself so, even under the influence of such a potent drug?"

"You were definitely alone, when you took it?" Hilton asked.

Maitland nodded. "Yes, absolutely. No young hippie girl."

"Incredible, incredible," Hilton muttered, shaking his head.

"There's one more thing I feel I should share with you."

"More?"

"Yes my friend. There's one last fact I failed to tell."

"Oh?"

"Forgive me, I did not inform you that the user of the Liao can not only project himself back into the past, but also forward into the future. You see, the unfortunate Private Prendergast, he was a soldier in World War Four!"

Pegleg and Paddy Save the World
JONATHAN MABERRY

I KNOW WHAT YOU'VE HEARD but Pat O'Leary's cow didn't have nothing to do with it. Not like they said in the papers. The way them reporters put it you'd thought the damn cow was playing with matches. I mean, sure, it started in the cowshed, but that cow was long dead by that point, and really it was Pat himself who lit it. I helped him do it. And that meteor shower some folks talked about—you see, that happened beforehand. It didn't start the fire either, but it sure as hell *caused* it.

You have to understand what the West Side of Chicago was like back then. Pat had a nice little place on DeKoven Street—just enough land to grow some spuds and raise a few chickens. The cow was a skinny old milker, and she was of that age where her milk was too sour and her beef would probably be too tough. Pat O'Leary wanted to sell her to some drovers who were looking to lay down some jerky for a drive down to Abilene, but the missus would have none of it.

"Elsie's like one of the family!" Catherine protested. "Aunt Sophie gave her to me when she was just a heifer."

I knew Pat had to bite his tongue not to ask if Catherine meant when the cow was a heifer or when Sophie was. By that point in their marriage Pat's tongue was crisscrossed with healed-over bite marks.

Catherine finished up by saying, "Selling that cow'd be like selling Aunt Sophie herself off by the pound."

Over whiskey that night Pat confided me that if he could find a buyer for Sophie he'd have loved to sell the old bitch. "She eats twice as much as the damn cow and don't smell half as good."

I agreed and we drank on it.

Shame the way she went. The cow, I mean. I wouldn't wish that on a three-legged dog. As for Sophie…well, I guess in a way I feel sorry for her, too. And for the rest of them that died that night, the ones who died in the fire…and the ones who died before.

The fire started Sunday night, but the problem started way sooner, just past midnight on a hot Tuesday morning. That was a strange autumn. Dryer than it should have been, and with a steady wind that you'd have thought blew straight in off a desert. I never saw anything like it except the Santa Ana's, but this was Illinois, not California. Father Callahan had a grand ol' time with it, saying that it was the hot breath of Hell blowing hard on all us sinners. Yeah, yeah, whatever. We wasn't sinning any worse that year than we had the year before and the year before that. Conner O'Malley was still sneaking into the widow Daley's backdoor every Saturday night, the Kennedy twins were still stealing hogs, and Pat and I were still making cheap whiskey and selling it in premium bottles to the pubs who sold it to travelers heading west. No reason Hell should have breathed any harder that year than any other.

What was different that year was not what we sinners were doing but what those saints were up to, 'cause we had shooting stars every night for a week. The good Father had something to say about that, too. It was the flaming sword of St. Michael and his lot, reminding us of why we were tossed out of Eden. That man could make a hellfire and brimstone sermon out of a field full of fuzzy bunnies, I swear to God.

On the first night there was just a handful of little ones, like Chinese fireworks way out over Lake Michigan. But the second night there was a big ball of light—Biela's Comet the reporter from the Tribune called it—and it just burst apart up there and balls of fire came a'raining down everywhere.

Pat and I were up at the still and we were trying to sort out how to make Mean-Dog Mulligan pay the six months worth of whiskey fees he owed us. Mean-Dog was a man who earned his nickname and he was bigger than both of us put together, so when we came asking for our cash and he told us to piss off, we did. We only said anything out loud about it when we were a good six blocks from his place.

"We've got to sort him out," I told Paddy, "or everyone'll take a cue from him and then where will we be?"

Pat was feeling low. Mean-Dog had smacked him around a bit, just for show, and my poor lad was in the doldrums. His wife was pretty but she was a nag; her Aunt Sophie was more terrifying than the red Indians who still haunting some of these woods, and Mean-Dog Mulligan was turning us into laughing stocks. Pat wanted to brood, and brooding over a still of fresh whiskey at least takes some of the sting out. It was after our fourth cup that we saw the comet.

Now, I've seen comets before. I seen them out at see before I lost my leg, and I seen 'em out over the plains when I was running with the Scobie gang. I know what they look like, but this one was just a bit different. It was green, for one thing. Comets don't burn green, not any I've seen or heard about. This one was a sickly green, too, the color of bad liver, and it scorched a path through the air. Most of it burned up in the atmosphere, and that's a good thing, but one piece of it came down hard by the edge of the lake, right smack down next to Aunt Sophie's cottage.

Pat and I were sitting out in our lean-to in a stand of pines, drinking toasts in honor of Mean-Dog developing a wasting sickness when the green thing came burning down out of the sky and smacked into the ground not fifty feet from Sophie's place. There was a sound like fifty cannons firing all at once and the shock rolled up the hill to where we sat. Knocked both of us off our stools and tipped over the still.

"Pegleg!" Pat yelled as he landed on his ass, "The brew!"

I lunged for the barrel and caught it before it tilted too far, but a gallon of it splashed me in the face and half-drowned me. That's just a comment, not a complaint. I steadied the pot as I stood up. My clothes were soaked with whiskey but I was too shocked to even suck my shirttails. I stood staring down the slope. Sophie's cottage still stood, but it was surrounded by towering flames. Green flames, and that wasn't the whiskey talking. There were real green flames licking at the night, catching the grass, burning the trees that edged her property line.

"That's Sophie's place," I said.

He wiped his face and squinted through the smoke. "Yeah, sure is."

"She's about to catch fire."

He belched. "If I'm lucky."

I grinned at him. It was easy to see his point. Except for Catherine there was nobody alive who could stand Aunt Sophie. She was fat and foul, and you couldn't please her if you handed here a deed to a gold mine. Not even Father Callahan liked her and he was sort of required to by license.

We stood there and watched as the green fire crept along the garden path toward her door. "Suppose we should go down there and kind of rescue her, like," I suggested.

He bent and picked up a tin cup, dipped it in the barrel, drank a slug and handed it to me. "I suppose."

"Catherine will be mighty upset if we let her burn."

"I expect."

We could hear her screaming now as she finally realized that Father Callahan's hellfire had come a'knocking. Considering her evil ways, she probably thought that's just what it was, and had it been, not even she could have found fault with the reasoning.

"Come on," Pat finally said, tugging on my sleeve, "I guess we'd better haul her fat ass outta there or I'll never hear the end of it from the wife."

"Be the Christian thing to do," I agreed, though truth to tell we didn't so much as hustle down the slope to her place as sort of saunter.

That's what saved our lives in the end, cause we were still only halfway down when the second piece of the comet hit. This time it hit her cottage fair and square.

It was like the fist of God—if His fist was ever green, mind—punching down from heaven and smashing right through her roof. The whole house just flew apart, the roof blew off, the windows turned to glittery dust and the log walls splintered into matchwood. The force of it was so strong that it just plain sucked the air out of the fire, like blowing out a candle.

Patrick started running about then, and since he has two legs and I got this peg I followed along as best I could. Took us maybe ten minutes to get all the way down there.

By that time Sophie Kilpatrick was deader'n a doornail.

We stopped outside the jagged edge of what had been her north wall and stared at her just lying there amid the wreckage. Her bed was smashed flat, the legs broke; the dresser and rocker were in pieces, all the crockery in fragments. In the midst of it, still wearing her white nightgown and bonnet, was Sophie, her arms and legs spread like a starfish, her mouth open like a bass, her goggle eyes staring straight up at heaven in the most accusing sort of way.

We exchanged a look and crept inside.

"She looks dead," he said.

"Of course she's dead, Pat, a comet done just fell on her."

The fire was out but there was still a bit of green glow coming off her and we crept closer still.

"What in tarnation is that?"

"Dunno," I said. There were bits and pieces of green rock scattered around her, and it glowed like it had a light inside. Kind of pulsed in a way, like a slow heartbeat. Sophie was dusted with glowing green powder. It was on her gown and her hands and her face. A little piece of the rock pulsed inside her mouth, like she'd gasped it in as it all happened.

"What's that green stuff?"

"Must be that comet they been talking about in the papers. Biela's Comet they been calling it."

"Why'd it fall on Sophie?"

"Well, Pat, I don't think it *meant* to."

He grunted as he stared down at her. The green pulsing of the rock made it seem like she was breathing and a couple of times he bent close to make sure.

"Damn," he said after he checked the third time, "I didn't think she'd ever die. Didn't think she could!"

"God kills everything," I said, quoting one of Father Callahan's cheerier observations. "Shame it didn't fall on Mean-Dog Mulligan."

"Yeah, but I thought Sophie was too damn ornery to die. Besides, I always figured the Devil'd do anything he could to keep her alive."

I looked at him. "Why's that?"

"He wouldn't want the competition. You know she ain't going to heaven and down in Hell…well, she'll be bossing around old Scratch and his demons before her body is even cold in the grave. Ain't nobody could be as persistently disagreeable as Aunt Sophie."

"Amen to that," I said and sucked some whiskey out of my sleeve. Pat noticed what I was doing and asked for a taste. I held my arm out to him. "So…what you think we should do?"

Pat looked around. The fire was out, but the house was a ruin. "We can't leave her out here."

"We can call the constable," I suggested. "Except that we both smell like whiskey."

"I think we should take her up to the house, Peg."

I stared at him. "To the house? She weighs nigh on half a ton."

"She can't be more than three hundred-weight. Catherine will kill me if I leave her out here to get gnawed on by every creature in the woods. She always says I was too hard on Sophie, too mean to her. She sees me bringing Sophie's body home, sees how I cared enough to do that for her only living aunt, then she'll think better of me."

"Oh, man...." I complained, but Pat was adamant. Besides, when he was in his cups Pat complained that Catherine was not being very "wifely" lately. I think he was hoping that this would somehow charm him back onto Catherine's side of the bed. Mind you, Pat was as drunk as a lord, so this made sense to him, and I was damn near pickled, so it more or less made sense to me, too. Father Callahan could have gotten a month's worth of hellfire sermons on the dangers of hard liquor out of the way Pat and I handled this affair. Of course, Father Callahan's dead now, so there's that.

Anyway, we wound up doing as Pat said and we near busted our guts picking up Sophie and slumping her onto a wheelbarrow. We dusted off the green stuff as best we could, but we forgot about the piece in her mouth and the action of dumping her on the 'barrow must have made that glowing green chunk slide right down her gullet. If we'd been a lot less drunk we'd have wondered about that, because on some level I was pretty sure I heard her swallow that chunk, but since she was dead and we were grunting and cursing trying to lift her, and it couldn't be real *anyway*, I didn't comment on it. All I did once she was loaded was peer at her for a second to see if that great big bosom of hers was rising and falling—which it wasn't—and then I took another suck on my sleeve.

It took near two hours to haul her fat ass up the hill and through the streets and down to Pat's little place on DeKoven Street. All the time I found myself looking queer at Sophie. I hadn't liked that sound, that gulping sound, even if I wasn't sober or ballsy enough to say anything to Pat. It made me wonder, though, about that glowing green piece of comet. What the hell was that stuff, and where'd it come from? It weren't nothing normal, that's for sure.

We stood out in the street for a bit with Pat just staring at his own front door, mopping sweat from his face, careful of the bruises from Mean-Dog. "I can't bring her in like this," he said, "it wouldn't be right."

"Let's put her in the cowshed," I suggested. "Lay her out on the straw and then we can fetch the doctor. Let him pronounce her dead all legal like."

For some reason that sounded sensible to both of us, so that's what we did. Neither of us could bear to try and lift her again so we tipped over the barrow and let her tumble out.

"Ooof!" she said.

"Excuse me," Pat said, and then we both froze.

He looked at me, and I looked at him, and we both looked at Aunt Sophie. My throat was suddenly as dry as an empty shot glass.

Pat's face looked like he'd seen a ghost and we were both wondering if that's what we'd just seen in fact. We crouched over her, me still holding the arms of the barrow, him holding one of Sophie's wrists.

"Tell me if you feel a pulse, Paddy my lad," I whispered.

"Not a single thump," he said.

"Then did you hear her say 'ooof' or some suchlike?"

"I'd be lying if I said I didn't."

"Lying's not always a sin," I observed.

He dropped her wrist, then looked at the pale green dust on his hands—the glow had faded—and wiped his palms on his coveralls.

"Is she dead or isn't she?" I asked.

He bent and with great reluctance pressed his ear to her chest. He listened for a long time. "There's no ghost of a heartbeat," he said.

"Be using a different word now, will ya?"

Pat nodded. "There's no heartbeat. No breath, nothing."

"Then she's dead?"

"Aye."

"But she made a sound."

Pat straightened, then snapped his fingers. "It's the death rattle," he said. "Sure and that's it. The dead exhaling a last breath."

"She's been dead these two hours and more. What's she been waiting for?"

He thought about that. "It was the stone. The green stone—it lodged in her throat and blocked the air. We must have dislodged it when we dumped her out and that last breath came out. Just late is all."

I was beginning to sober up and that didn't have the ring of logic it would have had an hour ago.

We stood over her for another five minutes, but Aunt Sophie just lay there, dead as can be.

"I got to go tell Catherine," Pat said eventually. "She's going to be in a state. You'd better scram. She'll know what we've been about."

"She'll know anyway. You smell as bad as I do."

"But Sophie smells worse," he said, and that was the truth of it.

So I scampered and he went in to break his wife's heart. I wasn't halfway down the street before I heard her scream.

∞∞⊙∞∞

I didn't come back until Thursday and as I came up the street, smoking my pipe, Pat came rushing around the side of the house. I swear he was wearing the same overalls and looked like he hadn't washed or anything. The bruises had faded to the color of a rotten eggplant but his lip was less swollen. He grabbed me by the wrist and fair wrenched my arm out dragging me back to the shed; but before he opened the door he stopped and looked me square in the eye.

"You got to promise me to keep a secret, Pegleg."

"I always keep your secrets," I lied, and he knew I was lying.

"No, you have to really keep this one. Swear by the baby Jesus."

Pat was borderline religious, so asking me to swear by anything holy was a big thing for him. The only other time he'd done it was right before he showed me the whiskey still.

"Okay, Paddy, I swear by the baby Jesus and his Holy Mother, too."

He stared at me for a moment before nodding; then he turned and looked up and down the alley as if all the world was leaning out to hear whatever Patrick O'Leary had to say. All I saw was a cat sitting on a stack of building bricks distractedly licking his bollocks. In a big whisper Pat said, "Something's happened to Sophie."

I blinked at him a few times. "Of course something happened to her, you daft bugger, a comet fell on her head and killed her."

He was shaking his head before I was even finished. "No... *since* then."

That's not a great way to ease into a conversation about the dead. "What?"

He fished a key out of his pocket, which is when I noticed the shiny new chain and padlock on the cowshed door. It must have cost Pat a week's worth of whiskey sales to buy that thing.

"Did Mean-Dog pay us now?"

Pat snorted. "He'd as soon kick me as pay us a penny of what he owes."

I nodded at the chain. "You afraid someone's going to steal her body?"

He gave me the funniest look. "I'm not afraid of anybody breaking *in.*"

Which is another of those things that don't sound good when someone says it before entering a room with a dead body in it.

He unlocked the lock, then he reached down to where his shillelagh leaned against the frame. It was made from a whopping great piece of oak root, all twisted and polished, the handle wrapped with leather.

"What's going on now, Paddy?" I asked, starting to back away, and remembering a dozen other things that needed doing. Like running and hiding and getting drunk.

"I think it was that green stuff from the comet," Paddy whispered as he slowly pushed open the door. "It did something to her. Something *unnatural.*"

"Everything about Sophie was unnatural," I reminded him.

The door swung inward with a creak and the light of day shone into the cowshed. It was ten feet wide by twenty feet deep, with a wooden rail, a manger, stalls for two cows—though Paddy only even owned just the one. The scrawny milk cow Catherine doted on was lying on her side in the middle of the floor.

I mean to say what was *left* of her was lying on the floor. I tried to scream but all that came out of my whiskey-raw throat was a crooked little screech.

The cow had been torn to pieces. Blood and gobs of meat littered the floor, and there were more splashes of blood on the wall. And right there in the middle of all that muck, sitting like the queen of all Damnation was Aunt Sophie. Her fat face and throat were covered with blood. Her cotton gown was torn and streaked with cow shit and gore. Flies buzzed around her and crawled on her face.

Aunt Sophie was gnawing on what looked like half a cow liver and when the sunlight fell across her from the open door she raised her head and looked right at us. Her skin was as gray-pale as the maggots that wriggled through little rips in her skin; but it was her eyes that took all the starch out of my knees. They were dry and milky but the pupils glowed an unnatural green, just like the piece of comet that had slid down her gullet.

"Oh…lordy-lordy-save a sinner!" I heard someone say in an old woman's voice, and then realized that it was me speaking.

Aunt Sophie lunged at us. All of sudden she went from sitting there like a fat dead slob eating Paddy's cow and then she was coming at us like a charging bull. I shrieked. I'm not proud; I'll admit it.

If it hadn't been for the length of chain Paddy had wound around her waist she'd have had me, too, 'cause I could no more move from where I was frozen than I could make leperchauns fly out of my bottom. Sophie's lunge was jerked to a stop with her yellow teeth not a foot from my throat.

Paddy stepped past me and raised the club. If Sophie saw it, or cared, she didn't show it.

"Get back, you fat sow!" he yelled and took to thumping her about the face and shoulders, which did no noticeable good.

"Paddy, my dear," I croaked, "I think I've soiled myself."

Paddy stepped back, his face running sweat. "No, that's her you smell. It's too hot in this shed. She's coming up ripe." He pulled me further back and we watched as Sophie snapped the air in our direction for a whole minute, then she lost interest and went back to gnawing on the cow.

"What's happened to her?"

"She's dead," he said.

"She can't be. I've seen dead folks before, lad, and she's a bit too spry."

He shook his head. "I checked and I checked. I even stuck her with the pitchfork. Just experimental like, and I got them tines all the way in but she didn't bleed."

"But…but…"

"Catherine came out here, too. Before Sophie woke back up, I mean. She took it hard and didn't want to hear about comets or nothing like that. She thinks we poisoned her with our whiskey."

"It's strong, I'll admit, but it's more likely to kill a person than make the dead wake back up again."

"I told her that and she commenced to hit me, and she hits as hard as Mean-Dog. She had a good handful of my hair and was swatting me a goodun' when Sophie just woke up."

"How'd Catherine take that?"

"Well, she took it poorly, the lass. At first she tried to comfort Sophie, but when the old bitch tried to bite her Catherine seemed to cool a bit toward her aunt. It wasn't until after Sophie tore the throat out of the cow that Catherine seemed to question whether Sophie was really her aunt or more of an old acquaintance of the family."

"What'd she say?"

"It's not what she said so much as it was her hitting Sophie in the back of the head with a shovel."

"That'll do 'er."

"It dropped Sophie for a while and I hustled out and bought some chain and locks. By the time I came back Catherine was in a complete state. Sophie kept waking up, you see, and she had to clout her a fair few times to keep her tractable."

"So where's the missus now?"

"Abed. Seems she's discovered the medicinal qualities of our whiskey."

"I've been saying it for years."

He nodded and we stood there, watching Sophie eat the cow.

"So, Paddy me old mate," I said softly, "what do you think we should do?"

"With Sophie?"

"Aye."

Paddy's bruised faced took on the one expression I would have thought impossible under the circumstances. He smiled. A great big smile that was every bit as hungry and nasty as Aunt Sophie.

∞∞∞⊖∞∞∞

It took three days of sweet talk and charm, of sweat-soaked promises and cajoling but we finally got him to come to Paddy's cowshed. And then there he was, the Mean-Dog himself, all six-and-a-half feet of him, flanked by Killer Muldoon and Razor Riley, the three of them standing in Paddy's yard late on Sunday afternoon.

My head was ringing from a courtesy smacking Mean-Dog had given me when I'd come to his office; and Pat lips were puffed out again—but Pat was still smiling.

"So, lads," Mean-Dog said quietly, "tell me again why I'm here in a yard that smells of pig-shit instead of at home drinking a beer."

"Cow shit," Pat corrected him, and got a clout for it.

"We have a new business partner, Mr. Mulligan," I said. "And she told us that we can't provide no more whiskey until you and she settle accounts."

"She? You're working with a woman?" His voice was filled with contempt. "Who's this woman, then? Sounds like she has more mouth than she can use."

"You might be saying that," Pat agreed softly. "It's my Aunt Sophie."

I have to admit, that did give even Mean-Dog a moment's pause. There are Cherokee war parties that would go twenty miles out to their way not to cross Sophie. And that was *before* the comet.

"Sophie Kilpatrick, eh?" He looked at his two bruisers. Neither of them knew her and they weren't impressed. "Where is she?"

"In the cowshed," Pat said. "She said she wanted to meet somewhere quiet."

"Shrewd," Mean-Dog agreed, but he was still uncertain. "Lads, go in and ask Miss Sophie to come out."

The two goons shrugged and went into the shed as I inched my way toward the side alley. Pat held his ground and I don't know whether it was all the clouting 'round the head he'd been getting, or the latest batch of whiskey, or maybe he'd just reached the bottom of his own cup and couldn't take no more from anyone, but Pat O'Leary stood there grinning at Mean-Dog as the two big men opened the shed door and went in.

Pat hadn't left a light on in there and it was a cloudy day. The goons had to feel their way in the dark. When they commenced screaming I figured they'd found their way to Sophie. This was Sunday by now and the cow was long gone. Sophie was feeling a might peckish.

Mean-Dog jumped back from the doorway and dragged out his pistol with one hand and took a handful of Pat's shirt with the other. "What the hell's happening? Who's in there?"

"Just Aunt Sophie," Pat said and actually held his hand to God as he said it.

Mean-Dog shoved him aside and kicked open the door. That was his first mistake because Razor Riley's head smacked him right in the face. Mean-Dog staggered back and then stood there in dumb shock as his leg-breaker's head bounced to the ground right at his feet. Riley's face wore an expression of profound shock.

"What?" Mean-Dog asked, as if anything Pat or I could say would be an adequate answer to that.

The second mistake Mean-Dog made was to get mad and go charging into the shed. We watched him enter and we both jumped as he fired two quick shots, then another, and another.

I don't know, even to this day, whether one of those shots clipped her chain or whether Sophie was even stronger than we thought she was, but a second later Mean-Dog came barreling out of the cowshed, running at full tilt, with Sophie Kilpatrick howling after him trailing six feet of chain. She was covered in blood and the sound she made would have made a banshee take a vow of silence. They were gone down the alley in a heartbeat and Pat and I stood there in shock for a moment, then we peered around the edge of the door into the shed.

The lower half of Razor Riley lay just about where the cow had been. Killer Muldoon was all in one piece, but there were pieces missing from him, if you follow. Sophie had her way with him and he lay dead as a mullet, his throat torn out and his blood pooled around him.

"Oh, lordy," I said. "This is bad for us, Pat. This is jail and skinny fellows like you and me have to wear petticoats in prison."

But there was a strange light in his eyes. Not a glowing green light, which was a comfort, but not a nice light either. He looked down at the bodies and then over his shoulder in the direction where Sophie and Mean-Dog had vanished. He licked his bruised lips and said, "You know, Pegleg…there are other sonsabitches who owe us money."

"Those are bad thoughts you're having, Paddy my dear."

"I'm not saying we feed them to Sophie. But if we let it get known, so to speak. Maybe show them what's left of these lads…"

"Patrick O'Leary you listen to me—we are not about being criminal masterminds here. I'm not half as smart as a fencepost and you're not half as smart as me, so let's not be planning anything extravagant."

Which is when Mean-Dog Mulligan came screaming *back* into Pat's yard. God only knows what twisted puzzle-path he took through the neighborhood but there he was running back toward us, his arms bleeding from a couple of bites and his big legs pumping to keep him just ahead of Sophie.

"Oh dear," Pat said in a voice that made it clear that the reality that his plan still had a few bugs to be sorted out.

"Shovel!" I said and lunged for the one Catherine had used on her aunt. Pat grabbed a pickaxe and we swung at the same time.

I hit Sophie fair and square in the face and the shock of it rang all the way up my arms and shivered the tool right out of my hands; but the force of the blow had its way with her and her green eyes were instantly blank. She stopped dead in her tracks and then pitched backward to measure her length on the ground.

Pat's swing had a different effect. The big spike of the pickaxe caught Mean-Dog square in the center of the chest and though everyone said the man had no heart, Pat and his pickaxe begged to differ. The gangster's last word was "Urk!" and he fell backward, as dead as Riley and Muldoon.

"Quick!" I said and we fetched the broken length of chain from the shed and wound it about Sophie, pinning her arms to her body and then snugging it all with the padlock. While Pat was checking the lock I fetched the wheelbarrow, and we grunted and cursed some more as we got her onto it.

"We have to hide the bodies," I said, and Pat, too stunned to speak, just nodded. He grabbed Mean-Dog's heels and dragged him into the shed while I played a quick game of football with Razor Riley's head. Soon the three toughs were hidden in the shed. Pat closed it and we locked the door.

That left Sophie sprawled on the barrow, and she was already starting to show signs of waking up.

"Sweet suffering Jesus!" I yelled. "Let's get her into the hills. We can chain her to a tree by the still until we figure out what to do."

"What about them?" Pat said, jerking a thumb at the shed.

"They're not going anywhere."

We took the safest route that we could manage quickly and if anyone did see us hauling a fat blood-covered struggling dead woman in chains out of town in a wheelbarrow it never made it into an official report. We chained her to a stout oak and then hurried back. It was already dark and we were scared and exhausted and I wanted a drink so badly I could cry.

"I had a jug in the shed," Pat whispered as we crept back into his yard.

"Then consider me on the wagon, lad."

"Don't be daft. There's nothing in there that can hurt us now. And we have to decide what to do with those lads."

"God...this is the sort of thing that could make the mother of Jesus eat fish on Friday."

He unlocked the door and we went inside, careful not to step in blood, careful not to look at the bodies. I lit his small lantern and we closed the door so we could drink for a bit and sort things out.

After we'd both had a few pulls on the bottle I said, "Pat, now be honest, my lad...you didn't think this through now did you?"

"It worked out differently in my head." He took a drink.

"How's that?"

"Mean-Dog got scared of us and paid us, and then everyone else heard about Sophie and got scared of us, too."

"Even though she was chained up in a cowshed?"

"Well, she got out, didn't she?"

"Was that part of the plan?"

"Not as such."

"So, in the plan we just scared people with a dead fat woman in a shed."

"It sounds better when it's only a thought."

"Most things do." We toasted on that.

Mean-Dog Mulligan said, "Ooof."

"Oh dear," I said, the jug halfway to my mouth.

We both turned and there he was, Mean-Dog himself with a pickaxe in his chest and no blood left in him, struggling to sit up. Next to him Killer Muldoon was starting to twitch. Mean-Dog looked at us and his eyes were already glowing green.

"Was this part of the plan, then?" I whispered.

Pat said "Eeep!" which was all he could manage.

That's how the whole lantern thing started, you see. It was never the cow, 'cause the cow was long dead by then. It was Patrick who grabbed the lantern and threw it, screaming all the while, right at Mean-Dog Mulligan.

I grabbed Pat by the shoulder and dragged him out of the shed and we slammed the door and leaned on it while Patrick fumbled the lock and chain into place.

It was another plan we hadn't thought all the way through. The shed didn't have a cow anymore, but it had plenty of straw. It fair burst into flame. We staggered back from it and then stood in his yard, feeling the hot wind blow past us, watching as the breeze blew the fire across the alley. Oddly, Pat's house never burned down, and Catherine slept through the whole thing.

It was about 9 p.m. when it started and by midnight the fire had spread all the way across the south branch of the river. We watched the business district burn—and with it all of the bars that bought our whiskey.

Maybe God was tired of our shenanigans, or maybe he had a little pity left for poor fools, but sometime after midnight it started to rain. They said later that if it hadn't rained then all of Chicago would have burned. As it was, it was only half the town. The church burned down, though, and Father Callahan was roasted like a Christmas goose. Sure and the Lord had His mysterious ways.

Two other things burned up that night. Our still and Aunt Sophie. All we ever found was her skeleton and the chains wrapped around the burned stump of the oak. On the ground between her charred feet was a small lump of green rock. Neither one of us dared touch it. We just dug a hole and swatted it in with the shovel, covered it over and fled. As far as I know it's still up there to this day.

When I think of what would have happened if we'd followed through with Pat's plan...or if Mean-Dog and Muldoon had gotten out and bitten someone else. Who knows how fast it could have spread, or how far. It also tends to make my knees knock when I think of how many other pieces of that green comet must have fallen...and where those stones are. Just thinking about it's enough to make a man want to take a drink.

I would like to say that Patrick and I changed our ways after that night, that we never rebuilt the still and never took nor sold another drop of whiskey. But that would be lying, and as we both know I never like to tell a lie.

∞∞∞⊙∞∞∞

Historical Note: There are several popular theories on how the Great Fire of Chicago got started. It is widely believed that it started in a cowshed behind the house of Patrick and Catherine O'Leary. Historian Richard Bales asserts that Daniel 'Pegleg' Sullivan started it while trying to steal some milk. Other theories blame a fallen lantern or a discarded cigar. One major theory, first floated in 1882 and which has gained a lot of ground lately, is that Biela's Comet rained down fragments as it broke up over the Midwest.

About the only thing experts and historians can agree on is that the cow had nothing to do with it.

SKN-3
STEVEN E. WEDEL

CHILDREN CROWDED the dirty street, some carrying bags or sacks of treats given by local residents, or stolen from other children in other parts of the borough. Older kids sat on the curb smoking pot or whatever their pusher sold them last. No mothers would call these kids home as the evening grew steadily darker. Screams filled the night, but that was not unusual for this neighborhood. Jack-o-lanterns that had not yet been smashed by the marauding children of the ghetto still glowed dully in the dirty night.

Reluctantly, the trick-or-treaters, drug users, and pushers, moved aside to let a battered old Mercury chug past them.

The long brown Mercury stopped in front of the house where Dr. Daniel Stillson had set up his medical practice. A tall white man got out from the driver's side and a huge Negro from the passenger side. The black man opened a back door and began pulling another white man from the seat. The driver came around the car to help his companion.

The man they extracted from the car was unconscious. He was well-dressed in his tailored gray suit, though his silk tie had come untucked from under his suit coat and flapped in the gentle breeze as the other two men—supporting him between them—dragged him through the yard to the front door of Dr. Stillson's home office. A scowling jack-o-lantern watched them from inside the window.

Once on the porch, the black man knocked heavily on the front door. A curtain in the window flickered before the door was pulled open and the three men admitted. The door closed quickly behind them.

"Bring him in here," Dr. Stillson said, waving for the other men to follow him. Daniel Stillson was a medium-sized man of about forty-five, though he looked at least ten years older due to life in the city's slums. He was losing his dark hair at the crown, but his eyes still burned with unspent life. Tonight they shone even brighter than usual. Tonight he was a man on the brink of revenge.

The doctor led his guests into his examination room, which was also the kitchen; it was the cleanest room in the house. White linoleum covered the floors. The many cabinets on the walls were painted white, though in many places the paint was faded and stained. The sink in the corner had rust stains around the drain, and the table where the doctor sat to talk with his patients was propped up by chipped bricks because one of the legs had been broken off by a patient who had gotten angry over a price. The only other piece of furniture in the room was the steel examination table, and it was un-remarkable, except for the fact that tonight it was equipped with pieces of nylon rope tied to each of the four legs.

"Undress him and put him on the table," Dr. Stillson instructed. "Then tie his wrists and ankles with those ropes. Make sure you get them tight. Stretch him out so he can't move." He stood by and watched as his orders were carried out. When he was satisfied, he tossed a bottle of pills to each of the two men.

"Remember," he warned, "You don't know anything."

"Right," they both agreed.

"Good. Now go." Stillson followed the two and locked the door behind them. He heard the cough and roar of the old Mercury as it was started and driven away. He peeked out the window again to make sure his visitors had not attracted any unwanted attention.

Just the usual scum, he decided. The little ones dressed in costumes were less monstrous than their reality tonight. He let the dingy curtain drop back into place and returned to the examination room.

He stood over the unconscious body on his table for a few minutes, studying the smooth, pale flesh and the peaceful look of the handsome face. Then, smiling to himself, he turned and walked away.

From a corner, he pulled out a small, wheeled cart with a gleaming metal tray for a top. He removed the utensils he would need from a drawer: a scalpel, a syringe, and a new needle in a plastic wrapper. He took a small, corked bottle of clear liquid from a cabinet, then placed all the items neatly on the tray of his cart and pushed them to the examination table. He brought a chair from the conference table and put it beside the tray, then sat down to wait for the man to regain his senses.

The wait wasn't long.

The man's head began to move, his well-groomed blond hair becoming mussed. He tried to raise an arm, and the ropes held it down. His head snapped up and he found Dr. Stillson's smiling face. The man's eyes widened in surprise.

"Hello, Jeffrey," Dr. Stillson said. "Or shall it still be Mister Davies? Like it was in the courtroom? No, I think here it will be just plain old Jeff. Is that all right with you?"

"What am I doing here, Stillson?" Jeff demanded. "Where the hell am I?"

"Why, Jeff," the doctor feigned surprise. "This is my new office. Don't you like it? It's the best I can do since you ruined my practice with that nasty law suit."

"You killed my wife," Jeff accused, again.

"It was an accident," the doctor said harshly. "I explained before the operation that there was the chance she wouldn't make it through. You didn't hesitate to give me the go-ahead."

"You killed her because she wouldn't have sex with you in the hospital room."

Dr. Stillson's face reddened. "She was mine. She needed me as much as I wanted her. You should have heard her begging me to fuck her that first day she came to me. She said her husband was too busy with his work at the bank to give her the dick when he came home, *if* he came home. She told me she had heard rumors of homosexual activity between you and a clerk in the vault. Did you like getting corn-holed while you were bent over stacks of hundred dollar bills? Huh, Jeffy?"

"Fuck you! Why am I naked? Where are my clothes?"

"They've been taken care of. Be happy with what you have on.

"I made love to Molly," Stillson confessed. "You never got me to admit that in court, did you? No. But I did. She was a wonderful lover. Exquisite, really. She was going to leave you before we found out the lump was cancerous. I wanted her to leave you immediately then, but she didn't want to go through a divorce until after the operation. We made love in her hospital room several times. Even after her hair fell out.

"I miss her," Dr. Stillson added. "I doubt you do."

"It's none of your business," Jeff said. "Why am I here?"

"I'm going to do an operation on you tonight, Jeff. I've never performed this particular operation on a human before, but I'm sure if Molly were here she would give me the okay, just like you did for her. Besides, you're not that much different than an animal. Are you?"

"You're not going to cut me," Jeff said. "You can't."

"Sure I can," Dr. Stillson said. He plucked the scalpel from his tray and showed it to his patient. "I'm all ready to go."

"No," Jeff said quietly. "No! Help! Somebody help me!"

"Nobody will help you because nobody cares!" Dr. Stillson shouted over the other man's voice. "We're in the slums, Jeff. The ghetto. The people out there, they've heard shouts coming from this house before. Most of my patients are thieves, gang members and their ilk. My neighbors won't care about your shouts."

"Nooo," Jeff moaned.

"Oh, yes," the doctor said in a reassuring tone. He took the syringe and the needle from his tray and fitted them together. He picked up the small bottle and stuck the needle through the cork, pulling the plunger up until the syringe was just over half full. He put the bottle back on the tray and shot a quick stream of the clear fluid into the air.

"Got to get the air bubbles out," Stillson said. "I don't want you dying of a heart attack. I have something much better in mind."

"What is that?"

"This?" Dr. Stillson brandished the syringe. "This is a concoction I made up. I call it SKN-3. The three is because the first two tries were unsuccessful. It's an amphetamine. Speed. Can you say trick-or-treat? I thought you could."

"Don't..." Jeff whined as Dr. Stillson brought the needle close to his arm. He winced as the steel penetrated his flesh. The plunger came down and the fluid was in his blood. "Now what?" Jeff asked, a tear coming from his eye.

"Now we wait," Dr. Stillson said, dropping the empty syringe onto the tray. "It should be just a few seconds before the drug takes effect."

"Then what?"

"Then, Jeff, I'm going to skin you alive. SKN-3 will keep you conscious for most of the operation. Won't it be interesting to watch as your flesh is peeled off?"

"*No!*" Jeff began yelling for help again. Dr. Stillson let him shout without trying to stop him. He sat calmly and watched his patient, smiling when he saw the drug was working. Jeff's eyes bulged in their sockets and his face turned red as if he were blushing deeply. He trembled slightly. His heart beat rapidly beneath his skin, causing the flesh of his chest to pulsate.

"My hair's crawling," Jeff said. "Are there bugs in it?"

"No, it just feels that way," the doctor told him. "I think we're ready to begin." He stood up, pushed the chair out of his way, lifted the scalpel from the tray, and pushed the cart back beside the discarded chair. He stepped close to the trembling man on his table.

"No. Please. I'll give you anything," Jeff begged, his voice hoarse with fright. "Anything you want."

"All I want from you, Jeff, is revenge," Dr. Stillson said. "And I'm about to have it."

Jeffrey Davies howled when the cold steel of the scalpel touched his super-sensitive skin. Dr. Stillson ignored the noise and concentrated on his cutting. He made an incision from a point a few inches below the Adam's apple to just above the start of the pubic hair. The cut swelled with ripe, red blood that soon spilled from its canal and ran down the man's hairless chest and stomach. Jeff continued to shriek with pain, and the doctor smiled to himself as he made his next cut along the inside of the left arm, then the right, and then the legs. He joined the slits on Jeff's limbs to the first cut on his torso, and peeled the flesh away from the carcass. Jeff's screams became louder and shriller, reaching an octave that Dr. Stillson would have believed impossible coming from the human throat.

Jeff's ropy red muscles glistened beneath the room's naked hundred-watt bulb. Within moments after his insides were exposed, Jeff passed out.

Dr. Stillson looked at his watch.

"Good," he judged. "You stayed awake for the best parts, Jeffy. Thanks to my little drug."

The doctor completed his job, his face a mask of concentration. He cut from the top of his first incision, below the Adam's apple, around the base of the neck as far as he could reach. He untied Jeff and rolled the body over so he could complete the cuts on the wrists and ankles, then, bringing the cut from the man's neck up around the hairline and back to the forehead.

Taking hold of Jeff's blond hair, Dr. Stillson pulled slowly and steadily. The scalp lifted, and with a little help, the rest of the man's flesh came away from his back with a wet, sucking sound. Dr. Stillson lifted the skin away from the calves carefully so as not to tear the trophy, and then spread the dripping hide on his floor, inside up.

Leaving the body on the table for a moment, the doctor went to a cabinet and took out several white rags. He knelt beside his prize skin and wiped away the blood. When the inside was clean, he flipped the hide over and wiped the streaks of crimson from the front.

The skinless body still glistened wetly on the table. Dr. Stillson stood looking at it for a long moment. He smiled. "Happy Halloween, Jeffy," he said. "I love your costume."

He brought a bone saw from a drawer. Quickly and expertly he cut Jeff's body into small pieces, which he put into two Hefty Cinch Sacks along with the bloody rags. He then cleaned his examination table and the floor around it, added the rags to the plastic bags, and closed them up. He pulled them to the far corner of the room to wait until he could hire a couple of junkies to dispose of them. Happy with a job well done, the doctor looked at the skin laid out on the floor.

"I feel better, Jeff," he said. "Thank you." He took the small bottle of SKN-3 from the tray and examined the remaining fluid. "And thank *you* for keeping him awake long enough to make my task thoroughly enjoyable." He tossed the glass vial into the air, holding his palm out to catch it.

The bottle went up, tumbling end over end, and began its descent. The fluid within rolled from cork to bottom and back as gravity demanded. The bottle hit Dr. Stillson's upturned palm and bounced up before he could close his fingers around it. Again the bottle sailed through the air. It hit the skin stretched on the floor and shattered on impact with the hard linoleum beneath. Glass fragments flew like sparks in all directions as the liquid spread in a small stain.

"Shit!" The doctor glared at the mess. He stooped, picking the pieces of glass off the skin and the floor; then he went for another rag to wipe up the formula. When he returned, the SKN-3 had soaked into the hide, leaving a small stain that looked like a birthmark.

"Oh well," Stillson said, "I suppose I didn't need the rest of it anyway." He dropped the rag onto his table and left the room, turning out the light.

He went to his bathroom and quickly showered, then to his bedroom and lay down, wearing only his underwear. He was asleep within minutes.

In his examination room, the skin began to move. At first the activity was only in the area where the fluid had stained the hide, a small rippling motion. Soon, however, the movement traveled outward until the entire hide was flowing, wave-like, from the headless scalp to the feetless legs and handless arms. The rippling became concentrated, and the skin began to inch its way across the floor toward the open doorway.

In the living room of the house it rolled itself into a turn and rippled past a worn chair, the outstretched arm brushing the leg of an end table. The jack-o-lantern in the window took no notice. The skin slithered into a short hallway and then over the threshold of Daniel Stillson's bedroom. It crossed the hardwood floor and was soon at the foot of the narrow bed. Snake-like, it raised itself up until the scalp seemed to be peeking over the edge of the bed. The top part of the skin flopped down onto the mattress and pulled the bottom of the torso and the legs up after it.

The skin quickly covered Dr. Stillson's nearly naked body, wrapping the empty husks of its arms and legs around the sleeping doctor. It began to squeeze.

Daniel Stillson woke up slowly, thinking at first that some of the neighborhood heavies had broken in and wanted drugs. He would give them something that would knock them on their asses for disturbing him. He looked through bleary eyes and saw the skin of Jeffrey Davies wrapped around him. He screamed.

The piece of flesh on the top end of the hide flopped forward. Dr. Stillson sucked Jeff's starchy hair down his throat and gagged.

As the doctor fought to free himself from the skin, the empty hide wrapped itself tighter around him, hugging out the small breaths he could draw around the hair in his throat. At last he lay still, his body limp, his gray eyes like specks of polished glass staring at the water-stained ceiling.

The skin continued squeezing for several hours, until all of Dr. Stillson's SKN-3 drug had evaporated from the flesh.

Fishing
JASON BRANNON

Just looking at it, the ocean seems pretty one-dimensional, empty, like crinkled cellophane flat over the earth. At first glance, all you see is a reflection or two, waves and froth and the occasional seagull. Sometimes a fish will surface, look at the world and decide that everything stinks of pollution, death, and immorality, before submerging itself once again. Smart creatures, those fish.

Sunlight glinting off of the mirrored surface makes it hard to see anything but quicksilver shapes doing the hula in front of yours eyes. But there's nothing else to see anyway. Right?

Wrong. There's plenty to see if you know where to look. The ocean is the world's biggest casket. Think about how many things live and die unseen beneath the surface. Think about the infinite number of creatures that shut their eyes for the last time in the thrall of dark currents without ever seeing the sun or the moon or the clouds that drift lazily overhead. Think about all the other things that aren't born of water that take their last breath and then sink to the bottom. Boats. Sailors. Fishermen. Wrecked planes. Lovers.

Lovers...

Now there's an odd choice to add to that list. But it's the main reason I'm here, sitting in the sand, summoning ghosts from the bottom of the sea. Some might call what I do necromancy. Others might call it sick and depraved. I call it desperate. All I'm really doing is looking for love. Isn't that what everyone does at some point or another? I'm just looking in a different place than most.

Truth be told, I had that perfect mate once and I lost her. Actually, I killed the woman I loved and dumped her in the middle of the ocean. It was a complicated time. My head was in another place. I could give a hundred other excuses. None of them would change what I did.

On the day we were sailing I was drunk, as was my normal custom. The day was beautiful. We had a picnic lunch out on the deck of my boat. Amber was wearing the floral-print bikini that I liked so much. A smile seemed to be permanently drawn onto her face. I couldn't help but feel happy as well. Everything was perfect.

Until Amber told me she was pregnant.

I snapped. I couldn't help it. I didn't want any explanations or consolations. I just wanted things to be like they were before Amber made her little confession. That, of course, wasn't going to happen.

It was like she was flaunting my own inadequacies in front of my face. I'm not normally the type to lose my temper, but this was different. This was a problem I had been struggling with for a long time, and here Amber was announcing that she was going to have a baby. Of course, she didn't know about my problem. It's not something I had ever discussed with her.

It was something we would never get the chance to talk about. Even now, thinking back, I don't remember putting my hands around her neck. But I must have done it. The marks around her throat told the story well enough.

Once Amber stopped flopping around the deck I panicked and threw her into the ocean. It's not the sort of thing you usually do to a loved one. Then again, neither is choking the life out of them. In the span of a few minutes I had done both.

All my life I've dealt with a certain gift, and I briefly considered using it as Amber bobbed up and down in the water like a fisherman's cork. I could have fixed everything, made every-thing right again. All it would have taken was a simple touch of my hand to send life flooding back into Amber's body.

So why didn't I?

I suppose it's complicated. A man doesn't really think too clearly when his head is full of booze and murderous thoughts and feelings of inadequacy. I guess the bottom line is that I panicked. It's not everyday that I murder someone in cold blood and throw them out to sea to be nibbled on by hungry fish.

It's not everyday I go fishing for corpses either.

Do you have any idea just how many dead things are in the ocean? Even I wasn't really aware of how monumental this task would be until the dead started emerging from tidal depths like bits of driftwood washing onto the beach.

To make things a little more clear, I have a certain affinity with the dead. Not in that 'I see dead people' kind of way, but in a different symbiotic way, like the relationship between a mind and body, one depending on the other. Mostly them depending on me. I can feel them out there, waiting to be used again, waiting to be filled up with a soul and a spirit. That's why they respond so well to me. I whisper promises to them, vowing to give them life and purpose again, and they come to me.

I've never called on the dead on such a grand scale as I've been doing for the past three days. Given the number of bodies lying at the bottom of the ocean, I wasn't even sure how to start or what to expect. What I didn't expect was to see the half-eaten bodies of sailors, fighter pilots who crashed into the ocean, swimmers who became lunch for the sharks, and even the sharks themselves. Some of them even had enough cohesion left about them to actually stagger ashore before realizing that the promises I whispered were mere lies.

With every new disappointment, I sat as still as I possibly could and listened hard, hoping to hear Amber's sweet voice calling to me from amongst the waves. Becalmed by the murmurings of the sea, I drew pictures in the sand with a bit of driftwood. The pictures were of Amber and me. And the baby.

I wonder how I'll react to the sight of her after days at the bottom of the sea. She won't look the same. Decay will have likely set in. The fish will have taken their nibbles. Curious varieties of marine plankton may have established their colonies on her skin.

I'd like to say things will be as they were before; that's what I hope. But I'm realistic. Things can never be as the same. They can be close. But not identical.

It will be like making a photocopy. The second chapter in our lives together will be like an incoming fax of the first. At first glance it will look basically the same. But there will be that fuzziness around the edges that makes it a little different, a little more grainy, a little less clear. I'll know that there's a baby in Amber's womb. I'll also know that the baby's not mine.

I won't bring it back from the dead unless Amber convinces me otherwise.

As I sit here, hooking and releasing the dead, a dolphin carcass washes ashore. It's been bitten in half. A shark has likely made a meal off of the poor, defenseless creature. One of its flippers waves to and fro like the hand of a wannabe beauty queen in a small-town parade. I feel sorry for it and kick it into the waters where something can finish it off. One black, forlorn eye stares back at me. I try to ignore it. But, somehow, that blank, lifeless stare reminds me of what the eyes of that unborn child must look like, peering around in that dismal prison that is Amber's womb, wondering what went wrong. I try to put it out of my mind and do so with some success.

Eventually the darkness wanes as the moon trades places with the sun. I can see the extent of the carnage I raised from sub-aquatic depths. The water is full of chunks of dead meat and the fins of hungry sharks. Detritus left over from murdered ships floats lazily on the currents. Still, no Amber. I clear my mind of everything and remember the good times we shared. The day we first said 'I love you.' The first time she slept in my bed. The first time we had that conversation about the rest of our lives, only to discover that we both had the same optimistic outlook.

That was all it took to summon her when the other feelings wouldn't do the trick.

She emerged from the oily black depths like the princess of some sub-aquatic kingdom, all glistening and wet and fresh like a baby out of the womb. I was a little surprised to see that her stomach was distended when she emerged from the dark water. There had been no indications before I killed her to suggest that Amber was pregnant and I couldn't figure out why there should be now. The baby wasn't still alive in there. I hadn't brought it back from the abyss.

Then I saw the smile on Amber's face and realized that she was flaunting her secret in my face. She thought it was funny that this was the way things had turned out.

Or maybe she was just so proud of the human cargo she carried inside of her that she couldn't rid her face of the smile that might have only been a death rictus.

"That's not mine, you know?" I said, pointing to Amber's stomach. One milky eye swiveled and turned to follow my finger.

"Yours," she hissed insistently.

"No," I said. "I'm infertile."

Amber looked at me oddly. "Yours," she said. "And no one else's."

"You just don't get it," I said.

"Why did you kill me and bring me back?"

And there it was, the very question I had been asking

myself. Even now, I wasn't sure I had the answer.

"I killed you because I knew you had been unfaithful to me. You betrayed me after all the good times we shared. I brought you back because I wanted you to know why I killed you. I wanted you to realize that I knew you were cheating on me."

"I didn't," she insisted. "No one else. You were the only one. I loved you."

"You're lying," I said, but I wasn't really sure anymore. Amber was dead now. There was nothing else I could do to her. She had no reason to lie at this juncture.

"You are the only one who could be the father," Amber insisted. Her blue lips trembled with each word she spoke.

"I am not physically capable of fathering a child," I stammered. "Don't you understand that?"

"Doctors make mistakes too," Amber said.

I wanted to say something else, but I knew she was right. Doctors weren't infallible. Even the best ones gave faulty diagnoses sometimes.

"Prove it to me," I said. "Show me that you're telling the truth."

She took the pocketknife from my hand and slowly inserted it into her abdomen. It reminded me of someone about to segment an orange. The knife was dull, but the flesh was rotten. The blade cut through the skin easily enough. Amber pulled the flaps of flesh back like curtains in front of a window.

That's when I saw my son for the first time and realized that Amber was, in fact, telling the truth. He looked just like me all the way down to the patrician slant of the nose, the prominent chin, and the wisps of black hair. I couldn't deny him.

I realized at that moment what I had thrown away in a fit of jealous anger. It seemed impossible that I could be the father of that withered fetus, but there was no getting around it.

It was like having a ready-made family. The only part needed was a father and husband. That role was mine.

I ran a trembling hand through my thinning hair and looked around at all the piles of bones that I had summoned from the deep in order to get to this point. I couldn't help thinking that things would have been a lot simpler had I just taken that extra moment to allow Amber an explanation rather than throttling her to death. I could have had a living family instead of this bone-yard byproduct.

Nonetheless, this is what I was meant to have. This was my family. These were the people I was meant to be with and love. I just took a circuitous route to get to this point.

"Can you ever forgive me for what I've done?" I asked Amber as tears rolled down my cheeks.

Amber smiled at me with blue lips. "We'll work it out," she rasped.

I pulled her close to me, barely noticing her rotten flesh and the way it felt like wet Styrofoam. I hardly winced at her saltwater stench.

"Bring him back too," Amber urged, putting her arm around my waist. In that moment, I knew what every delivery room father feels like when he sees his child open its eyes for the first time.

Amber smiled and parted the flaps of skin that covered the baby.

The little boy—my son—wriggled and squirmed.

Amber gently removed him from her abdomen and held him to her breast.

"Do you want to hold him?" she asked.

Of course, I did.

Most fishermen cast their lines and throw their nets in search of fish. Sometimes they catch something of value. Sometimes not. I think I beat even the best of them on their most successful day.

I've never met an angler who went out on the water and caught a family.

Groundwood
BEV VINCENT

FOR A WHILE it seemed like the tide had turned against us permanently. Since that dumb ass down in D.C. had deployed our soldiers to every corner of the planet except where they were needed, it took a while before we could mount a defence. I passed those tense days in front of the TV, tryin' to decide how to use the five bullets in the magazine of the Walther P38 my daddy brought home from Germany. If those god-forsaken creatures had reached a city, I believe it would have been all over for everyone back then, including Gilbert Marcoux—that's me.

After our guys finally got back from overseas, they killed every last one of 'em. I say "killed" like they was alive—but they weren't. Not really. Anyway, they stacked those abominations in fields like so much cordwood, under armed guard in case they happened to forget they was dead again. Most folks was afraid they'd come crawling out of the ground if they was buried, and I can't blame 'em. Happened once, after all—could happen again.

On television, smarter people'n me argued over what to do with 'em. The tree huggers got their panties in a twist when someone proposed burning, going on about poisoning the atmosphere and global warming as if we hadn't all just almost died on account of something far worse than carbon dioxide and meltin' icecaps.

No one had a jeezly clue where the infection came from or

how to make sure it was gone for good. Then a politician suggested grindin' the remains up and turning 'em into paper, the kind of idea you'd expect in a state covered with trees. The notion took hold. Even satisfied the eco-nutjobs. A green solution, they called it, and everyone was happy.

I've been making paper for nearly thirty years. Dropped out of school after my daddy got blinded by a part thrown from a machine and couldn't work no more. He didn't last long after that. At least he didn't wind up lumbering around with his arms stretched out like a scarecrow. There's that to be thankful for.

For the past decade, I worked groundwood, at the back of the second floor of the mill. A dozen lines stood maybe twenty feet apart, each with a metal conveyer belt. After the trees were cut and debarked out in the yard, six-foot lengths—some as thick as a man is tall—were dumped through holes in the roof into the lagoons at the front of the conveyers.

Two men worked each line, a hauler and a loader. The hauler stood in front of the low wall that kept the water in the lagoon, pulled floatin' logs close with an eight-foot peavey pole and slid 'em onto the metal conveyer with a picaroon. When a man found his rhythm, peavey in one hand, picaroon in the other, he kept a steady flow of logs comin' along the belt. If the log fall jammed, he had to balance on the narrow ledge between lagoons and poke at tons of timber hanging above him, trying to make it fall while praying he'd have time to get out of the way when it let go.

The loader tumbled logs into four pairs of magazines evenly spaced along the belt. These were metal boxes six feet square, standing three feet out of the floor. They went down another twenty feet to the grinders that turned logs into mulch that got turned into stock and pressed into paper. He filled the magazines from front to back, lining logs up as neat as matches in a box—or bullets in a clip—to keep 'em from jamming, and then made another pass, buildin' little pyramids on top to get as many logs into each magazine as possible. If the logs jammed, he had to reach down with a pole and yank heavy pieces of deadwood around while billows of steam used to soften the wood cooked him. I saw more than one man take early retirement because of a wrecked back from doin' that.

When all eight magazines were topped off, the team could head over to the cafeteria, grab a nap or whatever. A shift usually alternated forty-five minutes on, forty-five minutes off, dependin' on how high the grinders were turned up. If we let those bastards run empty, though, we'd spend the rest of the night strugglin' to keep 'em fed.

Maybe there are people in the world who look forward to goin' to work because each day is new and interesting, but that wasn't life on groundwood. Still, it wasn't a terrible way to earn a living for a man who didn't mind strenuous, steamy, wet, filthy, deafenin' work. In a way, we weren't so different from those mindless creatures. We lurched in, punched the time clock, filled the magazines, punched out, and lurched back home again.

One night management shut down Number Twelve and put up a tarp to keep out pryin' eyes while they ran tests. A paper mill doesn't exactly smell like a field of daisies, but the reek that greeted us at the top of the stairs that night 'bout knocked us off our feet. Reminded me of the time a guy died in the apartment building next to mine and nobody missed him for a while. The day they found him, that stench was everywhere. Once you get a whiff of death, you never forget it. It comes back to you at the strangest times.

About a month later, management called graveyard shift in half an hour early and told us things'd be different for a while. If anyone thought he'd have a problem stickin' a pick into those creatures, he'd be reassigned, no questions asked. They knew what they was doing. No one was gonna be a wimp in front of everyone else. The mill chews up and spits wimps out just like the grinders turn timber into mulch. Any man who asked out might as well have moved to Timbuktu, wherever the hell that is.

On the way outta the locker room there was two boxes—one with rubber gloves and the other with paper masks to cover our mouths and noses. The foreman stood next to the boxes, so we all took some and stuffed 'em into our pockets, but it seemed pretty clear to me no one had any intention of using 'em.

As we climbed the stairs to the lines, the building began to shake and rumble from the grinders startin' up. I pulled a pair of yellow foam earplugs from my shirt pocket, rolled 'em up and stuck 'em in my ears. When I reached the top of stairs, the stench caught me off guard. We only thought it'd been bad before. Remembering the way water from the lagoon splashed in my face during log falls, I pulled the paper mask out of my pocket and put it on. The others around me did the same.

That night, I was paired with Ernie Hamilton. He liked to pee in the magazines instead of going downstairs, and climbed up on the roof to sleep between loads. Lazy as the day is long. One time he didn't wake up and I had to get the foreman to help me when the grinders started runnin' empty. Why he didn't get a free pass to the unemployment office, I don't know. His wife must have been stepping out with the supervisor or something. Stuff like that happens in a small town.

I clambered over the metal stiles that spanned the conveyers until I got to Number Six, took a deep breath, put the new gloves on under my work gloves and turned toward the lagoon for the first time. Mixed in with the debarked logs were naked, decomposed bodies. They floated in the water and dangled behind the grotto ceiling like there'd been a hurricane or somethin'. They was all torn up, with missin' chunks of skin. I could see their muscles, bones, and innards. Their eyes gaped in what looked like amazement—those that still had eyes, that is.

Acid churned in my stomach and burned my throat. My flesh ran cold. We'd seen these things on TV, but to be this close was something else. I wanted to take a deep breath to settle my nerves, but the stench made that seem like a bad idea. One of 'em bobbed to the surface right in front of me. For a minute, I thought it was gonna crawl out of the lagoon and bite me. I took a step back, then I caught myself. I didn't know who might be watchin'. *They're just logs*, I told myself. *No different from the millions of others I've sent to the grinders over the years.* I swallowed hard, took off my helmet—against company regs, but who cared?—put on a little hat made out of newsprint, and wrenched a picaroon out of the overhead beam. *Just logs.*

Ernie was sittin' on the wooden bench beside the line, lookin' green around the gills and smokin' a cigarette—also against regs, but it probably helped mask the stench. When he noticed me starin' at him, he leapt up, ground his cigarette out under his foot and reached for one of the consoles that hung from the ceiling between each pair of magazines. At the push of a button, the conveyer sprang to life. It was show time.

The first object I struck with my peavey pole was solid. A log. I thanked God and all the saints, and pulled it close enough to get my picaroon into it. Water slopped over the edge of the lagoon and pooled at my feet as I hauled it onto the conveyor beside me. *Only eight more hours*, I told myself. *I can do this.*

The next one was a log, too, and I almost had myself convinced this wouldn't be so bad after all. Then my peavey hit somethin' that didn't feel the way any log did. It sank in with a dull thunk. I couldn't bring myself to look. I just hauled it close, dragged it onto the belt and focused on the logs bobbin' in the lagoon, tryin' to figure out how to avoid the nightmares floatin' among them. The first monster disappeared from my peripheral vision and I chased it with another log the same way

I chase scotch with a beer.

"Ah, crap," I heard Ernie say behind me, loud and clear through his facemask and my earplugs. I tried not to imagine him rollin' that thing off the line and into the magazine. Then I tried not to picture what the log did when it landed on top of it. Tried, and failed.

The first hour was grim. The creatures didn't take up as much room as logs did and the wood fallin' on top of 'em smashed 'em up even more, so it took longer to fill the magazines than usual.

When we finished the first load, I got out of there as quick as I could without looking like I was runnin' away. I ambled down the stairs and headed through the maze of machinery to the cafeteria, walking faster the farther away I got. I left my lunchbox in my locker. Nothing solid was gonna stay in my stomach, so I just had coffee. Gracie, who worked the cash, offered a tired smile. Usually I woulda flirted with her, but I wasn't in the mood. I didn't think she was, either. Everyone in the mill knew what we was doin'.

Since it wasn't break time for anyone else, the cafeteria was deserted. The night watchman saw me and sauntered over from his booth at the main entrance.

"Gil," he said.

I nodded and drank some coffee. It tasted like mud.

"As bad as they say?"

I looked up from my cup and nodded. He must have seen somethin' in my face, 'cos he didn't stick around. I glanced at the clock, dreadin' the moment when I had to go back. It came soon enough, though. I put in my earplugs, strapped on the facemask and slipped on the rubber gloves before I mounted the stairs to groundwood again.

It was Ernie's turn to haul, so I wore my hardhat, grabbed a picaroon and stationed myself at the front of the line. The first three things that came at me were logs. Then one of them things showed up. It was harder to handle than timber, soft and floppy, with limbs—and other parts that were never meant to dangle—danglin' all over the place. It almost got past me, and what a monumental disaster that would have been if it had reached the end of the belt and tumbled onto the floor with the oversized pieces someone would trim at the end of shift with a chainsaw.

I wrestled it into the magazine and right away there was another one. And another. It didn't really matter how they went in. Because they was flexible they couldn't jam up like logs. Still, old habits die hard. I lined them up like soldiers at attention when I could, and didn't look down when I dropped logs on top. My earplugs and the steady thrum of the grinders saved me from the sound of them bein' crushed and mangled by falling timber. Even so, my imagination did a pretty good job. I was just glad I wasn't downstairs to see what was comin' out of the grinders.

Men who work in a mill are used to getting used to things. At the end of the first shift, we kidded around a little, though nobody mentioned the gruesome sights we'd seen over the past eight hours. After two weeks, we was telling zombie jokes and playing tricks on each other with decomposed arms and legs. We got through it, because we had no choice. No one had a trade, and there was only so many jobs at Burger King. We all spent a little more time at the bar, and showered and washed our clothes more'n usual, but as long as the paychecks kept comin' we showed up and did our jobs.

After six weeks, it was all over. The box of masks and gloves disappeared. It still reeked on the lines—the smell had soaked into the timber beams and wooden floors—but we was used to it by then. I won't say we were sorry but, for a while, we had been more than just mindless cogs in the machine that churned out newspaper at the other end of the mill. Maybe we were a little disappointed we didn't have that any more.

I've worked from one end of this place to the other, from the steam plant to shipping, but I never really stopped to think about where all the paper we made ended up. New York, London, Tokyo—they was all just names to me. I went to Vegas once for a vacation and found big cities not to my likin'.

Outside of our little town, nobody knew what was in the newspapers they read at the breakfast table or on the subway on the way to work. People crumpled up our paper for packing material, lined their birdcages and litter boxes with it, and even wrapped their fish and chips up in it in some places, or so I'm told.

We spread that disease better'n any old bonfire ever could. Every time someone got a paper cut, or wiped their noses after reading the paper, they caught a dose. Every time someone shook hands with a friend or kissed a lover, they passed it on.

No one knew until the first newly infected dead person crawled out of his grave, so it had plenty of time to spread. By the time they figured out what had happened, it was too late. The tree-huggers never said a word when someone suggested burnin' the mill to the ground. For all I know, one of them struck the first match. That's how quickly priorities change.

And now, dear jeezus, they're everywhere—in every town and city on the planet. Maybe even in Timbuktu, for all I know. The tide has turned against us once more—for good.

So, now I'm filling the magazine again, one bullet at a time, and waitin'.

'Cos I know they're coming. It's only a matter of time.

This time it's the end.

About the
AUTHORS

JAMES ROY DALEY ~ *The Dead Parade,* James Roy Daley's first novel, was released in a trade paperback edition in 2008 by Permuted Press/Swarm Press. Within a few days of the release of *this* book, *The Dead Parade* will be released once again by Bad Moon Books in a limited edition hardcover edition. *Best New Zombie Tales, Volume One* is Daley's first anthology. Upcoming Books include his second novel, *Monsters, Zombies, Vampires & Ghouls* (Library of the Living Dead & Bad Moon Books), and *Best New Zombie Tales, Volume Two* (Books of the Dead). Visit him at: Jamesroydaley.com.

ROBERT ELROD ~ Award-winning illustrator and graphic designer, Robert Elrod, strives to embrace a variety of styles and genres. He works in acrylics, watercolours, inks, coloured-pencils, pencils, and digitally. He's active in local and national art shows and conventions, focusing primarily on images that depict horror, fantasy, and science fiction. His portfolio includes book covers, CD covers, comic books and pinup artwork. Robert's work can be found in *Vincent Price Presents* (Bluewater Comics), *New Horizons* (the British Fantasy Society), and in galleries across America.

RAY GARTON ~ Ray is the author of more than 50 books, including the novels *Ravenous, Bestial,* and the recently released, *Scissors.* Dozens of his short stories have appeared in magazines and anthologies, and have been collected in five volumes. His novel *Live Girls* was nominated for the Bram Stoker Award, and in 2006 Ray was presented with the Grand Master of Horror Award. He lives in northern California with his wife Dawn and their many cats.

MATT HULTS ~ Matt is a writer and artist living Minneapolis, Minnesota with his wife and two children. His drawings and fiction can be found lurking between the pages of such anthologies as *Fried! Fast Food, Slow Deaths; Harvest Hill; Undead: Skin & Bones; Horror Library Volume 2; Northern Haunts*, and *The Beast Within*, which he also edited. Track him down at Myspace.com/authormatthults and say hi.

JESSICA BROWN ~ Jessica is a lifelong fan of horror film and fiction and resides near Pittsburgh, Pennsylvania, only a few short miles from Living Dead ground zero. A short fiction writer and aspiring novelist, her work has been featured in Pill Hill Press' *Twisted Legends* collection and will be appearing in several Library of the Living Dead anthologies in the upcoming year. Her serial novel, *Rain*, can be found on Facebook and Textnovel.

KEALAN PATRICK BURKE ~ Described as 'a newcomer worth watching' (Publishers Weekly) and 'one of the most original authors in contemporary horror' (Booklist) Kealan Patrick Burke is the author of *The Turtle Boy, The Hides, Vessels, The Living, Midlisters, Masters of the Moors, Currency of Souls, Kin, Ravenous Ghosts*, and *The Number121 to Pennsylvania*, and the editor of the anthologies: *Taverns of the Dead, Night Visions 12, Quietly Now, Brimstone Turnpike*, and *Tales from the Gorezone*. Visit him at Kealanpatrickburke.com.

JEFF STRAND ~ Jeff's story in this anthology is so short that he'd feel guilty offering up more biographical information than a simple "His website is JeffStrand.com" so that's all he'll do.

ROBERT SWARTWOOD ~ Robert lives physically in Pennsylvania and lives virtually at Robertswartwood.com.

GARY MCMAHON ~ Gary's fiction has appeared in magazines and anthologies in the U.K. and U.S., and has been reprinted in both *The Mammoth Book Of Best New Horror* and *The Year's Best Fantasy & Horror*. He is the British-Fantasy-Award-nominated author of *Rough Cut, All Your Gods Are Dead, Dirty Prayers, How to Make Monsters, Rain Dogs, Different Skins, Pieces of Midnight, Hungry Hearts*, and has edited an anthology of original novelettes titled *We Fade to Grey*. Angry Robot/HarperCollins will publish the novels *Pretty Little Dead Things* and *Dead Bad Things* in 2010 and 2011. Visit Gary at: Garymcmahon.com.

HARRY SHANNON ~ Harry has been an actor, an Emmy nominated songwriter, a recording artist, music publisher, VP at Carolco Pictures, and a Music Supervisor on Basic Instinct and Universal Soldier. His novels include Night of the Beast, Night of the Werewolf, Daemon, Dead and Gone and The Pressure of Darkness, as well as the Mick Callahan suspense novels Memorial Day, Eye of the Burning Man, and One of the Wicked. His new collection A Host of Shadows is from Dark Region Press. Shannon has won the Tombstone Award, the Black Quill, and has been nominated for a Bram Stoker Award. Contact him at Harryshannon.com.

GORD ROLLO ~ Gord was born in St. Andrews, Scotland, but has lived in Ontario, Canada since 1971. His short stories and novella-length work have appeared in many pro and semipro publications throughout the genre. He is currently in the middle of a four book novel contract with Leisure Books in New York City. The Jigsaw Man was published in mass-market paperback in August of 2008 and his follow up, Crimson, was released in March 2009. His next two novels, Strange Magic, and Valley Of The Scarecrow are both being released in 2010. Besides novels, Gord edited the acclaimed evolutionary horror anthology, Unnatural Selection: A Collection of Darwinian Nightmares. He also co-edited Dreaming of Angels, a horror/fantasy anthology created to increase awareness of Down's syndrome and raise money for research. He's hard at work on his next novel and can be reached through his website at Gordqrollo.com.

BRIAN KNIGHT ~ Brian lives in Washington state, where he drinks too much coffee, smokes too many cigarettes, and collects Hawaiian shirts. Visit him at Brian-Knight.com.

SIMON McCAFFERY ~ Simon is a 46-year-old former magazine editor who sold his soul to high-tech corporate America. He lives in the Tulsa, Oklahoma area with his wife Angela and his three amazing children. Writing and selling fiction since 1990, he owes his love of zombies, science fiction, and things that go bump in the day (and night) to his father, James McCaffery, who taught Simon to read at an early age and gave him a box of paperback books when he was eleven. *Something Wicked This Way Comes* was among them.

JOHN GROVER ~ John is the author of *Feminine Wiles, Whispering Shadows, A Beckoning of Shadows*, and *Tandem of Terror*. Residing in Boston, Massachusetts, he previously studied creative writing online at Boston's Fisher College. He is also a member of the New England Horror Writers—a chapter of the Horror Writers Association. His short stories can be found in *Northern Haunts* (Shroud Publishing), Zombology (Library of the Living Dead), *Alien Skin Magazine, Morpheus Tales, Wrong World, The Willows,* and *Flesh and Blood Magazine*. For more information, feel free to visit his award-winning website, Shadowtales.com.

JEFF PARISH ~ Jeff is a 30-something native Texan who tries to pound a little bit of English into the skulls of high school seniors in Paris, Texas. He and his wife have a girl and two boys. He started writing in middle school, where he concentrated mostly on (bad) fantasy tales and (even worse) poetry. His writing skills developed over time, much to his delight and the relief of everyone he forced to read his work, and he gravitated to prose over poetry. He started work at a small newspaper in Greenville, Texas nearly a decade ago. But his newspaper career was suffocated in its sleep in 2006 after he realized journalism might be a noble profession, but slowly starving his family to death was not. He's had stories selected for Flashing Swords, Andromeda Spaceways Inflight Magazine, Triangulation: End of Time, Bits of the Dead, In Bad Dreams II and Dragons Composed, among others.

JOHN L. FRENCH ~ John is a crime scene supervisor with the Baltimore Police Department Crime Laboratory. In 1992 he began writing crime fiction, basing his stories on his experiences on the streets of what some have called one of the most dangerous cities in the country. His books include *The Devil of Harbor City, Souls On Fire, Past Sins* and the upcoming *Here There Be Monsters*. He is the editor of *Bad Cop, No Donut*, which features tales of police behaving badly.

KIM PAFFENROTH ~ Kim is Associate Professor of Religious Studies at Iona College. He grew up in New York, Virginia, and New Mexico, and attended St. John's College, Annapolis, MD (BA, 1988), Harvard Divinity School (MTS, 1990), and the University of Notre Dame (PhD, 1995). After writing several books on the Bible and theology, he turned his attention to the undead. He is the author of *Gospel of the Living Dead: George Romero's Visions of Hell on Earth* (Baylor, 2006) - Winner, 2006 Bram Stoker Award; *Dying to Live: A Novel of Life Among the Undead* (Permuted Press, 2007); and *Dying to Live: Life Sentence* (Permuted Press, 2008). He lives in upstate New York with his wife and two wonderful kids.

CHARLES BLACK ~ Charles is the editor of The Black Book of Horror anthology series. For more information of the series, visit: http://mortburypress.webs.com

JONATHAN MABERRY ~ Jonathan is the NY Times bestselling author of several novels, including *Ghost Road Blues* (winner of the Bram Stoker Award), *Dead Man's Song, Bad Moon Rising, The Wolfman, The Dragon Factory*, and *Rot & Ruin*. His nonfiction books include the Stoker winning *The Cryptopedia, Vampire Universe, They Bite, Zombie CSU* and *Wanted Undead or Alive*. He has a series of Joe Ledger thrillers is in development for TV, and is the founder of the Writers Coffeehouse and co-founder of The Liars Club—a group of critically acclaimed writers who work together to support libraries, booksellers, literacy programs and a love of reading. Jonathan is a popular speaker and panelist at writers conferences and genre cons across the country. Visit him online at Jonathanmaberry.com.

STEVEN E. WEDEL ~ Steven is a life-long Oklahoman best known for The Werewolf Saga books: *Murdered by Human Wolves,*

Shara, Ulrik and *Call to the Hunt* (Scrybe Press). His other books include *Darkscapes* (Fine Tooth Press), *Seven Days in Benevolence* (Scrybe Press) and *Little Graveyard on the Prairie* (Bad Moon Books). After many jobs, Steve is currently a high school English teacher; he holds a master's degree from the University of Oklahoma and a bachelor's degree from the University of Central Oklahoma. Steve lives in central Oklahoma with his wife and four children. Visit him online at Stevenewedel.com.

JASON BRANNON ~ Jason is the author of *The Cage, The Order of the Bull,* and *Winds of Change.* Several of his books have been translated into German and more are slated for the future. When not working on his new book, The Tears of Nero, he can be found reading horror novels and playing loud rock music in rural Mississippi where he resides. He currently maintains a website at Jbrannon.net where more information about his fiction can be found.

BEV VINCENT ~ Bev is the author of The Road to the *Dark Tower,* the Bram Stoker Award nominated companion to Stephen King's Dark Tower series, and *The Stephen King Illustrated Companion,* which was nominated for an Edgar Award and a Bram Stoker Award. His short fiction has appeared in places like *Ellery Queen's Mystery Magazine, Doctor Who: Destination Prague, Evolve, When the Night Comes Down, Borderlands 5* and *The Blue Religion.* He is a contributing editor with *Cemetery Dance* magazine, a member of the Storytellers Unplugged blogging community, and a book reviewer for Onyx Reviews. He lives in Texas and can be found online at bevvincent.com.

Thank you for reading this book!

CPSIA information can be obtained at www.ICGtesting.com
Printed in the USA
LVOW08s1315250913

354097LV00001B/8/P